CREATURES

Thirty Years of Monsters

CREATURES

Thirty Years of Monsters

Edited by John Langan

& Paul Tremblay

PRIME BOOKS

Creatures: Thirty Years of Monsters

ISBN: 978-1-60701-284-9

For our own little monsters: Cole, David, and Emma.

Contents

It Came and We Knew It

It's not just that we live in a culture of monsters—that Frankenstein's monster, say, shuffles from screen to graphic novel to breakfast cereal—but that we have always lived in a culture of monsters. Go back to *Beowulf*, and Grendel strips the flesh from a hapless warrior's bones with his hideous teeth. Go back further, to the *Book of Job*, and the God who speaks to Job from the whirlwind boasts of having subdued and broken Leviathan, bridling the vast beast through its smoking nostrils. Go back still further, to Egypt's Middle Kingdom, and the flint-headed Apep coils just below the horizon, his scaly jaws open wide to threaten the sun. And so on: from the ancient Chinese Xian Tian, whose giant, headless body shakes its sword and rattles its shield, to the contemporary Chupacabra, which stalks the border between Mexico and the United States, monsters are among the building blocks of our cultures, a legacy to accompany the languages we learn. We meet them in a variety of venues, from old movies rerun on TV to books read under the blanket by flashlight, from the bright panels of comic books to stories passed around the playground.

It should come as no surprise, then, how many monsters are familiar to us. Long before we have contemplated Godzilla as a trope for Japanese trauma over the atomic bombings of Hiroshima and Nagasaki, we hear the great reptile's metallic roar. Before we have read Frankenstein's monster as Mary Shelley's grief over her lost daughter, we see the pattern of stitches that hold the artificial man's body together. We experience our monsters first in all their strange and striking particularity, as the host of details that assembles into them. Only later do we see them as vessels fit for carrying a weight of meaning, as something other than literal. Perhaps this explains some of their continuing power, because, no matter how well we may think we explain them, they hail from a time in our lives when we did not know not to take them at face value.

No doubt, the current round of monster narratives that this anthology considers is indebted to the success of Stephen King's fiction. Several of the stories in his first collection, *Night Shift* (1978), employ monsters in a serious and frightening way, a practice his short novel, *The Mist* (1980), and longer novel, *It* (1986), solidify. At the same time, King follows in a line of American writers of the fantastic, reaching back through Philip K. Dick, Ray Bradbury, and Theodore Sturgeon to H.P. Lovecraft and beyond. In "The Father Thing" (1954), "The Fog-Horn" (1951), "It" (1940), and *At the Mountains of Madness* (1936), these writers place monsters center-stage in their fiction. In addition, British counterparts such as John Wyndham and E.F. Benson have brought their sensibilities to bear on the topic, while Franz Kafka, one of the giants of twentieth-century European literature, rests his career on a long story about a salesman who is metamorphosed into a monstrous insect. If there is one thing this range of fictions has in common, it is the decision to place the monster in a contemporary, realistically-portrayed setting, an imaginary toad in a real garden.

Frequently, the effect of such a move is comic, as is the case with several of the stories collected in the first section of this book. Joe R. Lansdale's "Godzilla's Twelve-Step Program" imagines the great monster and his fellows laboring to resist their destructive tendencies; while Jeffrey Ford's "After Moreau" retells and rewrites H.G. Wells's *Island of Dr. Moreau* (1896) from the point of view of one of the doctor's lesser-known creations, Hippopotamus Man; and Michael Kelly's "Kraken" presents the story of what might be called a were-kraken. However humorous their premises, each of these stories swerves, sometimes unexpectedly, towards the dark. In this, they are of a piece with the section's other selections. Both Jim Shepard's "The Creature from the Black Lagoon" and Alaya Dawn Johnson's "Among Their Bright Eyes" present monstrous narrators who are shot through with loneliness and melancholy, which their acts of often shocking violence do little to assuage. The monsters in Christopher Golden's breakneck "Under Cover of the Night" and Carrie Laben's offbeat "Underneath Me, Steady Air" are strange, savage entities antithetical to the humans they encounter; in this, they achieve something of the quality of the things that used to scrape the floor under our beds, to jangle the hangers in our closets. Yet in Golden and Laben's stories, the monsters the characters confront are not completely unknown; whether from folklore or literary history, the protagonists are able to identify them.

It is a critical commonplace—cliché, even—to see the monster as the embodiment of the other. Certainly there are enough stories for which this is the case to allow this interpretation to stand. But the seven stories which open this anthology suggest an additional possibility: that what might be most frightening is that we recognize, whether from a movie watched from between fingers, or a story that made our hearts pound, or from a toy that used to stare across the bedroom at us.

Godzilla's Twelve-Step Program
Joe R. Lansdale

ONE: HONEST WORK

Godzilla, on his way to work at the foundry, sees a large building that seems to be mostly made of shiny copper and dark, reflecting solar glass. He sees his image in the glass and thinks of the old days, wonders what it would be like to stomp on the building, to blow flames at it, kiss the windows black with his burning breath, then dance rapturously in the smoking debris.

One day at a time, he tells himself. One day at a time.

Godzilla makes himself look at the building hard. He passes it by. He goes to the foundry. He puts on his hard hat. He blows his fiery breath into the great vat full of used car parts, turns the car parts to molten metal. The metal runs through pipes and into new molds for new car parts. Doors. Roofs. Etc.

Godzilla feels some of the tension drain out.

TWO: RECREATION

After work Godzilla stays away from downtown. He feels tense. To stop blowing flames after work is difficult. He goes over to the BIG MONSTER RECREATION CENTER.

Gorgo is there. Drunk from oily seawater, as usual. Gorgo talks about the old days. She's like that. Always the old days.

They go out back and use their breath on the debris that is deposited there daily for the center's use. Kong is out back. Drunk as a monkey. He's playing with Barbie dolls. He does that all the time. Finally, he puts the Barbies away in his coat pocket, takes hold of his walker and wobbles past Godzilla and Gorgo.

Gorgo says, "Since the fall he ain't been worth shit. And what's with him and the little plastic broads anyway? Don't he know there's real women in the world."

13

Godzilla thinks Gorgo looks at Kong's departing walker-supported ass a little too wistfully. He's sure he sees wetness in Gorgo's eyes.

Godzilla blows some scrap to cinders for recreation, but it doesn't do much for him, as he's been blowing fire all day long and has, at best, merely taken the edge off his compulsions. This isn't even as satisfying as the foundry. He goes home.

THREE: SEX AND DESTRUCTION

That night there's a monster movie on television. The usual one. Big beasts wrecking havoc on city after city. Crushing pedestrians under foot.

Godzilla examines the bottom of his right foot, looks at the scar there from stomping cars flat. He remembers how it was to have people squish between his toes. He thinks about all of that and changes the channel. He watches twenty minutes of "Mr. Ed," turns off the TV, masturbates to the images of burning cities and squashing flesh.

Later, deep into the night, he awakens in a cold sweat. He goes to the bathroom and quickly carves crude human figures from bars of soap. He mashes the soap between his toes, closes his eyes and imagines. Tries to remember.

FOUR: BEACH TRIP AND THE BIG TURTLE

Saturday, Godzilla goes to the beach. A drunk monster that looks like a big turtle flies by and bumps Godzilla. The turtle calls Godzilla a name, looking for a fight. Godzilla remembers the turtle is called Gamera.

Gamera is always trouble. No one liked Gamera. The turtle was a real asshole.

Godzilla grits his teeth and holds back the flames. He turns his back and walks along the beach. He mutters a secret mantra given him by his sponsor. The giant turtle follows after, calling him names.

Godzilla packs up his beach stuff and goes home. At his back he hears the turtle, still cussing, still pushing. It's all he can do not to respond to the big dumb bastard. All he can do. He knows the turtle will be in the news tomorrow. He will have destroyed something, or will have been destroyed himself.

Godzilla thinks perhaps he should try and talk to the turtle, get him on the twelve-step program. That's what you're supposed to do. Help others. Maybe the turtle could find some peace.

But then again, you can only help those who help themselves. Godzilla realizes he cannot save all the monsters of the world. They have to make these decisions for themselves.

But he makes a mental note to go armed with leaflets about the twelve-step program from now on.

Later, he calls in to his sponsor. Tells him he's had a bad day. That he wanted to burn buildings and fight the big turtle. Reptilicus tells him it's okay. He's had days like that. Will have days like that once again.

Once a monster always a monster. But a recovering monster is where it's at. Take it one day at a time. It's the only way to be happy in the world. You can't burn and kill and chew up humans and their creations without paying the price of guilt and multiple artillery wounds.

Godzilla thanks Reptilicus and hangs up. He feels better for awhile, but deep down he wonders just how much guilt he really harbors. He thinks maybe it's the artillery and the rocket-firing jets he really hates, not the guilt.

Five: Off The Wagon

It happens suddenly. He falls off the wagon. Coming back from work he sees a small dog house with a sleeping dog sticking halfway out of a doorway. There's no one around. The dog looks old. It's on a chain. Probably miserable anyway. The water dish is empty. The dog is living a worthless life. Chained. Bored. No water.

Godzilla leaps and comes down on the dog house and squashes dog in all directions. He burns what's left of the dog house with a blast of his breath. He leaps and spins on tip-toe through the wreckage. Black cinders and cooked dog slip through his toes and remind him of the old days.

He gets away fast. No one has seen him. He feels giddy. He can hardly walk he's so intoxicated. He calls Reptilicus, gets his answering machine. "I'm not in right now. I'm out doing good. But please leave a message, and I'll get right back to you."

The machine beeps. Godzilla says, "Help."

Six: His Sponsor

The dog house rolls around in his head all the next day. While at work he thinks of the dog and the way it burned. He thinks of the little house and the way it crumbled. He thinks of the dance he did in the ruins.

The day drags on forever. He thinks maybe when work is through he might find another dog house, another dog.

On the way home he keeps an eye peeled, but no dog houses or dogs are seen.

When he gets home his answering machine light is blinking. It's a message from Reptilicus. Reptilicus's voice says, "Call me."

Godzilla does. He says, "Reptilicus. Forgive me, for I have sinned."

SEVEN: DISILLUSIONED. DISAPPOINTED.

Reptilicus's talk doesn't help much. Godzilla shreds all the twelve-step program leaflets. He wipes his butt on a couple and throws them out the window. He puts the scraps of the others in the sink and sets them on fire with his breath. He burns a coffee table and a chair, and when he's through, feels bad for it. He knows the landlady will expect him to replace them.

He turns on the radio and lies on the bed listening to an Oldies station. After a while, he falls asleep to Martha and the Vandellas singing "Heat Wave."

EIGHT: UNEMPLOYED

Godzilla dreams. In it God comes to him, all scaly and blowing fire. He tells Godzilla he's ashamed of him. He says he should do better. Godzilla awakes covered in sweat. No one is in the room.

Godzilla feels guilty. He has faint memories of waking up and going out to destroy part of the city. He really tied one on, but he can't remember everything he did. Maybe he'll read about it in the papers. He notices he smells like charred lumber and melted plastic. There's gooshy stuff between his toes, and something tells him it isn't soap.

He wants to kill himself. He goes to look for his gun, but he's too drunk to find it. He passes out on the floor. He dreams of the devil this time. He looks just like God except he has one eyebrow that goes over both eyes. The devil says he's come for Godzilla.

Godzilla moans and fights. He dreams he gets up and takes pokes at the devil, blows ineffective fire on him.

Godzilla rises late the next morning, hung over. He remembers the dream. He calls in to work sick. Sleeps off most of the day. That evening, he reads about himself in the papers. He really did some damage. Smoked a large part of the city. There's a very clear picture of him biting the head off of a woman.

He gets a call from the plant manager that night. The manager's seen the paper. He tells Godzilla he's fired.

NINE: ENTICEMENT

Next day some humans show up. They're wearing black suits and white shirts and polished shoes and they've got badges. They've got guns, too. One of them says, "You're a problem. Our government wants to send you back to Japan."

"They hate me there," says Godzilla. "I burned Tokyo down."

"You haven't done so good here either. Lucky that was a colored section of town you burned, or we'd be on your ass. As it is, we've got a job proposition for you."

"What?" Godzilla asks.

"You scratch our back, we'll scratch yours." Then the men tell him what they have in mind.

TEN: CHOOSING

Godzilla sleeps badly that night. He gets up and plays the monster mash on his little record player. He dances around the room as if he's enjoying himself, but knows he's not. He goes over to the BIG MONSTER RECREATION CENTER. He sees Kong there, on a stool, undressing one of his Barbies, fingering the smooth spot between her legs. He sees that Kong has drawn a crack there, like a vagina. It appears to have been drawn with a blue ink pen. He's feathered the central line with ink-drawn pubic hair. Godzilla thinks he should have got someone to do the work for him. It doesn't look all that natural.

God, he doesn't want to end up like Kong. Completely spaced. Then again, maybe if he had some dolls he could melt, maybe that would serve to relax him.

No. After the real thing, what was a Barbie? Some kind of form of Near Beer. That's what the debris out back was. Near Beer. The foundry. The Twelve-Step Program. All of it. Near Beer.

ELEVEN: WORKING FOR THE GOVERNMENT

Godzilla calls the government assholes. "All right," he says. "I'll do it."

"Good," says the government man. "We thought you would. Check your mail box. The map and instructions are there."

Godzilla goes outside and looks in his box. There's a manila envelope there. Inside are instructions. They say: "Burn all the spots you see on the map. You finish those, we'll find others. No penalties. Just make sure no one escapes. Any rioting starts, you finish them. To the last man, woman and child."

Godzilla unfolds the map. On it are red marks. Above the red marks are listings: *Nigger Town. Chink Village. White Trash Enclave. A Clutch of Queers. Mostly Democrats.*

Godzilla thinks about what he can do now. Unbidden. He can burn without guilt. He can stomp without guilt. Not only that, they'll send him a check. He has been hired by his adopted country to clean out the bad spots as they see them.

TWELVE: THE FINAL STEP

Godzilla stops near the first place on the list: *Nigger Town.* He sees kids playing in the streets. Dogs. Humans looking up at him, wondering what the hell he's doing here.

Godzilla suddenly feels something move inside him. He knows he's being used. He turns around and walks away. He heads toward the government section of town. He starts with the governor's mansion. He goes wild. Artillery is brought out, but it's no use, he's rampaging. Like the old days.

Reptilicus shows up with a megaphone, tries to talk Godzilla down from the top of the Great Monument Building, but Godzilla doesn't listen. He's burning the top of the building off with his breath, moving down, burning some more, moving down, burning some more, all the way to the ground.

Kong shows up and cheers him on. Kong drops his walker and crawls along the road on his belly and reaches a building and pulls himself up and starts climbing. Bullets spark all around the big ape.

Godzilla watches as Kong reaches the summit of the building and clings by one hand and waves the other, which contains a Barbie doll.

Kong puts the Barbie doll between his teeth. He reaches in his coat and brings out a naked Ken doll. Godzilla can see that Kong has made Ken some kind of penis out of silly putty or something. The penis is as big as Ken's leg.

Kong is yelling, "Yeah, that's right. That's right. I'm AC/DC, you sonsofabitches."

Jets appear and swoop down on Kong. The big ape catches a load of rocket right in the teeth. Barbie, teeth and brains decorate the graying sky. Kong falls.

Gorgo comes out of the crowd and bends over the ape, takes him in her arms and cries. Kong's hand slowly opens, revealing Ken, his penis broken off.

The flying turtle shows up and starts trying to steal Godzilla's thunder, but Godzilla isn't having it. He tears the top off the building Kong had mounted and beats Gamera with it. Even the cops and the army cheer over this.

Godzilla beats and beats the turtle, splattering turtle meat all over the place, like an overheated poodle in a microwave. A few quick pedestrians gather up chunks of the turtle meat to take home and cook, 'cause the rumor is it tastes just like chicken.

Godzilla takes a triple shot of rockets in the chest, staggers, goes down. Tanks gather around him.

Godzilla opens his bloody mouth and laughs. He thinks: If I'd have gotten finished here, then I'd have done the black people too. I'd have gotten the yellow people and the white trash and the homosexuals. I'm an equal opportunity destroyer. To hell with the twelve-step program. To hell with humanity.

Then Godzilla dies and makes a mess on the street. Military men tip-toe around the mess and hold their noses.

Later, Gorgo claims Kong's body and leaves.

Reptilicus, being interviewed by television reporters, says, "Zilla was almost there, man. Almost. If he could have completed the program, he'd have been all right. But the pressures of society were too much for him. You can't blame him for what society made of him."

On the way home, Reptilicus thinks about all the excitement. The burning buildings. The gunfire. Just like the old days when he and Zilla and Kong and that goon-ball turtle were young.

Reptilicus thinks of Kong's defiance, waving the Ken doll, the Barbie in his teeth. He thinks of Godzilla, laughing as he died.

Reptilicus finds a lot of old feelings resurfacing. They're hard to fight. He locates a lonesome spot and a dark house and urinates through an open window, then goes home.

The Creature from the Black Lagoon
Jim Shepard

Before they came, I went about my business in pond muck, slurry, roiling soups and thermoclines of particulate matter and anaerobiotic nits and scooters. I'd been alone for somewhere between 250 and 260 million years. I'd forgotten the exact date. Our prime had been the Devonian, and we'd been old news by the Permian. We'd become a joke by the Triassic and fish food by the Cretaceous. The Cenozoic had dragged by like the eon it was. At some point I'd looked around and everyone else was gone. I was still there, the spirit of a fish in the shape of a man. I breast-stroked back and forth, parting underwater meadows with taloned mitts. I watched species come and go. I glided a lot, vain about my swimming, and not as fluid with my stroking as I would have liked to have been. I suffered from negative buoyancy. I was out of my element.

Out of the water, I gaped. In the hundred percent humidity it felt like I should be able to breathe. My mouth moved like I was testing a broken jaw. My gills flexed and extended, to pull what I needed out of the impossible thinness of the air. The air felt elastic and warm at the entrance to my throat, as though it had breath behind it that never got through. The air was strands of warmth pulling apart, dissipating at my mouth.

My mouth was razored with shallow triangular teeth. I lived on fish that I was poorly equipped to catch. I killed a tapir out of boredom or curiosity but it tasted of dirt and parasites and dung. For regularity I ate the occasional water cabbage. I'd evolved to crack open ammonites and rake the meat from trilobites. Instead I flopped around after schools of fish that moved like light on leaves. They slipped away like memories. Every so often a lucky swipe left one taloned.

How long had it been since I'd seen one of my own? We hadn't done well where we'd been, and our attempt at a diaspora had been a washout.

I'd gotten pitying looks from the plesiosaurs.

Was I so unique? In the rainforest, the common was rare and the rare was common.

The lagoon changed over the years. It snaked out in various directions and receded in others. Most recently it had become about nine times as long as it was wide. The northern end was not so deep and the southern end fell away farther than I'd ever needed to go. Something with bug eyes and fanlike dorsals had swum up out of there once seventy-five hundred years ago, and hadn't been seen since.

Every so often the water tasted brackish or salty.

There was one crescent of sandy beach that came or went by the decade, depending on storms, a wearying expanse of reedy shoreline that flooded every spring (silver fish glided between the buttress-roots, gathering seeds), and a shallow-bottomed plateau of thickly cloaking sawgrass that turned out to be perfect for watching swimmers from concealment. There was a minor amphitheater of a rocky outcrop suitable for setting oneself off against when being probed for at night with searchlights (stagger up out of the waist-deep water, perform your blindness in the aggravating glare, swipe ineffectually at the beams). There were two seasonally roving schools of piranha with poor self-control, a swarm of unforgiving parasitic worms in a still water cul-de-sac, five or six uninviting channels that led to danger and mystery, one occasionally blocked main artery in from the bend of the Amazon, one secret underwater passageway which led to an oddly capacious and echo-y chamber of stone, and a gargantuan fallen stilt palm which seemed to be still growing despite its submarine status. From below, the water was the color of tea. From above, even on sunny days, the deeper levels looked black.

During the day, the air was humid and blood-warm. In the morning, orchid-smelling mists surrounded columns buttressed with creepers. Lines of small hunting vireos moved like waves through the trees. Wrens sang antiphonally, alternating the opening notes and completing phrases with their mates.

Night fell in minutes. Bats replaced birds, moths replaced butterflies. In the close darkness, howler monkeys roared defiance. Nectar-gathering bats side-slipped through the clearings. Fishing bats gaffed pickerel and ate them in flight.

I didn't go far. I entertained dim memories of thickets of stinging insects, poisonous snakes and spiders, and the yellow-eyed gleams of jaguars. Away from the water, all trees looked the same and there were no clues to help with orientation. Everything considered me with a diffident neutrality: the bushmaster in the leaf litter, the army ants in the hollow tree, the millipede spiraled into its defensive position. I chewed leguminous beans and certain fungi for the visions their hallucinogens provided. The visions stood in for insights.

One afternoon after 470 million years of quiet a boat chugged-chugged into the lagoon. Old rubber tires hung over its side. It leaked black oil and something more pungent that spread small rainbows over the water. It made a lot of unnecessary and fish-scaring noise. Once it settled into quiet, I fingered its bottom from below with a talon, scraping lines in the soft slime.

Later, across the lagoon, I hovered in the black water, invisible in the sun's glare. The figures on the boat had my shape. Naturally, I was curious.

They spoke over one another in headlong squabbles and seemed to have divided their tasks in obscure ways. Just what they were doing was something I could not untangle. Had I found Companions? Was I no longer completely alone? Had the universe singled me out for good fortune? My heart boomed terror.

I had not one single illusion about this group. Spears were unpacked. Nets. Other ominous-looking instruments. Nothing about any of this suggested diffident neutrality.

A smaller boat steadily brought minor hills of junk ashore. A canvas tent went up. Floating off by myself, savoring that moment of illusory coolness when I'd rise from the water in the early, early morning, I watched a bare-chested native lead a hurrying scientist in a Panama hat to an exposed bank of rock. They arrived to confront a conspicuous claw waving menacingly from the shale.

I paddled over for a listen.

What was it, Doctor? the native asked.

The Doctor admitted he didn't know. He was fumbling with a cumbersome flash camera. He said he'd never seen anything like it before.

Was it important? the native wondered.

The Doctor took pictures, his flash redundant in the sunlight. He said he thought it was. Very important. He set the camera aside and pickaxed the fossil arm right out of the rock. So much for the preciousness of the find.

He announced he was going to take it to the Institute. Luis and his friend were to wait here for his return.

First, he said, he had to make some Measurements. Then he fussed about for days.

There were four men: a figure with a hat who remained on the boat, and Luis, Andujar, and the Doctor on the shore, their sagging tent beside that still water cul-de-sac with the swarm of parasitic worms.

The foreclaw that they kept in the center of the tent in a box had some sentimental value for me. In the middle of the night at times I stood beside the open tent flaps, dripping, ruminating on whether or not to go in for it. The Doctor's breathing was clogged and he sounded like a marine toad.

In the morning they made their waste down the end of a trail leading to a stand of young palms that turned from orange to green as they matured.

One day the foreclaw was gone; I could feel it. The Doctor was gone with it. The boat was gone.

Luis and Andujar sang as they worked. They didn't work often. They played a game with a sharp knife they used to hack down plants.

I watched them and learned their idiosyncrasies. I learned about camp stools, and toilet paper. I learned about rifles. They enjoyed disassembling and oiling rifles. The procedure for loading rifles and killing animals with rifles was patiently walked through every morning, as though for the benefit of those creatures like myself watching interestedly from the bush. I was impressed with the rifles.

That night beside their camp I rose so slowly from the water that the surface meniscus distended before giving way. With my mouth still submerged, my eyes negotiated the glow of their lanterns. The tent canvas blocking the light was the color of embers. On a nearby hibiscus, the light refracted through an insect disguised as a water droplet.

I stood beside their tent in the darkness. One of them looked out and then withdrew his head.

Even with my scales glimmering moonlight and water seeping from my algae, I had a talent for invisibility, for sudden disappearance, the way blue butterflies in the canopy vanished when entering shade.

On the other side of the canvas Luis and Andujar nattered and thumped about. I waited as quietly as an upright bone. My chest was stirred by an obscurely homicidal restlessness.

They fell silent. This was more annoying than their noise. I stood before the closed flaps of the tent's entrance, spread a taloned claw, and extended it slowly into the light. No response.

I pulled the flap aside. Luis gaped, goggled, brandished one of the lanterns; threw it. Andujar sprang from his cot swinging the big sharp knife. They weren't as much exercise as the tapir.

I enjoyed throwing them about. I raked meat off the bone, lathed, splintered, and shredded; wrung, wrenched, rooted, and uprooted. I noted my lack of restraint. I opened them to the jungles. I unearthed their wet centers.

I sat outside the tent, not ready to return to the water. I held my claws away from my body. Space in the upper canopy turned blue and paled. Two tiny scarlet frogs wrestled beside me. Leaf-litter beneath them slipped and scattered. Along the water, one set of noisemakers retired and the next took its place.

I swam off my murderousness. I floated on my back in the center of the lagoon. Fish nipped at my feet. I had even less appetite than usual.

Days passed. Luis and Andujar, slung across shredded cots and canvas, became festive gathering places. In the evenings, even a jaguarundi stopped by. In the opened chest cavities, beetles swarmed and tumbled over one another. Compact clouds of emerald-eyed flies lifted off and resettled.

The big boat came chug-chugging back into the lagoon.

I watched it come from out of the east. My head ached. The sunrise spiked my vision.

I dove to the bottom, corkscrewed around in the muck, and startled some giant catfish.

I resurfaced. Once again, the boat stopped and settled into quiet. Once again there was oblique activity back and forth on deck. Once again the smaller boat was loaded and sent to shore.

The Doctor stood in the front. Three other men spread themselves across the back. They centered their attention on a slender figure between them that I could smell all the way across the water. She smelled like the center of bromeliads torn open, mixed with anteater musk and clay. Anteater musk for years had made me pace certain feeding trails, obscurely excited.

Female scent tented through the membranes in my skull. I gawped. I sounded. I hooted, their nightmare owl.

The group looked off in my direction, startled by the local color. The Doctor called for Luis and Andujar. Luis and Andujar weren't answering. The boat rocked and pitched and scuffed up onto the same muddy bank it had left. The Doctor clambered out and marched off toward his tent. The men called the female Kay and helped her out and followed.

I cruised over, a lazy trail of bubbles.

They made their discovery. I hovered nearby in the deeper water, stroking every so often to remain upright. A few of them picked up shattered objects and examined them. There were a number of urgent motions and decisive gestures. Kay was trundled back to the small boat and the entire group returned to the bigger one. On its deck, crates were wrenched open and still more rifles passed around. Rifles were exchanged and admired.

The sun toiled across the sky. Above the wavelets the steamy air was thick enough to bite. I dozed, watching them bustle.

The water cooled. The moon rose. Frogs made their early evening chucking noises. A giant damselfly pulled a big spider out of its web and bit it in half, dropping the head and legs and devouring the rest.

By the next day the visitors were again anxiety-free. In the morning they putt-putted back ashore in their small boat, and scooped and chipped away at the bank of rock. Fragments piled up and were sifted. The sifters complained.

Kay, reclining in the shade with her back to the work, looked entranced. "And I thought the Mississippi was something," she mused to her companions, who kept working, pouring sweat. In the afternoon, everyone returned to the bigger boat and slept like lizards on the deck in the heat, heads or arms sprawled over one another.

I decided to spend more time on the bottom of the lagoon. I was alternately appalled and bemused by my need to spy. I got the sulks. I kept my distance.

Over the years I'd been continuously taken aback by the ingenuity with which I could disappoint myself.

I heard a splash.

Kay swam on her back away from the boat in my direction, cutting widening wake-lines into the sunlight above her. I watched her cruise by. I left the bottom, and swam on *my* back beneath her for a stretch, as if her reflection.

When she stopped, I sank lower into the murk. She turned, did somer-saults; played, in some obscure way. Resting, she treaded water.

I ascended and drifted a talon into one of her kicking legs, which jerked upwards. I dove. She dove. Vegetative murk billowed up around us. She surfaced, and swam back to the boat. Suddenly ferocious, I followed. It was an exciting race, which I lost. She climbed a ladder out just ahead of my arrival.

Braced on the bottom in the ooze, I took the keel and uprooted it with both arms. Tons of displaced water surged and rocked. On the deck above, boxes slid and smashed and shinbones barked against wheelhouses.

I climbed up a convenient rope to give them a look. They each produced individualized noises of consternation. I made my peccary snarl and back-handed a lantern hanging on the rail into the water. Everyone held up their favorite rifle and I dove back in.

I surfaced on the other side of the boat. "The lantern must have frightened him," Kay said. In the middle of the afternoon.

Within minutes, two men came after me, with little masks on their faces and breathing tubes in their mouths. Bubbles bubbled from their heads. Back in the deep reeds, I watched them churn by overhead, a body's length away, and then swam the other direction. I backstroked through the weeds. They seemed to have trouble following. I did an underwater plié. They spotted me. Their legs thrashed and pounded inefficiently. More bubbles bubbled. This went on for some time.

And again the next day they went about their business.

I kept being *drawn* to them and their leaking hippo-belly of a boat.

This whole thing had affected me. My eye glands were secreting. I rubbed my face on tree bark. I urinated on my feet.

Normally for me the geologic periods came and went, and normally I had the tender melancholic patience of a floodplain, but with them in the lagoon I found myself foolish and hopeful, carp-toothed. I was a creature of two minds, one of them as unteachable as the swamp. I wanted to make this signal event a signal event. I wanted to *become* something.

To them I was the unknown Amazon embodied—*who knew what lay undis-covered in those hidden backwaters?*—and *still* they lounged and chatted. They flirted. They acted as if they were home.

At midday, one wilted crewmember stood guard. He exchanged vacant stares with a cotton-topped tamarin eating its stew of bugs and tree gum on a shoreline branch. The rest of the group squabbled below deck.

I hauled myself back up the rope—why didn't they just *pull up* the rope?—and schlumped past the porthole while they argued. I was dripping all over the planking. I grabbed the crewmember by both sides of his head and toppled us over the rail.

His internal workings ran down on shore later that night. I sat with him with my elbows on my knees. Every so often he got his breath back. A yellow tree boa angled forward from a branch but I waved it away. He called out to the boat. They called back.

They built a cage. Bamboo.

They rowed around in their smaller boat dumping powder all over their section of the lagoon. It paralyzed the fish, which floated to the surface. A few eyed me dazedly on the way up.

While they worked, I waited under their larger boat. It seemed safer there.

That night they lined the deck stem to stern under their lanterns, their rifles nosed out towards the darkness. I bobbed under the curve of the bow. Off in the distance, a giant tree fell, shearing its way through canyons of canopy, opening up new opportunities.

"Do you suppose he remembers being chased, and intends to take revenge?" Kay asked.

"I've got a hunch this creature remembers the past and more," her favorite male answered. He watched his own arms whenever he moved so I named him Baby Sloth.

I floated and listened while they tried to get under the rock of my primitive reasons. How sly was it possible I was? How instinctual? "Just what do you think we're dealing with here, Doctor?" I heard Baby Sloth ask.

I cleared my throat. I cleaned bone bits from my talons. Hours passed. I listened to the quiet crunch of beetle larvae chewing through the boat's hull. One by one, the talkers above me ran out of words and announced they were going to sleep. There were dull, resonant sounds of them settling in below. I sank, my neck back, only my face above the dark water. For some reason I thought of scorpions, those brainless aggravations who went back as far as I did.

Back up into the night air tiptoed Kay, with Baby Sloth. They whispered.

The sound carried. "How much more time do you think you'll need?" I heard her tease. "From where I'm sitting, a lifetime," I heard him answer. One more time, I hauled myself up the rope.

I slipped and tumbled over the railing, sending the shock of my greeting across the deck. Kay shrieked. She was within arm's reach. Baby Sloth swung, whonking me with his rifle butt. I knocked him overboard. Others came stumbling up from below. They ringed me as if everyone was ready to charge but no one harbored any unreasonable expectations.

I grabbed Kay and tilted us over the rope and into the water.

I surfaced to let her fill her lungs. There was splashing behind me. I dove and towed her through my secret underwater passageway. Particles of their powder were suspended in the water even at this depth and I could feel them befuddling me.

In my hidden cavern, I rose from the water and lugged her around. "Kay!" Baby Sloth called, hoarse from held breath. I splotched along in the shallow water puddling the rocks. "Kay!" he called again. I bellowed some response.

I had no stamina. Everything was too much work. I laid her out on a shelf and then, once he knelt next to her, surfaced from a convenient nearby pool. I approached him woozily, planning mayhem. He bounced a head-sized rock off my face. He stabbed at my chest. I lifted him up and started working my talons into his ribs. Gunshots, from all those rifles, made little fire tunnels through my back and shoulders. The others had found the land entrance to my lair. A headache came on. I put him down.

I turned from him. Kay gave another shriek, for someone's benefit. They all fired again. I staggered past them to the land entrance and out into the warmer air. "That's enough," I heard Baby Sloth tell the others. "Let him go."

Lianas patted and dabbed at my face. Day or night? I couldn't tell. I walked along bleeding and gaping. The path was greasy with mud. My feet were scuffling buckets filling with stones. I hallucinated friends. I could hear them all cautiously following. I headed for the lagoon.

What was less saddening, finally, than a narcissist's solitude? I'd been drawn to Kay the way insects singled out the younger shoots or leaves not yet toughened or toxic. I'd added nothing but judgment and violence to the world. If their law, like the lagoon's, was grim and casual, they at least took what they found and tried to make the best of it.

So they liked to disassemble their surroundings, and tinker with them. Was it such a shame that they didn't save all the parts?

Once in the water I sank to my knees down a slope, the muck giving way in clouds. I was happy they'd turned me out. I was rooting against me. I was less their shadow side than an oafish variant on a theme. Extinction was pouring over me like a warm flood, history swirling and eddying one last time before moving on, and I was like the pain of a needle frond in the foot: I filled the moment entirely, and then vanished.

After Moreau
Jeffrey Ford

I, Hippopotamus Man, can say without question that Moreau was a total asshole. Wells at least got that part right, but the rest of the story he told all wrong. He makes it seem like the Doctor was about trying to turn beasts into humans. The writer must have heard about it third-hand from some guy who knew a guy who knew something about the guy who escaped the island by raft. In fact, we were people first before we were kidnapped and brought to the island. I was living in a little town, Daysue City, on the coast in California. Sleepy doesn't half describe it. I owned the local hardware store, had a wife and two kids. One night I took my dog for a walk down by the sea, and as we passed along the trail through the woods, I was jumped from behind and hit on the head. I woke in a cage in the hold of a ship.

People from all over the place wound up on the island. Dog Girl was originally from the Bronx, Monkey Man Number Two was from Miami, and they snatched Bird Boy, in broad daylight, from a public beach in North Carolina. We all went through Moreau's horrifying course of injections together. The stuff was an angry wasp in the vein, and bloated me with putrid gases, made my brain itch unbearably. Still, I can't say I suffered more than the others. Forget House of Pain, it was more like a city block. When you wake from a deep, feverish sleep and find your mouth has become a beak, your hand a talon, it's terrifying. A scream comes forth as a bleat, a roar, a chirp. You can't conceive of it, because it's not make believe.

Go ahead, pet my snout, but watch the tusks. No one wants the impossible. What human part of us remained didn't want it either. It was a rough transition, coming to terms with the animal, but we helped each other. After we had time to settle into our hides, so to speak, there were some good times in the jungle. Moreau could only jab so many needles in your ass in a week, so the rest of the time we roamed the island. There was a lot of fucking too. I'll never forget the sight of Caribou Woman and

30

Skunk Man going at it on the beach, beneath the bright island sun. The only way I can describe it is by using a quote I remember from my school days, from Coleridge about metaphor, "the reconciliation of opposites." I know, it means nothing to you.

We all talked a lot and for some reason continued to understand each other. Everybody was pretty reasonable about getting along, and some of the smarter ones like Fish Guy helped to develop a general philosophy for the community of survivors. The Seven Precepts are simple and make perfect sense. I'll list them, but before I do I want to point something out. Keep in mind what it states in the list below and then compare that to the dark, twisted version that appears in Laughton's film version of the Wells novel, *Island of Lost Souls*. Monkey Man Number One and a couple of the others took the boat to Frisco, and by dark of night robbed a Macy's. One of the things they brought back was a projector and an 8-millimeter version of the flick. I believe it's Bela Lugosi who plays Speaker of the Law. I'll refrain from saying "hambone" for the sake of Pig Lady's feelings. That performance is an insult to the truth, but, on the other hand, Laughton, himself was so much Moreau it startled us to see the film. Here are the real Seven Precepts, the list of how we live:

1. Trust don't Trust
2. Sleep don't Sleep
3. Breathe don't Breathe
4. Laugh don't Laugh
5. Weep don't Weep
6. Eat don't Eat
7. Fuck Whenever You Want

You see what I mean? Animal clarity, clean and sharp, like an owl's gaze. Anyway, here we are, after Moreau. We've got the island to ourselves. There's plenty to eat—all the animals that resided naturally and the exotic beasts Moreau brought in for the transmission of somatic essence—the raw ingredients to make us them. A good number of the latter escaped the fire, took to the jungle and reproduced. There are herds of suburban house cats that have wiped out the natural ostrich population and herds of water oxen that aren't indigenous.

Actually, there's also a tiger that roams the lower slopes of the island's one mountain. Ocelot Boy thought he could communicate with the tiger. He tracked the cat to its lair in a cave in the side of the mountain, and sat outside the entrance exchanging growls and snarls with the beast until the sun went down. Then the tiger killed and ate him. The tiger roared that night and the sound of its voice echoed down the mountain slope. Panther Woman, who lay with me in my wallow, trembled and whispered that the tiger was laughing.

She also told me about how back in the days of the Doctor, when her tail and whiskers were still developing, she'd be brought naked to his kitchen and made to kneel and lap from a bowl of milk while Moreau, sitting in a chair with his pants around his ankles, boots still on, petted his knobby member. I asked Panther Woman why she thought he did it. She said, "He was so smart, he was stupid. I mean, what was he going for? People turning into animals part way? What kind of life goal is that? A big jerk-off." We laughed, lying there in the moonlight.

Where was I? I had to learn to love the water, but otherwise things weren't bad. I had friends to talk to, and we survived because we stuck together, we shared, we sacrificed for the common good. Do I have to explain? Of course I do, but I'm not going to. I can't remember where this was all headed. I had a point to make, here. What I can tell you right now is that Rooster Man went down today. He came to see me in the big river. I was bobbing in the flow with my real hippo friends when I noticed Rooster calling me from the bank. He was flapping a wing and his comb was moving in the breeze. Right behind him, he obviously had no idea, was a gigantic alligator. I could have called a warning to him, but I knew it was too late. Instead I just waved goodbye. He squawked bloody murder, and I finally dove under when I heard the crunch of his beak.

Tomorrow I've got tea with the Boar family. I ran into old man Boar and he invited me and Panther Woman over to their cave. The Boars are a strange group. They all still wear human clothes—the ones that can do anyway. Old man Boar wears Moreau's white suit and his Panama hat. It doesn't seem to faze him in the least that there's a big shit stain in the back of the pants. I've shared the Doctor's old cigars with Boar. He blows smoke like the boat's funnel and talks crazy politics not of this world. I just nod and say yes to him, because he puts honey in his tea. Panther and I crave honey.

The other day, when he offered the invitation, Boar told me under his breath that Giraffe Man was engaged in continuing experiments with Moreau's formulas and techniques. He said the situation was dire, like a coconut with legs. I had no idea what he meant. I asked around, and a couple of the beast people told me it was true. Giraffe couldn't leave well enough alone. He was injecting himself. Then a couple days after I confirmed old

Boar's claim, I heard they found Giraffe Man, on the floor of what remained of the old lab—a bubbling brown mass of putrescence.

We gathered at the site and Fish Guy shoveled up Giraffe's remains and buried them in the garden out back. Monkey Man Number Two played a requiem on the unburned half of the piano and Squirrel Girl, gray with age, read a poem that was a story of a tree that would grow in the spot Giraffe was buried and bear fruit that would allow us all to achieve complete animality. Everybody knew it would never happen but we all wished it would.

When I loll in the big river, I think about the cosmos as if it's a big river of stars. I eat fish and leaves and roots. Weasel Woman says it's a healthy diet, and I guess it is. How would she know, though, really? As long as I stay with the herd of real hippos, I'm safe from the alligators. There have been close calls, believe me. When standing on land in the hot sun, sometimes I bleed from all my pores to cool my hide. Panther Woman has admitted this aspect of my nature disgusts her. To me she is beautiful in every way. The fur . . . you can't imagine. She's a hot furry number, and she's gotten over her fear of water. I'm telling you, we do it in the river, with the stars watching, and it's a smooth animal.

If you find this message in this bottle, don't come looking for us. It would be pointless. I can't even remember what possessed me to write in the first place. You should see how pathetic it is to write with a hippo paw. My reason for writing is probably the same unknown thing that made Moreau want to turn people into beasts. Straight up human madness. No animal would do either.

Monkey Man Numbers One and Two are trying to talk some of the others into going back to civilization to stay. They approached me and I asked them, "Why would I want to live the rest of my life as a sideshow freak?"

Number Two said, "You know, eventually Panther Woman is going to turn on you. She'll eat your heart for breakfast."

"Tell me something I don't know," I said. Till then, it's roots and leaves, fucking in the wallow, and bobbing in the flow, dreaming of the cosmos. Infrequently, there's an uncertain memory of my family I left behind in the old life but the river's current mercifully whisks that vague impression of pale faces to the sea.

That should have been the end of the message, but I forgot to tell you something. This is important. We ate Moreau. That's right. He screamed like the bird of paradise when we took him down. I don't eat meat, but even I had a small toe. Sweet flesh for a bitter man. Mouse Person insisted on eating the brain, and no one cared to fight him for it. The only thing is, he got haunted inside from it. When we listened in his big ears, we heard voices. He kept telling us he was the Devil. At first we laughed, but he kept it up too long. A couple of us got together one night and pushed him off the sea cliff. The next day and for months after, we searched the shore for his body, but never found it. Monkey Man Number One sniffs the air and swears the half-rodent is still alive on the island. We've found droppings.

Among Their Bright Eyes
Alaya Dawn Johnson

"What I ask of you is reasonable and moderate; I demand a creature of another sex, but as hideous as myself . . . neither you nor any other human being shall ever see us again: I will go to the vast wilds of South America . . . My companion will be of the same nature as myself and will be content with the same . . ."

—The monster, *Frankenstein*

He doesn't understand what it's like, to hover at their edges without a light while he spends each dead day within shining distance of their eyes. I've seen my eyes in still pools after the rain. They have two different colors, blue and brown, but they're mismatched and they never shine. Even if I bring a fire right by my face, even if lightning strikes a few feet away, they never shine.

I wish that I could stop. I wish I could close my dull eyes and imagine them shining someplace else—someplace where my body is whole and he is gone forever. But instead I squat here by the river, looking through the trees as they sit by their fire, talking and laughing and eating and spraying light with the whites of their eyes.

He told me that we cannot die.

"Do you see that lightning?" he said, pointing with a finger a different color than the rest of his hand to distant storm clouds. "It senses our presence. It will come here, and strike us, and we will gain its energy."

"What if it doesn't strike us?" I asked.

"Eventually, we'll stop. It's the closest we'll ever get to death."

And I, who still didn't know that eyes could shine, hoped I would always find the lightning.

They worship him. Or, perhaps more accurately, they are afraid of him. They keep him in one of their shelters, where he sits rigidly day after day, surrounded by the tiny, shriveled heads of their enemies. His dull, open eyes—two different shades of brown—stare at nothing. His stolen lungs do not breathe, his pilfered heart does not pound. Yet his crudely stitched patchwork skin does not rot any further—the monster has stopped, but he is not dead.

I despise him for being so pityingly self-assured, so brave. He descended to the darkness, but I still chased the lightning, wishing I could stop even while that surreal light coursed through my body. He says that Christians are supposed to love their creator, but how could I love mine? I am an abomination, a wild assembly of wasted, fetid things—a whore of borrowed parts. How could I want this life? And yet, how can I end it?

I walk along the edge of the river towards the far end of their village, sneaking carefully behind the trees so they do not see me. I like invisibility, because I imagine it must be a little like death. I see the perfect, fist-sized trophy heads on their stakes before I actually see the hut. Each of the little men's mouths are open, as though they are engaged in a perpetual, silent gasp. Some of them seem to be falling apart, with hair peeling off in ragged patches from the shrunken skull. I cannot help but feel a kinship with these sad trophies: are we not, after all, the same thing?

When I squat in the shadow of a nearby tree, I see that he is not alone. The strange girl is there again, bobbing her head as she rakes over the earthen floor and shoes away the bird-eating spiders. Her hair is much too long for someone her age, and she has strange tattoos on her stomach that she periodically strokes with a malformed left hand. I've seen her here for the past moon—her pleasant face has brilliant, bone-white eyes with irises like charred wood, but the other villagers never look at her when they speak. They always seem afraid, but I don't know why.

A few minutes after I arrive, she pauses. Slowly, she uses her good hand to unravel her loincloth. Very deliberately, she sets it on the ground.

After shock, I feel an unexpected rush of warmth—even sympathy. Here, again, is a soul made of different parts. Below her ochre-stained breasts and her tattooed belly, I see what the loincloth has been hiding. The "woman" is neither woman nor man. Or, perhaps, both.

She turns and stares right at the tree I was sure hid my hideous form. "Will you . . . will you show yourself? Or do I offend you?" Her voice is very soft, but deeper than I expected.

My heart beats fast and irregular; my blood feels as though it is slowly leaking from my veins. I trace back to my very first memories—alone on a glacier with a half-frozen monster who had just realized that he couldn't die. *When people see us,* he told me then as he cradled my head like a baby, *they hate us. We are too hideous to live, but we cannot die. Never let them see you. I will take care of you.*

But he has abandoned me—his eyes are duller than those on the trophy heads beside him, and I have never longed for anything more than I suddenly long for this strange creature's acceptance.

"You do not want to see me," I say, slowly. The words feel foreign—this is the first time I have ever spoken their language, though I learned to understand it years ago. "You will hate me."

She laughs softly. "I couldn't. I've already shown you why. I know hate, but I could never feel it for you."

My skin feels taut. I want to go to her, but dull terror holds me back. "You must promise," I say, wishing my voice wouldn't rasp in my throat. "Not to look . . . never look at my eyes."

She seems surprised. Her hands still as she wraps the loincloth back around her waist. "Why?" she asks. "I only want to see you. Do you think your appearance would matter to me?"

"Just promise. Promise, or I'll leave here and never return." I never knew my voice could sound so threatening. I sound almost like him.

She glances down, but not before I see her surprise, her sudden wariness. "I promise," she says. "I won't look. Will you come out?"

I reach up to the tree above me and pull down one of its large leaves. I fasten the ends to my tangled, matted hair and pull it down so that it shades my eyes.

She takes a step back when I walk into the clearing. Her eyes rake my body—I stand there, exposed, as she takes in the crude stitches, the mismatched limbs, the filthy slaves' tunic that I stole from them so I would not have to see my own naked body. But at least, I think as my temples pound with fear, she cannot see my eyes.

Is she disgusted? I cannot tell, but when she raises her eyes, I see the beautiful, bright things are smiling and I am relieved.

"We really are the same," she says as she reaches out to touch the cleft of my rough chin. "I am called Kaapi. You?"

Already, she's touched an old sorrow. "I'm called nothing," I say.

"And the patchwork God?" she asks, gesturing to his rigid figure.

"They sometimes call him . . . monster."

She articulates the foreign word slowly and then smiles. Her right hand ventures to my face again, caressing the rough scars on my cheekbone. It drifts up my face until it touches the edge of the leaf shading my eyes.

My hand darts out and grips her wrist. She lets out a gasp of surprise and for a few terrifying, exhilarating moments I revel in the frantic pounding of her blood that beats against my palm. The knowledge of how easily I could crack the fragile bones beneath her skin makes my breath come fast and hard. Is this, I wonder, what he feels when he kills?

The thought snaps me back to myself, and I let go of her. She grips her wrist, but not before I see the angry red imprint of my oversized hand.

I stumble backwards and then flee into the forest.

That night, shivering in my hole as the rain pounded on my back, I vowed to never go back. But today I find myself beside the same tree again, staring at Kaapi's slow, meticulous movements as she cleans the shaman's tools. I am lost in every part of her—her long hair, her deformed left hand, her hybrid parts. Her right wrist has a livid, purple bruise and she winces occasionally when she bends it.

I shift my weight to lean forward, and a twig snaps beneath me. She looks up.

"I hoped you would come back," she says. "You're the only one who doesn't hate me." She pauses for a few moments. "I saw . . . monster before he became like this," she says. "He helped them attack my village. He had no axe, but he covered himself with blood. When it was over, they took me before they knew what I was . . . but it doesn't matter. It's no different here." She pointed to one of the trophy heads and laughed. "That's my cousin," she said. "He and I would have been married had I been whole, but now he guards the god who killed him. You're very different from monster, I think. When he killed, he looked . . . like there was joy in the death. You seem so much kinder."

I can't take my eyes off her wrist. I keep remembering how her blood felt beneath my palm, the abrupt exhilaration of my physical superiority, and the realization of just how sweet her death would feel by my hands.

"I am no different," I whisper.

Two days later, I finally see her again. I don't know where she has been, but her body is now covered with bruises and still bleeding cuts. She now no longer has even a ragged loincloth to cover herself. She huddles in a corner of the hut and sobs.

"Are you there?" she asks.

Before I can think better of it, I fasten another leaf to shade my eyes and approach her. She looks scared, but not of me. I wonder if she's a fool. I kneel by her and she touches me tentatively with her left hand. Then she leans forward and kisses my mouth.

His lips never felt like this—they were hard and awkward, demanding something they could never give. Kaapi's are tentative, but soft and so gentle I dare not touch her. She presses herself closer to me and we fall back. I taste her salt tears and blood mingling with the saliva in our mouths. The sudden taste of blood makes me grip her more convulsively, though I hate myself for it. She pulls up my tunic and I am unable to stop her.

The sight of her hair spilling across her face above me brings back an unfamiliar, hazy memory—Kaapi's features momentarily blend with those of a blonde woman with dark green eyes. I don't know her, but I recognize the flash as a shadow memory from the life of the man whose brain I now use.

Kaapi pauses. She must have noticed my expression. "Do you want to stop?" she asks.

Her hybrid part is warm and hard against my thigh. I shake my head.

It begins to rain, and in the distance I think I hear the beginning rumbles of thunder. I ignore them. Kaapi pounds into me, her expression intense. I imagine myself as a slab of meat, or a corpse with a million tiny ants skittering all over my body. Very soon, it is over. She pulls back out, curling herself against me. The thunder and its accompanying flashes of lightning seem to be coming closer, but I turn my head away.

Kaapi is still crying. "I want to die," she whispers. "I just want to die."

The lightning is dancing outside, begging me to come and find it, to be its slave once more, like I have been for all ten years of my life. I refuse to look.

"I do too," I tell her. "Would you like . . . would you like to die together?"

She hugs me silently. The lightning, acknowledging its defeat, moves on.

I killed the boy who had the canoe. He seemed surprised to see me. I did not have to kill him, but I did. My chest is filled with many joys and many horrors—the memory of his small, scared face as he gasped for air above my reckless hands is both. Without the lightning, I can feel myself begin to slow. In a few days, I will stop. Kaapi said nothing about the boy, though I half wish she would. I wish she would condemn me, but she looks at me with nothing but devotion. She leans against me when I am not steering the boat, kissing my most repulsive parts, though she does not lift the leaf that shades my eyes.

"When do we reach the fall?" Kaapi asks.

"Two days, I think."

She is silent for a while. "When we hit the rocks," she says, "our souls will be free of our hideous bodies. We will walk in paradise together."

He has told me we do not have souls, so I know her hopes are empty, but I still nod and pat her hand. Perhaps I will at least manage to achieve nothingness.

"I feel tired," I say. "I will sleep for a while."

I give her the pole to steer and lay down in the bottom of the boat.

My dreams are not my own. I see jumbled images of the green-eyed girl and the verdant bushes of a small cottage in a country I have never seen. The girl calls me Henry.

"He has your eyes, Henry," she says, jiggling a laughing baby on her lap. "Just that exact shade of blue." She tickles the baby's fuzzy scalp and smiles.

I try to turn my head away from her, because the whites of her eyes are almost blinding me, but I can't hide from the grief clawing up my throat.

The girl touches my arm, but her skin seems much darker. The world shudders, and I remember where I am.

"Are you okay?" Kaapi asks. I say nothing, instead choosing to watch her silently from under the shadow of the leaf. She leans in closer to me, and the moonlight reflects off of her eyes so brightly I can hardly see her irises. Instead, I see two reflected images of my own hideous face, mocking me in her bone-white brightness. I force myself still, struggling to control the anger that skitters beneath my skin.

"I am glad . . . to be dying with you," she whispers.

And then, she lifts the leaf.

In that brief, naked moment I see the shock, the unwilling repulsion in her eyes. Unreasoning anger explodes from beneath my tingling skin. She falls back in the violently rocking canoe, but I lunge at her and grab her throat.

"I told you not to look!" I yell. "Why did you look?" Hot tears leak from my eyes onto her face.

"I'm sorry," she gasps. "I didn't realize . . . I didn't know . . . "

"Didn't know what?" She is going limp beneath my hands, but I cannot seem to stop myself. She has stopped struggling.

"You have his eyes," she says, so softly I can barely hear her.

Abruptly, I let her go. She collapses on the bottom of the boat.

You have his eyes.

The dead eyes of a soulless god, whose only joy is death.

Kaapi awakes briefly, when we are minutes away from the falls. She doesn't speak—but the roar of the water would make it impossible to hear her, anyway. I hold her head in my lap, rigidly keeping my eyes off of her ruined neck. She can't seem to move her legs or arms, or even feel when I touch them.

She smiles. I catch the tears that leak from the corners of her eyes and lick them from my fingers.

"We're about to go over," I say, though I know she can't hear me.

Her still-loving stare punishes me, sears my insides until I wish I could vomit my self-revulsion into the churning water.

"I told you not to look," I whisper.

Her smile grows softer.

Suddenly, I can no longer stand the thought of being on this boat, alone with that smile, those eyes. I toss myself over the edge, and the small boat capsizes. Kaapi cannot even move her arms, but her eyes still somehow indict me just before she sinks below the water that last time.

I turn away from her and force my way across the current—the effort to reach the far bank exhausts even me, and I sit among the roots and mud, gasping in the damp air. I wonder, if I look over the edge of the falls, will I see Kaapi's body? I want to look, but when I try to move I discover that my limbs no longer obey me. The sun rises behind the waterfall, but even that spectacular vision grows dimmer with each second. It takes me a long time—too long—to understand.

I'm stopping.

At the last moment I close my eyes. I remember Kaapi—not her eyes, or my guilt, but the simple, animalistic pleasure of her pounding into me, the ants skittering across my skin.

I wish I were an ant. Dull eyes wouldn't matter to me then. And if I died, I could just be squashed flat—a featureless smear on loamy earth that not even lightning could revive.

Under Cover of Night
Christopher Golden

Long past midnight, Carl Weston sat in a ditch in the Sonoran Desert with his finger on the trigger of his M-16, waiting for something to happen. Growing up, he'd always played army, dreamed about traveling around the world and taking on the bad guys—the black hats who ran dictatorships, invaded neighboring countries, or tried exterminating whole subsets of the human race. That was what soldiering was all about. Taking care of business. Carrying the big stick and dishing out justice.

The National Guard might not be the army, but he had a feeling the end result wasn't much different. Turned out the world wasn't made up of black hats and white hats, and the only way to tell who was on your side was looking at which way their guns were facing. Weston spent thirteen months in the desert in Iraq, and for the last three he'd been part of a unit deployed to the Mexican border to back up the Border Patrol.

One fucking desert to another. Some of the guys he knew had been stationed in places like El Paso and San Diego. Weston would've killed for a little civilization. Instead, he got dirt and scrub, scorpions and snakes, land so ugly even the Texas Rangers had never spent that much time worrying about it.

Army or Guard, didn't matter that much in the scheme of things. None of it was anything like he'd imagined as a kid. If he'd earned a trip to Hell, he was living it. Never mind the heat, or the sand in his hair and every fucking orifice . . . the boredom was Hell enough. It was all just so much waiting around.

Once upon a time, he'd have been excited about a detail like tonight. Border Patrol and DEA were working together to take out a cocaine caravan, bouncing up from South America on the Mexican Trampoline. The traffickers were doing double duty—taking money from illegals to smuggle them across the border, and using them as mules, loading them up with coke to carry with them. Where the DEA got their Intel was none of Weston's business. He was just a grunt with a gun. But from the way the hours were ticking by, it didn't look good. They hadn't seen shit all night, and it had to be after two A.M.

South of the ditch, Weston couldn't see anything but desert. Out there in the dark, less than half a mile off, locals had strung a barbed wire fence that ran for miles in either direction. The idea that this might deter illegals from crossing the border made him want to laugh and puke all at the same time. Yeah, Border Patrol units traversed this part of the invisible line between Mexico and the U.S. on a regular basis, but if you were committed enough to try crossing the border through the desert, you had a decent shot at making it. Border Patrol captured or turned back hordes of illegals every day, but plenty still slipped through.

And that was just the poor bastards who didn't have transport, a bottle of water, or a spare sandwich. You had a little money and wanted to get some drugs across, all you needed was a ride to the border and a pair of wire-cutters. Came to it, you didn't need the cutters, either. If you drove a little way, you'd find an opening.

The whole thing was a game. That was what bothered Weston the most. Over in Iraq, the other guys were full of hate and trying to take as many Americans out of action as possible. That was war. This whole business, sitting around in the ditch, was hide-and-fucking-seek.

"Weston."

He blinked, turned and glanced at Brooksy. The guy hadn't been in Iraq with Weston's unit. He was brand new to the squad; eighteen years old and thinking this shit was war. Grim motherfucker, skinny as a crack whore, hair shaved down to bristle, and twitchy as hell. The squad leader—Ortiz—had made Weston the kid's babysitter, which meant they were sharing the ditch tonight. Six other guys in the squad, but Brooksy had to be Weston's responsibility. He wasn't sure if Ortiz was punishing him or complimenting him, making him look after the kid.

"Shut up," Weston said, voice low.

He held his M-16 at the ready and glanced around to see if anyone was picking up on their chatter. No sign of movement from the rest of the squad, never mind the Border Patrol grunts or the DEA crusaders.

"I gotta piss, man," Brooksy said.

Weston's nostrils flared. "Not in this ditch."

"What do I do?"

"Hold it, dumbass."

"And when I can't?"

"You piss in this ditch, I swear to God I'll shoot you."

Brooksy's eyes narrowed. He gripped his M-16 and scanned the desert in the direction of the border.

Weston rolled his eyes. He turned and looked north. In the moonlight, the black silhouettes of a dozen or so small buildings were visible. They were all single-story, slant-roof shacks, most of which had once been houses. One had been offices, one a gas station, and one a saloon. The tiny desert town had never had a name—though one clever prick had painted a sign and planted it at the south end of the cluster of shacks. It read WELCOME TO PARADISE.

From what Ortiz had told the squad, passed down from the DEA briefing, the place had been hopping back in the days when heroin production had been huge in Mexico—before they'd realized that their greatest asset wasn't crops, but the border itself, and started putting all of their efforts into trafficking instead. There'd been a big operation going in this little shithole, but the DEA had compromised it then and it had been abandoned ever since. The few people who'd actually tried to live there had long since wandered off.

Paradise Lost.

"Seriously, man," Brooksy began.

Weston laughed softly, reached out with his foot, and kicked the kid's pack. "Drain your canteen and piss in it."

"I'll never get it clean, man. I'll never be able to use it."

That might be true. Weston gave him a hard look. "Go in the corner over there. Dig yourself a little hole, piss in it, then cover it up again. And you better hope the wind doesn't shift."

Brooksy nodded, propped his weapon against the side of the ditch, and went over to the corner. He used the heel of his boot to dig into the ground, then got down and deepened the hole with his hands. When he stood and unzipped, Weston laughed.

"Keep your head down, Brooks."

The kid bent his head and his knees, half-crouched, and it was just about the most foolish-looking thing Weston had ever seen. For a few seconds, it seemed inevitable that Brooksy would stumble into his hand-dug latrine.

From out across the desert came the distant growl of an engine. Weston swung round, propped the barrel of his M-16 on the top of the ditch, and sighted into the darkness. The sound of the engine cut off abruptly. Maybe there had been more than one. Regardless, it had come from the other side of the border, and no way anyone was joyriding the Sonoran in the wee hours of the morning.

"It's on," he whispered.

Brooksy might have been a kid, but instead of losing his cool and flopping all over the place, he turned pro. Quietly, he sat backward on the floor of the ditch, used his boots to cover the hole he'd made with dirt, then lay back and zipped up. He was back at his post with his weapon up in a handful of seconds, eyes gleaming in the dark. All the nervous energy that made him so twitchy had gone away. Weston nodded to him, then settled in to wait. Maybe the kid wouldn't be a liability after all.

He imagined he could hear the twang of the barbed wire being cut, but at this distance, that might have been in his head. For long minutes they sat in the ditch, barely breathing. The other six members of the squad were broken into three two-man teams in different locations, but all on the obvious approach to the empty husks of Paradise.

At first, the rhythmic sound was so muffled that it could've been his own pulse in his ears. But when it grew louder, Weston knew the mules were on the move. Ortiz had told them the DEA expected a couple of dozen, but as the noise of running feet multiplied, it sounded like a hundred or more. The illegals would all have backpacks full of coke. They'd been warned some of them would be guards sent along to protect the coke—coyotes herding the mules—and those guys would be armed. Weston tried to do the math. If he figured twenty-five pounds of coke per mule—over ten kilos—at a hundred mules, they were talking about over a thousand kilos of cocaine.

How the DEA knew about the whole setup, he had no idea. That was their job. But obviously the traffickers had to be pretty confident to risk that kind of product on a bunch of desperate Mexicans looking for a better life in the goddamn desert.

Shadows out on the desert began to resolve into running figures. They were coming, but after crossing through the hole they'd cut in the fence, they'd spread out. DEA and Border Patrol were set up in the ramshackle buildings of Paradise, hiding behind and inside them, just waiting. There were big black Humvees and somewhere—not far off—a DEA chopper was waiting to be deployed.

Weston sighted down the barrel of his M-16. He almost felt bad for the mules. They didn't stand a chance. They expected to show up in Paradise, get a meal and a blanket, and transport deeper into the U.S. But their ride wasn't ever going to show up. DEA had already taken care of that.

A night wind blew over the desert and Weston shivered. During the day, the Sonoran was a frying pan. But at night, it could get cold as Hell.

He watched the tiny figures running closer, moving in and out of patches of moonlight. The night played tricks on the eyes. It was hard to track them closely from this distance. But the sounds of their running grew louder and pretty soon he motioned to Brooksy to duck down inside the ditch.

They slid down, their backs to the dirt wall. The mules started running by, some of them so close he could hear their labored breathing and their grunts of exertion. A voice snarled, let off a stream of abuse at one of the mules. Had to be one of the shipment's guards. Weston forced himself to take his finger off the trigger to fight the urge to rise up from the ditch and blow a hole in the bastard's skull.

He kept his own breathing steady. Their assignment was simple. Let the mules and the coyotes pass on by, then close ranks behind them so that when the shit hit the fan in Paradise, none of the coke fled back across the border. Simple.

Until the screaming started.

In the dark, he saw Brooksy glance at him, wondering who the fuck was screaming. There'd been no gunshots yet. Nobody was supposed to make a move until they got the go signal from DEA, and that wasn't intended to happen until all of the coke-carrying illegals and their guards had marched into Paradise, putting them between the DEA and Border Patrol on one side, and the National Guard on the other to keep them from retreating. But to the south, toward the border, a grown man had started shrieking like someone had just cut his dick off. It sent a chill up Weston's spine, and he wondered how the other guys would be taking it.

The sound of running footsteps slowed, became hesitant.

Voices barked, urging the illegals on. The guards couldn't let the mules change their minds now. Whoever was hurt or dying out there, it didn't concern the drug runners.

Then the screaming died abruptly, a second of silence followed, and several other voices started a chorus of screams. At least one of them had to be that of a child, badly injured or at least in terror.

"Damn," Weston whispered.

Brooksy flinched and stared at him, almost like the kid was judging him for breaking silence. Punk could fuck off as far as Weston was concerned.

You got to the point where the terrified, maybe dying screams of a child didn't rip your heart out, you might as well eat a bullet right there.

The comm unit in his ear crackled. "Go. Word is go."

Engines roared—the Humvees coming to life. Shouts began to arise, in English. "Go, go, go, go!" over and over. Weston took one glance at Brooksy and saw that, indeed, the twitchy motherfucker had vanished, leaving one stone cold bastard behind. No more babysitting for Weston.

"Go, go!" Brooksy chimed in.

They ran up out of the ditch, weapons up and ready. Instantly, Weston saw what had happened. The screams back there in the darkness of the border had made the flood of illegals hesitate. They'd slowed down. Some had maybe even started to turn back, going to check on friends or family members who were stragglers, worried that they were the source of the screams. Whatever it was, the DEA cowboys had gotten worried that they might lose part of their score—or they'd just gotten impatient, which was typical. Grunts like Weston were used to waiting around for the world to explode. From what Ortiz had said, DEA cowboys spent too much time in offices, doing paper-work, and got stir crazy enough that once they hit the field, they couldn't wait for shit to go down.

The mules started shouting in Spanish. Weston didn't have to be fluent to know what they were yelling. "Fuck. We're fucked. Get the fuck out of here." Pretty much a universal language.

The Mexicans started dropping the backpacks full of cocaine—mules couldn't run very fast with kilos of blow strapped to their shoulders—and turning toward the border full speed. One of the guards—they were better dressed, healthier looking, and didn't carry any coke—started screaming at them, raised a 9mm, and put a bullet in the head of the nearest mule who'd dared to dump his drugs.

Weston stitched him with a few rounds from his M-16 and the guy danced a little, spraying blood, and then sprawled onto the desert.

That didn't accomplish anything except to start more shouting and make them run all the faster, like a starter pistol. Only about two thirds of the hundred and fifty or so Mexicans had made their way past the ditches the National Guard squad had been waiting in, not even all the way into Paradise. Now they were fleeing.

"Stop right there!" Brooksy roared.

Like they were going to listen.

"Hustle!" Weston told him.

Brooksy fired a few rounds into the air and they started running along-side the illegals, watching for more coyotes—more guns. Not one of them slowed down. They all figured to take their chances that it would be some other guy who got dropped. Ortiz and the other guys in the squad were on the other side of the stampede. If it was only the eight of them, they'd have had to let most of them go.

"Get the guards," Weston said.

Brooksy nodded and they started scanning the throng.

Then the Humvees tore past them, half a dozen of the roaring machines kicking up clouds of desert sand as they began to herd the stampede. Two vehicles reached the far end and cut in, blocking the way. Doors popped open and DEA agents leaped out, jackets emblazoned with the bold yellow letters of their agency. Jeeps followed, loaded with Border Patrol.

The stampede slowed. The mules didn't know what to do with themselves. The guards were fucked. Now it was just a matter of containing the herd and getting them all into custody. For a minute, it had looked like the operation might fall apart. But the DEA and the Border Patrol guys had moved fast.

"Look at you," Brooksy said, eyes bright. "Taking that guy out. You had him fuckin' dancing, man."

Weston's nostrils flared. "I did what had to be done. That shit isn't fun for me."

"Would be for me," Brooksy replied, that skittery grin returning.

The comm in Weston's ear clicked and Ortiz came on, sounding like he'd climbed right inside his skull.

"Weston, come in."

He adjusted the comm so the mouthpiece was in place. "This is Weston."

"We've got plenty of runners, including at least a couple of coyotes. Take Brooks. Stop as many of the illegals still carrying as you can, but first priority are the guards. Do not let them back across the border. Improvise. You read me?"

"Affirmative, Sergeant."

"Go."

But Weston was already moving. He grabbed Brooksy by the arm and started dragging him away from the cluster of DEA and Border Patrol officers who were closing ranks around the corralled mules.

"What the fuck?"

"Come on. We're moving," Weston said.

"Where to?"

"Give me a minute."

Brooks fell into step and the two of them ran outside the circle of vehicles. A Border Patrol Jeep had slewed sideways in the sand and sat there, engine still purring. An officer stood beside the open door, talking into a two-way radio. From somewhere far off, Weston could hear the distant staccato of helicopter blades.

"Drive!" Weston snapped.

He ran around the Jeep and pulled the door open at the same time Brooksy was climbing into the back. The Border Patrol officer stared into his vehicle at them.

"Get the fuck out of there. What do you think you're doing?"

Weston leaned over and shot him a hard look. "We've got coyotes on the run and orders to stop them. You want to explain fucking that up, or you want to drive?"

The officer hesitated, but only for a second.

"Fine," he said as he slid into the driver's seat. "But I want your names."

He dropped the Jeep into gear and hit the gas, the tires spinning and spitting sand in plumes behind them as they tore off across the desert. Brooksy clutched his M-16 like he was bringing flowers to his mother.

"I'm Weston. This is Brooks."

"Austin," said the Border Patrol man. He drove past the last Humvee and then they were in open desert, headlights illuminating the ground straight ahead but somehow making the rest of the landscape around them even darker.

"That your first or last name?" Brooksy asked.

"We on a date?" Austin snapped.

He picked up the radio he'd tossed aside and got his boss on the line, told the guy he had two Guardsmen on board and they were running down the last of the coyotes the cartel had sent to protect the coke. He had the accelerator pinned. The Jeep jittered in the ruts and bounced across the ground, closing the gap between Paradise and the Mexican border. They passed a bunch of backpacks full of cocaine that had been tossed aside in favor of getting the hell out of the U.S.

Austin's boss told him to carry on, inter-agency cooperation, and some other bullshit that meant any pissing matches that were going to happen would take place above their pay grade. Let the DEA, Border Patrol, and the Guard work it out after the op was over and they jostled for credit or blame.

The first of the strays came in view up ahead. They should've rabbited in either direction but they kept going in a straight line, which confused Weston until he remembered the fence. They went right or left, they'd never get back across the border before they were caught. The opening in the fence was dead ahead.

An old man stumbled. A younger guy collided with him from behind, managed to stay on his feet, grabbed the old man by a fistful of white hair and shoved him out of the way. The old guy fell in a tangle of arms and legs, probably breaking something—bones were brittle at that age. The one who'd tossed him aside had a 9mm in one hand and was shouting to some of the other mules. Two young women and a small boy were just ahead of him. He raised his gun and fired once like he was trying to get them moving faster.

Instead, they stopped short.

"What the fuck?" Austin barked.

But Weston understood. The young guy—one of the guards—ran between them and kept on running. He'd commanded them to stop or he'd shoot them, made them stand still, block the Jeep to buy him a few seconds.

It worked. Austin hit the brakes, swerved around them, then gunned it again.

"We want that guy," Weston said. "Probably at least one more. But let's do this the easy way. Go right past him."

"What?" Brooksy snapped.

"Shut up." Weston glared back at him, then turned to Austin. "Just do it."

Austin held the wheel tightly, went around the guard. They caught a glimpse of his confused expression and he seemed to slow down, wondering what the hell was going on. They passed maybe a dozen others, all mules, some of them still wearing their backpacks.

"There's the fence," Austin said.

The headlights picked up the hole that had been cut in the border fence instantly. They caught just a glimpse of a few Mexicans returning to their homeland through the opening.

"Block it with the Jeep," Weston said.

"My thought exactly." Austin actually smiled. He'd been uptight about working with them, but now he was on the hunt, doing the job he'd signed up for. Weston thought maybe he wasn't an asshole after all.

The Jeep hurtled across the sand. Brooksy let out a rebel yell.

Austin hit the brake and cut the wheel. The Jeep slewed badly to the left and skidded on the desert sand, bumped right up against the fence, and then was still. Austin killed the engine and had the door open instantly. Weston knew he shouldn't even step across the border, which didn't leave him many options. The window of the Jeep was open but the door was almost up against the fence. He pushed himself out the window and climbed onto the rack on the Jeep's roof.

Brooksy and Austin brandished their weapons at the exhausted, pitiful, starving people who had already had their worst night ever. Weston had nothing against the Mexicans. They were breaking a shitload of laws, bringing coke into the U.S., never mind crossing the border illegally. If he lived their lives, he'd do the same goddamn thing. But the coyotes worked for the scum who couriered the drugs into the States and were taking advantage of desperate people at the same time. He would've loved to get his hands on the bosses, the guys who actually hired the guards. But since that wasn't going to happen—those guys weren't running coke mules across the border themselves—he'd make do with the guards.

The one they'd passed—the one who'd shoved the old man—had slowed to a walk and now held up his 9mm, hands raised in surrender. The mules dropped to their knees in exhaustion, knowing it was all over, that they'd likely be shipped back home, where they'd try to cross the border again as soon as possible.

In the moonlight, Weston studied one of the mules. He had no backpack, but a lot of them had dropped the drugs while running. But this guy wore a decent shirt and, though he had stubble on his cheeks, he'd had a haircut recently.

"Better watch—" he started to say.

The guy—a guard pretending to be a mule—pulled a pistol from the waistband of his pants and shot Austin in the face. The mules screamed and the echo carried across the Sonoran desert. For an instant, Weston could do nothing but listen to those screams and the echo of the gunshot, and he remembered the other screams they'd heard, right before the whole op went off the rails. Out there in the darkness of the border . . . not far from here.

"Fuck!" Brooksy shouted.

He put three rounds in the cartel guard's face and chest at close range. The back of the guy's head exploded, spattering a teenaged girl beside him with blood and flecks of bone and brain matter. She screamed, closed her eyes tightly, and crumbled to the ground as though wondering when she'd wake up from this nightmare.

Weston trained his M-16 on the other guard. "Drop it."

The coyote let the gun fall to the sand. Brooksy rushed over and picked it up, stuck it inside his jacket, then smashed the guard in the face with the butt of his M-16. The guy went down hard and didn't get up again. He was still breathing.

"Beautiful," Brooksy whispered.

"You're psycho, Brooks. We got a guy down, and this is beautiful?" Weston slid off the roof of the Jeep.

Brooksy sniffed. "Border Patrol, man. Sorry to see him go, but he ain't one of ours."

A chill ran through Weston.

Then the screams began again, from behind them this time—from beyond the border fence. Weston stepped to one side, trying to keep his weapon trained on the illegals even as he moved around the Jeep to get a look across the border.

Something thumped against the Jeep. He heard the chain link fence shake and a scrambling against the vehicle, and then a face came over the top.

"What the fuck?" Brooksy shouted.

A young guy, no more than twenty, crawled onto the roof of the Jeep. His face had been slashed, long wounds that pouted open, weeping blood. His eyes were wide with madness and fear—had to be crazy to try to cross the border by scaling a Border Patrol vehicle. But this guy wasn't even seeing the Jeep, barely even seeing them.

"Stop right there!" Weston shouted. "Alto! Alto!"

The wounded man noticed the guns, then. He stared at Weston, lower lip quavering in shock or terror, then glanced over his shoulder. With a low, Spanish curse, he turned toward them again, brought his legs up beneath him, and tensed to lunge at them.

Weston pulled the trigger.

The dead man staggered backward and fell off the Jeep. He heard the body hit the sand on the other side, then he turned to Brooksy.

"Cover them."

Brooksy nodded, training his weapon on the twelve or thirteen illegals they'd rounded up. He stood right beside Austin's body, one boot sunken into sand made wet by the Border Patrol officer's blood, but didn't seem to notice.

The whole thing was fucked. Weston hesitated only a second and then went around the Jeep. The last thing he needed was an incursion into

Mexican territory. But there was a space of about two feet between the Jeep and the fence. He hesitated a second and then slipped through that space to the opening in the fence. The corpse lay in the moonlight, and Weston saw that he'd suffered more wounds than the gashes in his face. The dead man had landed on his belly with his arms and legs splayed out. The back of his shirt had been torn to bloody ribbons, and it looked like the skin beneath it was just as badly damaged.

What the hell happened to this guy?

He remembered the other screams, the ones that had come from down here right before the op started going bad. Standing on the border, he looked out across the moonlit Sonoran. The Mexican side looked no different from the American side. It was all hellscape, no matter what country you were in. But the moonlight picked out dark forms crumpled on the sand. He counted at least six bodies out there, and there might have been more. One of them looked like only part of a person. If he'd had any thoughts that some of them still be alive, that banished them.

Something moved out there in the desert, a black silhouette that crouched like an animal, running from one body to the next. Weston stared at that strange, slender figure as it bent over a corpse. It moved its head in curious dips and sways like an animal, but walked on two feet. In that crouched position, it lifted a dead man from the sand with ease, as though the body weighed nothing. In the moonlight, Weston saw its head rear back and a long, thin tongue dart out. The sound that carried to him across that killing ground was the dry crack of bone, followed by a terrible, wet slap.

The thing had driven its tongue right through the dead man's skull, and now it began to suck. The noise made him retch, but he forced himself not to vomit, not to look away from the horror unfolding out there on the desert. These people had to have been the source of the earlier screams. This thing had murdered them and now it was moving from body to body, feasting on the dead.

"Weston, what's up?" Brooksy called from the other side of the Jeep.

The creature froze, cocked its head, listening. It thrust out its tongue, tasting the night air. Slowly, it turned to look right at Weston.

He couldn't breathe. Long seconds passed while the thing stared at him. At last it turned away, dropped the body, and scurried across the desert to the next corpse to start the whole process again.

Weston raised his M-16 and sighted on the creature, but his finger paused on the trigger. If he missed it, somehow, or if there were more of them, he would be endangering the civilians now in his care. They might be illegals, but they were still people and were his responsibility.

Silently, he slid once more between Jeep and fence and moved around the front of the vehicle. It felt like stepping between worlds. Brooksy looked up sharply.

"Where you—?" he started.

Weston silenced him with a look and a raised hand. "Get them in the Jeep," he whispered, gesturing to the Mexicans and then to the vehicle. He glanced again toward the other side of the border and when he looked back, Brooksy had a dubious expression on his face, like he might challenge that order or take it upon himself to go see what they were running from.

"Go," Weston whispered.

Brooksy must have heard the edge in his voice, then, for he started moving as quickly and quietly as he could. A fortyish guy tried talking to them in thickly accented English, but Weston hushed him and gestured for him to get into the vehicle. The man did, and others followed. Quickly enough, the Jeep was full, leaving six illegals still on foot. The girl who'd nearly been killed by one of the cartel guards looked at him in confusion and fear, her face still dappled with drying blood.

"You drive," Weston whispered to Brooks. "I'll escort the others. Don't rev it. No lights. Roll out quiet and dark."

"What's going on?" Brooksy asked, a little twitchy but not smiling.

Weston shook his head. "Later. Just go."

"What about Austin?" He pointed to the dead Border Patrol officer.

"We'll come back," Weston whispered.

Brooksy shrugged. He got behind the wheel of the Jeep, closed the door as quietly as possible, then fired up the engine. To Weston, it seemed the loudest thing he'd ever heard. But then it dropped to a purr and he heard Brooksy put it into gear.

"Vaminos. Let's go," he said, using the barrel of his M-16 to gesture toward Paradise. He put a finger to his lips and shushed them. "Quietly."

The Jeep pulled away from the opening in the fence and for a second, Weston was sure one or more of the Mexican men with him would bolt for the border. The girl wasn't going anywhere, and he didn't think the older woman would try to run it out. But the men . . .

He glanced back toward the bodies scattered on the desert and saw that slender silhouette again. It crouched by a corpse with its head cocked and in the moonlight he saw the glint of its eyes, watching the Jeep pull away.

His pulse raced and his finger twitched on the trigger. Weston forced himself not to run, instead urging the others on. They were focused on him, and he had to keep them from panicking. They all fell in step alongside the Jeep, which rolled slowly back toward the ghost town. The sound of helicopter rotors came from that direction. The headlights of Jeeps and Humvees had made a circle, like a wagon train preparing for attack. If they could just get back there, they would be safe.

Finally on the move, he snapped the mouth piece of his comm unit into place. "Weston for Squad Leader. Weston for Squad Leader."

Seconds ticked by and he was about to radio again when he heard a pop on the line. "What the hell are you whispering for, Weston? It's all over but the paperwork."

"Maybe not, sir."

"What happened? You didn't catch the coyotes?"

"Got 'em, sergeant, but it's a mess." He glanced back, saw the thing—the scavenger—framed in the opening in the fence, standing in the very same spot he'd been in just a minute ago, watching them. Fear ran up the back of his neck and prickled his skin. "And there's . . . there's something else over here, sarge. We're not alone."

"What the hell are you talking about?"

Weston thought about that a second. He looked back again.

Only that gaping hole across the border remained, and beyond it the scattered dead. The creature had vanished.

It darted out of the night so swiftly that he barely had time to aim the M-16. The creature came from the left, a paintstroke of fluid black across the moonlit landscape, grabbed hold of the Mexican at the front of their little march and tore open his throat and abdomen in a single pass.

The screaming started.

Weston ran past the others, up to the front of the Jeep, and squeezed off a couple of rounds without a chance in Hell of hitting the thing. It blended too well with the desert and the dark.

"What the hell?" Brooksy roared from behind the wheel of the Jeep.

"Weston. Do you read? Are you under fire?" Ortiz barked in the comm in his ear.

"Under attack!" Weston snapped back. "Not under fire. That was me shooting."

Ortiz asked half a dozen questions in as many seconds, but Weston wasn't listening anymore. He pulled the comm from his ear and tossed it to the sand. They were three or four hundred yards from the lights and vehicles and weapons of the DEA and Border Patrol. Not far at all.

Not far, he told himself.

But those Mexicans hadn't made it very far, back at the border. They'd been picked off one by one, the stragglers, killed quickly. The thing only slowed down to start its banquet when they were all dead and the screaming was over.

Weston swung the barrel of his M-16, searching the darkness all around, knowing the thing could come from anywhere. The Mexicans not inside the Jeep huddled nearby him. Afraid as they were, no way were they making a break for the border now.

"Damn it, Weston, what was that?" Brooksy asked.

"I don't know," he said, without sparing the other grunt a glance.

"Fuck this."

Brooksy gunned it. The Jeep's engine roared and the tires spit sand as the vehicle leaped forward.

"God damn it, no!" Weston yelled.

Two of the Mexican men started running after the Jeep, shouting. The others hesitated only a second before following. Weston yelled for them to stop, but they were beyond listening. Exhaustion, starvation, and despair had plagued them earlier—people who'd been taken advantage of by nearly everyone they'd encountered—but now fear drove them to madness.

Weston pursued them. The night loomed up on either side of him. He could feel the vulnerability of his unprotected back, but knew that they were all vulnerable. The darkness shifted. Every shadow, every depression in the desert floor, seemed about to coalesce and take shape and rush at him with its claws out.

The illegals were stretched out in a line, scattered in their pursuit of the Jeep. The thing came out of the night and killed the woman, punching a hole in her chest. Weston brought up his weapon and fired at it. Two bullets hit the woman as her corpse fell. The thing flinched and he thought he'd winged it, but it rushed off into the dark again, merging with the night.

The taillights of the Jeep grew smaller.

Weston swore, catching up with the four survivors. The teenaged girl fell to her knees beside the dead woman, and Weston heard her saying "Tia" over and over, and knew she had been the girl's aunt.

They all clustered around the sobbing girl. Weston heard the Humvees revving. One of them pulled away from Paradise, headlights turning their way.

"We'll be all right," he said. "They're coming."

But his fingers felt frozen on his weapon. Ortiz would be coming to get them, maybe with inter-agency backup, but seconds counted. He swung the M-16 around, jerking at every sound—real or imagined—from the desert. The survivors stayed low, out of his way. Maybe they hoped the thing would come for him next.

One of the men had begun to cry with the girl.

When Weston saw it, at first he didn't even know what he was looking at. The thing stood forty feet away, entirely motionless. On instinct he raised the M-16 and squeezed the trigger. The thing darted aside, slipping through the darkness, too fast to hit. It stopped, studied him again, cocked its head and gazed with a terrible intelligence. It thrust out that long, thin, snaking tongue and tasted the air with it.

"El Chupacabra," one of the men whispered.

Engines roared and headlights splashed across them. A pair of Humvees arrived, one on either side of the group, bathing the Chupacabra in yellow light. It bolted instantly, heading for that gap in the border fence.

"Oh no you don't," Weston whispered.

Fast as it was, the thing was making a run for the fence in a straight line. He sighted on its back as Humvee doors popped open and DEA agents jumped out. Ortiz's voice called out, so Weston knew his squad leader was with them.

Once again the creature paused, framed in that opening in the fence.

Weston squeezed the trigger.

An arm came up under the barrel, knocking the gun's nose up, and the bullets fired into the desert sky.

Enraged, Weston spun on a man wearing a DEA jacket.

"Back off!" he snapped, shoving the man away. When he glanced back toward the fence, the creature had vanished once more, and he knew that the opportunity had passed. "What's wrong with you? Did you see that thing? Do you have any idea what it just did? What you let get away?"

Ortiz had come up by then. The DEA agent grinned and Weston wanted to break his face with the butt of his M-16. But the Squad Leader glared at him.

"Stand down, Weston."

Weston glared at the DEA prick. "Tell me you saw that thing."

"I didn't see anything." The grin remained. "And neither did you. We've got thousands of miles of border to worry about. If there's something else that keeps them from trying to get across, then it's doing us a favor."

Behind Weston, the teenaged girl still sobbed over the corpse of her dead aunt. She'd wanted a new beginning, but instead she'd found an ending to so much of her life. All he could think about was that if the girl had been torn open by that thing out in the desert, this son of a bitch would have kept grinning.

Doing us a favor.

Weston looked at the grim, cautious expression on Ortiz's face. The staff sergeant was silently warning him to keep his mouth shut. More than anything, that made him wonder. Was the grinning DEA man just happy the scavenger was out there in the desert, helping him do his job, or had he and his people put the thing there in the first place? And if they had, were there others?

But he did not ask those questions.

"A Border Patrol officer—Austin—one of the coyotes shot him. He's down by the fence, DOA," he said.

"A tragedy," said the grinning man. "Died in the firefight that cost the lives of a number of illegals as they attempted to enter the country carrying cartel cocaine. A hero of the border wars, this Austin. You were lucky to survive yourself."

Weston slung his M-16 across his back. One last time he glanced at Ortiz. They already had their version of tonight's op ready to go. If he tried telling it differently, who would listen?

Slowly, Weston nodded.

"Sir, yes sir."

The Kraken
Michael Kelly

The Kraken, scaly and oozing slime, was on the kitchen counter. It pulsed and moved across the Formica and eased itself onto the bottom of the food-encrusted stainless steel sink.

I stood on wobbly knees, staring down at the bulbous creature. Two round eyes swung up, stared at me with a keen alien intelligence, unblinking, waiting. I thought I recognized those sad eyes. Tentacles reached, feeling along the bottom of the sink. One slimy appendage found a bit of lasagna stuck to the wall of the sink, tugged it off and shoved it into its dark wet mouth.

My stomach roiled. My head spun. My legs buckled. I grabbed the end of the counter and held fast. I felt like a small ship tossed around in a violent sea.

My own fault, really. Can't handle the booze like I once could. Christ, what a mistake. Kenny's fault, too, I guess. Hadn't seen the bastard in years and he calls me up, out of the blue, says he wants to get together, like old time's sake. The two of us, tearing up the town. Like back in college.

Except we are not in college anymore and I'm not a kid anymore. And holy mother of fuck, I can't remember the last time I drank that much beer.

But, yeah, Kenny was always able to talk me into almost anything. Like the time we set off a smoke bomb in biology class. Crazy-ass shit, you know. Always preceded by a few hits off the bong or hash pipe. It made Kenny all moon-eyed and mystical. Not the crazy-ass shit; the drugs. Turned him all gooey and sentimental.

Another time we snuck into the observatory, after hours, so Kenny could use the giant telescope, so he could peer up into the night sky. Bastard was always looking up at the stars, expectant. It wasn't like he was watching for something, no, it was more like he was waiting for something. Him and his gooey eyes.

"There's something out there," Kenny said, wistful. "Something else." And he turned to me, shaking, his voice all syrupy. "There has to be."

Last time I saw the crazy fucker was when we went down to the marina in the dead of night and broke into the main clubhouse, took out that ring of keys and found that sleek boat, the Cat, and, yeah, took the damn thing out onto the lake, the water all dark and shiny, full of green mystery, and shards of moonlight sparkling of its surface. More crazy-ass shit. Kenny and me surging along the water, throttle thrown open, the spray rising up, soaking us, and us laughing, neither one of us ever having driven a boat before, you know, and it's funny, really funny, because this is stupid, but we don't care, because, yeah, we're high or drunk or both. Pirates. That's what we are. Fucking pirates. Adventurers on the high seas. And I tell Kenny that, I say, "We're on the high seas. Get it?"

And Kenny, sweet doe-eyed Kenny, screws his face up, thinking. Thinking real hard. Then he gets it, you know, *high* seas, and cackles like, well, a peg-legged pirate with one good eye and a foul-mouthed parrot. Like any respectable pirate. A hearty chortle. Avast ye matesy!

We take turns at the wheel, shooting along like the madmen we are, turning circles, doubling back, jumping the wakes. Up, then thunk. Man, it's some funny shit. Really. At least for a little while.

Soon we are so wet and stoned that it's not fun any more. You know the feeling, right? You're high, and pretty much anything seems like a good idea. Anything. But that feeling, like all feelings, dissipates, fritters away. So we stop the boat. And now we are floating on the lake, and the boat starts bobbing. And I'm reminded of when I was a kid and the one time my dad took me fishing, before he decided that a wife and kid were too much for one man and bailed on us. Dad got me to cast a line out, and attached to the line is a small red and white ball, called a bob, oddly enough, and I get a bite, and the bob starts, well, bobbing. Up, then down. And the boat, this slick little thing we've, um, borrowed, starts sort of going up and down, like that little red and white bob, you know? And my stomach is doing the same, rising, falling, and the bile in the back of my throat is like corrosive acid.

Kenny looks green. He jumps up, wobbles to the edge of the boat and leans over. He gags and a stream of yellow puke shoots from his mouth. He straightens, wipes his mouth, turns and grins at me. Puke-eating grin, all green and yellow and crusty. He's a sight, yeah.

"How about another hit?" he asks, reaching into his wet pocket and retrieving a small foil pouch. And then this huge tentacle reaches up, all scaly and slimy and smelling of puke. I blink. Yup, there is it, rising up, a huge fucking tentacle, dripping fish guts, and it wraps around Kenny's waist, yanks him off his feet, and his puke-eating grin vanishes, and his eyes bug out, fish eyes, and then, briefly, he's smiling, eyes and mouth wide and I've never seen him so happy, so animated. Then whoosh, he's gone, overboard, and all that is left is a small foil package on the boat's floorboards, you know, and the smell of dead fish guts and vomit.

So, being the friend I am, I stand there and blink. I'm good at that. I blink again. Still no Kenny. Still gone. But I blink, shake my head, because, really, it's the hash or shrooms or whatever the hell we ingested from that foil pouch. I probably should have asked Kenny what it was. But it didn't matter. He always got good shit, and it hadn't killed me yet.

Kenny doesn't return. He's gone. Vanished. Poof!

I stagger to the edge of the boat. My stomach clenches. I retch. Nothing comes up. The water below is still, gleaming darkly. No sign of Kenny and no sign of the Kraken.

Kraken? What the fuck is a Kraken, I think. And where the hell did that come from? Then I remember: Me and Kenny used to listen to this Scandinavian death metal, you know. And one of the bands was The Kraken. All the cover art on their CDs had this beast, a big huge mother-fucking Octopus that lives in the deep sea and attacks ships. Pirate ships. Avast mateys!

But there can't be a Kraken, can't be a beast. No. It's the drugs, baby, the hallucinogens. Kenny has fallen over. And he's probably dead now because I'm here thinking about Norwegian death metal when I should be saving my friend.

So, I jump overboard, into the lake—and it's a lake for goddamn sakes, not a fucking sea, so there can't be a Kraken—and it is cold, you know. Cold. And I sober up real fast, and swim about, but I can't see when I'm under, it's too dark. And it is so cold I'm beginning to tighten up, my arms and legs like lead, or some sort of heavy metal, or Scandinavian death metal, dig? And I'm chuckling because it's funny and scary and fucked up. And I guess I'm not all that sober because I'm making self-referential jokes while Kenny is drowning. But I'm sinking too. So I struggle over to the side of the boat and manage to pull my wet, skinny-ass body back onboard.

No sign of Kenny. Nothing. The lake is calm, motionless, a thing at rest.

And that was the last time I saw Kenny. Until last night.

When he called, I didn't recognize his voice. It was garbled. Bad cell phone connection.

But it was him all right. We chatted about old times, as if nothing had happened, nothing had changed, his voice warbling in and out as if there was some sort of interference on the line. I told him I thought he was dead and he laughed. Laughed like a madman, like a drunken pirate.

See, I didn't report anything. I was scared, you know. Who wouldn't be? Fucking crazy-ass shit. Kind of surreal. Almost convinced myself none of it happened. And I guess it didn't, because here was Kenny on the other end of the line and he sure as hell wasn't dead. You know?

Yeah, I was a fucking coward. Selfish bastard.

Here's his story: He fell overboard. Fuck, surprised we both didn't, truth be told. That was some mighty fine mushrooms we'd consumed. He told me he went under and that he could see things really clearly, like a new world opening up to him, and he swam around for a while, like he was born to water, you know. After a bit, he surfaced, but I was gone. Or he couldn't find the boat. (Whatever, you know? I wasn't going to tell him that I panicked, bolted, ran the boat up onto the shore and scuttled off into the night. That I was abandoning my friend, like my old man abandoned me.) So he swam to shore. It wasn't that difficult. It was easy, he said. The most natural thing in the world. But, he laid low. Because he'd changed. Something deep inside him broke open. Something new and wondrous and alien. And he knew the world wasn't ready for it, for him. This was his chance to start fresh. So he moved around, changed his life. He wasn't the same old person. Not even close. This was his second chance.

Some story, eh?

So we arranged to meet up at this pub down by the docks to catch some music, some Norwegian black/death metal thing. It wasn't quite my bag anymore—I'm no kid, you see—but, fuck, it'd be great to see Kenny. Great to hear his voice.

The place was loud, dark, smoky, and smelled of the sea. Smelled of dead fish guts and puke. A three piece band was on the tiny stage, pounding out some vaguely familiar speed thrash.

Kenny was in a corner. He waved, a long arm beckoning. I sauntered over, took a seat. He couldn't have picked a darker corner of the bar. I couldn't see Kenny at all, he was a hazy shape, shifting. Then he leaned forward and I saw his eyes, only his eyes, those same sad doe eyes.

I flagged down a server, ordered some pitchers of beer. It was too damn loud to talk, so I drank and listened to the band. Kenny didn't touch his beer. I drank enough for the two of us. Eventually, the band took a break, and I turned to Kenny, raised my glass. "Cheers," I said. An arm snaked out, and we clinked glasses.

I gulped down half a beer, wiped an arm across my mouth like a thirsty pirate. "Man, I'm glad to see you," I said. "I really thought you were dead."

Kenny's dark shadow stirred. I could smell seaweed. He spoke, and his voice vacillated between a watery tremble and a sonorous rumble. A voice of deep seas and even deeper night skies.

"I've never been so alive," he said. "Before, I never quite fit in. I was different. I don't think I ever really belonged here. And I was right. There was something else out there. Something for me." He gestured, and through the smoky darkness I caught a faint glimmer of an arm waving upward. "But it wasn't up there," he said. "It was the sea." I imagined I heard a watery chuckle. "I'm a pirate, of sorts."

Then Kenny leaned in, across the table, and I saw him for what he'd become, for what he really was. "But even pirates get lonely," he said.

And I thought about what it means to be a friend, to be there for someone. Thought about what I was, what I'd become. Kenny was proof that people change. That I could change.

So I took Kenny home.

Kenny the Kraken smiled, wide. His mouth was large and deep and black. Dead things swam in its depths. His eyes were bulbous fish eyes, and they regarded me with sad, alien innocence.

I reached over, plugged the sink, turned on the tap. Kenny lolled in the water. I plucked a can of sardines from the refrigerator and began to feed them to Kenny. It was the least I could do for my friend.

Underneath Me, Steady Air
Carrie Laben

Rosemary's is always this dark, but it's a good dark. If you come here at night to drink with the hipsters and hipster-watchers, it's illuminated by strings of year-round Christmas lights and the dull glow of the jukebox. If you come in the afternoon to drink with the old men with tracheotomies and slumped backs, the sun never reaches the third bar stool. Squint a little and you can believe you're in a bunker underground. I still feel safe here, after everything.

I drank at Rosemary's with Ginger and Carol and Steve the night before. I started around five with the vague plan that I'd cut it off and leave myself plenty of time to sleep, since I had to work the next day. Then I started drinking to forget that I had to work the next day. Then I did forget that I had to work the next day.

This is a long way of explaining why my story might sound unfocused, spotty. And, let's be honest, self-centered. There's nothing that inspires more self-centeredness than a hangover, and I was shitty hung over that day.

I made it out of the house on autopilot, it hit me in the subway: tightness in the skin over my skull, feet irritable in my cheap-cute rubber rain boots, and most of all the blue pain of hunger in a slightly nauseated stomach. But I was two trains into the commute by then, which made it harder to turn back than to go on.

The rain had mostly stopped by the time I got there. As I emerged from the subway station, I caught a flash of movement and looked up. I would have split my skull on the sun if it hadn't been for a little cloud—a scrap of fog, really—just above the building that turned the light all pinkish-gray.

As it was, I winced and blinked and, seeing nothing important, turned my focus back to the pavement and cigarette butts and sodden pages of the *Post*.

The elevators in that building were saunas, prone to breaking down. I remember thinking that I could maybe claim that I'd been stuck in one; I looked shitty enough. It was something I often thought about trying. But I figured they could check with the maintenance guys, I'd get busted, which would be even more embarrassing.

As soon as I stepped through the door of the office I was struck by how quiet it was. To the point that I wondered if I'd somehow forgotten a day off. But Rosemary's redecorates for every holiday known to humankind, including Arbor Day. I'd have noticed.

I came around the corner of the first row of cubes and spotted my boss and my boss's boss. They couldn't miss me. I tried to brace myself, but that would have required something to brace, and I felt invertebrate.

Neither of them said anything as I approached. Neither of them even looked up. They weren't talking, I remember thinking they both looked sad, sore. I wondered if they'd decided to fire me.

"Hey," I said, trying to sound casual, actually sounding dehydrated. "Good morning." And they each nodded slowly, but neither of them replied as I entered my cubicle. By the time my computer finished starting up, a peek over the wall revealed that they'd drifted away.

I figured something in email might account for their behavior, but no—the company hadn't been sold, or sued, or the server farm set on fire, there hadn't been any layoffs. There were no new emails at all except the autogenerated one I got every Monday reminding me to update my time sheets.

I got some coffee, read some blogs. The worst of the pounding and lurching inside faded away. By lunchtime, I was ready to risk the break room.

As I came back along the corridor, I heard a dull hiss, the sound of something scraping over the dense industrial carpet. A moment later the receptionist, Jeannette, came around the corner pushing a box of printer paper along the floor.

It started my brain and stomach pulsing again, the way she was bent like something out of Bosch with her knees crooked and her bowed back in the air. Normally she could lift three of those boxes. She was flushed a shade of orange I'd never seen on a human being before, beyond the worst nightmares of spray tan, and the tip of her tongue was protruding from her mouth.

As bad off as I was, I knew I needed to help her. But before the words could wriggle down from my brain and through my clamped jaw, she fell over. Not collapsed, not fell down—fell over, to the side, stiffly.

I knelt on the floor beside her, put my coffee against the wall—where

I promptly kicked it over—and felt for her pulse. Her wrist was slick with greasy sweat and I couldn't find it. But she was still alive, because she was still breathing, because something was making that moaning noise and pushing the horrible greenish foamy drool out.

I couldn't figure out what to do, and then I thought she might be contagious, and I was kneeling in now-cold coffee-damp pants on the now-cold coffee-damp rug. I reached in my pocket for my phone, but of course I'd left it in my bag, back at my desk.

"I'm sorry," I said to Jeanette, though I doubted she could hear me, and heaved myself back to my feet. Walking backwards, unwilling to take my eyes off her, I found myself among the cubes of the QA team.

"Someone better call 911." No one answered, and for a moment I wondered if I'd only thought it, but then I turned around and saw Angel slumped at her desk and Karl at his, both foaming and staring blankly, both as orange as Jeanette.

I don't know how I made myself reach across Karl and pick up his phone. I don't remember what I said to the woman who answered. Sometime between when I hung up and when the EMTs arrived, I got back to my desk. I even retrieved my empty mug along the way.

Yeah, some inspiring story of survival. Honestly, it's probably a good thing that I lost so much of my hospital stay. I'm not sure who broke it to me that I was the only survivor to come out of the office. I have vague memories of people interrogating me and yelling about bioterrorism. And then later different people telling me that it had all been some kind of weird gas leak, and that I didn't need to talk to the press if I didn't want to, and that, by the way, I definitely didn't want to. That I might be confused or have hallucinations. That they'd given me some kind of weird experimental drug that was supposed to prevent PTSD but also fucked with my short-term memory kind of a lot.

But I remembered enough to bet that what I'd seen wasn't a gas leak, even before the weird crap started happening.

You'd think I wouldn't keep coming back here, wouldn't you? I was on this exact fucking stool the first time I got one of those calls. You'd think I'd have the good goddamn sense to be creeped out. But I get angry and think, why *should* I let them scare me off? It was my bar first.

Yeah, the calls were what started it. They didn't start until almost three months after I got out of the hospital, but then again, for most of that time

I didn't have a phone. My old phone, along with everything in my bag and my office, my wallet, my keys, my coffee mug, my boots, got swept into the maw of evidence control and were never heard from again.

If it hadn't been for Ginger I'd probably still be living on cash and self-pity, but she got me through the convoluted process of getting everything back in order. Out of all my friends, she was the one who kept up with me instead of coming to visit a couple of times and then getting weirded out by the hamster wheel of no explanations that my brain was on and drifting away. She was the one who told the reporters to fuck off and leave me alone when they tracked me down. She was the one who smiled at the cops when they came by after the reporters left, and assured them that everything was just fine, officer. She listened to me when I explained what I'd seen, or thought I'd seen. And then when I didn't want to talk about it she didn't bring it up.

She also let me stay with her, which was really key because I wasn't sleeping so great in my old apartment by myself. Her place was right on Bedford Avenue and we came down to Rosemary's almost every night, to take the edge off.

One night, when the edge had been blunted, my phone rang.

At first I thought I was just confused by the noise of conversation and the blaring jukebox. I shouted "Hello" three times, then realized I was talking to a recording. But it wasn't about one of my many unpaid bills or a political candidate. It wasn't about anything, it didn't make any sense no matter how I tried to push through the beer and concentrate.

The voice didn't have a gender or age that I could pin down, and it didn't sound like any machine voice I'd ever heard either. When I tried to understand it, the syllables slid away. Yet there was a tone of urgency that made me keep trying. I finally got up and left Ginger watching my drink and took it outside.

On the sidewalk the words were still evasive, but eventually I got them. That didn't really help, though.

Numbers. No nouns or verbs or context, no discernible pattern. Just an endless string of numbers in that slippery voice.

I don't know how long I stood out there, waiting for it to end or say something else or for some kind of pattern to emerge. Eventually I felt a tap on my shoulder, flinched away, and turned to find Ginger behind me.

"The hell?" she said. "Are you ok?"

"Listen to this." I shoved the phone at her, and she put it to her ear and frowned.

Then she laughed and hung up. "That's the stupidest prank call I've ever heard. Do you even know anyone with a" she glanced at the phone, "406 number?"

I shook my head.

We went back inside and ordered new drinks. It being a Tuesday, we were even able to get our stools back.

Sonovia, the bartender, smiled at me and then glanced at the phone. I didn't remember putting it on the bar instead of back in my bag, but there it was and I was fidgeting with it.

"Everything alright?"

I nodded and managed a smile, but not a very convincing one, because the next thing I knew she was giving me a buyback on a shot of Jameson.

The calls weren't every night, at least not at first. If they had been I would have just flushed the phone down the toilet like a prom baby, or turned it off. No, they were sporadic, and yet somehow only came when I was drunk enough to answer, thinking this time it might make sense.

It didn't, and finally Ginger demanded custody of the phone because me running in and out of the bar getting more agitated was not the point of the exercise. I was happy to hand it over. She let everything go to voicemail.

Now we're coming to a part of the story where I look kind of stupid. Stupider.

So, it was a week after I'd given up on my cell phone making any sense, more than four months after the gas leak, or whatever you wanted to call it. That's when I see that asshole Doyle for the first time.

He waited until I was five beers in. Then he walked up as though he'd just come in off Bedford Avenue, he even had a foil-wrapped lamb shawarma in his hand, and he plopped down on the vacant bar stool next to me when Ginger went to the bathroom. But he blew it with his first line.

"There are tigers in the air," he said.

He looked at me as though he expected me to supply the other half of a secret password, while the yogurt sauce dripped through the foil and onto his fingers.

"Tigers? In the beer?" I gazed into the foam at the bottom of my pint glass, then back at him. Then I decided that maybe this was some kind of PETA thing, like the sea kittens, even though I could smell the delicious dead baby sheep in his hand.

The whole point was that I was drunk enough to take the burden off of things to make sense, after all.

I didn't want anything to do with any save-the-yeasts campaign, so I turned away and asked Sonovia for another drink. Then I turned back to tell this tiger guy to get out of Ginger's seat. But he was already gone.

I shrugged and when Ginger got back we laughed about it. But that didn't mean that I wasn't irritated when I saw him again the next evening, sitting in the backmost booth. I'm sure he thought it was a good place to observe without being observed, but it was next to the bathrooms. Poor dumb fuck.

"He's here," I said to Ginger when I got back from the facilities, leaning over close to her ear.

"Who?"

"Tiger dude."

"Where?"

"Last booth."

"What, the guy with the beard and the five-head?"

"That's the one."

Ginger stared, so blatantly he couldn't have missed her. I gave up trying to resist and stared too. His untrimmed beard and bulging cranium, combined with his narrow cheeks, made his head look like a giant had pinched it. His eyes were ridiculously huge, dirty-ice gray, and bloodshot. Although to be fair Rosemary's lighting scheme tends to make everyone's eyes look that way.

"Creeper," Ginger said after a moment's consideration.

"You can't say that just based on the fact that he doesn't own a beard trimmer."

"My instincts are never wrong," she said, and to be fair this was accurate in my experience. Also I had no interest in defending the dude.

We turned away. For the rest of the night my shoulders were tense waiting for him to come up behind me, but he didn't.

That was too good to last, though, and a few days later we walked in and he was just standing at the end of the bar, grinning through his beard at us.

"Looks like someone gave him the talk about how self-confidence is attractive," Ginger muttered.

"Look, I'm sorry," he said as we approached, and held up his hand so that I had to stop if I didn't want to touch him. "I'm not trying to be dense on purpose. I thought you knew."

I was drawn into the question like quicksand. "Knew what?"

"About the air jungles. About those weird phone calls you've been getting. About what killed all those people in your office."

Ginger stepped around me to get between us. "She doesn't want to talk about that shit."

"I'm not a reporter," he said, side-stepping her. "In fact," he looked directly at me again, "you don't have to talk at all. You listen, I'll tell you what I know. You can decide if I sound like a reporter, or someone who actually knows what's going on."

"Not right now," I said, "I need a beer."

But you can't hear something like that and not wonder. Besides, if I didn't talk, and Ginger was right there, everything would be fine.

The stupidest thought I ever had in my life. And I've drunk-dialed my mom at midnight to win an argument, flirted with the tracheotomy guys, cried about Jeanette and Karl and Angel in public even though I know I couldn't have done anything different.

Anyhow, when a bar stool opened up next to me a couple of hours later, he slid in immediately.

"Get lost," Ginger said without looking up.

"No, let him stay," I said. Judas asshole me. She gave me a look that would have killed me if I had any sense. Anyway, I said, "Let's see if he's actually as smart as he says."

He smiled again. His teeth were weird. All there, all white and shiny, but they seemed off-center somehow.

"Thanks. I'm Henry Doyle. And like I said, you don't have to tell me anything. The people in your office didn't die of any gas leak."

I didn't move, didn't nod my head or twitch my hand. It could be a set-up, despite his insistence that I didn't have to talk.

Besides, if he was the kind of person he looked to be, he'd go on in the absence of any encouragement.

"What most people don't know about the history of aviation . . . " He stopped, waved his hand vaguely. "What most people don't know about the history of aviation fills books. But even the books don't tell about Harold Conrad, or Lieutenant Ash, or Randolph Joyner-Leigh."

It wasn't hard to keep looking at him blankly.

"Why should anyone remember? They were only three martyrs, out of many martyrs . . . but my great-great uncle remembered. You might have heard of him." He paused, took a little sip of his PBR, and for a moment I thought Williamsburg suited him very well. "Arthur Conan Doyle."

"Yeah, the writer," Ginger said. "Who wrote *fiction*."

"Sometimes. And sometimes when he wrote the truth, the government asked him to publish it as fiction, with the names and details changed to throw the public off track. He did what they asked. But in the family, we passed it down for generations. There's a reason none of us will get on an airplane. I personally spent days getting here on a Greyhound bus next to the most awful gum-chewing old woman who wanted me to pray with her every time she opened a snack cake, rather than risk flying."

Sonovia came by and Doyle interrupted his rant to order us all another round, although he hadn't finished the one he already had. As soon as she stepped away to pull the taps he plunged back in, still in the groove.

"What the history books, and the science books, and the governments of this and every other nation won't tell you is that there are jungles in the air."

"With tigers?" I said. I couldn't help myself. At least one minor thing made more sense now.

"With every sort of creature that belongs in an ecosystem, from tiny herbivores to massive predators. All amorphous or supported by gas bladders, all adapted to living in the upper atmosphere. Early aeronauts ran into these creatures from time to time as they got high enough. Or when the creatures get low enough, because sometimes they get knocked down somehow. The Crawfordsville monster, to name one, was probably a smaller and less dangerous . . . "

"Horseshit," Ginger cut in. "If that were true, we'd have planes and things getting attacked all the time."

He seemed to be prepared for that. "Does the fact that normal tigers don't eat people in downtown Mumbai prove that the normal jungle doesn't exist? Does the fact that you aren't currently being eaten by a black bear prove that there's no such thing? No. The fact is, when the governments of the world saw how key a role aircraft could play in warfare, if only they could get up there without getting their heads eaten, they took it upon themselves to civilize the skies. The tigers like the head best, you know. And the tongue best out of the head."

"Yum," said Ginger.

He frowned at her. "The air tigers were slaughtered or repelled by the numbers stations. They exist now mostly over remote, uninhabited parts of the world that no major power bothers with."

"Numbers." I needed to stop doing that, but when I wasn't talking I had nothing to do with myself but drink and my latest beer was already almost gone. I could feel my brain shuffling and reshuffling all this information, trying to make the pieces fit, and I didn't like the futility of the feeling.

"Yes, have you heard of numbers stations? Broadcasting eternally on a wavelength no one listens to, impossible to jam, sending out a string of numbers to the atmosphere—numbers that mean nothing to a human, but repel the air-beasts like citronella repels a mosquito."

"Ginger," I said, "give me my phone." There were seven missed calls blinking, and when I hit the callback button, the *Carmina Burana* started playing in Doyle's pocket.

He chuckled. "Caught me. I wanted to see how you'd react to that. I thought it would tell me how much you already know."

"Thanks a lot, asshole."

He brushed that off. "So, like the tigers in earth jungles, these were out of sight and out of mind—maybe killing some hikers in the Urals, grabbing a hunter in Vermont, causing a plane crash or two over what the rubes call the Bermuda Triangle, but mostly not a problem. Except for the rare instances where they come down over a major, populated area. Like they did a few months ago."

He waved Sonovia over. "You look like you could use another drink."

I was shaking like a chihuahua I was so pissed off. "Yeah, no kidding."

"Put it on my tab," he said to Sonovia, and then he tapped on the bar. "I'll be right back." He headed for the bathroom, and went into the ladies' by mistake.

"What a dipshit," Ginger said.

"For real. I was about to buy it for a while, with the numbers thing."

"You should have decked him for that." She gulped beer; she was pissed for real, even if she was joking. "You still can if you'd like, I'll hold his arms."

"Not even worth it." I sighed. "I don't know why I fell for it. It's not like Jeanette or any of them had their heads eaten, or their tongues, or whatever."

We sat in silence for a moment, and then she grinned and said, "Do it."

"Don't tempt me. I don't need any more reasons for the police to yell at me."

"They'd give you the keys to the city for it if they had any sense. Put you on the cover of the *Post*."

After what seemed like a ridiculously long time for a pee, Doyle came back.

"Ok, my turn," Ginger said, and as she walked by me whispered, "Don't smack him while I'm gone, I want to see this."

Doyle didn't hear, and didn't seem to sense the shift in the wind. "A lot of us believe that most of the UFO flaps in history are actually sightings of air beasts. If you look at the older reports, they tend to suggest something organic—it's only when the Air Force gets involved during and right after World War Two that you start to see witnesses jumping to mechanistic explanations for what they saw."

"Who is us, exactly?"

He looked at me and smiled so I could see those awful teeth again. "There are a lot of us who know the truth. More than the government would like, for sure." He pulled his beer towards him, and knocked my cell phone off the bar. I ducked down to retrieve it.

After I came back up and took another sip of beer, my memories get all wobbly.

Yeah, not the smartest night of my life.

I woke up, sort of, with streetlights flashing over my face. The side of my head hurt where it was pressed against the cold window glass, and I'd drooled on my sleeve.

"I'm thirsty," I said, pulling myself upright.

"That's to be expected." It was Doyle. I'd known it would be. Ginger doesn't even own a car. "There's a bottle of water in the cup holder. It's still sealed."

"Too late now."

He chuckled. "You really had me going, you know. Whoever covered up your ties to the government did a good job. And I thought you might honestly not know what I was talking about for a little while there. "

"There's a reason for that."

"Drop the act. You're the only person who wasn't eaten in that office. You know how to survive. That kind of thing doesn't happen by accident."

"No one was eaten!"

"I said drop it. You gave yourself away when you tried to get names out of me."

We were going about eighty miles an hour, thought the road didn't seem built for it. I wasn't sure if I could survive jumping out of the car or not. If I'd really been a government agent, I would know things like that.

"Would you mind telling me which branch you were in? We've never been quite sure whose bailiwick the air tigers are—I've always felt it would be Air Force, but some of my friends think it's more the C.I.A.'s type of thing. Or even the N.S.A."

I opened the water bottle and took a slurp.

"Of course, it's just idle curiosity on my part. It's all the same in the end."

"Why," I said slowly, trying to sound non-confrontational, "allowing that these air tigers exist at all, why would the government want to cover them up? They don't cover up real tigers."

He looked over at me. His expression was unclear behind the beard but I felt safe assuming it was a smirk. "I suppose I might as well admit that we don't know. It's the subject of a lot of speculation in our groups. Probably at first it was to prevent panic that would discourage aeronautic exploration, and later because secrecy is self-perpetuating in the halls of power. Am I close?"

I slurped again. If I told him I had to pee, would he let me out long enough to make a break for it? Probably not.

"Now it's my turn to ask a question, and of course you won't answer, but it doesn't matter because I've learned to read your face. Why let any through? Is it some kind of green nonsense, like those idiots who put the wolves back in Yellowstone? Is it to keep people panicked? Has the government decided to bankrupt the airlines so it can nationalize them?"

I realized after a few seconds that if I didn't say something, he was going to keep watching me instead of the road.

"Well, when I was talking to the police after the attack on my office, they did keep asking about bioterrorism."

He nodded. "That's what I thought. It all makes sense. Frightened people are sheep."

Baaah, I thought, and didn't jump out of the car.

Doyle shut up and I tried to puzzle out where the hell we were. Clearly outside of the city. The streetlights had ended abruptly and now we were driving uphill with trees closer than I liked on either side and large areas of unnerving emptiness that I guessed must be meadows, or marshes, or glimpses of the Hudson. Or maybe off the edge of world. You'd think there would be something. Deer, owls, then, if this is the country. A light from a window in the distance. But no.

I was nauseous from just the water by the time we stopped, and my head was pounding again. Doyle could obviously tell that I was doing bad. He let me walk behind without anything tying me to him except the need to stay in the circle of his flashlight.

"Luckily for you," he said as we walked out of sight of the car on an unpaved path, "we don't need to go all the way to the top. This tiger is coming to unprecedented lows, or so my guy with the tracking equipment says."

"Then why are we here?"

"I'll tell you when this is all over."

"According to you, when this is all over we'll be eaten. Or at least our tongues will." Right now that didn't even sound like such a bad option.

Doyle waited for me to catch up, but he didn't answer. I didn't have the breath for much more conversation anyway, and it did feel as though making noise under these pine trees in this dark would bring something down on us, even if air tigers were bullshit.

Finally, after I'd drained the rest of the water bottle and developed blisters on top of my blisters, we came to an open space.

"This is the spot," Doyle said. "Or within a quarter-mile of here anyway."

He clicked off the flashlight, and I felt that I had no option but to sit down too.

I felt pretty calm, like people who've been kidnapped often say. I thought maybe he'd doze off and I could grab the flashlight, make a break for the car. Maybe when morning came and we were still alive and had our tongues I'd be able to talk him down. Maybe I could call 911. It seemed improbable that I'd have a signal, but maybe luck would be with me, if he'd just fall asleep so he wouldn't see the light from my phone.

To distract myself from the pain and how chilly the night was, I stared up at the stars. Out here they looked close. I could pick out the Big Dipper, and the North Star, and . . . well, that was it, actually. So I looked at that, until a cloud drifted by.

The cloud passed on, and over the moon, and Doyle gasped. He fumbled a bit, stood up, turned the flashlight back on and pointed it at the ground.

When I looked back up from that distraction, the cloud was bigger. And expanding, every second. The stars behind it turned pinkish-gray.

Yeah. Not expanding. Dropping.

I glanced over at Doyle. He planned to survive, and I was going to take my cues from him on that even if he was a crazy kidnapping fuck.

He was staring back at me. Waiting to see what I would do, with a big old shit-eating wrong-toothed grin on his face like he was the smartest damn conspiracy theory buff ever.

I scrambled to my feet and turned to run, but he got to me before I could get anywhere and pinned me against a tree.

"Too late to run now anyway," he said. "It'll be on us in thirty seconds max. Do your stuff."

"I don't have any stuff to do, you dumb shit!"

He looked stunned, and let go of me. Stepped back into the middle of the clearing to stare at me as if I'd let him down, not even turning over his shoulder to see the translucent but now clearly defined mass of death heading for us.

I knew it was no use now, but I didn't want my body to rot up on the mountain next to this jackass's, so I pulled out my cell phone anyway. And it did have a signal. God from a machine.

My hands were shaking and my brain was on autopilot, and I wasn't looking down. I was looking at the thing, which I will not call an air tiger. It looked like a large, pearly amoeba with fine eyelash-hairs all over and a slight pink tinge. It made a moaning sound as it came down on Doyle, who had spread his arms in a Jesus Christ pose, I suppose to die as big a douche as he had lived, all tragic around the red-rimmed eyes. I hit a few buttons that weren't 9-1-1.

My voicemail started playing back. The volume was turned up all the way, the better to be heard in the noisy womb of Rosemary's.

The numbers seemed tiny in the woods, tiny compared to the thing on top of Doyle, but it shuddered. The moaning went up a note, the little hairs all quivered in unison. Slowly, like an elephant climbing out of a wallow, it began to rise.

When the first message ended I frantically skipped to the next. It was twice as high as the trees when I had to start replaying from the beginning, and that's when the clearing was flooded with light and a dozen uniformed, armed men burst from the trees.

Two of them grabbed me, and held me up when my legs decided they were checking out. Another two tackled Doyle.

A pony-tailed woman came up behind them with a pair of binoculars and a long rifle. She looked at the pearly thing still hovering just above us, then shook her head.

"It's too late," she said to the man next to her, and he nodded. She raised the rifle, sighted, fired.

I expected the bullet to go right through, but it made a sound like *wumph*, like it had hit a pillow, and exploded like a tiny firework inside the thing.

The moaning, Jesus Christ. Like Jeanette had moaned that day dying on the dirty brown carpet. It listed towards the side it'd been shot on, then tried to right itself, tipped too far the other way, went over and belly up. And then it dissolved into the air, into the tops of the trees, barely-pink fragments snowing down. A couple of the men raised bandannas to their faces, but most of us, including the woman with the gun, just watched in silence.

When there was nothing more to witness, they jerked Doyle to his feet and we headed back down the mountain. Someone shut down the floodlight behind us, but that was ok because the sun was coming up.

Doyle seemed triumphant, despite the burly guy on either side of him and the cuffs on his wrists.

"It's too late," he whispered at me when they shoved him into the back seat of the cop car next to me. "Now that I know how you did it, I'm going to make sure everyone knows. All along we thought it was something about the radio waves, but it turns out it's just the voice."

"But . . . " No. Let him figure it out how that couldn't work on his own, if he was so smart. It'd only taken me a minute once I had time to think, once I wasn't terrified for my life. In the meantime, if he wanted to believe he'd got one over on me, more power to him.

Besides, since that couldn't have worked, I wasn't sure what had.

Doyle was silent as we headed back downstate, which was a relief. But then, just as we passed out of the south boundary of Adirondack State Park, he slumped over onto me.

"Hey!" I pushed him, and he flopped over the other way. His skin had flushed orange, and as his head jerked his tongue lolled out.

"Crap." The man riding shotgun looked back at us. "It touched him, huh?"

"It was settled on him for . . . " I didn't know for sure, though, although later by playing my messages and timing them I figured it must have been a solid five minutes.

They pulled over and dragged Doyle out to lie on the pine needles on the shoulder of the road. Another car stopped and emitted the pony-tailed woman.

"She says it was on him for awhile," the man said, and jerked his chin at me.

"Poor thing. No wonder it was so bad off."

"Don't beat yourself up. You know there's nothing we can do." Doyle was in the foaming stage, and they both looked down at him with a combination of pity and disgust. "For anyone concerned."

I walked back to the car and didn't look at Doyle again. No one tried to stop me.

They gave me more of their so-called anti-PTSD drugs, but I don't think those work like they're supposed to on me. Maybe it's all the booze in my system. I pretended to forget it all, though.

The hardest part was getting Ginger to forgive me for ignoring her creepdar and screwing us both. She'd been beat up pretty bad by Doyle's confederate who jumped her in the bathroom, but Sonovia spotted something wrong when I left with Doyle and went to investigate. The police got things put together pretty quickly, since Doyle had used the same credit card for everything from his Greyhound ticket to his fleabag hostel bed, the same card he'd left behind when he took me out of Rosemary's without paying our tab. It didn't take Sherlock Holmes to figure that out.

Yeah, I'm sorry. Not that funny.

I erased all the messages. I told Ginger I'd been a schmuck and an asshole and I bought her dinner at Momofuku. We still live together, and she still drinks with me, although not every night now that she has a new job. But she'll definitely notice if I don't come home. Just so you know. In case you're one of Doyle's "us."

But I doubt you are. I doubt you'll even remember this conversation tomorrow, since you've been pacing me all night. But if you do, maybe you'll be able to figure out everything Doyle mistakenly thought he knew and I never did grasp. Maybe it'll click in your brain, even though it keeps buzzing in circles in mine.

IT CAME AND
WE COULD NOT STOP IT

What makes a monster monstrous may be less a matter of any distinguishing physical feature and more a matter of certain intangible qualities. Chief among these would have to be its persistence, its relentless pursuit of whatever its goal. That goal likely entails some threat to us, either direct or incidental, and the monster likely combines its single-mindedness with a capacity to endure whatever attacks we hurl at it. If the monster can be defeated, it will be by an artifact or invention whose uniqueness only underscores the creature's singularity.

This iteration of the monster narrative seems the polar opposite of the power fantasy that animates so many stories of the fantastic. Here, what is on display is not omnipotence, but fatal vulnerability. The particulars of what we are liable to may change with the given story, as the narratives gathered in this second section demonstrate. Clive Barker's "Rawhead Rex" presents a monster of unbridled male aggression, while David J. Schow's "Not from Around Here" joins a monster of more general sexual excess with a concern for suburban alienation. Cherie Priest and Jeff VanderMeer focus on monsters for whom our bodies are little more than raw material to be used for their own, strange arts. Norman Partridge's "The Hollow Man" expands on this idea, giving us a creature whose amusement lies in making us its puppets, while Al Sarrontonio's "The Ropy Thing" addresses the perils of infatuation.

Whatever their surface differences, however, these stories are united by a sense, an anxiety, about the recalcitrance of the world, about those aspects of our existence over which we have no control, against which we struggle in vain. And underneath that plenitude lurks a common fact, that of our own, inevitable end. Asking himself whether he understands death, Mark Petrie, the boy-hero of Stephen King's *'Salem's Lot* (1975), thinks, "Sure. That was when the monsters got you." The stories in this section of *Creatures* bear him out.

Rawhead Rex
Clive Barker

Of all the conquering armies that had tramped the streets of Zeal down the centuries, it was finally the mild tread of the Sunday tripper that brought the village to its knees. It had suffered Roman legions, and the Norman conquest, it had survived the agonies of Civil War, all without losing its identity to the occupying forces. But after centuries of boot and blade it was to be the tourists—the new barbarians—that bested Zeal, their weapons courtesy and hard cash.

It was ideally suited for the invasion. Forty miles southeast of London, amongst the orchards and hopfields of the Kentish Weald, it was far enough from the city to make the trip an adventure, yet close enough to beat a quick retreat if the weather turned foul. Every weekend between May and October Zeal was a watering hole for parched Londoners. They would swarm through the village on each Saturday that promised sun, bringing their dogs, their plastic balls, their litters of children, and their children's litter, disgorging them in bawling hordes on to the village green, then returning to "The Tall Man" to compare traffic stories over glasses of warm beer.

For their part the Zealots weren't unduly distressed by the Sunday trippers; at least they didn't spill blood. But their very lack of aggression made the invasion all the more insidious.

Gradually these city-weary people began to work a gentle but permanent change on the village. Many of them set their hearts on a home in the country; they were charmed by stone cottages set amongst churning oaks, they were enchanted by doves in the churchyard yews. Even the air, they'd say as they inhaled deeply, even the air smells fresher here. It smells of England.

At first a few, then many, began to make bids for the empty barns and deserted houses that littered Zeal and its outskirts. They could be seen every fine weekend, standing in the nettles and rubble, planning how to have a kitchen extension built, and where to install the jacuzzi. And although many of them, once back in the comfort of Kilburn or St John's Wood, chose to stay there, every year one or two of them would strike a reasonable bargain with one of the villagers, and buy themselves an acre of the good life.

So, as the years passed and the natives of Zeal were picked off by old age, the civil savages took over in their stead. The occupation was subtle, but the change was plain to the knowing eye. It was there in the newspapers the Post Office began to stock—what native of Zeal had ever purchased a copy of "Harpers and Queen" magazine, or leafed through "The Times Literary Supplement"? It was there, that change, in the bright new cars that clogged the one narrow street, laughingly called the High Road, that was Zeal's backbone. It was there too in the buzz of gossip at "The Tall Man," a sure sign that the affairs of the foreigners had become fit subject for debate and mockery.

Indeed, as time went by the invaders found a yet more permanent place in the heart of Zeal, as the perennial demons of their hectic lives, Cancer and Heart Disease, took their toll, following their victims even into this newfound land. Like the Romans before them, like the Normans, like all invaders, the commuters made their profoundest mark upon this usurped turf not by building on it, but by being buried under it.

It was clammy the middle of that September; Zeal's last September.

Thomas Garrow, the only son of the late Thomas Garrow, was sweating up a healthy thirst as he dug in the corner of the Three Acre Field. There'd been a violent rainstorm the previous day, Thursday, and the earth was sodden. Clearing the ground for sowing next year hadn't been the easy job Thomas thought it'd be, but he'd sworn blind he'd have the field finished by the end of the week. It was heavy labour, clearing stones, and sorting out the detritus of out-of-date machinery his father, lazy bastard, had left to rust where it lay. Must have been some good years, Thomas thought, some pretty fine damn years, that his father could afford to let good machinery waste away. Come to think of it, that he could have afforded to leave the best part of three acres unploughed; good healthy soil too. This was the Garden of England after all: land was money. Leaving three acres fallow was a luxury nobody could afford in these straitened times. But Jesus, it was hard work: the kind of work his father had put him to in his youth, and he'd hated with a vengeance ever since.

Still, it had to be done.

And the day had begun well. The tractor was healthier after its overhaul, and the morning sky was rife with gulls, across from the coast for a meal of freshly turned worms. They'd kept him raucous company as he worked, their insolence and their short tempers always entertaining. But then, when he came back to the field after a liquid lunch in "The Tall Man," things began to go wrong. The engine started to cut out for one, the same problem that he'd just spent £200 having seen to; and then, when he'd only been back at work a few minutes, he'd found the stone.

It was an unspectacular lump of stuff: poking out of the soil perhaps a foot, its visible diameter a few inches short of a yard, its surface smooth and bare. No lichen even; just a few grooves in its face that might have once been words. A love letter perhaps, a "Kilroy was here" more likely, a date and a name likeliest of all. Whatever it had once been, monument or milestone, it was in the way now. He'd have to dig it up, or next year he'd lose a good three yards of ploughable land. There was no way a plough could skirt around a boulder that size.

Thomas was surprised that the damn thing had been left in the field for so long without anyone bothering to remove it. But then it was a long spell since the Three Acre Field had been planted: certainly not in his thirty-six years. And maybe, now he came to think of it, not in his father's lifetime either. For some reason (if he'd ever known the reason he'd forgotten it) this stretch of Garrow land had been left fallow for a good many seasons, maybe even for generations. In fact there was a suspicion tickling the back of his skull that someone, probably his father, had said no crop would ever grow in that particular spot. But that was plain nonsense. If anything plant life, albeit nettles and convolvulus, grew thicker and ranker in this forsaken three acres than in any other plot in the district. So there was no reason on earth why hops shouldn't flourish here. Maybe even an orchard: though that took more patience and love than Thomas suspected he possessed. Whatever he chose to plant, it would surely spring up from such rich ground with a rare enthusiasm, and he'd have reclaimed three acres of good land to bolster his shaky finances.

If he could just dig out that bloody stone.

He'd half thought of hiring in one of the earth movers from the building site at the North End of the village, just to haul itself across here and get its mechanical jaws working on the problem. Have the stone out and away in two seconds flat. But his pride resisted the idea of running for help at the first sign of a blister. The job was too small anyhow. He'd dig it out himself, the way his father would have done. That's what he'd decided. Now, two and a half hours later, he was regretting his haste.

The ripening warmth of the afternoon had soured in that time, and the air, without much of a breeze to stir it around, had become stifling. Over from the Downs came a stuttering roll of thunder, and Thomas could feel the static crawling at the nape of his neck, making the short hairs there stand up. The sky above the field was empty now: the gulls, too fickle to hang around once the fun was over, had taken some salt-smelling thermal.

Even the earth, that had given up a sweet-sharp flavour as the blades turned it that morning, now smelt joyless; and as he dug the black soil out from around the stone his mind returned helplessly to the putrefaction that made it so very rich. His thoughts circled vacuously on the countless little deaths on every spadeful of soil he dug. This wasn't the way he was used to thinking, and the morbidity of it distressed him. He stopped for a moment, leaning on his spade, and regretting the fourth pint of Guinness he'd downed at lunch. That was normally a harmless enough ration, but today it swilled around in his belly, he could hear it, as dark as the soil on his spade, working up a scum of stomach acid and half-digested food.

Think of something else, he told himself, or you'll get to puking. To take his mind off his belly, he looked at the field. It was nothing out of the ordinary; just a rough square of land bounded by an untrimmed hawthorn hedge. One or two dead animals lying in the shadow of the hawthorn: a starling; something else, too far gone to be recognisable. There was a sense of absence, but that wasn't so unusual. It would soon be autumn, and the summer had been too long, too hot for comfort.

Looking up higher than the hedge he watched the mongol-headed cloud discharge a flicker of lightning to the hills. What had been the brightness of the afternoon was now pressed into a thin line of blue at the horizon. Rain soon, he thought, and the thought was welcome. Cool rain; perhaps a downpour like the previous day. Maybe this time it would clear the air good and proper.

Thomas stared back down at the unyielding stone, and struck it with his spade. A tiny arc of white flame flew off. He cursed, loudly and inventively: the stone, himself, the field. The stone just sat there in the moat he'd dug around it, defying him. He'd almost run out of options: the earth around the thing had been dug out two feet down; he'd hammered stakes under it, chained it and then got the tractor going to haul it out. No joy. Obviously he'd have to dig the moat deeper, drive the stakes further down. He wasn't going to let the damn thing beat him.

Grunting his determination he set to digging again. A fleck of rain hit the back of his hand, but he scarcely noticed it. He knew by experience that labour like this took singularity of purpose: head down, ignore all distractions. He made his mind blank. There was just the earth, the spade, the stone and his body.

Push down, scoop up. Push down, scoop up, a hypnotic rhythm of effort. The trance was so total he wasn't sure how long he worked before the stone began to shift.

The movement woke him. He stood upright, his vertebrae clicking, not quite certain that the shift was anything more than a twitch in his eye. Putting his heel against the stone, he pushed. Yes, it rocked in its grave. He was too drained to smile, but he felt victory close. He had the bugger.

The rain was starting to come on heavier now, and it felt fine on his face. He drove a couple more stakes in around the stone to unseat it a little further: he was going to get the better of the thing. You'll see, he said, you'll see. The third stake went deeper than the first two, and it seemed to puncture a bubble of gas beneath the stone, a yellowish cloud smelling so foul he stepped away from the hole to snatch a breath of purer air. There was none to be had. All he could do was hawk up a wad of phlegm to clear his throat and lungs. Whatever was under the stone, and there was something animal in the stench, it was very rotten.

He forced himself back down to the work, taking gasps of the air into his mouth, not through his nostrils. His head felt tight, as though his brain was swelling and straining against the dome of his skull, pushing to be let out.

"Fuck you," he said and beat another stake under the stone. His back felt as though it was about to break. On his right hand a blister had bust. A cleg sat on his arm and feasted itself, unswatted.

"Do it. Do it. Do it." He beat the last stake in without knowing he was doing it.

And then, the stone began to roll.

He wasn't even touching it. The stone was being pushed out of its seating from beneath. He reached for his spade, which was still wedged beneath the stone. He suddenly felt possessive of it; it was his, a part of him, and he didn't want it near the hole. Not now; not with the stone rocking like it had a geyser under it about to blow. Not with the air yellow, and his brain swelling up like a marrow in August.

He pulled hard on his spade: it wouldn't come. He cursed it, and took two hands to the job, keeping at arm's length from the hole as he hauled, the increasing motion of the stone slinging up showers of soil, lice, and pebbles.

He heaved at the spade again, but it wouldn't give. He didn't stop to analyse the situation. The work had sickened him, all he wanted was to get his spade, *his* spade, out of the hole and get the hell out of there.

The stone bucked, but still he wouldn't let go of the spade, it had become fixed in his head that he had to have it before he could leave. Only when it was back in his hands, safe and sound, would he obey his bowels, and run.

Beneath his feet the ground began to erupt. The stone rolled away from the tomb as if feather-light, a second cloud of gas, more obnoxious than the first, seemed to blow it on its way. At the same time the spade came out of the hole, and Thomas saw what had hold of it.

Suddenly there was no sense in heaven or earth.

There was a hand, a living hand, clutching the spade, a hand so wide it could grasp the blade with ease.

Thomas knew the moment well. The splitting earth: the hand: the stench. He knew it from some nightmare he'd heard at his father's knee.

Now he wanted to let go of the spade, but he no longer had the will. All he could do was obey some imperative from underground, to haul until his ligaments tore and his sinews bled.

Beneath the thin crust of earth, Rawhead smelt the sky. It was pure ether to his dulled senses, making him sick with pleasure. Kingdoms for the taking, just a few inches away. After so many years, after the endless suffocation, there was light on his eyes again, and the taste of human terror on his tongue.

His head was breaking surface now, his black hair wreathed with worms, his scalp seething with tiny red spiders. They'd irritated him a hundred years, those spiders burrowing into his marrow, and he longed to crush them out. Pull, pull, he willed the human, and Thomas Garrow pulled until his pitiful body had no strength left, and inch by inch Rawhead was hoisted out of his grave in a shroud of prayers.

The stone that had pressed on him for so long had been removed, and he was dragging himself up easily now, sloughing off the grave earth like a snake its skin. His torso was free. Shoulders twice as broad as a man's; lean, scarred arms stronger than any human. His limbs were pumping with blood like a butterfly's wings, juicing with resurrection. His long, lethal fingers rhythmically clawed the ground as they gained strength.

Thomas Garrow just stood and watched. There was nothing in him but awe. Fear was for those who still had a chance of life: he had none.

Rawhead was out of his grave completely. He began to stand upright for the first time in centuries. Clods of damp soil fell from his torso as he stretched to his full height, a yard above Garrow's six feet.

Thomas Garrow stood in Rawhead's shadow with his eyes still fixed on the gaping hole the King had risen from. In his right hand he still clutched his spade. Rawhead picked him up by the hair. His scalp tore under the weight of his body, so Rawhead seized Garrow round the neck, his vast hand easily enclosing it.

Blood ran down Garrow's face from his scalp, and the sensation stirred him. Death was imminent, and he knew it. He looked down at his legs, thrashing uselessly below him, then he looked up and stared directly into Rawhead's pitiless face.

It was huge, like the harvest moon, huge and amber. But this moon had eyes that burned in its pallid, pitted face. They were for all the world like wounds, those eyes, as though somebody had gouged them in the flesh of Rawhead's face then set two candles to flicker in the holes.

Garrow was entranced by the vastness of this moon. He looked from eye to eye, and then to the wet slits that were its nose, and finally, in a childish terror, down to the mouth. God, that mouth. It was so wide, so cavernous it seemed to split the head in two as it opened. That was Thomas Garrow's last thought. That the moon was splitting in two, and falling out of the sky on top of him.

Then the King inverted the body, as had always been his way with his dead enemies, and drove Thomas head first into the hole, winding him down into the very grave his forefathers had intended to bury Rawhead in forever.

By the time the thunderstorm proper broke over Zeal, the King was a mile away from the Three Acre Field, sheltering in the Nicholson barn. In the village everyone went about their business, rain or no rain. Ignorance was bliss. There was no Cassandra amongst them, nor had "Your Future in the Stars" in that week's "Gazette" even hinted at the sudden deaths to come to a Gemini, three Leos, a Sagittarian and a minor star-system of others in the next few days.

The rain had come with the thunder, fat cool spots of it, which rapidly turned into a downpour of monsoonal ferocity. Only when the gutters became torrents did people begin to take shelter.

On the building site the earth-mover that had been roughly landscaping Ronnie Milton's back garden sat idling in the rain, receiving a second wash-down in two days. The driver had taken the downpour as a signal to retire into the hut to talk racehorses and women.

In the doorway of the Post Office three of the villagers watched the drains backing up, and tutted that this always happened when it rained, and in half an hour there'd be a pool of water in the dip at the bottom of the High Street so deep you could sail a boat on it.

And down in the dip itself, in the vestry of St Peter's, Declan Ewan, the Verger, watched the rain pelting down the hill in eager rivulets, and gathering into a little sea outside the vestry gate. Soon be deep enough to drown in, he thought, and then, puzzled by why he imagined drowning, he turned away from the window and went back to the business of folding vestments. A strange excitement was in him today: and he couldn't, wouldn't, didn't want to suppress it. It was nothing to do with the thunderstorm, though he'd always loved them since he was a child. No: there was something else stirring him up, and he was damned if he knew what. It was like being a child again. As if it was Christmas, and any minute Santa, the first Lord he'd ever believed in, would be at the door. The very idea made him want to laugh out loud, but the vestry was too sober a place for laughter, and he stopped himself, letting the smile curl inside him, a secret hope.

While everyone else took refuge from the rain, Gwen Nicholson was getting thoroughly drenched. She was still in the yard behind the house, coaxing Amelia's pony towards the barn. The thunder had made the stupid beast jittery, and it didn't want to budge. Now Gwen was soaked and angry.

"Will you come on, you brute?" she yelled at it over the noise of the storm. The rain lashed the yard, and pummeled the top of her head. Her hair was flattened. *"Come on! Come on!"*

The pony refused to budge. Its eyes showed crescents of white in its fear. And the more the thunder rolled and crackled around the yard the less it wanted to move. Angrily, Gwen slapped it across the backside, harder than she strictly needed to. It took a couple of steps in response to the blow, dropping steaming turds as it went, and Gwen took the advantage. Once she had it moving she could drag it the rest of the way.

"Warm barn," she promised it. "Come on, it's wet out here, you don't want to stay out here."

The barn door was slightly ajar. Surely it must look like an inviting prospect, she thought, even to a pea-brained pony. She dragged it to within spitting distance of the barn, and one more slap got it through the door.

As she'd promised the damn thing, the interior of the barn was sweet and dry, though the air smelt metallic with the storm. Gwen tied the pony to the crossbar in its stall and roughly threw a blanket over its glistening hide. She was damned if she was going to swab the creature down, that was Amelia's job. That was the bargain she'd made with her daughter when they'd agreed to buy the pony: that all the grooming and clearing out would be Amelia's responsibility, and to be fair to her, she'd done what she promised, more or less.

The pony was still panicking. It stamped and rolled its eyes like a bad tragedian. There were flecks of foam on its lips. A little apologetically Gwen patted its flank. She'd lost her temper. Time of the month. Now she regretted it. She only hoped Amelia hadn't been at her bedroom window watching.

A gust of wind caught the barn door and it swung closed. The sound of rain on the yard outside was abruptly muted. It was suddenly dark.

The pony stopped stamping. Gwen stopped stroking its side. Everything stopped: her heart too, it seemed. Behind her a figure that was almost twice her size rose from beyond the bales of hay. Gwen didn't see the giant, but her innards churned. Damn periods, she thought, rubbing her lower belly in a slow circle. She was normally as regular as clockwork, but this month she'd come on a day early. She should go back to the house, get changed, get clean.

Rawhead stood and looked at the nape of Gwen Nicholson's neck, where a single nip would easily kill. But there was no way he could bring himself to touch this woman; not today. She had the blood cycle on her, he could taste its tang, and it sickened him. It was taboo, that blood, and he had never taken a woman poisoned by its presence.

Feeling the damp between her legs, Gwen hurried out of the barn without looking behind her, and ran through the downpour back to the house, leaving the fretting pony in the darkness of the barn.

Rawhead heard the woman's feet recede, heard the house door slam.

He waited, to be sure she wouldn't come back, then he padded across to the animal, reached down and took hold of it. The pony kicked and complained, but Rawhead had in his time taken animals far bigger and far better armed than this.

He opened his mouth. The gums were suffused with blood as the teeth emerged from them, like claws unsheathed from a cat's paw. There were two rows on each jaw, two dozen needle-sharp points. They gleamed as they closed around the meat of the pony's neck. Thick, fresh blood poured down Rawhead's throat; he gulped it greedily. The hot taste of the world. It made him feel strong and wise. This was only the first of many meals he would take, he'd gorge on anything that took his fancy and nobody would stop him, not this time. And when he was ready he'd throw those pretenders off his throne, he'd cremate them in their houses, he'd slaughter their children and wear their infants' bowels as necklaces. *This place was his.* Just because they'd tamed the wilderness for a while didn't mean they owned the earth. It was his, and nobody would take it from him, not even the holiness. He was wise to that too. They'd never subdue him again.

He sat cross-legged on the floor of the barn, the grey-pink intestines of the pony coiled around him, planning his tactics as best he could. He'd never been a great thinker. Too much appetite: it overwhelmed his reason. He lived in the eternal present of his hunger and his strength, feeling only the crude territorial instinct that would sooner or later blossom into carnage.

The rain didn't let up for over an hour.

Ron Milton was becoming impatient: a flaw in his nature that had given him an ulcer and a top flight job in Design Consultancy. What Milton could get done for you, couldn't be done quicker. He was the best: and he hated sloth in other people as much as in himself. Take this damn house, for instance. They'd promised it would be finished by mid-July, garden land-scaped, driveway laid, everything, and here he was, two months after that date, looking at a house that was still far from habitable. Half the windows without glass, the front door missing, the garden an assault course, the driveway a mire.

This was to be his castle: his retreat from a world that made him dyspeptic and rich. A haven away from the hassles of the city, where Maggie could grow roses, and the children could breathe clean air. Except that it wasn't ready. Damn it, at this rate he wouldn't be in until next spring. Another winter in London: the thought made his heart sink.

Maggie joined him, sheltering him under her red umbrella.

"Where are the kids?" he asked.

She grimaced. "Back at the hotel, driving Mrs. Blatter crazy."

Enid Blatter had borne their cavorting for half a dozen weekends through the summer. She'd had kids of her own, and she handled Debbie and Ian with aplomb. But there was a limit, even to her fund of mirth and merriment.

"We'd better get back to town."

"No. Please let's stay another day or two. We can go back on Sunday evening. I want us all to go to the Harvest Festival Service on Sunday."

Now it was Ron's turn to grimace.

"Oh hell."

"It's all part of village life, Ronnie. If we're going to live here, we have to become part of the community."

He whined like a little boy when he was in this kind of mood. She knew him so well she could hear his next words before he said them.

"I don't want to."

"Well, we've no choice."

"We can go back tonight."

"Ronnie—"

"There's nothing we can do here. The kids are bored, you're miserable . . . "

Maggie had set her features in concrete; she wasn't going to budge an inch. He knew that face as well as she knew his whining.

He studied the puddles that were forming in what might one day be their front garden, unable to imagine grass there, roses there. It all suddenly seemed impossible.

"You go back to town if you like, Ronnie. Take the kids. I'll stay here. Train it home on Sunday night."

Clever, he thought, to give him a get-out that's more unattractive than staying put. Two days in town looking after the kids alone? No thank you.

"OK. You win. We'll go to the Harvest-bloody-Festival."

"Martyr."

"As long as I don't have to pray."

Amelia Nicholson ran into the kitchen, her round face white, and collapsed in front of her mother. There was greasy vomit on her green plastic mackintosh, and blood on her green plastic Wellingtons.

Gwen yelled for Denny. Their little girl was shivering in her faint, her mouth chewing at a word, or words, that wouldn't come.

"What is it?"

Denny was thundering down the stairs.

"For Christ's sake—"

Amelia was vomiting again. Her face was practically blue.

"What's wrong with her?"

"She just came in. You'd better ring for an ambulance."

Denny put his hand on her cheek.

"She's in shock."

"Ambulance, Denny . . . " Gwen was taking off the green mackintosh, and loosening the child's blouse. Slowly, Denny stood up. Through the rain-laced window he could see into the yard: the barn door flapped open and closed in the wind. Somebody was inside; he glimpsed movement.

"For Christ's sake—ambulance!" Gwen said again.

Denny wasn't listening. There was somebody in his barn, on his property, and he had a strict ritual for trespassers.

The barn door opened again, teasing. Yes! Retreating into the dark. Interloper.

He picked up the rifle beside the door, keeping his eyes on the yard as much as he could. Behind him, Gwen had left Amelia on the kitchen floor and was dialing for help. The girl was moaning now: she was going to be OK. Just some filthy trespasser scaring her, that's all. On his land.

He opened the door and stepped into the yard. He was in his shirtsleeves and the wind was bitingly cold, but the rain had stopped. Underfoot the ground glistened, and drips fell from every eave and portico, a fidgety percussion that accompanied him across the yard.

The barn door swung listlessly ajar again, and this time stayed open. He could see nothing inside. Half wondered if a trick of the light had—

But no. He'd seen someone moving in here. The barn wasn't empty. Something (not the pony) was watching him even now. They'd see the rifle in his hands, and they'd sweat. Let them. Come into his place like that. Let them think he was going to blow their balls off.

He covered the distance in a half a dozen confident strides and stepped into the barn.

The pony's stomach was beneath his shoe, one of its legs to his right, the upper shank gnawed to the bone. Pools of thickening blood reflected the holes in the roof. The mutilation made him want to heave.

"All right," he challenged the shadows. "Come out." He raised his rifle. "You hear me, you bastard? Out I said, or I'll blow you to Kingdom Come."

He meant it too.

At the far end of the barn something stirred amongst the bales.

Now I've got the son of a bitch, thought Denny. The trespasser got up, all nine feet of him, and stared at Denny.

"Jee-sus."

And without warning it was coming at him, coming like a locomotive smooth and efficient. He fired into it, and the bullet struck its upper chest, but the wound hardly slowed it.

Nicholson turned and ran. The stones of the yard were slippery beneath his shoes, and he had no turn of speed to outrun it. It was at his back in two beats, and on him in another.

Gwen dropped the phone when she heard the shot. She raced to the window in time to see her sweet Denny eclipsed by a gargantuan form. It howled as it took him, and threw him up into the air like a sack of feathers. She watched helplessly as his body twisted at the apex of its journey before plummeting back down to earth again. It hit the yard with a thud she felt in her every bone, and the giant was at his body like a shot, treading his loving face to muck.

She screamed; trying to silence herself with her hand. Too late. The sound was out and the giant was looking at her, straight at her, its malice piercing the window. Oh God, it had seen her, and now it was coming for her, loping across the yard, a naked engine, and grinning a promise at her as it came.

Gwen snatched Amelia off the floor and hugged her close, pressing the girl's face against her neck. Maybe she wouldn't see: she mustn't see. The sound of its feet slapping on the wet yard got louder. Its shadow filled the kitchen.

"Jesus help me."

It was pressing at the window, its body so wide that it cancelled out the light, its lewd, revolting face smeared on the watery pane. Then it was smashing through, ignoring the glass that bit into its flesh. It smelled child meat. It wanted child meat. It would *have* child meat.

Its teeth were spilling into view, widening that smile into an obscene laugh. Ropes of saliva hung from its jaw as it clawed the air, like a cat after a mouse in a cage, pressing further and further in, each swipe closer to the morsel.

Gwen flung open the door into the hall as the thing lost patience with snatching and began to demolish the window frame and clamber through. She locked the door after her while crockery smashed and wood splintered on the other side, then she began to load all the hall furniture against it. Tables, chairs, coat stand, knowing even as she did it, that it would be matchwood in two seconds flat. Amelia was kneeling on the hall floor where Gwen had set her down. Her face was a thankful blank.

All right, that was all she could do. Now, upstairs. She picked up her daughter, who was suddenly air-light, and took the stairs two at a time. Halfway up, the noise in the kitchen below stopped utterly.

She suddenly had a reality crisis. On the landing where she stood all was peace and calm. Dust gathered minutely on the windowsills, flowers wilted; all the infinitesimal domestic procedures went on as though nothing had happened.

"Dreaming it," she said. God, yes: dreaming it.

She sat down on the bed Denny and she had slept in together for eight years, and tried to think straight.

Some vile menstrual nightmare, that's what it was, some rape fantasy out of all control. She lay Amelia on the pink eiderdown (Denny hated pink, but suffered it for her sake) and stroked the girl's clammy forehead.

"Dreaming it."

Then the room darkened, and she looked up knowing what she'd see.

It was there, the nightmare, all over the upper windows, its spidery arms spanning the width of the glass, clinging like an acrobat to the frame, its repellent teeth sheathing and unsheathing as it gawped at her terror.

In one swooping movement she snatched Amelia up from the bed and dived towards the door. Behind her, glass shattered, and a gust of cold air swept into the bedroom. It was coming.

She ran across the landing to the top of the stairs but it was after her in a heart's beat, ducking through the bedroom door, its mouth a tunnel. It whooped as it reached to steal the mute parcel in her arms, huge in the confined space of the landing.

She couldn't outrun it, she couldn't outfight it. Its hands fixed on Amelia with insolent ease, and tugged.

The child screamed as it took her, her fingernails raking four furrows across her mother's face as she left her arms.

Gwen stumbled back, dizzied by the unthinkable sight in front of her, and lost balance at the top of the stairs. As she fell backwards she saw Amelia's tear-stained face, doll-stiff, being fed between those rows of teeth. Then her head hit the banister, and her neck broke. She bounced down the last six steps a corpse.

The rainwater had drained away a little by early evening, but the artificial lake at the bottom of the dip still flooded the road to a depth of several inches. Serenely, it reflected the sky. Pretty, but inconvenient. Reverend Coot quietly reminded Declan Ewan to report the blocked drains to the County Council. It was the third time of asking, and Declan blushed at the request.

"Sorry, I'll . . ."

"All right. No problem, Declan. But we really must get them cleared."

A vacant look. A beat. A thought.

"Autumn fall always clogs them again, of course."

Coot made a roughly cyclical gesture, intending a son of observation about how it really wouldn't make that much difference when or if the Council cleared the drains, then the thought disappeared. There were more pressing issues. For one, the Sunday Sermon. For a second, the reason why he couldn't make much sense of sermon writing this evening. There was an unease in the air today, that made every reassuring word he committed to paper curdle as he wrote it. Coot went to the window, back to Declan, and scratched his palms. They itched: maybe an attack of eczema again. If he could only speak; find some words to shape his distress. Never, in his forty-five years, had he felt so incapable of communication; and never in those years had it been so vital that he talk.

"Shall I go now?" Declan asked.

Coot shook his head.

"A moment longer. If you would."

He turned to the Verger. Declan Ewan was twenty-nine, though he had the face of a much older man. Bland, pale features: his hair receding prematurely.

What will this egg-face make of my revelation? thought Coot. He'll probably laugh. That's why I can't find the words, because I don't want to. I'm afraid of looking stupid. Here I am, a man of the cloth, dedicated to the Christian Mysteries. For the first time in forty odd years I've had a real glimpse of something, a vision maybe, and I'm scared of being laughed at. Stupid man, Coot, stupid, stupid man.

He took off his glasses. Declan's empty features became a blur. Now at least he didn't have to look at the smirking.

"Declan, this morning I had what I can only describe as a . . . as a . . . visitation."

Declan said nothing, nor did the blur move.

"I don't quite know how to say this . . . our vocabulary's impoverished when it comes to these sorts of things . . . but frankly I've never had such a direct, such an unequivocal, manifestation of—"

Coot stopped. Did he mean God?

"God," he said, not sure that he did.

Declan said nothing for a moment. Coot risked returning his glasses to their place. The egg hadn't cracked.

"Can you say what it was like?" Declan asked, his equilibrium absolutely unspoiled.

Coot shook his head; he'd been trying to find the words all day, but the phrases all seemed so predictable.

"What was it like?" Declan insisted.

Why didn't he understand that there were no words? I must try, thought Coot, I *must*.

"I was at the Altar after Morning Prayer . . . " he began, "and I felt something going through me. Like electricity almost. It made my hair stand on end. Literally on end."

Coot's hand was running through his short-cropped hair as he remembered the sensation. The hair standing bolt upright, like a field of grey-ginger corn. And that buzzing at the temples, in his lungs, at his groin. It had actually given him a hard-on; not that he was going to be able to tell Declan that. But he'd stood there at the Altar with an erection so powerful it was like discovering the joy of lust all over again.

"I won't claim . . . I *can't* claim it was our Lord God—" (Though he wanted to believe that; that his God was the Lord of the Hardon.) "—I can't even claim it was Christian. But something happened today. I felt it."

Declan's face was still impenetrable. Coot watched it for several seconds, impatient for its disdain.

"Well?" he demanded.

"Well what?"

"Nothing to say?"

The egg frowned for a moment, a furrow in its shell. Then it said:

"God help us," almost in a whisper.

"What?"

"I felt it too. Not quite as you describe: not quite an electric shock. But something."

"Why God help us, Declan? Are you afraid of something?"

He made no reply.

"If you know something about these experiences that I don't . . . please tell me. I want to know, to understand. God, I *have* to understand."

Declan pursed his lips. "Well . . . " his eyes became more indecipherable than ever; and for the first time Coot caught a glimpse of a ghost behind Declan's eyes. Was it despair, perhaps?

"There's a lot of history to this place you know," he said, "a history of things . . . on this site."

Coot knew Declan had been delving into Zeal's history. Harmless enough pastime: the past was the past.

"There's been a settlement here for centuries, stretches back well before Roman occupation. No one knows how long. There's probably always been a temple on this site."

"Nothing odd about that." Coot offered up a smile, inviting Declan to reassure him. A part of him wanted to be told everything was well with his world: even if it was a lie.

Declan's face darkened. He had no reassurance to give. "And there was a forest here. Huge. The Wild Woods." Was it still despair behind the eyes? Or was it nostalgia? "Not some tame little orchard. A forest you could lose a city in; full of beasts . . . "

"Wolves, you mean? Bears?"

Declan shook his head.

"There were things that owned this land. Before Christ. Before civilisation. Most of them didn't survive the destruction of their natural habitat: too primitive I suppose. But strong. Not like us; not human. Something else altogether."

"So what?"

"One of them survived as late as the fourteen hundreds. There's a carving of it being buried. It's on the Altar."

"On the Altar?"

"Underneath the cloth. I found it a while ago: never thought much of it. Till today. Today I . . . tried to touch it."

He produced his fist, and unclenched it. The flesh of his palm was blistered. Pus ran from the broken skin.

"It doesn't hurt," he said. "In fact it's quite numb. Serves me right, really. I should have known."

Coot's first thought was that the man was lying. His second was that there was some logical explanation. His third was his father's dictum: "Logic is the last refuge of a coward."

Declan was speaking again. This time he was seeping excitement.

"They called it Rawhead."

"What?"

"The beast they buried. It's in the history books. Rawhead it was called, because its head was huge, and the colour of the moon, and raw, like meat."

Declan couldn't stop himself now. He was beginning to smile.

"It ate children," he said, and beamed like a baby about to receive its mother's tit.

It wasn't until early on the Saturday morning that the atrocity at the Nicholson Farm was discovered. Mick Glossop had been driving up to London, and he'd taken the road that ran beside the farm, ("Don't know why. Don't usually. Funny really.") and Nicholson's Friesian herd was kicking up a row at the gate, their udders distended. They'd clearly not been milked in twenty-four hours. Glossop had stopped his jeep on the road and gone into the yard.

The body of Denny Nicholson was already crawling with flies, though the sun had barely been up an hour. Inside the house the only remains of Amelia Nicholson were shreds of a dress and a casually discarded foot. Gwen Nicholson's unmutilated body lay at the bottom of the stairs. There was no sign of a wound or any sexual interference with the corpse.

By nine-thirty Zeal was swarming with police, and the shock of the incident registered on every face in the street. Though there were conflicting reports as to the state of the bodies there was no doubt of the brutality of the murders. Especially the child, dismembered presumably. Her body taken away by her killer for God knows what purpose.

The Murder Squad set up a Unit at "The Tall Man," while house to house interviews were conducted throughout the village. Nothing came immediately to light. No strangers seen in the locality; no more suspicious behaviour from anyone than was normal for a poacher or a bent building merchant. It was Enid Blatter, she of the ample bust and the motherly manner, who mentioned that she hadn't seen Thorn Garrow for over twenty-four hours.

They found him where his killer had left him, the worse for a few hours of picking. Worms at his head and gulls at his legs. The flesh of his shins, where his trousers had slid out of his boots, was pecked to the bone. When he was dug up families of refugee lice scurried from his ears.

The atmosphere in the hotel that night was subdued. In the bar Detective Sergeant Gissing, down from London to head the investigation, had found a willing ear in Ron Milton. He was glad to be conversing with a fellow Londoner, and Milton kept them both in Scotch and water for the best part of three hours.

"Twenty years in the force," Gissing kept repeating, "and I've never seen anything like it."

Which wasn't strictly true. There'd been that whore (or selected highlights thereof) he'd found in a suitcase at Euston's left luggage department, a good decade ago. And the addict who'd taken it upon himself to hypnotise a polar bear at London Zoo: he'd been a sight for sore eyes when they dredged him out of the pool. He'd seen a good deal, had Stanley Gissing—

"But this . . . never seen anything like it," he insisted. "Fair made me want to puke."

Ron wasn't quite sure why he listened to Gissing; it was just something to while the night away. Ron, who'd been a radical in his younger days, had never liked policemen much, and there was some quirky satisfaction to be had from getting this self-satisfied prat pissed out of his tiny skull.

"He's a fucking lunatic," Gissing said, "you can take my word for it. We'll have him easy. A man like that isn't in control, you see. Doesn't bother to cover his tracks, doesn't even care if he lives or dies. God knows, any man who can tear a seven-year-old girl to shreds like that, he's on the verge of going bang. Seen 'em."

"Yes?"

"Oh yes. Seen 'em weep like children, blood all over 'em like they was just out of the abattoir, and tears on their faces. Pathetic."

"So, you'll have him."

"Like that," said Gissing, and snapped his fingers. He got to his feet, a little unsteadily, "Sure as God made little apples, we'll have him." He glanced at his watch and then at the empty glass.

Ron made no further offers of refills.

"Well," said Gissing, "I must be getting back to town. Put in my report."

He swayed to the door and left Milton to the bill.

Rawhead watched Gissing's car crawl out of the village and along the north road, the headlights making very little impression on the night. The noise of the engine made Rawhead nervous though, as it over-revved up the hill past the Nicholson Farm. It roared and coughed like no beast he had encountered before, and somehow the homo sapiens had control of it. If the Kingdom was to be taken back from the usurpers, sooner or later he would have to best one of these beasts. Rawhead swallowed his fear and prepared for the confrontation.

The moon grew teeth.

In the back of the car Stanley was near as damnit asleep, dreaming of little girls. In his dreams these charming nymphettes were climbing a ladder on their way to bed, and he was on duty beside the ladder watching them climb, catching glimpses of their slightly soiled knickers as they disappeared into the sky. It was a familiar dream, one that he would never have admitted to, not even drunk. Not that he was ashamed exactly; he knew for a fact many of his colleagues entertained peccadilloes every bit as offbeat as, and some a good deal less savoury than, his. But he was possessive of it: it was his particular dream, and he wasn't about to share it with anyone.

In the driving seat the young officer who had been chauffeuring Gissing around for the best part of six months was waiting for the old man to fall well and truly asleep. Then and only then could he risk turning the radio on to catch up with the cricket scores. Australia were well down in the Test: a late rally seemed unlikely. Ah, now there was a career, he thought as he drove. Beats this routine into a cocked hat.

Both lost in their reveries, driver and passenger, neither caught sight of Rawhead. He was stalking the car now, his giant's stride easily keeping pace with it as it navigated the winding, unlit road.

All at once his anger flared, and roaring, he left the field for the tarmac.

The driver swerved to avoid the immense form that skipped into the burning headlights, its mouth issuing a howl like a pack of rabid dogs.

The car skidded on the wet ground, its left wing grazing the bushes that ran along the side of the road, a tangle of branches lashing the windscreen as it careered on its way. On the back seat Gissing fell off the ladder he was climbing, just as the car came to the end of its hedgerow tour and met an iron gate. Gissing was flung against the front seat, winded but uninjured. The impact took the driver over the wheel and through the window in two short seconds. His feet, now in Gissing's face, twitched.

From the road Rawhead watched the death of the metal box. Its tortured voice, the howl of its wrenched flank, the shattering of its face, frightened him. But it was dead.

He waited a few cautious moments before advancing up the road to sniff the crumpled body. There was an aromatic smell in the air, which pricked his sinuses, and the cause of it, the blood of the box, was dribbling out of its broken torso, and running away down the road. Certain now that it must be finished, he approached.

There was someone alive in the box. None of the sweet child flesh he savoured so much, just tough male meat. It was a comical face that peered at him. Round, wild eyes. Its silly mouth opened and closed like a fish's. He kicked the box to make it open, and when that didn't work he wrenched off the doors. Then he reached and drew the whimpering male out of his refuge. Was this one of the species that had subdued him? This fearful mite, with its jelly lips? He laughed at its pleas, then turned Gissing on his head, and held him upside down by one foot. He waited until the cries died down, then reached between the twitching legs and found the mite's manhood. Not large. Quite shrunk, in fact, by fear. Gissing was blathering all kinds of stuff: none of it made any sense. The only sound Rawhead understood from the mouth of the man was this sound he was hearing now, this high-pitched shriek that always attended a gelding. Once finished, he dropped Gissing beside the car.

A fire had begun in the smashed engine, he could smell it. He was not so much a beast that he feared fire. Respected it yes: but not feared. Fire was a tool, he'd used it many times: to burn out enemies, to cremate them in their beds.

Now he stepped back from the car as the flame found the petrol and fire erupted into the air. Heat bailed towards him, and he smelt the hair on the front of his body crisp, but he was too entranced by the spectacle not to look. The fire followed the blood of the beast, consuming Gissing, and licking along the rivers of petrol like an eager dog after a trail of piss. Rawhead watched, and learned a new and lethal lesson.

In the chaos of his study Coot was unsuccessfully fighting off sleep. He'd spent a good deal of the evening at the Altar, some of it with Declan. Tonight there'd be no praying, just sketching. Now he had a copy of the Altar carving on his desk in front of him, and he'd spent an hour just staring at it. The exercise had been fruitless. Either the carving was too ambiguous, or his imagination lacked breadth. Whichever, he could make very little sense of the image. It pictured a burial certainly, but that was about all he was able to work out. Maybe the body was a little bigger than that of the mourners, but nothing exceptional. He thought of Zeal's pub, "The Tall Man," and smiled. It might well have pleased some Mediaeval wit to picture the burial of a brewer under the Altar cloth.

In the hall, the sick clock struck twelve-fifteen, which meant it was almost one. Coot got up from his desk, stretched, and switched off the lamp. He was surprised by the brilliance of the moonlight streaming through the crack in the curtain. It was a full, harvest moon, and the light, though cold, was luxuriant.

He put the guard in front of the fire, and stepped into the darkened hallway, closing the door behind him. The clock ticked loudly. Somewhere over towards Goudhurst, he heard the sound of an ambulance siren.

What's happening? he wondered, and opened the front door to see what he could see. There were car headlights on the hill, and the distant throb of blue police lights, more rhythmical than the ticking at his back. Accident on the north road. Early for ice, and surely not cold enough. He watched the lights, set on the hill like jewels on the back of a whale, winking away. It was quite chilly, come to think of it. No weather to be standing in the—

He frowned; something caught his eye, a movement in the far corner of the churchyard, underneath the trees. The moonlight etched the scene in monochrome. Black yews, grey stones, a white chrysanthemum strewing its petals on a grave. And black in the shadow of the yews, but outlined clearly against the slab of a marble tomb beyond, a giant.

Coot stepped out of the house in slippered feet.

The giant was not alone. Somebody was kneeling in front of it, a smaller, more human shape, its face raised and clear in the light. It was Declan. Even from a distance it was clear that he was smiling up at his master.

Coot wanted to get closer; a better look at the nightmare. As he took his third step his foot crunched on a piece of gravel.

The giant seemed to shift in the shadows. Was it turning to look at him? Coot chewed on his heart. No, let it be deaf; please God, let it not see me, make me invisible.

The prayer was apparently answered. The giant made no sign of having seen his approach. Taking courage Coot advanced across the pavement of gravestones, dodging from tomb to tomb for cover, barely daring to breathe. He was within a few feet of the tableau now and he could see the way the creature's head was bowed towards Declan; he could hear the sound like sandpaper on stone it was making at the back of its throat. But there was more to the scene.

Declan's vestments were torn and dirtied, his thin chest bare. Moonlight caught his sternum, his ribs. His state, and his position, were unequivocal. This was adoration—pure and simple. Then Coot heard the splashing; he stepped closer and saw that the giant was directing a glistening rope of its urine onto Declan's upturned face. It splashed into his slackly opened mouth, it ran over his torso. The gleam of joy didn't leave Declan's eyes for a moment as he received this baptism, indeed he turned his head from side to side in his eagerness to be totally defiled.

The smell of the creature's discharge wafted across to Coot. It was acidic, vile. How could Declan bear to have a drop of it on him, much less bathe in it? Coot wanted to cry out, stop the depravity, but even in the shadow of the yew the shape of the beast was terrifying. It was too tall and too broad to be human.

This was surely the Beast of the Wild Woods Declan had been trying to describe; this was the child-devourer. Had Declan guessed, when he eulogised about this monster, what power it would have over his imagination? Had he known all along that if the beast were to come sniffing for him he'd kneel in front of it, call it Lord (before Christ, before Civilisation, he'd said), let it discharge its bladder on to him, and smile?

Yes. Oh yes.

And so let him have his moment. Don't risk your neck for him, Coot thought, he's where he wants to be. Very slowly he backed off towards the Vestry, his eyes still fixed on the degradation in front of him. The baptism dribbled to a halt, but Declan's hands, cupped in front of him, still held a quantity of fluid. He put the heels of his hands to his mouth, and drank.

Coot gagged, unable to prevent himself. For an instant he closed his eyes to shut out the sight, and opened them again to see that the shadowy head had turned towards him and was looking at him with eyes that burned in the blackness.

"Christ Almighty."

It saw him. For certain this time, it saw him. It roared, and its head changed shape in the shadow, its mouth opened so horribly wide.

"Sweet Jesus."

Already it was charging towards him, antelope-lithe, leaving its acolyte slumped beneath the tree. Coot turned and ran, ran as he hadn't in many a long year, hurdling the graves as he fled. It was just a few yards: the door, some kind of safety. Not for long maybe, but time to think, to find a weapon. Run, you old bastard. Christ the race, Christ the prize. Four yards.

Run.

The door was open.

Almost there; a yard to go—

He crossed the threshold and swung round to slam the door on his pursuer. But no! Rawhead had shot his hand through the door, a hand three times the size of a human hand. It was snatching at the empty air, trying to find Coot, the roars relentless.

Coot threw his full weight against the oak door. The door stile, edged with iron, bit into Rawhead's forearm. The roar became a howl: venom and agony mingled in a din that was heard from one end of Zeal to the other.

It stained the night up as far as the north road, where the remains of Gissing and his driver were being scraped up and parcelled in plastic. It echoed round the icy walls of the Chapel of Rest where Denny and Gwen Nicholson were already beginning to degenerate. It was heard too in the bedrooms of Zeal, where living couples lay side by side, maybe an arm numbed under the other's body; where the old lay awake working out the geography of the ceiling; where children dreamt of the womb, and babies mourned it. It was heard again and again and again as Rawhead raged at the door.

The howl made Coot's head swim. His mouth babbled prayers, but the much needed support from on high showed no sign of coming. He felt his strength ebbing away. The giant was steadily gaining access, pressing the door open inch by inch. Coot's feet slid on the too-well-polished floor, his muscles were fluttering as they faltered. This was a contest he had no chance of winning, not if he tried to match his strength to that of the beast, sinew for sinew. If he was to see tomorrow morning, he needed some strategy.

Coot pressed harder against the wood, his eyes darting around the hallway looking for a weapon. It mustn't get in: it mustn't have mastery over him. A bitter smell was in his nostrils. For a moment he saw himself naked and kneeling in front of the giant, with its piss beating on his skull. Hard on the heels of that picture, came another flurry of depravities. It was all he could do not to let it in, let the obscenities get a permanent hold. Its mind was working its way into his, a thick wedge of filth pressing its way through his memories, encouraging buried thoughts to the surface. Wouldn't it ask for worship, just like any God? And wouldn't its demands be plain, and real? Not ambiguous, like those of the Lord he'd served up 'til now. That was a fine thought: to give himself up to this certainty that beat on the other side of the door, and lie open in front of it, and let it ravage him.

Rawhead. Its name was a pulse in his ear—Raw. Head.

In desperation, knowing his fragile mental defences were within an ace of collapsing, his eyes alighted on the clothes stand to the left of the door.

Raw. Head. Raw. Head. The name was an imperative. Raw. Head. Raw. Head. It evoked a skinned head, its defences peeled back, a thing close to bursting, no telling if it was pain or pleasure. But easy to find out—

It almost had possession of him, he knew it: it was now or never. He took one arm from the door and stretched towards the rack for a walking stick. There was one amongst them he wanted in particular. He called it his cross-country stick, a yard and a half of stripped ash, well used and resilient. His fingers coaxed it towards him.

Rawhead had taken advantage of the lack of force behind the door; its leathery arm was working its way in, indifferent to the way the door jamb scored the skin. The hand, its fingers strong as steel, had caught the folds of Coot's jacket.

Coot raised the ash stick and brought it down on Rawhead's elbow, where the bone was vulnerably close to the surface. The weapon splintered on impact, but it did its job. On the other side of the door the howl began again, and Rawhead's arm was rapidly withdrawn. As the fingers slid out Coot slammed the door and bolted it. There was a short hiatus, seconds only, before the attack began again, this time a two-fisted beating on the door. The hinges began to buckle; the wood groaned. It would be a short time, a very short time, before it gained access. It was strong; and now it was furious too.

Coot crossed the hall and picked up the phone. Police, he said, and began to dial. How long before it put two and two together, gave up on the door, and moved to the windows? They were leaded, but that wouldn't keep it out for long. He had minutes at the most, probably seconds, depending on its brain power.

His mind, loosed from Rawhead's grasp, was a chorus of fragmented prayers and demands. If I die, he found himself thinking, will I be rewarded in Heaven for dying more brutally than any country vicar might reasonably expect? Is there compensation in paradise for being disembowelled in the front hall of your own Vestry?

There was only one officer left on duty at the Police Station: the rest were up on the north road, clearing up after Gissing's party. The poor man could make very little sense of Reverend Coot's pleas, but there was no mistaking the sound of splintering wood that accompanied the babbles, nor the howling in the background.

The officer put the phone down and radioed for help. The patrol on the north road took twenty, maybe twenty-five seconds to answer. In that time Rawhead had smashed the central panel of the Vestry door, and was now demolishing the rest. Not that the patrol knew that. After the sights they'd faced up there, the chauffeur's charred body, Gissing's missing manhood, they had become insolent with experience, like hour-old war veterans. It took the officer at the Station a good minute to convince them of the urgency in Coot's voice. In that time Rawhead had gained access.

In the hotel Ron Milton watched the parade of lights blinking on the hill, heard the sirens, and Rawhead's howls, and was besieged by doubts. Was this really the quiet country village he had intended to settle himself and his family in? He looked down at Maggie, who had been woken by the noise but was now asleep again, her bottle of sleeping tablets almost empty on the bedside cabinet. He felt, though she would have laughed at him for it, protective towards her: he wanted to be her hero. She was the one who took the self-defence night classes however, while he grew overweight on expense account lunches. It made him inexplicably sad to watch her sleep, knowing he had so little power over life and death.

Rawhead stood in the hall of the Vestry in a confetti of shattered wood. His torso was pin-pricked with splinters, and dozens of tiny wounds bled down his heaving bulk. His sour sweat permeated the hall like incense.

He sniffed the air for the man, but he was nowhere near. Rawhead bared his teeth in frustration, expelling a thin whistle of air from the back of his throat, and loped down the hall towards the study. There was warmth there, his nerves could feel it at twenty yards, and there was comfort too. He over-turned the desk and shattered two of the chairs, partly to make more room for himself, mostly out of sheer destructiveness, then threw away the fire guard and sat down. Warmth surrounded him: healing, living warmth. He luxuriated in the sensation as it embraced his face, his lean belly, his limbs. He felt it heat his blood too, and so stir memories of other fires, fires he'd set in fields of burgeoning wheat.

And he recalled another fire, the memory of which his mind tried to dodge and duck, but he couldn't avoid thinking about it: the humiliation of that night would be with him forever. They'd picked their season so care-fully: high summer, and no rain in two months. The undergrowth of the Wild Woods was tinder dry, even the living tree caught the flame easily. He had been flushed out of his fortress with streaming eyes, confused and fearful, to be met with spikes and nets on every side, and that . . . *thing* they had, that sight that could subdue him.

Of course they weren't courageous enough to kill him; they were too superstitious for that. Besides, didn't they recognise his authority, even as they wounded him, their terror a homage to it? So they buried him alive: and that was worse than death. Wasn't that the very worst? Because he could live an age, ages, and never die, not even locked in the earth. Just left to wait a hundred years, and suffer, and another hundred and another, while the generations walked the ground above his head and lived and died and forgot him. Perhaps the women didn't forget him: he could smell them even through the earth, when they came close to his grave, and though they might not have known it they felt anxious, they persuaded their men to abandon the place altogether, so he was left absolutely alone, with not even a gleaner for company. Loneliness was their revenge on him, he thought, for the times he and his brothers had taken women into the woods, spread them out, spiked and loosed them again, bleeding but fertile. They would die having the children of those rapes; no woman's anatomy could survive the thrashing of a hybrid, its teeth, its anguish. That was the only revenge he and his brothers ever had on the big-bellied sex.

Rawhead stroked himself and looked up at the gilded reproduction of "The Light of the World" that hung above Coot's mantelpiece. The image woke no tremors of fear or remorse in him: it was a picture of a sexless martyr, doe-eyed and woebegone. No challenge there. The true power, the only power that could defeat him, was apparently gone: lost beyond recall, its place usurped by a virgin shepherd. He ejaculated, silently, his thin semen hissing on the hearth. The world was his to rule unchallenged. He would have warmth, and food in abundance. Babies even. Yes, baby meat, that was the best. Just dropped mites, still blind from the womb.

He stretched, sighing in anticipation of that delicacy, his brain awash with atrocities.

From his refuge in the crypt Coot heard the police cars squealing to a halt outside the Vestry, then the sound of feet on the gravel path. He judged there to be at least half a dozen. It would be enough, surely.

Cautiously he moved through the darkness towards the stairs.

Something touched him: he almost yelled, biting his tongue a moment before the cry escaped.

"Don't go now," a voice said from behind him. It was Declan, and he was speaking altogether too loudly for comfort. The thing was above them, somewhere, it would hear them if he wasn't careful. Oh God, it mustn't hear.

"It's up above us," said Coot in a whisper.

"I know."

The voice seemed to come from his bowels not from his throat; it was bubbled through filth.

"Let's have him come down here shall we? He wants you, you know. He wants me to—"

"What's happened to you?"

Declan's face was just visible in the dark. It grinned; lunatic.

"I think he might want to baptise you too. How'd you like that? Like that would you? He pissed on me: you see him? And that wasn't all. Oh no, he wants more than that. He wants everything. Hear me? Everything."

Declan grabbed hold of Coot, a bear hug that stank of the creature's urine.

"Come with me?" he leered in Coot's face.

"I put my trust in God."

Declan laughed. Not a hollow laugh; there was genuine compassion in it for this lost soul.

"He *is* God," he said. "He was here before this fucking shithouse was built, you know that."

"So were dogs."

"Uh?"

"Doesn't mean I'd let them cock their legs on me."

"Clever old fucker aren't you?" said Declan, the smile inverted. "He'll show you. You'll change."

"No, Declan. Let go of me—"

The embrace was too strong.

"Come on up the stairs, fuckface. Mustn't keep God waiting."

He pulled Coot up the stairs, arms still locked round him. Words, all logical argument, eluded Coot: was there nothing he could say to make the man see his degradation? They made an ungainly entrance into the Church, and Coot automatically looked towards the altar, hoping for some reassurance, but he got none. The altar had been desecrated. The cloths had been torn and smeared with excrement, the cross and candlesticks were in the middle of a fire of prayer books that burned healthily on the altar steps. Smuts floated around the Church, the air was grimy with smoke.

"You did this?"

Declan grunted.

"He wants me to destroy it all. Take it apart stone by stone if I have to."

"He wouldn't dare."

"Oh he'd dare. He's not scared of Jesus, he's not scared of . . . "

The certainty lapsed for a telling instant, and Coot leapt on the hesitation.

"There's something here he *is* scared of, though, isn't there, or he'd have come in here himself, done it all himself . . . "

Declan wasn't looking at Coot. His eyes had glazed.

"What is it, Declan? What is it he doesn't like? You can tell me—"

Declan spat in Coot's face, a wad of thick phlegm that hung on his cheek like a slug.

"None of your business."

"In the name of Christ, Declan, look at what he's done to you."

"I know my master when I see him—"

Declan was shaking.

"—and so will you."

He turned Coot round to face the south door. It was open, and the creature was there on the threshold, stooping gracefully to duck under the porch. For the first time Coot saw Rawhead in a good light, and the terrors began in earnest. He had avoided thinking too much of its size, its stare, its origins. Now, as it came towards him with slow, even stately steps, his heart conceded its mastery. It was no mere beast, despite its mane, and its awesome array of teeth; its eyes lanced him through and through, gleaming with a depth of contempt no animal could ever muster. Its mouth opened wider and wider, the teeth gliding from the gums, two, three inches long, and still the mouth was gaping wider. When there was nowhere to run, Declan let Coot go. Not that Coot could have moved anyway: the stare was too insistent. Rawhead reached out and picked Coot up. The world turned on its head—

There were seven officers, not six as Coot had guessed. Three of them were armed, their weapons brought down from London on the order of Detective Sergeant Gissing. The late, soon to be decorated posthumously, Detective Sergeant Gissing. They were led, these seven good men and true, by Sergeant Ivanhoe Baker. Ivanhoe was not an heroic man, either by inclination or education. His voice, which he had prayed would give the appropriate orders when the time came without betraying him, came out as a strangled yelp as Rawhead appeared from the interior of the Church.

"I can see it!" he said. Everybody could: it was nine feet tall, covered in blood, and it looked like Hell on legs. Nobody needed it pointed out. The guns were raised without Ivanhoe's instruction: and the unarmed men, suddenly feeling naked, kissed their truncheons and prayed. One of them ran.

"Hold your ground!" Ivanhoe shrieked; if those sons of bitches turned tail he'd be left on his own. They hadn't issued him with a gun, just authority, and that was not much comfort.

Rawhead was still holding Coot up, at arm's length, by the neck. The Reverend's legs dangled a foot above the ground, his head lolled back, his eyes were closed. The monster displayed the body for his enemies, proof of power.

"Shall we . . . please . . . can we . . . shoot the bastard?" One of the gunmen inquired.

Ivanhoe swallowed before answering. "We'll hit the vicar."

"He's dead already," said the gunman.

"We don't know that."

"He must be dead. Look at him—"

Rawhead was shaking Coot like an eiderdown, and his stuffing was falling out, much to Ivanhoe's intense disgust. Then, almost lazily, Rawhead flung Coot at the police. The body hit the gravel a little way from the gate and lay still. Ivanhoe found his voice—

"Shoot!"

The gunmen needed no encouragement; their fingers were depressing the triggers before the syllable was out of his mouth.

Rawhead was hit by three, four, five bullets in quick succession, most of them in the chest. They stung him and he put up an arm to protect his face, covering his balls with the other hand. This was a pain he hadn't anticipated. The wound he'd received from Nicholson's rifle had been forgotten in the bliss of the bloodletting that came soon after, but these barbs hurt him, and they kept coming. He felt a twinge of fear. His instinct was to fly in the face of these popping, flashing rods, but the pain was too much. Instead, he turned and made his retreat, leaping over the tombs as he fled towards the safety of the hills. There were copses he knew, burrows and caves, where he could hide and find time to think this new problem through. But first he had to elude them.

They were after him quickly, flushed with the ease of their victory, leaving Ivanhoe to find a vase on one of the graves, empty it of chrysanthemums, and be sick.

Out of the dip there were no lights along the road, and Rawhead began to feel safer. He could melt into the darkness, into the earth, he'd done it a thousand times. He cut across a field. The barley was still unharvested, and heavy with its grain. He trampled it as he ran, grinding seed and stalk. At his back his pursuers were already losing the chase. The car they'd piled into had stopped in the road, he could see its lights, one blue, two white, way behind him. The enemy was shouting a confusion of orders, words Rawhead didn't understand. No matter; he knew men. They were easily frightened. They would not look far for him tonight; they'd use the dark as an excuse to call off the search, telling themselves that his wounds were probably fatal anyhow. Trusting children that they were.

He climbed to the top of the hill and looked down into the valley. Below the snake of the road, its eyes the headlights of the enemy's car, the village was a wheel of warm light, with flashing blues and reds at its hub. Beyond, in every direction, the impenetrable black of the hills, over which the stars hung in loops and clusters. By day this would seem a counterpane valley, toy town small. By night it was fathomless, more his than theirs.

His enemies were already returning to their hovels, as he'd known they would. The chase was over for the night.

He lay down on the earth and watched a meteor burn up as it fell to the southwest. It was a brief, bright streak, which edge-lit a cloud, then went out. Morning was many long, healing hours in the future. He would soon be strong again: and then, then—she'd burn them all away.

Coot was not dead: but so close to death it scarcely made any difference. Eighty per cent of the bones in his body were fractured or broken: his face and neck were a maze of lacerations: one of his hands was crushed almost beyond recognition. He would certainly die. It was purely a matter of time and inclination.

In the village those who had glimpsed so much as a fragment of the events in the dip were already elaborating on their stories: and the evidence of the naked eye lent credence to the most fantastic inventions. The chaos in the churchyard, the smashed door of the Vestry: the cordoned-off car on the north road, Whatever had happened that Saturday night it was going to take a long time to forget.

There was no harvest festival service, which came as no surprise to anyone.

Maggie was insistent: "I want us all to go back to London."

"A day ago you wanted us to stay here. Got to be part of the community."

"That was on Friday, before all this . . . this . . . There's a maniac loose, Ron."

"If we go now, we won't come back."

"What are you talking about; of course we'll come back."

"If we leave once the place is threatened, we give up on it altogether."

"That's ridiculous."

"You were the one who was so keen on us being visible, being seen to join in village life. Well, we'll have to join in the deaths too. And I'm going to stay—see it through. You can go back to London. Take the kids."

"No."

He sighed, heavily.

"I want to see him caught: whoever he is. I want to know it's all been cleared up, see it with my own eyes. That's the only way we'll ever feel safe here."

Reluctantly, she nodded.

"At least let's get out of the hotel for a while. Mrs. Blatter's going loopy. Can't we go for a drive? Get some air—"

"Yes, why not?"

It was a balmy September day: the countryside, always willing to spring a surprise, was gleaming with life. Late flowers shone in the roadside hedges, birds dipped over the road as they drove. The sky was azure, the clouds a fantasia in cream. A few miles outside the village all the horrors of the previous night began to evaporate and the sheer exuberance of the day began to raise the family's spirits. With every mile they drove out of Zeal Ron's fears diminished. Soon, he was singing.

On the back seat Debbie was being difficult. One moment "I'm hot Daddy", the next: "I want an orange juice, Daddy;" the next: "I have to pee."

Ron stopped the car on an empty stretch of road, and played the indulgent father. The kids had been through a lot; today they could be spoiled.

"All right, darling, you can have a pee here, then we'll go and find an ice cream for you."

"Where's the la la?" she said. Damn stupid phrase; mother-in-law's euphemism.

Maggie chipped in. She was better with Debbie in these moods than Ron. "You can go behind the hedge," she said.

Debbie looked horrified. Ron exchanged a half-smile with Ian.

The boy had a put-upon look on his face. Grimacing, he went back to his dog-eared comic.

"Hurry up, can't you?" he muttered. "Then we can go somewhere proper."

Somewhere proper, thought Ron. He means a town. He's a city kid: its going to take a while to convince him that a hill with a view *is* somewhere proper. Debbie was still being difficult.

"I can't go here, Mummy—"

"Why not?"

"Somebody might see me."

"Nobody's going to see you, darling," Ron reassured her. "Now do as your Mummy says." He turned to Maggie. "Go with her, love."

Maggie wasn't budging. "She's OK."

"She can't climb over the gate on her own."

"Well, you go, then."

Ron was determined not to argue; he forced a smile. "Come on," he said.

Debbie got out of the car and Ron helped her over the iron gate into the field beyond. It was already harvested. It smelt . . . earthy.

"Don't look," she admonished him, wide eyed, "you *mustn't* look."

She was already a manipulator, at the ripe old age of nine. She could play him better than the piano she was taking lessons on. He knew it, and so did she. He smiled at her and closed his eyes.

"All right. See? I've got my eyes closed. Now hurry up, Debbie. Please."

"Promise you won't peek."

"I won't peek." My God, he thought, she's certainly making a production number out of this. "Hurry up."

He glanced back towards the car. Ian was sitting in the back, still reading, engrossed in some cheap heroics, his face set as he stared into the adventure. The boy was so serious: the occasional half-smile was all Ron could ever win from him. It wasn't a put-on, it wasn't a fake air of mystery. He seemed content to leave all the performing to his sister.

Behind the hedge Debbie pulled down her Sunday knickers and squatted, but after all the fuss her pee wouldn't come. She concentrated but that just made it worse.

Ron looked up the field towards the horizon. There were gulls up there, squabbling over a tit-bit. He watched them awhile, impatience growing.

"Come on, love," he said.

He looked back at the car, and Ian was watching him now, his face slack with boredom; or something like it. Was there something else there: a deep resignation? Ron thought. The boy looked back to his comic book "Utopia" without acknowledging his father's gaze.

Then Debbie screamed: an ear-piercing shriek.

"Christ!" Ron was clambering over the gate in an instant, and Maggie wasn't far behind him.

"Debbie!"

Ron found her standing against the hedge, staring at the ground, blubbering, face red. "What's wrong, for God's sake?"

She was yabbering incoherently. Ron followed her eye.

"What's happened?" Maggie was having difficulty getting over the gate.

"It's all right . . . it's all right."

There was a dead mole almost buried in the tangle at the edge of the field, its eyes pecked out, its rotting hide crawling with flies.

"Oh God, Ron." Maggie looked at him accusingly, as though he'd put the damn thing there with malice aforethought.

"It's all right, sweetheart," she said, elbowing past her husband and wrapping Debbie up in her arms.

Her sobs quieted a bit. City kids, thought Ron. They're going to have to get used to that sort of thing if they're going to live in the country. No road sweepers here to brush up the run over cats every morning. Maggie was rocking her, and the worst of the tears were apparently over.

"She'll be all right," Ron said.

"Of course she will, won't you, darling?" Maggie helped her pull up her knickers. She was still snivelling, her need for privacy forgotten in her unhappiness.

In the back of the car Ian listened to his sister's caterwauling and tried to concentrate on his comic. Anything for attention, he thought. Well, she's welcome.

Suddenly, it went dark.

He looked up from the page, his heart loud. At his shoulder, six inches away from him, something stooped to peer into the car, its face like Hell. He couldn't scream, his tongue refused to move. All he could do was flood the seat and kick uselessly as the long, scarred arms reached through the window towards him. The nails of the beast gouged his ankles, tore his sock. One of his new shoes fell off in the struggle. Now it had his foot and he was being dragged across the wet seat towards the window. He found his voice. Not quite *his* voice, it was a pathetic, a silly-sounding voice, not the equal of the mortal terror he felt. And all too late anyway; it was dragging his legs through the window, and his bottom was almost through now. He looked through the back window as it hauled his torso into the open air and in a dream he saw Daddy at the gate, his face looking so, so ridiculous. He was climbing the gate, coming to help, coming to save him but he was far too slow. Ian knew he was beyond salvation from the beginning, because he'd died this way in his sleep on a hundred occasions and Daddy never got there in time. The mouth was wider even than he'd dreamed it, a hole which he was being delivered into, head first. It smelt like the dustbins at the back of the school canteen, times a million. He was sick down its throat, as it bit the top of his head off.

Ron had never screamed in his life. The scream had always belonged to the other sex, until that instant. Then, watching the monster stand up and close its jaws around his son's head, there was no sound appropriate but a scream.

Rawhead heard the cry, and turned, without a trace of fear on his face, to look at the source. Their eyes met. The King's glance penetrated Milton like a spike, freezing him to the road and to the marrow. It was Maggie who broke its hold, her voice a dirge.

"Oh . . . please . . . no."

Ron shook Rawhead's look from his head, and started towards the car, towards his son. But the hesitation had given Rawhead a moment's grace he scarcely needed anyway, and he was already away, his catch clamped between his jaws, spilling out to right and left. The breeze carried motes of Ian's blood back down the road towards Ron; he felt them spot his face in a gentle shower.

Declan stood in the chancel of St Peter's and listened for the hum. It was still there. Sooner or later he'd have to go to the source of that sound and destroy it, even if it meant, as it well might, his own death. His new master would demand it. But that was par for the course; and the thought of death didn't distress him; far from it. In the last few days he'd realised ambitions that he'd nurtured (unspoken, even unthought) for years.

Looking up at the black bulk of the monster as it rained piss on him he'd found the purest joy. If that experience, which would once have disgusted him, could be so consummate, what might death be like? rarer still. And if he could contrive to die by Rawhead's hand, by that wide hand that smelt so rank, wouldn't that be the rarest of the rare?

He looked up at the altar, and at the remains of the fire the police had extinguished. They'd searched for him after Coot's death, but he had a dozen hiding places they would never find, and they'd soon given up. Bigger fish to fry. He collected a fresh armful of *Songs of Praise* and threw them down amongst the damp ashes. The candlesticks were warped, but still recognisable. The cross had disappeared, either shrivelled away or removed by some light-fingered officer of the law. He tore a few handfuls of hymns from the books, and lit a match. The old songs caught easily.

Ron Milton was tasting tears, and it was a taste he'd forgotten. It was many years since he'd wept, especially in front of other males. But he didn't care any longer: these bastard policemen weren't human anyway. They just looked at him while he poured out his story, and nodded like idiots.

"We've drafted men in from every division within fifty miles, Mr. Milton," said the bland face with the understanding eyes. "The hills are being scoured. We'll have it, whatever it is."

"It took my child, you understand me? It killed him, in front of me—"

They didn't seem to appreciate the horror of it all.

"We're doing what we can."

"It's not enough. This thing . . . it's not human."

Ivanhoe, with the understanding eyes, knew bloody well how unhuman it was.

"There's people coming from the Ministry of Defence: we can't do much more 'til they've had a look at the evidence," he said. Then added, as a sop: "It's all public money, sir."

"You fucking idiot! What does it matter what it costs to kill it? It's not human. It's out of Hell."

Ivanhoe's look lost compassion.

"If it came out of Hell, sir," he said, "I don't think it would have found the Reverend Coot such easy pickings."

Coot: that was his man. Why hadn't he thought of that before? Coot.

Ron had never been much of a man of God. But he was prepared to be open minded, and now that he'd seen the opposition, or one of its troops, he was ready to reform his opinions. He'd believe anything, anything at all, if it gave him a weapon against the Devil.

He must get to Coot.

"What about your wife?" the officer called after him. Maggie was sitting in one of the side offices, dumb with sedation, Debbie asleep beside her. There was nothing he could do for them. They were as safe here as anywhere.

He must get to Coot, before he died.

He'd know, whatever Reverends know; and he'd understand the pain better than these monkeys. Dead sons were the crux of the Church after all.

As he got into the car it seemed for a moment he smelt his son: the boy who would have carried his name (Ian Ronald Milton he'd been christened), the boy who was his sperm made flesh, who he'd had circumcised like himself. The quiet child who'd looked out of the car at him with such resignation in his eyes.

This time the tears didn't begin. This time there was just an anger that was almost wonderful.

It was half past eleven at night. Rawhead Rex lay under the moon in one of the harvested fields to the southwest of the Nicholson Farm. The stubble was darkening now, and there was a tantalising smell of rotting vegetable matter off the earth. Beside him lay his dinner, Ian Ronald Milton, face up on the field, his midriff torn open. Occasionally the beast would lean up on one elbow and paddle its fingers in the cooling soup of the boy-child's body, fishing for a delicacy.

Here, under the full moon, bathing in silver, stretching his limbs and eating the flesh of human kind, he felt irresistible. His fingers drew a kidney off the plate beside him and he swallowed it whole.

Sweet.

Coot was awake, despite the sedation. He knew he was dying, and the time was too precious to doze through. He didn't know the name of the face that was interrogating him in the yellow gloom of his room, but the voice was so politely insistent he had to listen, even though it interrupted his peace-making with God. Besides, they had questions in common: and they all circled, those questions, on the beast that had reduced him to this pulp.

"It took my son," the man said. "What do you know about the thing? Please tell me. I'll believe whatever you tell me—" Now *there* was desperation— "Just explain—"

Time and again, as he'd lain on that hot pillow, confused thoughts had raced through Coot's mind. Declan's baptism; the embrace of the beast; the altar; his hair rising and his flesh too. Maybe there was something he could tell the father at his bedside.

" . . . in the church . . . "

Ron leaned closer to Coot; he smelt of earth already.

" . . . the altar . . . it's afraid . . . the altar . . . "

"You mean the cross? It's afraid of the cross?"

"No . . . not—"

"Not—"

The body creaked once, and stopped. Ron watched death come over the face: the saliva dry on Coot's lips, the iris of his remaining eye contract. He watched a long while before he rang for the nurse, then quietly made his escape.

There was somebody in the Church. The door, which had been padlocked by the police, was ajar, the lock smashed. Ron pushed it open a few inches and slid inside. There were no lights on in the Church, the only illumination was a bonfire on the altar steps. It was being tended by a young man Ron had seen on and off in the village. He looked up from his fire-watching, but kept feeding the flames the guts of books.

"What can I do for you?" he asked, without interest.

"I came to—" Ron hesitated. What to tell this man: the truth? No, there was something wrong here.

"I asked you a frigging question," said the man. "What do you want?"

As he walked down the aisle towards the fire Ron began to see the questioner in more detail. There were stains, like mud, on his clothes, and his eyes had sunk in their orbits as if his brain had sucked them in.

"You've got no right to be in here—"

"I thought anyone could come into a church," said Ron, staring at the burning pages as they blackened.

"Not tonight. You get the fuck out of here." Ron kept walking towards the altar.

"You get the fuck out, I said!"

The face in front of Ron was alive with leers and grimaces: there was lunacy in it.

"I came to see the altar; I'll go when I've seen it, and not before."

"You've been talking to Coot. That it?"

"Coot?"

"What did the old wanker tell you? It's all a lie, whatever it was; he never told the truth in his frigging life, you know that? You take it from he. He used to get up there—" he threw a prayer book at the pulpit "—and tell fucking lies!"

"I want to see the altar for myself. We'll see if he was telling lies—"

"No, you won't!"

The man threw another handful of books on to the fire and stepped down to block Ron's path. He smelt not of mud but of shit. Without warning, he pounced. His hands seized Ron's neck, and the two of them toppled over. Declan's fingers reaching to gouge at Ron's eyes: his teeth snapping at his nose.

Ron was surprised at the weakness of his own arms; why hadn't he played squash the way Maggie had suggested, why were his muscles so ineffectual? If he wasn't careful this man was going to kill him.

Suddenly a light, so bright it could have been a midnight dawn, splashed through the west window. A cloud of screams followed close on it. Fire-light, dwarfing the bonfire on the altar steps, dyed the air. The stained glass danced.

Declan forgot his victim for an instant, and Ron rallied. He pushed the man's chin back, and got a knee under his torso, then he kicked hard. The enemy went reeling, and Ron was up and after him, a fistful of hair securing the target while the ball of his other hand hammered at the lunatic's face 'til it broke. It wasn't enough to see the bastard's nose bleed, or to hear the cartilage mashed; Ron kept beating and beating until his fist bled. Only then did he let Declan drop.

Outside, Zeal was ablaze.

Rawhead had made fires before, many fires. But petrol was a new weapon, and he was still getting the hang of it. It didn't take him long to learn. The trick was to wound the wheeled boxes, that was easy. Open their flanks and out their blood would pour, blood that made his head ache. The boxes were easy prey, lined up on the pavement like bullocks to be slaughtered. He went amongst them demented with death, splashing their blood down the High Street and igniting it. Streams of liquid fire poured into gardens, over thresholds. Thatches caught; wood-beamed cottages went up. In minutes Zeal was burning from end to end.

In St. Peter's, Ron dragged the filthied cloth off the altar, trying to block out all thoughts of Debbie and Margaret. The police would move them to a place of safety, for certain. The issue at hand must take precedence.

Beneath the cloth was a large box, its front panel roughly carved. He took no notice of the design; there were more urgent matters to attend to. Outside, the beast was loose. He could hear its triumphant roars, and he felt eager, yes eager, to go to it. To kill it or be killed. But first, the box. It contained power, no doubt about that; a power that was even now raising the hairs on his head, that was working at his cock, giving him an aching hard-on. His flesh seemed to seethe with it, it elated him like love. Hungry, he put his hands on the box, and a shock that seemed to cook his joints ran up both his arms. He fell back, and for a moment he wondered if he was going to remain conscious, the pain was so bad, but it subsided, in moments. He cast around for a tool, something to get him into the box without laying flesh to it.

In desperation he wrapped his hand with a piece of the altar cloth and snatched one of the brass candleholders from the edge of the fire. The cloth began to smoulder as the heat worked its way through to his hand. He stepped back to the altar and beat at the wood like a madman until it began to splinter. His hands were numb now; if the heated candlesticks were burning his palms he couldn't feel it. What did it matter anyhow? There was a weapon here: a few inches away from him, if only he could get to it, to wield it. His erection throbbed, his balls tingled.

"Come to me," he found himself saying, "come on, come on. Come to me. Come to me." Like he was willing it into his embrace, this treasure, like it was a girl he wanted, his hard-on wanted, and he was hypnotising her into his bed.

"Come to me, come to me—"

The wood facade was breaking. Panting now, he used the corners of the candlestick base to lever larger chunks of timber away. The altar was hollow, as he'd known it would be. And empty.

Empty.

Except for a ball of stone, the size of a small football. Was this his prize? He couldn't believe how insignificant it looked: and yet the air was still electric around him; his blood still danced. He reached through the hole he'd made in the altar and picked the relic up.

Outside, Rawhead was jubilating.

Images flashed before Ron's eyes as he weighed the stone in his deadened hand. A corpse with its feet burning. A flaming cot. A dog, running along the street, a living ball of fire. It was all outside, waiting to unfold.

Against the perpetrator, he had this stone.

He'd trusted God, just for half a day, and he got shat on. It was just a stone: just a fucking *stone*. He turned the football over and over in his hand, trying to make some sense of its furrows and its mounds. Was it meant to be something, perhaps; was he missing its deeper significance?

There was a knot of noise at the other end of the church; a crash, a cry, from beyond the door a whoosh of flame. Two people staggered in, followed by smoke and pleas. "He's burning the village," said a voice Ron knew. It was that benign policeman who hadn't believed in Hell; he was trying to keep his act together, perhaps for the benefit of his companion, Mrs. Blatter from the hotel. The nightdress she'd run into the street wearing was torn. Her breasts were exposed; they shook with her sobs; she didn't seem to know she was naked, didn't even know where she was.

"Christ in Heaven help us," said Ivanhoe.

"There's no fucking Christ in here," came Declan's voice. He was standing up, and reeling towards the intruders. Ron couldn't see his face from where he stood, but he knew it must be near as damn it unrecognisable. Mrs. Blatter avoided him as he staggered towards the door, and she ran towards the altar. She'd been married here: on the very spot he'd built the fire.

Ron stared at her body entranced.

She was considerably overweight, her breasts sagging, her belly overshadowing her cunt so he doubted if she could even see it. But it was for this his cock head throbbed, for this his head reeled—

Her image was in his hand. God yes, she was there in his hand, she was the living equivalent of what he held. A woman. The stone was the statue of a woman, a Venus grosser than Mrs. Blatter, her belly swelling with children, tits like mountains, cunt a valley that began at her navel and gaped to the world. All this time, under the cloth and the cross, they'd bowed their heads to a goddess.

Ron stepped off the altar and began to run down the aisle, pushing Mrs. Blatter, the policeman and the lunatic aside.

"Don't go out," said Ivanhoe, "It's right outside."

Ron held the Venus tight, feeling her weight in his hands and taking security from her. Behind him, the Verger was screeching a warning to his Lord. Yes, it was a warning for sure.

Ron kicked open the door. On every side, fire. A flaming cot, a corpse (it was the postmaster) with its feet burning, a dog skinned by fire, hurtling past. And Rawhead, of course, silhouetted against a panorama of flames. It looked round, perhaps because it heard the warnings the Verger was yelling, but more likely, he thought, because it knew, knew without being told, that the woman had been found.

"Here!" Ron yelled, "I'm here! I'm here!"

It was coming for him now, with the steady gait of a victor closing in to claim its final and absolute victory. Doubt surged up in Ron. Why did it come so surely to meet him, not seeming to care about the weapon he carried in his hands?

Hadn't it seen, hadn't it heard the warning?

Unless—

Oh God in Heaven.

—Unless Coot had been wrong. Unless it was only a stone he held in his hand, a useless, meaningless lump of stone.

Then a pair of hands grabbed him around the neck.

The lunatic.

A low voice spat the word "Fucker" in his ear.

Ron watched Rawhead approaching, heard the lunatic screeching now: "Here he is. Fetch him. Kill him. Here he is."

Without warning the grip slackened, and Ron half-turned to see Ivanhoe dragging the lunatic back against the Church wall. The mouth in the Verger's broken face continued to screech.

"He's here! Here!"

Ron looked back at Rawhead: the beast was almost on him, and he was too slow to raise the stone in self-defence. But Rawhead had no intention of taking him. It was Declan he was smelling and hearing. Ivanhoe released Declan as Rawhead's huge hands veered past Ron and fumbled for the lunatic. What followed was unwatchable. Ron couldn't bear to see the hands take Declan apart: but he heard the gabble of pleas become whoops of disbelieving grief. When he next looked round there was nothing recognisably human on ground or wall—

—And Rawhead was coming for him now, coming to do the same or worse. The huge head craned round to fix on Ron, its maw gaping, and Ron saw how the fire had wounded Rawhead. The beast had been careless in the enthusiasm for destruction: fire had caught its face and upper torso. Its body hair was crisped, its mane was stubble, and the flesh on the left hand side of its face was black and blistered. The flames had roasted its eyeballs, they were swimming in a gum of mucus and tears. That was why it had followed Declan's voice and bypassed Ron; it could scarcely see.

But it must see now. It must.

"Here . . . here . . . " said Ron, "Here I am!" Rawhead heard. He looked without seeing, his eyes trying to focus.

"Here! I'm here!"

Rawhead growled in his chest. His burned face pained him; he wanted to be away from here, away in the cool of a birch thicket, moon-washed.

His dimmed eyes found the stone; the homo sapien was nursing it like a baby. It was difficult for Rawhead to see clearly, but he knew. It ached in his mind, that image. It pricked him, it teased him.

It was just a symbol, of course, a sign of the power, not the power itself, but his mind made no such distinction. To him the stone was the thing he feared most: the bleeding woman, her gaping hole eating seed and spitting children. It was life, that hole, that woman, it was endless fecundity. It terrified him.

Rawhead stepped back, his own shit running freely down his leg. The fear on his face gave Ron strength. He pressed home his advantage, closing in after the retreating beast, dimly aware that Ivanhoe was rallying allies around him, armed figures waiting at the corners of his vision, eager to bring the fireraiser down.

His own strength was failing him. The stone, lifted high above his head so Rawhead could see it plainly, seemed heavier by the moment.

"Go on," he said quietly to the gathering Zealots. "Go on, take him. Take him . . ."

They began to close in, even before he finished speaking.

Rawhead smelt them more than saw them: his hurting eyes were fixed on the woman.

His teeth slid from their sheaths in preparation for the attack. The stench of humanity closed in around him from every direction.

Panic overcame his superstitions for one moment and he snatched down towards Ron, steeling himself against the stone. The attack took Ron by surprise. The claws sank in his scalp, blood poured down over his face.

Then the crowd closed in. Human hands, weak, white human hands were laid on Rawhead's body. Fists beat on his spine, nails raked his skin.

He let Ron go as somebody took a knife to the backs of his legs and hamstrung him. The agony made him howl the sky down, or so it seemed. In Rawhead's roasted eyes the stars reeled as he fell backwards on to the road, his back cracking under him. They took the advantage immediately, over-powering him by sheer weight of numbers. He snapped off a finger here, a face there, but they would not be stopped now. Their hatred was old; in their bones, did they but know it.

He thrashed under their assaults for as long as he could, but he knew death was certain. There would be no resurrection this time, no waiting in the earth for an age until their descendants forgot him. He'd be snuffed out absolutely, and there would be nothingness.

He became quieter at the thought, and looked up as best he could to where the little father was standing. Their eyes met, as they had on the road when he'd taken the boy. But now Rawhead's look had lost its power to transfix. His face was empty and sterile as the moon, defeated long before Ron slammed the stone down between his eyes. The skull was soft: it buckled inwards and a slop of brain splattered the road.

The King went out. It was suddenly over, without ceremony or celebration. Out, once and for all. There was no cry.

Ron left the stone where it lay, half buried in the face of the beast. He stood up groggily, and felt his head. His scalp was loose, his fingertips touched his skull, blood came and came. But there were arms to support him, and nothing to fear if he slept.

It went unnoticed, but in death Rawhead's bladder was emptying. A stream of urine pulsed from the corpse and ran down the road. The rivulet steamed in the chilling air, its scummy nose sniffing left and right as it looked for a place to drain. After a few feet it found the gutter and ran along it awhile to a crack in the tarmac; there it drained off into the welcoming earth.

Wishbones
Cherie Priest

At the Andersonville camp there is a great, stinking dread. The Confederates don't have enough food of their own, so they sure as hell aren't feeding their prisoners of war; and the prisoners who aren't wasting away are dying of diseases faster than they can be replaced. Here, the world smells like bloody shit and coal smoke. It reeks of body odor and piss, and sweat.

South Georgia is nowhere to live by choice, and nowhere to die by starving.

The remains—the bodies of the ones who finally fell and couldn't rise again—they lie in naked piles, leather over skeletons as thin as hat racks. They lie in stacks waiting to be put into the ground. They collect in the back buildings because no one is strong enough to dig anymore, not blue nor gray.

This does not explain why, at night and sometimes between the watches, the piles are shrinking.

Some of us thought, at first, how people were hungry enough that even the old meat-leather on the bones out back . . . it might be better than nothing. We talked amongst ourselves in riddles that rationalized unthinkable things. We wondered about our friends and fellow soldiers who were dead there, piled like cordwood. We said, of old Bill this—or old Frank that—how he'd wish we weren't so hungry, if he were still here. We agreed, we nodded our heads, and we thought about how we'd make our secret ways back to the long, low shed.

But best as I know it, no one ever worked up the courage to do it. No one took any knives and crept back there, away from the guards who were half-starved themselves. How would we have cooked it, anyway? How do you smoke or carve a human being, an old friend?

Even so, the numbered dead began a backward count. One by one, the bodies went gone, and when fifteen or twenty had most definitely been taken, or lost, that's when we began to hear the noise at night. It was hard to calculate, hard to pinpoint. Hard to explain, or indicate.

But it rattled like the bones of death himself, beneath a robe or within loose-hanging skin. It wobbled and clattered back behind the sheds where the dead were kept.

It walked. It crept.

It gathered.

"Pete's Porno Palace, this is Scott, how can I help you?"

"Jesus," Dean shook his head. "Pete is going to fire your ass one of these days."

Scott wiggled the receiver next to his head and grinned. "Pizza Palace, ma'am. Of course that's what I said. Best in Plains, don't you know it? And what can I get for you today?"

"Jesus," Dean mumbled again and walked away. He untied his apron and wadded it up around his hand, then left it on the counter. His cigarettes were in his jacket pocket, hanging by the back door.

He took the smokes and left the jacket. Dead of winter in south Georgia doesn't usually call for anything heavier than a sweater, but sometimes when you own jackets, you just want to wear them—so you wait until it's barely cold enough, and you drag them out anyway.

So the jacket stayed on the peg and Dean stepped outside.

Dark was coming, but not bad yet; and the backwoods pitch black would hold off for another hour at least. Even so, when he struck the wheel of the lighter the sparks were briefly blinding. Maybe it was darker already than he'd thought. Or maybe he should quit working double shifts, no matter how cute Lisa was, or how hard she swung her eyelashes at him when she asked him to cover for her.

He wrapped his lips around the cigarette and sucked it gently while the flame took hold. The bricks of the old pizza joint were almost warm against his back when he leaned there, beside the back door, facing the dumpster and the edge of the woods.

A crackling noise—small footsteps, or shuffling—rustled underneath the big metal trash container.

"Scram," Dean commanded, but the soft crunching continued. He reached down by his feet and picked up the first thing he felt—an empty can that once held tomato sauce. He chucked it like a knuckleball and something squeaked, and scuttled.

"Stupid raccoons. Rats. Whatever."

"One of these days," Scott slipped through the doorway and shimmied sideways to stand next to him. "One of these days, it's going to be a bear, and you're going to get your face chewed off. Give me one?"

Dean palmed the pack to the delivery driver. "Help yourself. Bears. Stop shitting me. You ever see a bear out here?"

"No. But I've never seen a submarine, either, and I believe they exist in the world, someplace."

"You do, huh?"

"Yeah. Seen pictures. Anyway, I'm just saying, and shit, it's dark. We need to put a lamp out here or something. Can't see a damn thing." He lit a cigarette for himself and passed the pack back to Dean, who set it down on top of a crate.

"You got somewhere to go?"

Scott nodded. "Two large sausage and mushrooms. Going towards no man's land, out towards Andersonville. Fucking hate that, driving out there."

"Why?"

He popped his neck and sighed, taking another drag. "I always figure that's where I'll get a flat tire, or that's where the transmission will finally drop out of the Civic. It's only a matter of time, man, and I know my luck. It'll happen there."

"So what if it does? You've got a cell. I'd come and get you, or Pete would."

"I don't like it, is all. My sister's boyfriend, you know Ben, he used to live out that way, and he talked about it like it was weird. You know. Because of the camp."

Dean leaned his head back. "Oh yeah. The camp. I guess, sure. That could be weird. I think it'd be worse to live up north, near the battlefields. You hear cannons and artillery and shit. The camp was just . . . I don't know. Jail for POWs. And it's a park now. You seen it? It's all pretty and mowed."

"Man, people *died* there."

"People die everywhere." Dean crushed the cigarette against the wall, even though it was only half smoked.

Henry saw it first. He said he saw it, anyway. He said it was there, back by the sheds where they stored up the dried out dead until they could be dumped into a pit. According to him, it was a man-sized thing with black hole eyes and no soul inside it. According to him and his starved-up brain, the thing moved all jerky, like it wasn't used to having limbs. Like it wasn't used to having legs, or feet, or nothing like that.

Like it was man-sized, but no man.

"It staggers," Henry said. "It shuffles along and it takes them—it pulls them out the low windows, pulls them out in pieces and it, Jesus Lord, amen."

"What'd you see, anyway?" we asked, all gathered around close.

"It had an arm or something. A leg maybe. We get so skinny you can't tell, by looking in the dark. You can't see if that's a hand or a foot on the end of it, just that it's long and there's a joint in the middle. But the thing I saw, it had a limb of some kind, and it didn't bite it, didn't eat it or anything like that. It peeled it, just like a banana. It used these white, long fingers to pick the skin and just strip it on down until there was nothing there but bone."

The rest of us gasped, and one or two of us gagged. "Why?" I asked him.

"I haven't the foggiest. I haven't any idea, but that's how it happened. That's what it did. And then, when it finished yanking the skin away, it hugged on the bones what were left. It pulled them against its chest, and it's like they stuck there. It's like it pulled them against himself and they stayed there, and became part of him."

"Why would it do something like that—and better still, what would do something like that? It doesn't make any sense."

"I don't know," he said, and he was shaking. "But I'll tell you this—I'd gotten to thinking, these days, that maybe dying wasn't the worst thing that could happen. You know how it is, here. You know how sometimes you see another one drop and you almost feel, for a few minutes, a little envy for him."

"But not now," I said.

"No, not now."

"Lisa called in again," Scott said, putting the phone down and looking like he wanted to swear. "Third time in two weeks. Remind me again why she's still on the payroll? She's not *that* hot."

Dean shrugged into his apron and kept one eye on the cash register, where Lisa usually worked. "She's been sick, I think. Something wrong with her. She's been throwing up; I heard her in the bathroom a couple of days ago. That means we're short again, right?"

"You're not going to cover for her this time?"

"Can't." Dean adjusted the temperature dial on the side of the big pizza oven and felt a kick of heat when the old motor sparked to life.

"Can't? Or won't?"

"Whichever. I've got things to do tonight. I covered her with a double the last two times. You take this one."

"No. And you can't make me."

"Well then, I guess they'll be short tonight. It can't always be my problem," he complained, even though he knew why everyone acted like it was. He and Lisa had gone on a couple of dates once, and everyone treated them like it had been a secret office romance or something.

But Pete's wasn't an office, the dates hadn't been secret, and there wasn't anything much in the way of romance going on. Dean liked Lisa and he called her a friend, but it didn't seem very mutual unless she couldn't make it to work. He wondered if she was really sick and hiding it, like it was something worse than the flu.

The phone rang again as soon as Scott put it back on the hook.

"Christ," he complained. "We don't even open for another ten minutes. You answer it."

"No. You get it. If it's Lisa I don't want to talk to her. She'll try to rope me into covering for her, and I won't do it."

"Fine." He lifted the phone and said, with his mouth too close to the receiver, "Pete's Pizza Place, would you like to try two medium pizzas with two toppings for ten bucks?"

Dean walked away, back towards the refrigerator. He yanked the silvertone lever that opened the big walk-in; he stepped inside took the first two plastic cartons he found—green peppers, and onions, respectively. Both sliced. Whoever had closed had done a good job, he thought. Then he remembered that he hadn't gone home until one in the morning, and that the handiwork was his own.

"I'm here too damn much," he said to the olives. The olives didn't answer, but they implied their agreement by floating merrily in their own juices.

He stacked the olives on top of the green peppers and onions so that the three containers fit beneath his chin. With his hip, he opened the door again and carried the toppings out to the set-up counter and began to lay them out.

"Fucking *A*," Scott swore, still scribbling something down on the order pad kept next to the phone. "Another one."

"Another one what?"

"Another delivery, all the way out in Andersonville."

"That's not that far."

"Yeah, well. You know why I don't like it."

Dean cocked his head, dropping the olives into their usual spot with a sliding click. "Because you're a superstitious bastard?"

"That is correct, sir. It's the same house, I think. I told the guy he couldn't have his order for another hour at least, but he didn't care. So. Fine, I guess. I'll drive it out once we finally get open, and at least it's still daylight. Where's Pete?"

"He's not coming in until noon. He'll be here then, though."

"Okay. Cool. So it's just us until then?"

"Yep." Dean abandoned the conversation for the refrigerator again. This time he emerged with crumbly sausage balls and a fat sliced stack of pepperoni. He wasn't concerned about the lack of help; they'd opened the store alone before, and it wasn't too bad.

"I thought I heard someone out back, a few minutes ago. I thought maybe it was Lisa, but I don't know why."

"Lisa just called in, though."

"Yeah, I know. I don't know why I thought it was her. It turned out to be nobody, I guess." He stopped talking there, even though it sounded like he wanted to say more.

Dean dropped the pepperoni rounds into their appropriate spot and wiped a little bit of grease on his apron. "Out back? By the dumpster?"

"Yeah."

"Maybe it was a bear."

"You're an asshole. It wasn't a bear."

"It wasn't Lisa, either."

"Smelled like her."

Dean frowned. "What?"

"It smelled like her, I think that's what it was." Scott tweaked the pen and the order pad between his hands and leaned back against the counter. "She wears that rose perfume sometimes, she puts it in her hair."

"How often do you get close enough to tell?"

Scott slapped the order pad against the counter and left it there. "You know what I mean—she wears it strong because she doesn't want her mom to know she smokes. You can smell it in the back, in the kitchen, when she goes through there to take a break."

"I know what you mean, yeah. Okay."

"Well, that's it. That's what I smelled. But she wasn't there."

"Nobody was there."

"That's what I said. Nobody was there. But I felt like someone was watching me."

Dean raised an eyebrow that didn't care one way or another, and went back towards the refrigerator for another armload of toppings. "Must've been that goddamn mythical bear."

The thing out back, behind the sheds, it's getting bigger. Charles has seen it now, and the Sergeant too—they both say it's bigger than a man, and either Henry's been lying or the thing is getting bigger.

We talk about it more than we should, maybe. But there's nothing else to talk about, except how we want to go home and how much we'd love a meal. So we tell each other about the thing like it's a campfire story, as if we're little boys trying to scare each other. Except we don't want to anymore, really. We're scared enough already, and now we're just trying to understand what new, fresh horror has been imposed upon us.

As if this were not enough.

We are all so hungry, and we know there's no prayer for food since our captors haven't got any either, even for themselves. If the guards can't feed themselves, then we prisoners are done for.

In our bunks, smelling like summer in a charnel house, we gather and talk and wait. At night, we cluster close together even though all of us stink of death and bodies that haven't seen a bath in months. It's better than cowering alone and listening to the knock-kneed haint come walking by.

We think it grows by consuming us—it eats the starved ones up and walks on borrowed bones ill-fit together. And so many of us have wasted away, and so many more are bound to follow.

In another month, that thing will be a god.

"Hey," Lisa said. Her long brown hair was tied back behind her ears, elf-style, and her eyes were more bloodshot than blue.

Dean thought maybe she was looking thinner every day, like her collarbones jutted sharper out of her tank top and maybe her tits were settling closer to her ribcage. "Hey. Welcome back."

"Sure," she said, but it didn't make much sense as a response.

At supper rush she manned the cash register at the end of the counter, and Scott leaned in over Dean's shoulder. "She looks like hell."

"Yeah she does. Told you. She's been sick."

"That doesn't look like sick to me, exactly."

Dean shifted his arms to push Scott back, out of his personal space. "What do you think it looks like, then? What are you saying? You think it's drugs or something?"

"You said it, not me. It looks like it, though. Look at her. And you know what—she's gone to the bathroom three times in the last five hours."

"You've been counting? That's fucked up, man."

"I've been counting because I've been covering the register while you've been making pizzas. It's not like I've been taking inventory of her bladder or anything." He tapped his foot against the counter's support and chewed his lower lip. "I'm thinking, it could be crystal meth, or something like that. Meth makes you skinny."

"Meth makes you wired too," Dean argued. "She's been dragging. I think she's just been sick. I wonder if, do you think it's something like cancer? Christ, what if she has AIDS or something?"

"Did you ever fuck her?"

"No. Didn't go together that long."

Scott raised a shoulder and crushed his lips together in a dismissive grimace. "Then who cares?"

"I do, sort of. She's all right. Don't be an asshole about her. Hey—the phone's ringing. It's for you."

"I don't want to answer it."

"Well, you're going to." Dean turned his back completely, absorbing himself in the scattering of green things onto the crust and paste.

After a few seconds of being ignored, Scott took the hint and picked up the phone. "Pete's Party Palace, what's your request?"

Dean returned to making pizzas and shoveling them onto the slow-moving conveyor belt in the oven. Lisa stayed at the register and didn't seem to notice much of anything that wasn't right in front of her.

He watched, though. He waited for her to take a break, and then he followed her—back outside to where the dumpsters are pillaged by the creatures who come up from the edge of the woods.

By the time he reached the doorway she was struggling with a cigarette lighter, so he offered her his.

"Thanks," she said, and she leaned against the bricks.

Dean joined her. "I've been wanting to ask you," he started, but she cut him off.

"Thanks for covering for me the other night. I appreciated it. I wasn't feeling good, is all."

"That's cool. No big deal. I wanted to ask you, though, if something's wrong. I mean, *really* wrong. I know we're not that tight or anything, but if you need something, all you have to do is say so."

Lisa took a short drag on the cigarette, one that couldn't have earned her much nicotine. "What are you trying to ask me? You talking your way around something?"

He studied her closely, trying to think of how to ask what he meant. She was shaky—not in a hard way like she was shivering, but in a low-grade hum that meant her whole body was moving, very slightly.

When her fingers squeezed themselves around the cigarette, her chipped pearl nail polish looked ill and yellow against the paper. She glared out at the dumpster, and out past it. She glared into the coming dark like it might tell her important things, but she didn't really expect it to.

"Are you sick? I can't ask it any better than that. You've looked, I mean, you haven't looked good the last few times you've been here. Like you're weak, or like you've got a fever. I was wondering if maybe there wasn't something really wrong and you hadn't felt like telling us."

"Like what?"

"Like, I don't know. Cancer or something." He didn't mention Scott's meth theory because it seemed even ruder than telling a girl she looked terrible. He rolled on his shoulder to face her. "Look, you—you look like you're wasting away. You've been losing weight, enough weight that Scott even noticed, and he didn't notice it when you cut your hair off and dyed it black last year. It's pretty dramatic."

It was strange and not at all pleasant, the small smile that lifted a corner of her mouth beside the cigarette. "Bless your heart," she breathed. Then, a little louder, "You think I'm shrinking? You didn't have to say it like you were asking if I was dying. Most women like it if you point out they're losing weight."

"Yeah, but . . . " He couldn't figure out a tactful way to phrase the obvious rest.

"It's been good, lately. I've been getting into clothes I haven't worn since junior high."

"That's good?"

"It might be. I think it's good. I could still stand to—" she stopped herself, and changed her mind. "It's not the end of the world, dropping a few pounds. It's a good thing. I don't mind it, and I wish I could take another few down, so stop worrying. That's all it is. I'm on a diet."

"What kind of diet? Like a starvation diet, or what? You got some kind of eating disorder now, is that how it is?"

"There's nothing disordered about it. It's the most orderly thing I've ever done." She crushed the lit end of the cigarette against the wall, leaving a black streak on the brick and a mangled butt on the ground as she went back inside.

There's a Chinaman here in camp, a small fellow who looks like he might be a thousand years old. Someone told me he came from out west, out across the frontier—someone said he'd come east from California, but I can't imagine why.

He says he's no Chinaman, and he seems to get offended if you call him one, even though I don't think he understands one word of English out of three.

I don't know his name or what he's doing here, except that he runs errands between the officers. He washes pots and clothes for the Confederates when there's water to wash them, and I guess that's not strange since there aren't any women around.

The little old fellow is mostly quiet. He mostly listens and keeps his head low, not wanting to draw any attention to himself. Henry says he looks strange and wise, and I don't know if that's right or not, but the Chinaman sure has these black, sharp eyes that always seem to know something.

He came up on us, the other night while we were talking about the thing that eats the bones out back. Like I told it, I don't know how much of our talk he understands—but he got the idea. He saw our fear, and he watched the way we pointed and whispered at the sheds out back.

One of the guards heard us too, and he told us to shut ourselves up and be quiet, we were just trying to start trouble. He was complaining how we didn't need any more trouble than we'd already got, and he was right, but that didn't change anything.

When he was gone, the Chinaman approached us with small steps and a hunched back that bowed when he tiptoed forward. He nodded, yes. He nodded like he understood. He pointed one long, wrinkled finger towards the sheds where the dead are stored and where they wait to be buried.

"Gashadokuro," he said. It was a funny, long word filled with sharp edges.

We stared up at him, blank faces not comprehending very well. He looked back at us, frustrated that he could not make us comprehend. "Gashadokuro," he said again, pointing harder.

And then I nodded, trying to repeat the piece of foreign tongue and probably mangling it past recognition. I tried to convey my realization, that yes—the thing was there, and yes—it had a name, and it was a foreign name from across the country, and across the ocean, because white men like us wouldn't know what to call it.

Gashadokuro.

We can't even say it.

After Lisa was gone, Dean kept smoking and he said to the empty back lot, "You don't eat with us anymore. We all used to eat together after shift."

A creak answered him, with a twisting squeal of metal and a gentle knocking.

He jumped, and settled. The dumpster again. Something inside it. No, something behind it. Dean held his dwindling cigarette out like a weapon, or a pointer.

"Scram," he said, but he didn't say it loud. "Scram, you goddamn rats. Raccoons." It wasn't worth adding "bears" to the list, because he still thought Scott was full of shit.

But it was dark enough, and the woods were a black line of soldier-straight trees, hiding everything beyond or past them. He stepped forward, just a pace or two. Towards the dumpster, and the rattling shuffle that came from behind it, or beside it—somewhere near it.

"Get lost," he said with a touch more volume as another possibility occurred to him. Plains didn't have too many homeless people; it didn't have too many people of any sort, truth to tell. But there was always the chance of a passing human scavenger. You never knew, in this day and age.

The noise was louder as he got closer—tracking it with his ears to a spot behind the dumpster, close to the trees. It wasn't all scratching, either. It was something muffled and banging together—something like pool balls clattering in felt, or inside a leather bag. He couldn't pinpoint it, no matter how hard he listened.

Scott's head popped into the doorway, casting a giant round shadow against Dean's back. "Who're you talking to out here? Yourself again?"

"Sure." He turned and squinted at the doorway, where the world suddenly looked much brighter within that rectangle.

"I've got to make another run out to my favorite spot in all of Georgia. You coming back inside or what? I can't leave until someone takes the ovens, and baby, that needs to be *you*."

Dean looked back into the woods, past the dumpster where the noise had stopped as soon as Scott appeared. "Back towards the old prison camp?"

"Of course. Why can't that guy always call during the day, huh? Why's he got to wait until the creeps come out?"

"Why would you put it that way?" Dean asked, a hint of petulance framing the words. "There aren't any creeps. There's just the old camp, and there's nothing there anymore."

"Then why don't you drive it, if you're so fucking unperturbable. I hate going out there, it's—"

"It's not even two miles, you chickenshit. You could practically walk them the pizza in the time you've stood here complaining about it."

"Practically, but never. I'm serious. You do it, if that's what it's about. I'll take the ovens and the onion-smelling hands for a few minutes. *You* go brave the ghosts from the old camp."

"I will, then. Fine. Give me the address." He pulled himself back inside and swiped the sheet of paper out of Scott's hand.

The gash-beast is hungry; it is as hungry as we are. As it grows, so does its appetite. As it grows, and we diminish, it becomes ravenous. It outpaces us.

For us, the hunger comes and goes—and comes again.

It's when it comes again that we know, we know that it won't be dysentery or cholera or pneumonia that takes us. We know it will be the hunger. When first we go without food the days drag and stretch, and the belly is all we can think of. But in a few days, after a week or so, the hunger fades. The body adjusts. The stomach shrinks and thoughts of food are sharply sweet, but no longer dire.

It when the hunger comes again that we know.

It takes some time—maybe a month, maybe less. But when the weeks have slid by and there's nothing yet to fill us, when the hunger returns it returns with a message: "Now," it says, "you are dying. Now your body consumes itself from the inside, out. This is what will kill you."

The gash-monster knows. It hovers close, a clattering angel of death that follows the weakest ones after dark. It hums and taps, drumming its bone-fingers against the walls and waiting by the doors. It is impatient. And we are all afraid, even those of us whose stomachs have balled themselves into tight little knots that don't cry out just yet—we are all afraid that the gash-monster's impatience will get the better of it.

We are all afraid that the time will come when the dead aren't quite enough, and it comes to chase the living, starving, withering souls whose hearts still beat with a feeble persistence.

We are all afraid that the time will come when it pulls our still-living limbs apart, and peels our skin away, and eats our bones while we bleed and cry on the ground.

We keep ourselves quiet when the hunger returns.

We do not want it to hear us.

When Dean returned, he reclaimed his apron and went back to the pizza line. "Hey look," he told Scott. "Nothing snuck up and ate me."

"Bite me, big boy. Speaking of eating, we're shutting down in ten—no, eight minutes, and there are two large leftovers with our names on 'em. Pete said they're ours if we want them."

"Good to know. What's on them?"

"Gross shit. Pineapples and onion on the one, and sausage, chicken and anchovy on the other—that's your three major meat groups, right there. Three of the four, anyway. It'd need hamburger too, to make a good square meal of meat."

"Jesus." Dean made a face.

Scott mirrored the grimace and put the pizzas on the outside edge of the oven to stay warm. "Yeah. If I weren't so hungry, I'd leave them out back for the bears, but I've been here since before lunch and I'm either going to eat one of these fuckers, or my own hand—whichever holds still first and longest. Lisa—hey string bean there—we'll save some for you, baby. You could stand a little grease on those bones. It'll fatten you up. Put hair on your chest."

Lisa pushed a button on the cash register to open the drawer. "You don't know a damn thing about women, do you, Scott?"

"Probably not. Anyway, you want some?"

She reached beneath the drawer and scooped out the twenties, gathering them into a little stack. "No."

Dean watched her count for a few seconds, then said, "You didn't take a break for supper."

"So?"

"So you've been here as long as the rest of us. And you're not starving?"

"No. Mind your own business. No, I'm not starving."

She went back to her counting, and made a point of not paying any further attention to either of the other closers. When she wrapped up the drawer's contents, she put a rubber band around them and slipped them into a zippered bag that she then deposited into the safe.

"Aren't you jumping the gun a tad with that?" Dean asked, but she shrugged back at him.

"There's nobody here. Who cares? Turn off the sign. Let's close up."

"Where are you going?"

"Bathroom, to change clothes. I'm not walking home smelling like this. It's gross."

Dean took a rag and started wiping down the pizza line. "Smelling like food? It's not the grossest thing in the world, not by a long shot."

"I don't like it," she said. She lifted up the counter blocker that kept customers from wandering back into the kitchen and it almost looked like too much effort for those bird-frail arms. She shuddered when it dropped it back down behind her, when it fell back to its slot with a clang.

"Lisa?" Dean asked, thinking maybe he'd follow her or ask more questions, but she saw it coming and she waved him away.

"Don't," she ordered. "Just . . . don't."

"Stick around a few minutes, I'll drive you home when we're finished eating. I'll give you a lift—I mean, you really don't look like you're in any shape to walk back to the 'burbs."

"I'm in plenty good shape to walk anywhere I want. Thanks, though." She added the last part as she rounded the corner, taking a backpack with her. The bathroom door clicked itself shut behind her.

Dean jerked his hands into the air. "I give up," he declared.

"It's about time," Scott said. The words were already muffled around a mouth full of pizza. "Come and get it. More for us."

"Okay. Yeah, okay."

The back door was open, propped that way for the sake of air flow. Dean went back through the kitchen, back beside the refrigerator, and back to that open door that looked out over the empty lot—and the woods beyond it.

Scott was right. They needed a lamp.

The dumpster loomed black before the lot. It stank of rust, rot, and the decay of uneaten things that should've long ago been picked up. Trash service was spotty out there sometimes, and the bin was starting to fill. Maybe the collectors would come by before the morning.

It was as good an excuse as any not to take out the trash.

A clatter popped, loud beside his head.

Dean jerked—staring around and trying not to look too frantic, in case it was just Scott being an asshole. But Scott was inside, he could hear him. He'd turned up the radio past the point of ambient noise; and he'd tuned it to a louder station than Pete ever subjected the customers to. Inside, Scott was singing along to Skinny Puppy with his mouth full.

The clatter wasn't Scott.

It was hard to place, like before—hard to tell exactly where the sound was, or exactly what it sounded like. It sounded so close to so many things, but not precisely like any of them. The clicking was loud but muffled. Next to his head, between the building and the dumpster, and high. Up higher, he thought, higher than the edge of the window sill were the pattering knocks when they sounded again.

"Is somebody out here?" Dean asked, not loud enough to even pretend he wanted a response.

The clattering continued, high and muffled, and rhythmic—there was a balance to it, a swinging, swaying, like the pendulum on a large clock moving back and forth. Or like hips, loosely jointed and walking in lanky-legged steps.

"I . . . " There should've been more to say, but the noise—all rounded edges and heavy bones—was only coming closer.

He retreated back into the doorway, still seeing nothing except, maybe, at the edge of his sight something pale in a jagged flash. Whatever it was, he wanted no more of it; he tumbled over himself to get back inside, and he shut the door fast—hard. He drew the bolt back and stepped away, staring down at the door's lever handle, waiting for it to wiggle or slide.

"Dude?" Scott called. "Something wrong? You're panting like a sick dog in here; I can hear you all the way in the kitchen."

"I'm not panting!" Dean all but shouted, and as he objected he could hear his own breath dragging unevenly from his chest and out his mouth. "I'm not—there was something outside. Don't look at me like that, I'm serious. There's something out there and it's not a goddamn *bear*."

"Okay, calm down. What, then? Another raccoon or rat?"

"Fuck off, man. I don't know what. I don't know what, but I'm not going back to look."

"Let me see," he said but it was less a request than an announcement that he was going to look outside.

"Don't," Dean commanded, stepping between his coworker and the bolted metal door. "Don't. Whatever it was, we don't want it in here. It was, it was *big*—and I don't know what. Just leave it shut. It'll go away, later."

"You're actually scared?"

"Yes, I'm scared. What is there—there's rabies and shit, man. And big things with big teeth in the woods. Fine, a bear, if you want to call it that—if you want to wonder or worry about that."

Scott snorted. "Puss."

"Less a puss than *you*, motherfucker. At least I'm afraid of actual *things*, and not ghosts, like dead people from the Civil War. That ain't a ghost out there, whatever it is. It's something that came in from the woods, is what. And I'd just as soon not get eaten on the way home from work, so leave the door closed or you'll let it in."

"Fine," Scott held out his hands in surrender. "Fine, Christ. If it's that big a deal to you. Calm down, already. Don't get crazy."

"I'm not crazy, I think I've heard it out there before," he said, and he realized as the words came out that he was serious—he *had* heard it before, but not so loud and not so close.

It had been working itself up, working itself close. Homing in.

Dean shuddered, and peeled his apron off. He tossed it at the pegs where the coats were usually kept and it stuck, then straggled itself down to the floor. "Forget it. I'm not hungry anymore. I'm going home."

"With the monster outside? Ooh, you're *brave*."

"I'm going out the front," Dean growled. "Where there's a nice open parking lot and a big ol' streetlamp."

"Before you go—are you giving Lisa a ride? I think she needs one."

"What? She said no. She said she didn't want one."

Scott cocked his head towards the front of the restaurant, in the vague, general direction of the bathrooms. "She's still in the bathroom. Don't leave her with me; she's not my problem."

"Not mine either."

"You care more than I do. Go knock on the door or something."

Dean stood still and scowled, weighing the options and his own worry. "Fine. I'll go get her."

If nothing else, it gave him something else to think about; it gave him a few more seconds to calm his heartbeat and another problem to think about. He grabbed his light coat and shifted his shoulders into it, then pulled his keys out of his jeans pocket and went to the door of the ladies room.

He pressed his head against it, listening for any signs of life within. He rapped the back of his knuckles against the wood, lightly—politely. "Hey Lisa. You in there, still?"

She didn't answer, so he knocked again.

"You in there? Hey, I'm going home now. I'm tired and I'm not as hungry as I thought I was. Open up. I'll give you a ride home. Hey. Are you in there?" He knew she must be, but there was no hint of life. No water running, no toilets flushing. Again he knocked, but there wasn't any answer. "Do you need help? You'd better say something, or else I'm going to come in there. Do you hear me?"

Nothing.

Until there was the crash.

The sound of splintering, shattering glass rang out behind the closed door, jolting Dean so badly he leaped away. "Lisa?" he shouted, and he reached for the knob. It moved a click left and right, but didn't open. "Lisa?"

Scott came tearing around through the dining area. "Did you hear that? What was that?"

"In there—" Dean pointed at the locked door. "It came from inside the bathroom. The thing outside, I think it's gotten in—that's all I can think of," he trailed off, kicking at the door. Glass wasn't breaking anymore, but it was being pushed around—scraped around, and yes, there was that tell-tale knocking, rattling, clapping together of hard things with worn edges. He could hear it through the door.

"What's that sound in there?"

"Same sound I heard outside."

"Well, what is it?" Scott's voice was rising, creeping up towards shrill as the ruckus in the bathroom continued and the clacking rattles filled more and more of the space inside the restaurant. "What's that crazy sound?"

"I told you, I don't know!" Dean retreated a few feet and slammed himself forward, hip against the door. Something splintered, but nothing broke. He did it again, and motioned for Scott to join him. "Lisa, what's going on in there? *Lisa?*"

Nothing and no one answered, so the guys pushed together and then, when both their bodies met the wood at once, the door caved in and they caved in after it—tumbling forward and slipping on cool tiles.

"Lisa?" they said together.

"Lisa?" Dean asked again, but the bathroom was empty and there was no sound at all—not even the running of a commode out of order, or the whistle of warm January wind through the broken glass of the small square window.

"Could she—could she have gotten through there? Through that?" Scott asked, now as breathless as Dean and just as confused. He meant the window, all smashed and hanging open. It wasn't meant for escaping, or anything half so glamorous. It was installed for ventilation, or for light. It was too small for a normal-sized woman to fit through, or climb through.

But Dean could still hear, in his head more than in the night, the smattering beats of the knobby creature that crouched in the dark beyond the dumpster.

He climbed up onto counter, stepping past the sink and prying himself up high to see out the window. A hulking shape all corners and shadows was walking, retreating, removing itself from the restaurant.

It stopped.

It halted like it had snagged itself on something. It swiveled an oversized head on a twig-thin neck, and it lifted its face to gaze at the window from which Dean watched.

Not one head, but many together. Not one thing, but parts of a hundred—a thousand others. A skull made of skulls, ribs made of ribs, it was fleshless and breathless. Its ivory limbs quivered together, chattering a low-frequency buzz of bone on bone, dangling loose from unfinished joints.

Dean's breath caught in his throat.

The thing turned away. It loped slowly towards the trees, into the woods. It wandered into the sheltering darkness of the park, towards the old camp at Andersonville.

The Hollow Man
Norman Partridge

Four. Yes, that's how many there were. Come to my home. Come to my home in the hills. Come in the middle of feast, when the skin had been peeled back and I was ready to sup. Interrupting, disrupting. Stealing the comfortable bloat of a full belly, the black scent of clean bones burning dry on glowing embers. Four.

Yes. That's how many there were. I watched them through the stretched-skin window, saw them standing cold in the snow with their guns at their sides.

The hollow man saw them too. He heard the ice dogs bark and raised his sunken face, peering at the men through the blue-veined window. He gasped, expectant, and I had to draw my claws from their fleshy sheaths and jab deep into his blackened muscles to keep him from saying words that weren't mine. Outside, they shouted, *Hullo! Hullo in the cabin!* and the hollow man sprang for the door. I jumped on his back and tugged the metal rings pinned into his neck. He jerked and whirled away from the latch, but I was left with the sickening sound of his hopeful moans.

Once again, control was mine, but not like before. The hollow man was full of strength that he hadn't possessed in weeks, and the feast was ruined. They had ruined it.

"Hullo! We're tired and need food!"

The hollow man strained forward, his fingers groping for the door latch. My scaled legs flexed hard around his middle. His sweaty stomach sizzled and he cried at the heat of me. A rib snapped. Another. He sank backward and, with a dry flutter of wings, I pulled him away from the window, back into the dark.

"Could we share your fire? It's so damn cold!"

"We'd give you money, but we ain't got any. There ain't a nickel in a thousand miles of here. . . . "

Small screams tore the hollow man's beaten lips. There was blood. I cursed the waste and twisted a handful of metal rings. He sank to his knees and quieted.

"We'll leave our guns. We don't mean no harm!"

I jerked one ring, then another. I cooed against the hollow man's skinless shoulder and made him pick up his rifle. When he had it loaded, cocked, and aimed through a slot in the door, I whispered in his ear and made him laugh.

And then I screamed out at them, "You dirty bastards! You stay away! You ain't comin' in here!"

Gunshots exploded. We only got one of them, not clean but bad enough. The others pulled him into the forest, where the dense trees muffled his screams and kept us from getting another clear shot.

The rifle clattered to the floor, smoking faintly, smelling good. We walked to the window. I jingled his neck rings and the hollow man squinted through the tangle of veins, to the spot where a red streak was freezing in the snow.

I made the hollow man smile.

So four. Still four, when night came and moonlight dripped like melting wax over the snow-capped ridges to the west. Four to make me forget the one nearly drained. Four to make me impatient while soft time crept toward the leaden hour, grain by grain, breath by breath . . .

The hour descended. I twisted rings and plucked black muscles, and the hollow man fed the fire and barred the door. I released him and he huddled in a corner, exhausted.

I rose through the chimney and thrust myself away from the cabin. My wings fought the biting wind as I climbed high, searching the black forest below. I soared the length of a high mountain glacier and dove away, banking back toward the heart of the valley. Shadows that stretched forever, and then, deep in a jagged ravine that stabbed at a river, a sputtering glimmer of orange. A campfire.

So bold. So typical of their kind. I extended my wings and drifted down like a bat, corning to rest in the branches of a giant redwood. Its live green stench nearly made me retch. Huddling in my wings for warmth, I clawed through the bark with a wish to make the ancient monster scream. The tree quivered against the icy wind. Grinning, satisfied, I looked down.

Two strong, but different. One weak. One as good as dead.

Three.

Grizzly sat in silence, his black face as motionless as a tombstone. Instantly, I liked him best. Mammoth, wrapped in a bristling grizzly coat he looked even bigger, almost as big as a grizzly. He sat by the fire, staring at his reflection in a gleaming ax blade. He made me anxious. He could last for months.

Across from Grizzly, Redbeard turned a pot and boiled coffee. He straightened his fox-head cap and stroked his beard, clearing it of ice. I didn't like him. His milky squint was too much like my own. But any fool could see that he hated Grizzly, and that made me smile.

Away from them both, crouching under a tree with the whimpering ice dogs, Rabbit wept through swollen eyes. He dug deep in his plastic coat and produced a crucifix. I almost laughed out loud.

And in a tent, wrapped in sweat-damp wool and expensive eiderdown that couldn't keep him warm anymore, still clinging to life, was the dead man, who didn't matter.

But maybe I could make him matter.

And then there would only be two.

When the clouds came, when they suffocated the unblinking moon and brought sleep to the camp, I swept down to the dying fire and rolled comfortably in the crab-colored coals. The hush of the river crept over me as I decided what to do.

To make three into two.

Three men, and the dead man. Two tents: Grizzly and Redbeard in one, Rabbit and the dead man in the other. Easy. No worries, except for the dogs. (For ice dogs are wise. Their beast hearts hide simple secrets. . . .)

The packed snow sizzled beneath my feet as I crept toward Rabbit's tent. The dead man's face pressed against one corner of the tent, molding his swollen features in yellow plastic. Each rattling breath gently puffed the thin material away from his face, and each weak gasp slowly drew it back. It was a steady, pleasant sound I concentrated on it until it was mine.

No time for metal rings. No time for naked muscle and feast. Slowly, I reached out and took hold of Rabbit's mind, digging deep until I found his darkest nightmare. I pulled it loose and let it breathe. At first it frightened him, but I tugged its midnight corners straight and banished its monsters, and soon Rabbit was full of bliss, awake without even knowing it.

I circled the tent and pushed against the other side. The dead man rolled across, cold against the warmth of Rabbit's unbridled nightmare.

"Jesus, you're freezin', Charlie," whispered Rabbit as he moved closer. "But don't worry. I'll keep you warm, buddy. I've gotta keep you warm."

But in the safety of his nightmare, that wasn't what Rabbit wanted at all.

I waited in the tree until Grizzly found them the next morning, wrapped together in the dead man's bag. He shot Rabbit in the head and left him for the ice dogs.

Redbeard buried the dead man in a silky snowdrift.

That day was nothing. Grizzly and Redbeard sat at the edge of the clearing and wasted their only chance. Grizzly stared hungrily at the cabin, seeing only what I wanted him to see. Thick, safe walls. A puffing chimney. A home. But Redbeard, damned Redbeard, wise with fear and full of caution, sensed other things. The dead man's fevered rattle whispering through the trees. An ice dog gnawing a fresh, gristly bone. And bear traps, rusty with blood.

Redbeard rose and walked away. Soon Grizzly followed.

And then there was only the hollow man, rocking gently in his chair. The soles of his boots buffed the splintery floor and his legs swung back and forth, back and forth.

Two. Now two, as the second night was born, a silent twin to the first. Only two, as again I twisted rings and plucked muscles and put the hollow man to sleep. Just two, as my wings beat the night and I flew once more from the sooty chimney to the ravine that stabbed a river.

There they sat, as before, grizzly and fox. And there I watched, waiting, with nothing left to do but listen for the sweet arrival of the leaden hour.

Grizzly chopped wood and fed the fire. Redbeard positioned blackened pots and watched them boil. Both planned silently while they ate, and afterwards their mute desperation grew, knotting their minds into coils of anger. Grizzly charged the dying embers with whole branches and did not smile until the flames leaped wildly. The heat slapped at Redbeard in waves, harsh against the pleasant brandy-warmth that swam in his gut and slowed his racing thoughts.

"Tomorrow mornin'," blurted Redbeard, "we're gettin' away from here. I'm not dealin' with no crazy hermit."

Grizzly stared at his ax-blade reflection and smiled. "We're gonna kill us a crazy hermit," he said. "Tomorrow mornin'."

Soon the old words came, taut and cold, and then Grizzly sprang through the leaping flames, his black coat billowing, and Redbeard's fox-head cap flew from his head as he whirled around. Ax rang against knife. A white fist tore open a black lip, and the teeth below ripped into a pale knuckle. Knife split ebony cheek. Blood hissed through the flames and sizzled against burning embers. A sharp crack as the ax sank home in a tangle of ribs. Redbeard coughed a misty breath past Grizzly's ear, and the bigger man spun the smaller around, freed his ax, and watched his opponent stumble into the fire.

I laughed above the crackling roar. The ice dogs scattered into the forest, barking, wild with fear and the sour smell of death.

So Grizzly had survived. He stood still, his singed coat smoking, his cut cheek oozing blood. His mind was empty—there was no remorse, only a feeling that he was the strongest, he was the best.

Knowing that, I flew home happy.

There was not much in the cabin that I could use. I found only a single whalebone needle, yellow with age, and no thread at all. I watched the veined window as I searched impatiently for a substitute, and at last I discovered a spool of fishing line in a rusty metal box. Humming, I went about my work. First I drew strips of the hollow man's pallid skin over his shrunken shoulder muscles, fastening them along his backbone with a cross stitch. Then I bunched the flabby tissue at the base of his skull and made the final secret passes with my needle.

Now he was nothing. I tore the metal rings out of his neck and the hollow man twitched as if shocked.

A bullet ripped through the cabin door. "I'm gonna get you, you bastard," cried Grizzly, his voice loud but worn. "You hear me? I'm gonna *get* you!"

The hollow man sprang from the rocker; his withered legs betrayed him and he fell to the floor. I balanced on the back of the chair and hissed at him, spreading my wings in mock menace. With a laughable scream, he flung himself at the door.

Grizzly must have been confused by the hollow man's ravings, for he didn't fire again until the fool was nearly upon him. An instant of pain, another of relief, and the hollow man crumpled, finished.

And then Grizzly just sat in the snow, his eyes fixed on the open cabin door. I watched him from a corner of the veined window, afraid to move. He took out his ax and stared at his reflection in the glistening blade. After a time Grizzly pocketed the ax, and then he pulled his great coat around him, disappearing into its bristling black folds.

In the afternoon I grew fearful. While the redwoods stretched their heavy shadows over the cabin, Grizzly rose and followed the waning sun up a slight ridge. He cleaned his gun. He even slept for a few moments. Then he slapped his numb face awake and rubbed snow over his sliced cheek.

Grizzly came home.

I hid above the doorway. Grizzly sighed as he crossed the threshold, and I bit back my laughter. The door swung shut. Grizzly stooped and tossed a thick log onto the dying embers. He grinned as it crackled aflame.

I pushed off hard and dove from the ceiling. My claws ripped through grizzly hide and then into human hide. Grizzly bucked awfully, even tried to smash me against the hearth, but the heat only gave me power and as my legs burned into his stomach Grizzly screamed. I drove my claws into a shivering bulge of muscle and brought him to his knees.

The metal rings came next. I pinned them into his neck: one, two, three, four.

After I had supped, I sat the hollow man in the rocker and whispered to him as we looked through the veined window. A storm was rising in the west. We watched it come for a long time. Soon, a fresh dusting of snow covered the husk of man lying out on the ridge.

I told Grizzly that he had been my favorite. I told him that he would last a long time.

Not From Around Here
David J. Schow

This morning I saw an alley cat busily disemboweling a rail lizard. I watched much longer than I had to in order to get the point.

Townies call little hamlets like Point Pitt "bedroom communities." Look west from San Francisco, and you'll see the Pacific Ocean. Twenty minutes by car to any other compass point will bring you to the population-signless borders of a bedroom community. El Granada. Dos Piedras. Half Moon Bay. Summit. Pumpkin Valley (no kidding).

Point Pitt rated a dot on the roadmaps only because of a NASA tracking dish, fenced off on a stone jetty, anchored rock-solid against gales, its microwave ear turned toward the universe. Gatewood was four and three-quarter miles to the north. To drive from Point Pitt to Gatewood you passed a sprawling, loamy-smelling acreage of flat fields and greenhouses, where itinerant Mexicans picked mushrooms for about a buck an hour. I saw them working every morning. They were visible through my right passenger window as I took the coast road up to San Francisco, and to my left every evening when I drove home. On the opposite side of the road, the ocean marked time. The pickers never gazed out toward the sea; they lacked the leisure. My first week of commuting eroded my notice of them. The panorama of incoming surf proved more useful for drive-time meditation. I no longer lacked the leisure.

You had to lean out a bit, but you could also see the Pacific from the balcony rail of our new upstairs bedroom, framed between two gargantuan California pines at least eighty years old. Suzanne fell for the house as soon as we toured it under the wing of the realtor. Our three-year-old, Jilly, squealed "Cave!" and jumped up and down in place, in hyperactive circles of little kid astonishment. Hard to believe, that this cavernous place was ours, that we weren't visiting a higher social class and would soon have to go home. This *was* home, and we were in love . . . goofy as that may sound.

I did not fall in love with the idea that all the decent movies, restaurants, and other urban diversions were still up in San Francisco. Gatewood boasted a single grease-griddle coffee shop that opened two hours before my morning alarm razzed and went dark promptly at five—up here, dinner was obviously a meal eaten at home, with family. Nearby was a mom-and-pop grocery that locked up at 9:00 P.M. Several miles away, in Dos Piedras, was an all-nighter where you could get chips and beer and bread and milk.

It sure wasn't the city. As a town, it wasn't vast enough to merit a stop-light. Point Pitt was no more than a rustic clot of well-built older homes tucked into a mountainside, with an ocean view. Voilà—bedroom commu-nity. Any encapsulation made it sound like a travel-folder wet dream, or an ideal environment in which to raise a child. I suspect my shrink knew this. He fomented this conspiracy, with my doctor, to get me away from my beloved city for the sake of my not-so beloved ulcers.

I became a commuter. The drive was usually soothing, contemplative. I calmed my gut by chugging a lot of milk from the all-night market. We popped for cable TV—sixty channels. We adjusted fast.

It was required that I buy a barn-shaped rural mailbox. Suzanne jazzed it up with our name in stick-on weatherproof lettering: TASKE. The first Sunday after we moved in, I bolted it to the gang post by the feeder road, next to the boxes of our nearest neighbors. The hillside lots were widely sepa-rated by distance and altitude, fences and weald. There was much privacy to be had here. The good life, I guessed.

When a long shadow fell across the gang post from behind, I looked up at Creighton Dunwoody for the first time. His box read MR. & MRS. C. DUNWOODY. He had the sun behind him; I was on my knees, wrestling with a screwdriver. It just wouldn't have played for me to say, *You have me at a disadvantage, sir,* so I gave him something else sparkling, like, "Uh . . . hello?"

He squinted at my shiny white mailbox, next to his rusty steel one. It had a large, ancient dent in the top. "You're Taske?" He pronounced it like *passkey*; it was a mistake I'd endured since the first grade.

I gently corrected him. "Carl Taske, right." I stood and shifted, foot-to-foot, the essence of nervous schmuckdom, and finally stuck out my hand. Carl Taske, alien being, here.

I almost thought he was going to ignore it when he leaned forward and clasped it emotionlessly. "Dunwoody. You're in Meyer Olson's old house. Good house." He was taller than me, a gaunt farmer type. His skin was stretched over his bones in that brownly weathered way that makes thirty look like fifty, and fifty like a hundred and ten. Like a good neighbor coasting through meaningless chat, I was about to inquire as to the fate of Meyer Olson when Dunwoody cut in, point-blank, "You got any kids?"

"My daughter Jill's the only one so far." And Jilly had been well-planned. I couldn't help thinking of farm families with fourteen kids, like litters.

He chewed on that a bit. His attention seemed to stray. This was country speed, not city rush, but I felt like jumping in and filling the dead space. It wouldn't do to appear pushy. I might have to do this a lot with the hayseed set from now on.

"Any pets?" he said.

"Not today." A partial lie. Suzanne had found an orphaned Alsatian at the animal shelter and was making the drive to collect it the next day.

"Any guns in your house?"

"Don't believe in guns." I shook my head and kept my eyes on his. The languid, directional focus of his questions made my guard pop up automatically. This was starting to sound like more than the standard greenhorn feel-up.

"That's good. That you don't." We traded idiotic, uncomfortable smiles.

In my new master bedroom there were his and hers closets. A zippered case in the back of mine held a twelve-gauge Remington pumpgun loaded with five three-inch Nitro Mag shells. My father had taught me that this was the only way to avoid killing yourself accidentally with an "unloaded" gun, and Suzanne was giving me hell about it now that Jilly was walking around by herself. It was none of Dunwoody's business, anyway.

"How old's your girl?"

"Three, this past May."

"She's not a baby anymore, then."

"Well, technically, no." I smiled again and it hurt my face. The sun was waning and the sky had gone mauve. Everything seemed to glow in the brief starkness of twilight gray.

Dunwoody nodded as though I'd given the correct answers on a geography test. "That's good. That you have your little girl." He was about to add something else when his gaze tilted past my shoulder.

I turned around and saw nothing. Then I caught a wink of reflected gold light. Looking more intently, I could see what looked to be a pretty large cat, cradled in the crotch of a towering eucalyptus tree uphill in the distance. Its eyes tossed back the sunset as it watched us.

Dunwoody was off, walking quickly up the slope without further comment. Maybe he had to feed the cat. "I guess I'll see . . . you later," I said to his back. I doubt if he heard me. His house stood in shadow off a sharp switchback in the road. A wandering, deeply-etched dirt path wound up to the front porch.

Not exactly rudeness. Not the city brand, at least.

The moon emerged to hang full and orange on the horizon, like an ebbing sun. High in its arc it shrank to a hard silver coin, its white brilliance filtering down through the treetops and shimmering on the sea-ripple. Suzanne hopped from bed and strode naked to the balcony, moving out through the French doors. Moonbeams made foliage patterns on her skin; the cool night-time breeze buffeted her hair, in a gentle contest.

Her thin summer nightgown was tangled up in my feet, beneath the sheets. We'd dispensed with it about midnight. The one advantage to becoming a homeowner I'd never anticipated was the nude perfection of Suzanne on the balcony. She was a blue silhouette, weight on one foot and shoulders tilted in an unconsciously classical pose. After bearing Jilly and dropping the surplus weight of pregnancy, her ass and pelvis had resolved into a lascivious fullness that I could not keep my hands away from for long.

We fancied ourselves progressive parents, and Jilly had been installed in our living room from the first. We kept our single bedroom to ourselves. On hair triggers for the vaguest noise of infant distress, Mommy and Daddy were then besieged with the usual wee-hour fire drills and some spectacular demonstrations of eliminatory functions. Marital spats over the baby came and went like paper cuts; that was normal, too. Pain that might spoil a whole day, but was not permanent. Jilly's crib was swapped for a loveseat that opened into a single bed. And now she did not require constant surveillance, and was happily ensconced in her first private, real-life room.

Recently, Suzanne had shed all self-consciousness about sex, becoming adventurous again. There was no birth control to fret over. That was a hitch we still didn't discuss too often, because of the quiet pain involved—the permanent kind.

"Carl, come here and look." She spoke in a rapid hush, having spied something odd. "Hurry up!"

I padded out to embrace her from behind, nuzzling into the bouquet of her hair, then looking past her shoulder.

A big man was meandering slowly up the road. The nearest streetlamp was more than a block away, and we saw him as he passed through its pool of light, down by the junction with the coast highway. He was large and fleshy and fat and as naked as we were.

I pulled Suzanne back two paces, into the darkness of the bedroom. The balcony was amply private. Neither of us wanted to be caught peeking.

He seemed to grow as he got closer, until he was enormous. He was bald, with sloping mountain shoulders and vast pizza-dough pilings of flesh pulled into pendant bags by gravity. His knotted boxer's brow hid his eyes in shadow, as his pale belly hung to obscure his sex, except for a faint smudge of pubic hair. The load had bowed his knees inward, and his *lumpen* thighs jiggled as he ponderously hauled up one leg to drop in front of the other. We heard his bare feet slapping the pavement. His tits swam to and fro.

"There's something wrong with him," I whispered. Before Suzanne could give me a shot in the ribs for being a smartass, I added, "No—something else. *Look* at him. Closely."

We hurried across to the bedroom's south window so we could follow his progress past the mailboxes in front of the house. He was staring up into the sky us he walked, and his chin was wet. He was drooling. His arms hung dead dumb at his sides as he gazed upward, turning his head slowly one way, then another, as though trying to record distant stars through faulty receiving equipment.

"He's like a great big *baby*." Suzanne was aghast.

"That's what I was thinking." I recalled Jilly, when she was only a month out of the womb. The slack, stunned expression of the man below reminded me of the way a baby stares at a crib trinket—one that glitters, or revolves, or otherwise captures the eye of a being who is seeing this world for the first time.

"Maybe he's retarded."

A shudder wormed its way up my backbone but I successfully hid it. "Maybe he's a local boy they let run loose at night, y'know, like putting out the cat."

"Yeeugh, don't say that." She backed against me and my hands enfolded her, crossing to cup her breasts. Her body was alive with goosebumps; her nipples condensed to solid little nubs. She relaxed her head into the hollow of my shoulder and locked her arms behind me. Thus entangled, we watched the naked pilgrim drift up the street and beyond the light. My hands did their bit and she purred, closing her eyes. Her gorgeous rump settled in. "Hm. I seem to be riding the rail again," she said, and chuckled.

She loved having her breasts kneaded, and we didn't lapse into the dialogue

I'd expected. The one about how her bosom *could* be a *little bit* larger, didn't I think so? (What I thought was that every woman I'd ever known had memorized this routine, like a mantra. Suzanne played it back every six weeks or so.) Nor did she lapse into the post-sex melancholy she sometimes suffered when she thought of the other thing, the painful one.

Eighteen months after Jilly was born, Suzanne's doctor discovered ovarian cysts. Three, medium-sized, successfully removed. The consensus was that Jilly would be our only child, and Suzanne believed only children were maladjusted. While there was regret that our power of choice had been excised, Suzanne still held out hope for a happy accident someday. I was more pragmatic, or maybe more selfish. I wasn't sure I wanted more than one child, and in a sense this metabolic happenstance had neatly relieved me of the responsibility of the vasectomy I'd been contemplating. I was hung up on getting my virility surgically removed in an operation that was, to me, a one-way gamble with no guarantees. Frightening. I prefer guarantees—hardline, black-and-white, duly notarized. A hot tip from a realtor on a sheer steal of a house had more to do with reality than the caprices of a body that turns traitor and hampers your emotional life.

And when Suzanne's tumors were a bad memory, a plague of superstitions followed. For several months she was convinced that I considered her leprous, sexually unclean. From her late mother she had assimilated the irrational fear that says once doctors slice into your body with a scalpel, it's only a matter of borrowed time before the Big *D* comes pounding at the drawbridge.

The whole topic was a tightly twined nest of vipers neither of us cared to trespass upon anymore. God, how she could bounce back.

Passion cranked up its heat, and she shimmied around so we were face-to-face. The way we fit together in embrace was comfortingly safe. Her hand filled and fondled, and I got a loving squeeze below. "This gets enough of a workout," she slyly opined. Then she patted my waistline. "But we need to exert this. When we get the dog, you can go out running with it, like me."

It was depressingly true. Bucking a desk chair had caused a thickening I did not appreciate. "Too much competition, I muttered. I was afraid to challenge the ulcerations eating my stomach wall too soon. She was in much better physical shape than me. Those excuses served, for now. Her legs were short, well-proportioned, and athletic. Her calves were solid and sleek. Another turn-on.

"Mmm." Her hands slid up, around, and all over. "In that case, come back to bed. I've got a new taste sensation I know you're just dying to try."

The following morning, I met the huge bald man.

He was wearing a circus-tent-sized denim coverall, gum-soled work boots, and an old cotton shirt, blazing white and yellowed at the armpits. He was busily rummaging in Dunwoody's mailbox.

I played it straight, clearing my throat too loudly and standing by.

He started, looking up and yanking his hand out of the box. His head narrowed at the hat-brim line and bulged up and out in the back, as though his skull had been bound in infancy, ritually deformed. His tiny black eyes settled on me and a wide grin split his face. Too wide.

"G'morn," he said with a voice like a foghorn. My skin contracted. I got the feeling he was sniffing me from afar. His lips continued meaningless movements while he stared.

"*Ormly!*"

Creighton Dunwoody was hustling down the path from his house. The hillside was steep enough to put his cellar floor above the level of our roof. He wore an undershirt and had a towel draped around his neck; he had obviously interrupted his morning shave to come out and yell. Drooping suspenders danced around his legs as he mountaineered down the path.

Ormly cringed at the sound of his name, but did not move. Birds twittered away the morning, and he grinned hugely at their music.

For one frozen moment we faced off, a triangle with Ormly at the mail-boxes. I thought of the three-way showdown at the climax of *The Good, the Bad and the Ugly*.

Dunwoody stopped to scope us out, made his decision with a grunt, and resumed his brisk oldster's stride toward me. He realized the burden of explanation was his, and he motioned me to approach the mailboxes. His mouth was a tight moue of anger or embarrassment. Maybe disgust. But he bulled it through.

"Mister Taske. This here's Ormly. My boy." He nodded from him to me and back again. "Ormly. Mister Taske is from the city. You should shake his hand."

Dunwoody's presence did not make it any easier to move into Ormly's range. Without the workboots he would still be a foot taller than I was. I watched as his brain obediently motivated his hand toward me. It was like burying my own hand in a catcher's mitt. He was still grinning.

The social amenities executed, Dunwoody said, "You get on back up the house now. Mail ain't till later."

Ormly minded. I've seen more raw intelligence in the eyes of goldfish. As he clumped home, I saw a puckered fist of scar tissue nested behind his left ear. It was a baseball-sized hemisphere, deeply fissured and bone white. A big bite of brains was missing there. Maybe his pituitary gland had been damaged as part of the deal.

Dundy batted shut the lid to his mailbox; it made a hollow *chunk* sound. "S'okay," he said. "Ormly's not right in the head."

I was suddenly embarrassed for the older man.

"Sometimes he gets out. He's peaceful, though. He has peace. Ain't nothing to be afraid of."

I took a chance and mentioned what I'd seen last night. His eyes darted up to lock onto mine for the first time.

"And what were *you* doin' up that time of night anyhow, Mister Taske?" That almost colonial mistrust of newcomers was back.

"I woke up. Thought I heard something crashing around in the woods." The lie slipped smoothly out. So far, I'd aimed more lies at Dunwoody than truth. It was stupid for me to stand there in my C&R three-piece, calfhide attaché case in hand, judging his standards of honesty.

"This ain't the city. Animals come down from the hills to forage. Make sure your garbage can lids are locked down or you'll have a mess to clean up."

I caught a comic picture of opening the kitchen door late at night and saying howdy-do to a grizzly bear. Not funny. Nearly forty yards up the hill, I watched Ormly duck the front door lintel and vanish inside. Dunwoody's house cried out for new paint. It was as decrepit as his mailbox.

Dunwoody marked my expression. "Ormly's all I got left. My little girl, Sarah, died a long time ago. The crib death. Primmy—that's my wife; her name was Primrose—is dead, too. She just didn't take to these parts . . ." His voice trailed off.

I felt like the shallow, yuppie city slicker I was. I wanted to say something healing, something that would diminish the gap between me and this old rustic. He was tough as a scrub bristle. His T-shirt was frayed but clean. There was shaving lather drying on his face, and he had lost a wife, a daughter, and from what I'd seen, ninety percent of a son. I *wanted* to say something. But then I saw his bare arms, and the blood drained from my face in a flood.

He didn't notice, or didn't care.

I checked my watch, in an artificial, diversionary move Dunwoody saw right through. It was a Cartier tank watch. I felt myself sinking deeper.

"Mind if I ask you a question?"

"Uh-no." I shot my cuff to hide the watch, which had turned ostentatious and loud.

"Why do you folks want to live here?" There it was: bald hostility, countrified, but still as potent as snake venom. I tried to puzzle out some politic response to this when he continued. "I mean, why live here when it makes you so late for everything?" His eyes went to my shirtsleeve, which concealed my overpriced watch.

He shrugged and turned toward his house with no leave takings, as before. All I could register in my brain were his arms. From the wrists to where they met his undershirt, Dunwoody's arms were seeded with more tiny puncture marks than you would have found on two hundred junkies up in the Mission district. Thousands and thousands of scarred holes.

My trusty BMW waited, a sanctuary until the scent of leather upholstery brought on new heartstabs of class guilt. It was simple to insulate oneself with the trappings of upward mobility, with *things*. My grand exit was marred by sloppy shifting. The closer I drew to the city the better I felt, and my death-grip on the wheel's racing sleeve gradually relaxed.

Maybe our other neighbors would make themselves apparent in time. Oh bliss oh joy.

Brix became the dog's name by consensus. I stayed as far away from that decision as politely possible. Dad the diplomat.

Jilly had thrilled to its reddish-brown coat, which put her in mind of "bricks," you see. Suzanne went at tedious length about how Alsatians reacted best to monosyllabic names containing a lot of hard consonants. In a word, that was Brix—and he was already huge enough for Jilly to ride bareback. He could gallop rings around Suzanne while she jogged. He never got winded or tired. He looked great next to the fireplace. A Christmas card snapshot of our idyllic family unit would have made you barf from the cuteness: shapely, amber-haired Mom; angelic blond Jillian Heather; Brix the Faithful Canine . . . and sourpuss Dad with his corporate razor cut and incipient ulcers. We were totally nuclear.

I didn't bother with Dunwoody or Ormly again until the night Brix got killed.

It was predestined that the dog's sleeping mat would go at the foot of Jilly's hide-a-bed. While Suzanne and I struggled patiently to indoctrinate the animal to his new name and surroundings, he'd snap to and seek Jilly the instant she called him. They were inseparable, and that was fine. The dog got a piece of Jilly's life; Suzanne and I were fair—traded a small chunk of the personal time we'd sacrificed in order to be called Mommy and Daddy. This payoff would accrue interest, year by year, until the day our daughter walked out the door to play grownup for the rest of her life. It was a bittersweet revelation: starting right now, more and more of her would be lost to us. On the other hand, the way she flung her arms around Brix's ruff and hugged him tight made me want to cry, too.

Since we'd assumed residence in Point Pitt, our lives really *had* begun to arrange more agreeably. Our city tensions bled off. We were settling, healing. Sometimes I must be forced to drink the water I lead myself to.

Brix quickly cultivated one peculiar regimen. At Jilly's bedtime he'd plunk his muzzle down on the mat and play prone sentry until her breathing became deep and metered. Then he'd lope quietly out to hang with the other humans. When our lights went down, he'd pull an about-face and trot back to his post in Jilly's room. Once or twice I heard him pacing out the size of the house in the middle of the night, and when the forest made its grizzly-bear commotions, Brix would return one or two barks of warning. He never did this while in Jilly's room, which was considerate of him. Barks sufficed. In his canine way, he kept back the dangers of the night.

So when he went thundering down the stairs barking loudly enough to buzz the woodwork, I woke up knowing something was not normal. Suzanne moaned and rolled over, sinking her face into the pillows. I extricated myself from the sleepy grasp of her free arm in order to punch in as Daddy the night watchman. The digital clock merrily announced 3:44 A.M. And counting.

Point Pitt was not a place where residents bolted their doors at night, although that was one habit I was in no danger of losing, ever. Because the worst of summer still lingered, we had taken to leaving a few windows open. It wasn't completely foolish to assume some thief might be cruising for a likely smash-and-grab spot. By the time the sheriffs (the district's only real law enforcement) could be summoned, even an inept burglar would have ample time to rip off all the goodies in the house and come back for seconds. While this sort of social shortcoming was traditionally reserved for the big bad city, there was no telling who might start a trend, or when.

Besides, if there were no bad guys, I might be treated to the surreal sight of a live bear consuming my rubbish.

Downstairs a window noisily ceased existence. Breaking glass is one of the ugliest sounds there is. I picked up speed highballing down the stairs.

I thought of the claw hammer Suzanne had been using while hanging plants in her little conservatory and hung the corner wildly, skidding to a stop and embedding a flat wedge of glass into the ball of my right foot. I howled, keeled over, and obliterated a dieffenbachia mounted in a wire tripod. The entire middle section of leaded-glass panes was blown out into the night. Pots swung crookedly in their macramé slings where Brix had leapt through.

Somewhere in the backyard he was having it rabidly out with the interloper, scrabbling and snapping.

Grimacing, I stumped into the kitchen and hit the backyard light switches. Nothing. The floodlamps were still lined up on the counter in their store cartons, with a Post-it note stuck to the center one, reminding me of another undone chore. Outside the fight churned and boiled and I couldn't see a damned thing.

My next thought was of the shotgun. I limped back to the stairs, leaving single footprints in blood on the hardwood floor. Brix had stopped barking.

"Carl?"

"I'm okay," I called toward the landing. To my left was the shattered conservatory window, and the toothless black gullet of the night beyond it. "*Brix!* Hey, Brix! C'mon, guy! Party's over!"

Only one sound came in response. To this day I can't describe it accurately. It was like the peal of tearing cellophane, amplified a thousand times, or the grating rasp a glass cutter makes. It made my teeth twinge and brought every follicle on my body to full alert.

"Carl!" Suzanne was robed and halfway down the stairs.

"Get me a bandage and some peroxide, would you? I've hacked my goddamn foot wide open. Don't go outside. Get my tennis shoes."

I sat down on the second stair with a thump. When Suzanne extracted the trapezoidal chunk of glass, I nearly puked. There was a gash two inches wide, leaking blood and throbbing with each slam of my heartbeat. I thought I could feel cold air seeking tiny, exposed bones down there.

"Jesus, Carl." She made a face, as though I'd done this just to stir up a boring night. "Brixy whiffs a bobcat, or some fucking dog game, and you have to ruin our new floor by bleeding all over it . . . "

"Something turned him on enough to take out the conservatory window. Jesus Christ in a Handi-Van. Ouch! Even if it is a bobcat, those things are too bad to mess with."

She swept her hair back, leaving a smear of blood on her forehead. She handed over the peroxide and left my foot half taped. "You finish. Let me deal with Jilly before she freaks out."

"Mommy?" Jilly's voice was tiny and sleep-clogged. She'd missed the circus. I sure hadn't heard her roll out of the sack, but Suzanne apparently had. Mommy vibes, she'd tell me later.

After gingerly pulling on my shoes, I stumped to the kitchen door and disordered some drawers looking for a flashlight. Upstairs, Suzanne was murmuring a soothing story about how Daddy had himself an accident and fell on his ass.

I didn't have to look far to find Brix. He was gutted and strewn all over the backyard. The first part I found was his left rear leg, lying in the dirt like a gruesome drumstick with a blood-slicked jag of bone jutting from it. My damaged foot stubbed it; pain shot up my ass and blasted through the top of my head. His carcass was folded backward over the east fence, belly torn lengthwise, organs ripped out. The dripping cavern in the top of his head showed me where his brain had been until ten minutes ago.

The metallic, shrieking noise sailed down from the hills.

And the lights were on up at Dunwoody's place.

When the sheriffs told me Brix's evisceration was nothing abnormal, I almost lost it and started punching. Calling the cops had been automatic city behavior; a conditioned reaction that no longer had any real purpose. Atavistic. There hadn't been enough of Brix left to fill a Hefty bag. What wasn't in the bag was missing, presumed eaten. Predators, they shrugged.

In one way I was thankful we'd only had the dog a few days. Jilly was still too young to be really stunned by the loss of him, though she spent the day retreated into that horrible quiet that seizes children on the level of pure instinct. I immediately promised her another pet. Maybe that was impulsive and wrong, but I wasn't tracking on all channels myself. It did light her face briefly up.

I felt worse for Suzanne. She had been spared most of the visceral evidence of the slaughter, but those morsels she could not avoid seeing had hollowed her eyes and slackened her jaw. She had taken to Brix immediately, and had always militated against anything that caused pain to animals. There was no way to bleach out the solid and sickeningly large bloodstain on the fence, and I finally kicked out the offending planks. Looking at the hole was just as depressing.

The sheriffs were cloyed, too fat and secure in their jobs. All I had done was bring myself to their attention, which is one place no sane person wants to be. Annoyed at my cowardly waste of their time, they marked up my floor with their boots and felt up my wife with their eyes.

Things were done differently here. That was what impelled me to Dunwoody's place, at a brisk limp.

I had not expected Ormly to answer the door; I couldn't fathom what tasks were outside his capabilities and simply assumed he was too stupid to wipe his own ass. He filled up the doorway, immense and ugly, his face blank as a pine plank (with a knot on the flip side, I knew). He was dressed exactly as before. Perhaps he had not changed. It took a couple of long beats, but he did recognize me.

"Fur paw," he said.

The back of my neck bristled. When Ormly's brain changed stations, he haunted the forest, starkers, in the dead of night; what other pastimes might his damaged imagination offer him? When he spoke, I half expected him to produce one of Brix's unaccounted-for shanks from his back pocket and gnaw on it. Then I realized what he had said: *For pa*.

"Yeah." I tried to clear the idiocy out of my throat. "Is he home?"

"Home. Yuh." He lurched dutifully out of the foyer, Frankenstein's Monster in search of a battery charge.

I waited on the stoop, thinking it unwise to go where I wasn't specifically beckoned or invited. Another urban prejudice. Wait for the protocol, go through the official motions. Put it through channels. That routine was what had won me the white-lipped holes blooming in my stomach.

Dunwoody weaved out of the stale-smelling dimness holding half a glass of peppermint schnapps. He was wearing a long-sleeved workshirt with the cuffs buttoned.

"I'm sorry to bother you, Mr. Dunwoody, but my dog was killed last night." No reaction. He showed the same disinterest the cops had, and that brought my simmering anger a notch closer to boiling. "More to the point, he was pelted and hung on my back fence with his head scooped out and his guts spread all over the yard. The fence bordering *your* property, Mr. Dunwoody."

"I heard him barking." He looked down away. "Saw you kick the slats out." His words billowed toward me in minty clouds; he was tying on a nice, out-of-focus afternoon drunk. "You said you didn't have no pets."

It was an accusation: *If you hadn't lied, this would not have happened.*

I felt obligated to be pissed off, but my soul wasn't really in it. My need to know was stronger. "Sorry—but look, you mentioned wildcats coming out of the hills. Or bears. Maybe I'm no authority on wildlife feeding habits, but what happened was . . . " I flashed on Brix's corpse again and my voice hitched. "That was far beyond killing for food."

"I didn't see it." His voice wasn't a full slur. Not yet, but soon. "Woke me up. But I didn't see it. I'm glad I didn't. That part I don't fancy, sir." He scratched an eyebrow. "I think y'all should leave. Go."

"You mean leave Point Pitt?"

"Move somewhere else. Don't live here." He took a long drag on his glass and grimaced, as though choking down cough medicine. "See what happens? This ain't for boys like you, with your fag hairdo's and your little Japanese cars and your satellite TV . . . aahhh, Christ . . . "

Ormly loomed behind him, recording all the pain with oddly sad eyes, so much like a dog himself.

A cloudy tear slipped down Dunwoody's face, but his own eyes were clear and decisive as they looked from me to the north. "Go home," he said. "Just go home, please." Then he shut the door in my face.

Dinner was flavorless, by rote. Suzanne had tried to nap and only gotten haggard. Jilly told me she missed Brix.

After bestowing my customary bedtime smackeroo, Jilly asked again about getting another pet *right now*. Her mom had run the same idea past me downstairs. Between them I'd finally be goaded into some reparation.

Suzanne reached for me as soon as I hit my side of the bed. She had already divested herself of clothing, and her movements were brazen and urgent. She wanted to outrun the last twenty-four hours in a steambath of good therapeutic fucking. Her nerves were rawed, and close to the surface; she climaxed with very little effort and kept me inside her for a long, comforting while. Then she kissed me very tenderly, ate two sleeping pills, and chased oblivion in another direction.

My foot felt as if I had stomped on a sharpened pencil. I hobbled to the bathroom, pretending I was Chester in *Gunsmoke*. The dressing was yellowed from drainage and shadowed with dry brown blood. It gave off a carrion odor. I took my time washing and swabbing and winding on new gauze. I was still pleasantly numb everywhere else.

There was a low thrumming, like that of a large truck idling on the street outside. I felt it before I actually heard it. I checked the window across from the bathroom door, but there was nothing, not even Ormly making his uniformless predawn rounds. With my Bay City paranoid's devotion to ritual, I hobbled downstairs and jiggled all the locked doors. The boarded-up plant nook was secure. I sneaked a couple of slugs of milk straight from the carton. Ulcer maintenance.

Jilly's room was on the far side of the bathroom. When I peeked stealthily in, the vibrational noise got noticeably louder.

Triplechecking everything constantly was as much a habit of new parent-hood as security insecurity. Jilly was wound up in her Sesame Street sheets. I decided to shut the window, which was curtained, but half-open.

The sheet-shape was grotesque enough to suggest that Jilly's entire platoon of stuffed animals was bunking with her tonight. I'd tucked in Wile E. Coyote myself. No more Brix. My throat started to close up with self pity. I crept closer to plant a sleeptime kiss on Jilly's temple—another parental privilege, so Suzanne told me. Jilly's hair was just beginning to shade closer to the coloring of my own.

The low, fluttering noise was coming from beneath her sheets. And some-thing smelled bad in the room. Perhaps she had soiled herself in sleep.

Hunched into Jilly's back was a mass of oily black fur as big as she was. At first my brain rang with a replay of Brix's horrifying inside-out death. The thing spooning with my daughter had one fat paw draped over her sleeping shoulder, and was alive. And purring.

I had the sheet peeled halfway down to reveal more of it when it twisted around and bit me on the wrist.

I took one panicked backward step, jerking sway. Jilly's plush bronto-saurus was feet-up on the floor; I stumbled over it, savaging my injured foot and crashing, sprawl-assed, down on Brix's rug, which smelled doggish and was dusted with his red hair. I had to get up, fast, tear the thing from her back, get the shotgun, to—

I tried to chock my good leg under me and could not. Both had gone thick and unresponsively numb. Then, shockingly, warmth spread at my crotch as my belly was seized by a sudden and powerful orgasm. My arms became as stupid as my legs. Then even my neck muscles lost it, and my forehead thunked into Brix's rug. And I came again.

And again.

Within seconds it was like receiving a thorough professional battering. I was having one orgasm for every three beats of my heart. My useless legs twitched. Saliva ran from the corner of my mouth to pool in my ear; even my vocal cords were iced into nonfunction. And while I lay curled up on the floor, coming and shuddering and coming, the creature that had been in bed with my daughter climbed down to watch.

Its eyes were bronze coins, reflecting candlefire. I thought of the thing I had seen monitoring me from the tree on my first day as a Point Pitt resident.

It was bigger than a bobcat, stockier, low-slung. The fur or hair was back-swept, spiky-stiff and glistening, as though heavily lubricated. Thick legs sprouted out from the body rather than down, making its carriage ground-gripping and reptilian. I heard hard leather pads scuff the floor as it neared, saw hooked claws, hooded in pink ligatures, close in on my face.

It was still purring. The head was a cat's, all golden eyes and pointed felt ears, but the snout was elongated into a canine coffin shape. The chatoyant pupils were X-shaped, deep-glowing crosscuts in the iris of each eye, and they widened like opening wounds to drink me in. It yawned. Less than a foot from my face I saw two bent needle fangs, backed by triangular, sharkish teeth in double rows. Its breath was worse than the stink of the congealed bandage I had stripped from my foot.

One galvanic sexual climax after another wrenched my insides apart. I was dry-coming; about to ejaculate blood. The creature dipped its head to lick some spittle from my cheek. Its tongue was sandpapery.

I had to kill it, bludgeon its monster skull to mush, blast it again and again until its carcass could hold no more shot. I orgasmed again. I could barely breathe.

It ceased tasting me and the hideous eyes sparked alive, hot yellow now. It padded back to the bed and leaped silently up. Jilly remained limp. I didn't even know if she was already dead or not.

It looked, to make sure I could see. Then it settled in, gripping Jilly's shoulders from above with its claws and licking her hair. It opened its mouth. Cartilage cracked softly as its jawbones separated, and the elastic black lips stretched taut to engulf the top of her head.

It sensed how much I hated it. Hate glittered back at me from those molten gash-eyes—my own hate, absorbed, made primal and total, and sent back to me.

Of hate, it knew.

My traitorous body continued its knifing spasms, and tears of pain blurred the view that I was incapable of commanding my eyelids to block out. The lips wormed forward, side-to-side, the slanted teeth seating, then pulling backward. The mouth elongated to full bore and the eyes fixed in a forward stare, glazed as though intoxicated by this meal.

With a mindless alien malice, it looked like it was smiling.

Blackness sucked me down before I could hear the abrasive, porcelain sound of those teeth grinding together, meeting at last through the pale flesh of my little girl's throat.

Moonlight delineated the window in blue-white.

I tried to sit up and rub my face. I was sweat-soaked, and lacquered in scales of dry semen. My balls were crushed grapes. Half my mind tried to wheedle me back into unconsciousness, begging to flee from what it had recorded. The less craven half had kicked me until I awoke, feeling like a frayed net loaded with broken bones, unable to stand or walk. I crawled on my belly to Jilly's bed. Lowering groans slipped from my throat.

I've seen snakes eat their prey. I didn't have to see what was left in Jilly's bed to know what had happened. But to get my legs back, and finish the work begun this night, I forced myself to look.

I took it all in without even a gasp. Only the drapes whispered furtively together, unable to remain still or quiet.

So much blood, blackening the Sesame Street sheets. Her tiny outthrust hand was speckled with it, and cold to the touch. Her pillow was a saturated dark sponge.

I slumped and vomited into my own lap. Nothing much came up as my guts were rent, the sore muscles pulling themselves to tatters. My hand went out and skidded into something like warm gelatin next to the bedpost.

It was the skin of our visitor, piled there like an enormous scalp, greasy black spines rooted in an opaque membrane. It reminded me of Brix's empty pelt. Here was the broad, flat sheath of the back; here, the sleeve of each leg. The reversed tissue was coated with a kind of thick, veined afterbirth that smelled like shit and rotten hamburger. My stomach clenched at the hot stink, and the pain almost put me under again. I swallowed a surge of bile and held.

It was slippery, as heavy as a waterlogged throw rug when I dragged it out of the room.

I knew there was a handful of speed and painkillers waiting for me in the bathroom. I filled the basin from the cold tap and immersed my head. I stared into the clean white gorge of the toilet and decided not to heave.

Suzanne was still safe in the depths of drugged sleep, where there are no true nightmares. On wobbly wino's feet I locked the balcony doors. The bedroom door had a two-way skeleton-key lock that could be engaged from the outside.

My Levi's jacket and shoes were downstairs on the sofa. And the shotgun was where it had been patiently waiting since the day we moved in.

Dunwoody's house was just up the hill.

My shoulder stung as the Remington's recoil pad kicked it, and the works on Dunwoody's back door, mostly shit, blew away to floating wood chaff and fused shrapnel. The door skewed open on its upper hinge, and the inside knob rebounded from the kitchen wall with a clacking cueball noise. It spun madly in place until its energy was used up. The echo of the blast returned softly from the hills.

Two rooms down a narrow hallway, Dunwoody sat watching a black-and-white television that displayed only test-pattern hairs, The screen bounced rectangles of light off his wire-rim glasses and made his old-fashioned undershirt glow blue in the darkness. He turned to look at the intruder stepping through the hanging wreckage of his back door, his gaze settling with resigned indifference on the twelve-gauge in my hand. He sighed.

My right wrist was throbbing as though fractured; mean red coronas of inflammation had blossomed around the twin punctures there, and I didn't know how many more shots it could stand before breaking. The smell of dry puke swam richly through my head, chased by the fetor of my prize. My eyes were pinpricks; the black capsules were doing their dirty work in the solvents of my stomach. It was the dope as much as the backwash of nausea that made me giddy—dark, toxic waves slopping up on a polluted beach, then receding.

Stiff-legged, lead-footed, I moved into the house. I knew where I was going and what to do when I arrived. My life had a purpose.

I jacked back the slide to reload, retrieved the reeking mess of shed skin with my free hand, and clumped forward. I was going to nestle the barrel right on the bridge of Dunwoody's thin hickory nose. He just sat there, watching my approach. There were no hidey-holes, and Ormly was probably out cruising at this time of night.

"You look foolish with that pumpgun, city boy."

"Foolish enough to spread your reedy old ass all over the wallpaper." My voice was dry and coarse, a rusted thing.

"You want all kind of answers." He spoke like the keeper of knowledge and wisdom, shifting in his easy chair with a snort of contempt. "Big-city know-it-all finds out he *don't* know it all. Don't know shit." He gulped schnapps from a fingerprint glass.

I couldn't buy his casual disdain for the gun. Perhaps he thought I wouldn't use it. To dash that little misconception from his mind, I stepped into the room and brought the shotgun to bear.

It tore violently out of my grasp like a runaway rocket, skinning my index finger on the trigger guard. Momentum yanked me the rest of tile way into the room, and I got my crippled foot down to keep from falling. It wasn't worth it.

Ormly had been stationed in ambush behind the doorway and had acted with a speed startling for his bulk and presumed intellect. He stood there with the shotgun locked in his bulldozer grip, upside down, while Dunwoody watched drops of blood from my hand speckle the floor like small change.

"Get Mister Taske a cloth for his hand, Ormly." Each order was slow, metered, portioned out at rural speed. "Take care of his pumpgun; I'm sure he paid a lot of money for it. And bring me my bottle. You might as well have a seat, Mister Taske. And we'll talk."

The tar-colored pelt had slithered from my grasp and piled up in an oily heap on the floor. It slid around itself, never settling, as if it refused to give up the life it once contained. Dunwoody looked at it.

"It's stronger now, quicker. At its best, since it dropped a hide. Don't gawp at me like *I'm* nuts. You saw it the first day you was here, and you didn't pay it no mind."

"I thought it was . . . some kind of cat," I stammered lamely. "Mountain lion, or . . . "

"Yeah, well, you know so goddamn much about mountain cats, now don't you?" he said with derision. "You said you didn't have no pets, no guns. See what happens? It ain't no cat."

Jesus. Anybody with two dendrites of intelligence could see that it *weren't no cat*. Arguing that now would only keep the old man off the track. I decided to shut up, and he seemed satisfied that I was going to let him talk without any know-it all city-boy interruptions. Ormly lumbered back with the schnapps, which Dunwoody offered to me perfunctorily. *Let's retch!* my stomach announced, and I waved the bottle away.

Ormly backed into his corner like the world's largest Saint Bernard sentry, keeping his eyes on me.

"Ormly was whip-smart," Dunwoody began. "He was my Primmy's favorite. Then she had Sarah. Little Sarah. You'da seen that baby girl, Mister Taske, she woulda busted your heart left and right, she was so perfect. Like your little girl."

"Jilly's dead." It was shockingly easy to say it so soon. "It—that thing, it—"

"I know. And I know you think me and Ormly is up to something, squirreled away up here, that we're somehow responsible. We ain't. I'd never hurt a little girl, and Ormly's never harmed no person nor animal. It's just . . . there's a certain order of things, here."

I had begun watching the ugly shed skin, still yielding, relaxing. It might reinflate and attack.

"Primmy and I kept a henhouse. We loved fryers and fresh eggs. One day I went out and all our chickens had been killed." The drama replayed behind his eyes. "You know how chickens run around after you cut off their heads, too dumb to know they're dead? Christ almighty. Twenty chickens, and half of them still strutting around when I got there. Without heads. It came down that night to eat the heads. And left the chickens. We'd been living in Point Pitt about two months."

My brain dipped sickeningly toward blackout. It was an almost pleasing sensation. Ebb tide of the mind; time to go to sleep. I sat down hard in the chair next to Dunwoody's and swallowed some schnapps without even tasting it.

"I had two hounds, Homer and Jethro, and an old Savage and Fox double-barrel, not as fancy as that pumpgun you got, but mean enough to stop a runaway truck dead. I laid up in the chicken coop the next night. 'Long about two in the morning, it stuck its head in and I let it have both barrels in the face. It was as close as you are to me. It yowled and ran off into the woods, and I set Homer and Jethro on it. Next morning, I found them. That thing took two loads of double-ought buckshot in the face and still gutted both my dogs. Ormly loved them old mutts."

I remembered the sound it made, the ground-glass screech. I didn't have to ask whether Dunwoody's dogs had been found with their heads intact.

Dunwoody cleared his throat phlegmatically and hefted himself out of the chair, to pry open a stuck bureau drawer behind the TV set. "Next night, it came back again. Walked into my home bold as you please and took my baby Sarah. It was slow getting out the window. Sluggish, with its belly full. I shot it again like a fool. Didn't do no good. Let me show you something."

He handed across a brown-edged, fuzzy piece of sketchbook paper. "Careful with it. It's real old."

It was a pencil rendering of the Dunwoody house, done in a stark and very sophisticated woodcut style. The trim and moldings stood out in relief. The building was done in calm earth tones, complimented by trees in full bloom. The forest shaded up the hillside in diminishing perspective. The strokes and chiaroscuro were assured. The drawing deserved a good matte and frame. I tilted it toward the light of the television and made out a faded signature in the lower right, done with a modest but not egocentric flourish.

O. Dunwoody.

He handed me a photograph, also slightly foxed, in black-and-white with waffled snapshot borders. A furry diagonal crease bisected a robustly pregnant woman packed into a paisley maternity dress. She had the bun hairdo and slight bulb nose that had always evoked the 1940s for me—World War II wives, the Andrews Sisters, all of that. Hugging her ferociously was a slim, dark-haired boy of nine or so, smiling wide and unselfconsciously. He had his father's eyes, and they blazed with what Dunwoody would call the smarts.

I tried to equate the boy in the photo with Ormly's overgrown, cartoonish body, or to the imbecilic expression on his face as he stood placidly in his corner. No match.

"Night after it took baby Sarah, it came back. We were laying to bush-whack it outside. It flanked us. Ormly came in for a drink of water, and there it was, all black and bristly and eating away on his mamma. He couldn't do nothing but stand there and scream; all the starch had run right out of him. He looked kinda like you do right now. I ran back in. That was the first time it bit me."

I extended my wrist for him to see, and his eyes lowered with guilt.

"Then you know that part already," he said.

Ormly stood parked like a wax dummy while his father went to him and looked over the wasteland of his son, hoping, perhaps to read a glimmer of the past in the dull eyes. There was no light there, only the reflected snow of the TV set, now tuned to nothingness.

"Ormly was crazy with fear and wanted to run. He loved his mamma and his little sister and the dogs, but he knew the sense in running. I was full up with ideas of what a man should do. A man didn't go beggin' to the police. The police don't understand nothing; they don't care and don't want to. A man should settle with his own grief, I thought, and Ormly wanted to be a man, so he hung with me."

Brave kid, I thought. *Braver than me.*

"Ormly came up with the idea of setting it on fire. He'd seen some monster movie where'd they'd doused the monster with kerosene and touched it off with a flare gun. We set up for it. We knew it was coming back, because it knew we didn't like it and would try to kill it. It *knew* how we felt. We were the ones that had intruded on its territory, and when you do that, you either make peace or you make a stand. Or you run. And that's what we shoulda done, because we were prideful and we didn't know what we were up against. We shoulda run like hell."

Dunwoody was stoking his own coals now, like a stump revival preacher getting ready to rip Satan a new asshole.

"Sure enough, the son of a bitch came down after us that night. You couldn't have convinced me there was another human soul in Point Pitt. All the houses were dark. They all knew, that is, everyone but me. When I spotted it crossing the backyard, in the moonlight, it was different than before. It'd dropped its hide, just like a bullsnake." He indicated the rancid leftover on the floor with a weak wave of his hand, not wanting to see it.

He did not look at Ormly, either, even as he spoke of him.

"The boy was perfect, by god. He stepped out from his hiding place, exposed himself to danger just so he could dump his pail of gasoline right smack into that thing's open mouth. I set my propane torch to it and it tagged me on the back of the hand—just a scratch, no venom. Or maybe the gas all over my hand neutralized it. We watched it shag ass into the hills, shrieking and dropping embers, setting little fires in the bushes as it ran. We hooted and jumped and clapped each other on the back like we were big heroes or something, and the next morning we tried to find it. All we turned up was a shed skin, like that one. And when the sun went down again, it came back. For Ormly. I swear to you, Mister Taske, it knew who had thought of burning it. But it didn't kill Ormly." The memory shined in Dunwoody's swelling eyes. He had witnessed what had happened. "Didn't kill him. It took a big, red mouthful out of the back of his head, and . . . and . . . "

He extended his scarred arms toward me, Christ-like, seeking some absolution I could not give. Bite marks peppered them everywhere, holes scabbing atop older holes.

"You get so you can't go without," he said dully. "You won't want to. You'll see."

I was aware of speaking in an almost sub-aural whisper. "Why didn't you leave?"

He shook his head sadly, ignoring me. "One day it just showed up. That's all anybody knows. Whether it came down out of the hills or crawled out of the ocean don't really matter. What matters is it came here and decided to stay. Maybe somebody fed it."

The speed maxed out in my bloodstream, hitting its spike point. The murky room resolved to sharp-edged clarity around me in a single headlong second. I'd broken through, and rage sprang me from my chair, to brace Dunwoody so he could no longer retreat into obfuscations or babble.

"*Why the hell didn't you leave?*" I screamed in his face.

He flinched, then considered his ruined arms again, and avoided the easy answer. "We don't like the city."

I remembered Suzanne, browsing the house. All her remarks about getting back to nature, slowing down, escaping the killer smog, hightailing it from the city as though it was some monster that had corrupted us internally and conspired to consume us. The big, bad neon nightmare. What penetrated now was the truth—that the state of nature is the last thing any thinking being would want. The true state of nature is not romantic. It is savage, primal, unforgivingly hostile. Mercy is a quality of civilization. Out here, stuck halfway between the wilds and the cities, a man had to settle his own grief. And if he could not . . .

My father, the guy who'd taught me to keep all guns loaded, had another adage I'd never had to take seriously yet: *If you can't kill it with a gun, son—run.*

"You've squared off with it," Dunwoody said. "That choice was yours. Believe me when I say it knows you don't like it." The provincial superiority was seeping back into his tone. "Have you figured it out yet, or has all that toe-food crap turned your brain to marl?"

Near the nub of his right elbow, the old man had sustained a fresh bite. It was all I could see. The thing had bitten Dunwoody recently—and Dunwoody had let it.

He sighed at my thickness. "It's coming back. Might even come back tonight. You're new here, after all."

I bolted then, with a strangled little cry. It was a high sound, childish, womanish. A coward's bleat, I thought.

Ormly had left my shotgun on the kitchen table, and I snatched it up as I ran, hurdling the demolished door, heedless of the stabbing pains in my hand, or the blood I could feel welling from the ruptured wound on my foot. My shoe had turned crimson. I ran so fast I did not see Dunwoody nodding to himself, like a man who has made the desired impression, and I missed his final words to his huge, dullwitted son.

"Ormly, you go on with Mister Taske, now. You know what you have to do."

Three feet more.

Three feet more, and the world would be set right. Three feet more to reach the hole in the fence, where Brix had died. Then came three more feet to reach the back door, to the stairs, to our bedroom. Three seconds more and I could shake Suzanne awake, pack her into the BMW, and bust posted limits red-lining it out of this nightmare. If the city wanted us back, no problem. We could scoot by on our plastic for months. My life was not a spaghetti western; I did not bash through my degree and get ulcers so I could do symbol-laden combat with monsters.

And Jilly . . .

The south window had been shoved neatly up. The drapes fluttered and there was no hint of broken glass, of the horrorshow trespass my brain had pictured for me. The creature was snuggled between Suzanne's legs on the bed. Eating. It looked very different without its skin.

Thick braids of exposed sinew coiled up each of its legs, filament cable that bunched and flexed. The knobs of its spine were strapped down by double wrapping of inflated, powerful muscle tissue as smoothly grooved and perfect as plastic. It no longer required an envelope of skin. An absurd little triangular flap covered its anus like a pointed tail.

Suzanne's eyes were slitted, locked. She was beyond feeling what was being done to her. Another orgasm hissed past her teeth, gutturally. Nothing more.

The skeleton key dropped from my trembling fingers and bounced on the hardwood floor. The thing on the bed had cranked its blood-slathered muzzle around to dismiss me. I was no big deal.

With a sidelong yank of its head, it worried loose some morsel anchored by stubborn tendons to the chest cavity. It was about halfway to its favorite part. The scraps it had sampled and discarded littered the bed wetly. If it had chanced across any tumors during its methodical progress toward the brain, I was sure it had crunched them up like popcorn. Piggishly, it lapped and slurped.

Suzanne looked at me as she came again, convulsing as much as her sundered body would let her. A thin stringer of frothy lung blood leapt onto her chest.

I kept my eyes in contact with hers as I snapped the trigger of the Remington, thinking how much I loved her.

The Nitro Mag load tore our bed to smithereens. Suzanne's dead arm jerked up, flopped back. Bloodstained goosedown took to the air, drifting. I worked the slide one-handed and fired again. The French doors disintegrated. Rickrack jumped from the bedstands to shatter on the floor.

The creature eased out its caked snout and saw what had just befallen that part of the feast it had been saving for last. Its impossibly wide, hinged maw dropped open to screech at me, as though I owed it something and had reneged. I shot it in the face, as Dunwoody had years ago. It snapped at the incoming shot like a bloodhound at gnats, then obstinately sank its nose back into its grisly dinner.

Suzanne was no longer on the bed. The corpse was not identifiable as anything but dead, butchered meat.

I slammed the bedroom door hard; don't ask why. There was an instant when I might have jammed the barrel between my teeth and swallowed that last shot myself. Instead, a pungent odor hauled me, staggering, to the stair landing.

Downstairs, the floor was wet and sloppy, glistening. Ormly waited for me, a ten-gallon jerry can of gasoline in each massive hand, smiling.

The buffeting heat was so intense that we had to back across the street to avoid getting our eyebrows flash-fried.

I watched the south window of our bedroom grow dreamy behind a sheet of orange flame. There was absolutely no exterior access. The thing had crawled up the front of the house like a fly, and clinging, had opened the window with one paw.

Neither of us saw it jump out, trailing sparks. The expression on Ormly's face frightened me. It was the closest thing to a glimmer of abstract thought I'd yet seen mar his slablike, mannequin countenance. He stared, unblinking, into the skyrocketing licks of fire.

"Hotter," he said. "Stronger. Better this time."

By dawn we were down to smoldering debris. I did not want to scrutinize the wreckage too closely, for fear of recognizing blackened bones.

Ormly stood in the backyard, his face dead with a kind of infinite sadness. I followed his gaze to the ground, and saw a deeply-dug, charred clawprint. The foot that had embossed itself there had been so hot that the grass had been cooked into an unmistakable pattern.

Ormly's mitt-sized hands pushed me toward my BMW, parked past the mailboxes. When I dug in my heels, he plucked me up and carried me. It was too easy to know why.

When night fell, the ground-glass shriek would waft down from the forest, and Point Pitt's new god would return.

Back in the arms of the city, I waited around for fate to come crashing down on my head with charges of murder and arson. Civilized accusations. No one came knocking.

Like I said earlier, this morning I sat and watched a cat disembowel a rail lizard. I watched much longer than I had to in order to get the point. Then my eyelids pushed down to allow swatches of stop-and-go sleep.

The nightmares of my past replaced those of the here and now.

A week after I'd turned thirteen, the school sadist at my junior high decreed that the day had come to pound every last speck of shit out of my pasty white body. Ross Delaney was the eldest son of a local garbageman—to be fair, he took a lot of socially maladjusting crap just for that. He was coasting through his third encore performance at the seventh-grade level. A seventh-grader who had a down mustache, drove his own jalopy to school, smoked, and hung out with peers destined for big things: aggravated assault, rape, grand theft auto . . .

Ross had made me loan him a pen once in study hall and he'd dismantled it after scrawling on the back of my shirt and laughing like I was the world's biggest a-hole. My buddy Blake and I had discovered a bunch of disposable hypodermic needles while scrounging for intriguing goodies in the trash dumpster of a health clinic, reasoning that it was against some law for them to throw out anything really *dangerous*, right? Those hypos made primo mini-squirt guns, and that's all Blake and I thought of using them for. They were tech, they were cool. They were enormously appealing to Ross, who threatened to put out my eye with a Lucky if I didn't give him one. Right before lunch, Ross was scooped up by Mr. Shanks, *El Principal* of the humorless specs and full-length gray plastic raincoat. Needles in school were serious business, and I soon found myself being paged for an interview. I denied everything. Ross' eyes, yellow-brown, settled on me like a pronouncement of execution by hanging.

He laid for me in the parking lot. There was no way around him. He loomed above me. I wanted to say something pacifying, babble that might exonerate us both as rebels cornered by an unfair system. Ross' brain lacked the logic links such a ploy needed to work. Trying to appease him had always been a pussy's game with an automatic loser. Guess who.

The next thing I knew, I was catching Ross' hand with my face.

My neckbones popped as my head snapped around, and my hand made the mistake of contracting into a fist. My left eye filled up with knuckles and stopped seeing. He snagged a handful of my hair and used his knee to loosen all the molars on the side of my head nearest the pavement. I bit tarmac and tasted blood. I curled up. He stared kicking me with his Mexican pimp boots, shouting incoherently, his face totally glazed.

My deck was discarded, so I called for my mom. I honestly thought it was my moment to die, and so reverted to instant babyhood, bawling and dribbling and yowling for my mother. Ross' cohorts ate it up. What a queer, what a pussy, he wants his momma. Ross kicked again and I felt a lung try to jump out my throat. He yelled for me to shut up. Something cracked sharply inside me.

Then something *burst* inside me.

It wasn't my liver exploding. It was something slag-hot, bursting brightly outward, filling me, popping on full bore like sprinkler systems during a fire, or an airbag in a car crash. The only sensation I can compare it to is the time my cardiologist broke an ampule of amyl nitrate under my nose, to test my pump. Only my internal ampule was full of something more like PCP. I was flooded to the brim—WHAM! My fingertips tingled. Both hands locked into fists. I scared the crap out of myself; I think I yelped. Instead of stopping the tip of Ross' next incoming bonebreaker, I rolled out, stood up, and faced him.

Then I kicked the shit out of him, impossibly enough.

Hesitation scampered behind his eyes when he saw me get up. But there was no mystery in it for him. The medulla section of his primate mind saw an opportunity to stomp some serious ass and would not be denied. If I could stand, the massacre would just be more interesting. Ross roared and came in like a freight train. His fist was black and sooty and callused.

I snatched that meteor out of the air and diverted his momentum, planting my elbow in his mouth, then whip-cracking him into a one-eighty snap that left his gonads open to my foot. They decompressed with a squish and he hit the pavement on hands and knees . . . and then *I* was kicking *him*, blood flushing my face. Every bullshit, picayune adolescent injustice ever suffered now rushed home, and I went at Ross like a berserk wolverine spiked on crank. Ribs staved inward. Snot and blood lathered his chin.

And I felt *good*.

Mr. Shanks, the principal, yanked me off of Ross Delaney, school tyrant. He was too horrified by the damage he saw to wonder how I'd done it. I got my fine white ass suspended.

That school had been my introduction to life in the city. Since then, the city had treated me right. My apartment never got robbed; my car never got boosted. Degree. Master's. Wife. Promotion. Child. Success. Suzanne and

Jilly had been excited by our move to Point Pitt; I had been the reluctant one.

Now my city had repudiated me. I'd come crawling back after giving it the finger, and the only thing it would show me was an ugly orange tabby tearing the intestines out of a lizard that wasn't dead all the way yet.

In its reptile eyes, the suffering as it was eaten.

I wanted to file a complaint. To protest that none of this was my fault. I didn't want to leave; they made me do it. That would be like trying to make nice to Ross Delaney. Too late for that.

I had spent the night in a parking lot and there was dry snot on my lace, from crying. Returning to the city had not erased Suzanne or Jilly or poor old goddamn Brix. So much for the snapshot.

The BMW's motor caught on the third try. I noticed blood staining the walnut of the gearshift as I backed out of the alleyway.

I wanted my mommy. But she wasn't around this time, either. Not here.

The blackened garbage dump that, yesterday, had been my new home had cooled. If anyone had come out to investigate, they were gone now. Birds twittered in the forest, above all this folly.

Dunwoody finally spotted me and came out; I have to credit him for having that much iron left. He motioned me into his squalid little home and we sat drinking until the sun went down. I watched Ormly shamble about. Such a waste, there.

The shrieking I expected began to peal down from the woods after dusk. My hands quivered on the arms of Dunwoody's dusty easy chair. They had not stopped shaking since last night.

"You forgot your pumpgun," said Dunwoody. "Had Ormly fetch it. Only two loads innit though." He drained his schnapps glass and burped, half-in, half-out, a state he clearly wanted to maintain.

The clear liquor trickled into me like kerosene. I thought of it as fuel. I noticed the barrels of the shotgun were warm; that seemed odd, somehow.

Clutching the Remington, I left limping, favoring my gashed foot. Breathing was a chore. My eyes pulsed in time to the pounding of my metabolism as I picked my way to the center of my burned-out grave of a home. One end of the barbequed sofa jutted from the debris like the stern of a sinking ship. Here was the banister—fissured, carbonized, its stored heat energy bled free. Over here, smashed shards of terra cotta from Suzanne's conservatory. Skeletal junk, all exuding the reek of an overflowing ashtray. Soft clouds of soot puffed up with each step I took.

On the border of the feeder road, the streetlamp sputtered blue, then white, throwing tombstone shadows down from the row of mailboxes. The residents of Point Pitt had drawn their curtains. The houses on the hillside were dark against whatever might come in the night. Not secure. Just lacking light and any form of human sympathy.

Dunwoody was the exception. I saw his drawn face appear in a crack of drape, then zip away, then return. I'd lost my Cartier watch, so I used Dunwoody's periodic surveillance to mark time. I couldn't recall losing the watch, not that it mattered. Night vapors tingled the hair on my arms. My last bath had been yesterday afternoon, eons ago, and by now I was as aromatic as stale beef bouillon.

"Come on, come *on*!" I lashed out at a fire-ravaged plank and it crumbled into brittle charcoal cinders. My voice echoed back from the treeline twice.

Lava-colored eyes emerged to assess me from behind the still-standing brick chimney. Chatoyant pupils tossed back the street light in dual crosscut shapes.

A conventional defensive move would draw it out, confident of its own invincibility. I chambered a round as loudly as I could. "This is for you! Come on—it's what you want, right?"

Motion, hesitant, like Ross Delaney, unsure. There was a smear of bright bronze as the eyes darted to a new vantage.

"Come on, bag of shit!" Fuck reaction time. The gun went boom and a mean bite leapt out of the chimney. Pointed chunks of brick flew into the creature's face. It did not blink. The Remington's report settled debris all around.

I dropped the gun into the ashes.

Its outer tissue was pinkish, as though battened with blood from an earlier feed. The alien eyes blazed. When it saw me lose the shotgun, it decided, and in three huge bounds the distance between us was reduced to nothing. I saw it in midair, rippling, its thorny claws extruded from their cowls and coming for my face.

I braced myself, the memory of grabbing Ross Delaney's deadly fist still hot. I spoke softly to the woods, to the forest in the distance, to the sea behind me.

"Help me. Mother."

It smashed me down like a truck pasting an old lady in a crosswalk. The opaque talons sank to their moorings in my shoulder. I grabbed, to keep the jaws from my throat, and its fangs pierced the palm of my hand, one-two.

"Mother! Help me!"

I got my other hand up and seized its snout, which was feverishly hot. Stale blood-breath misted into my eyes and the black lips yawned wide for me. Those lips had caressed my daughter's face as they engulfed her. They had made an intimate, ghastly smorgasbord of Suzanne.

I clenched my fist. It tried to jerk its paw back to slash me into confetti, but the claws were trapped in my muscle tissue and would not slide free. The X-shaped eyes dimmed in surprise. It backpedaled, preparing to dig in with its hind legs and free my intestines.

I sat up with its movement, taking a firmer grip and twisting until its lower jaw came away in my hand. Think of halving a head of lettuce; that was the sound it made. Think of pulling a drumstick from a whole tom turkey. It jammed, then wrenched loose, dripping, trailing ruptured tatters of sinew.

It shrieked. Without a mouth, in pain.

Purple blood, thick and gelid, spurted into my face. Under the vapor lamp it looked like chocolate syrup; it stank of vomit or hydrochloric acid. The eyes went from golden to dead ochre, the color of dry leaves.

"You're done here," I rasped in its face. Still holding the snout, I punched my fist down the ruined wet maw of glottus. My fingers locked around something slick and throbbing and I tore it out. The body on top of me shuddered hideously and lost tension. The legs scrabbled, then went slack, pitching more feebly.

I stared fixedly into the eyes as their incandescence waned.

The residents of Point Pitt had come out at last, to watch. My new neighbors. They dotted the street, milling uncertainly, none daring closer than the mailboxes. They watched as their old god screeched and died. As with department-store mannequins, it had been so simple for them to be led, to be arranged.

What difference? That was ended now.

When I extracted the claws from my shoulder, my own blood jetted briefly out. I was still that human. Eyes cold, the limp and stinking carcass slid as I rose. Another shedding. A steel rail of an erection was trying to fight its way out of my pants.

They all stood, nothing more declarative. Silently they waited. The last to arrive were Dunwoody and Ormly, coming down the trail from their home. No one else moved to attack, or assist, or anything. It was not their place to.

Thank you . . .

Reflexively, the dead claws had folded in upon themselves. When I picked up the corpse, it crackled, still seeming to weigh too much for its mass. I remembered the awful sound its discarded skin had made. Purple goo dripped from the jawless mouth. The flat paws dangled harmlessly as I lifted the fatal wound to my lips and drank in long, soul-kiss draughts, quaffing with a passion almost primitive in its purity.

Thank you. Mother.

My communion raced through me to work its changes. My arm ceased bleeding and clotted up. I stopped shaking at last; all of me at once. My vision began to blur. Soon I would be able to see things imperceptible to normal, circular pupils.

I motioned to Ormly and he dutifully clumped forward. He had to be the first one. There was plenty for everybody, but Ormly had to be first.

Things evolve. Always have. Even in the country, things change when it's time. There was growth potential here.

Dunwoody nodded his old man's brand of approval. If I needed any indication that I was going to be benevolent, that was it.

The Ropy Thing
Al Sarrantonio

The ropy thing got most of the neighborhood while Suzie and Jerry were watching Saturday morning cartoons on TV. Then the cable went out and Jerry's Dad put on the radio but then that went out too. By then Suzie and Jerry were watching the ropy thing from the big picture window in Jerry's living room. The ropy thing was very fast, and sometimes they saw only its tip stretched high and straight, or formed into a loop, or snaking over a house or between trees or moving over cars. It hesitated, then shot into the moving van in front of Suzie's house across the street, pulling the fat uniformed mover out, coiling around him head to toe like a mummy and then yanking him down into the ground. It pulled Suzie's Mom into the ground too, catching her as she tried to run back into the house from where she had been directing the movers from the curb.

"We're getting out!" Jerry's Dad shouted, giving Jerry a strange look, and the ropy thing got him in the front yard between the garage and the car. Behind him was Jerry's Mom, with an armful of pillows, and the ropy thing got her too. It got Jerry's sister Jane as she was sneaking away from the house to be with her boyfriend Brad down the block. Suzie and Jerry watched the ropy thing jump out of the bushes in front of Brad's house like a coiled black spring, getting Jane right in front of Brad, just as she reached to hold his hand. Brad turned to run but it got him too, shooting up out of the lawn and over the sidewalk, thin and fast. It whipped around Brad and squeezed him into two pieces, top and bottom, then pulled both halves down.

Suzie and Jerry ran up to the attic, and the ropy thing snaked up around the house but didn't climb that high and then went away. From the small octagonal attic window they watched it wrap around the Myers' house and pull the Myers' baby from the second story window. Then it curled like a cat around the Myers' house's foundation, circling three times around and twitching, and stayed there.

"This is just like—" Jerry said, turning to Suzie, fear in his voice.

"I know," Suzie said, hushing him.

When they looked back at the Myers' house all the windows were broken and the porch posts had been ripped away, and the ropy thing was gone. They spied it down the block to the right, waving lazily in the air before whipping down; then they saw it up the block to the left, moving between two houses into the street to catch a running boy that looked like Billy Carson.

The day rose, a summer morning with nothing but heat.

The afternoon was hotter, an oven in the attic.

The ropy thing continued its work.

They discovered that the ropy thing could climb as high as it wanted when they retrieved Jerry's Dad's binoculars and found the ropy thing wrapped like a boa constrictor around the steeple of the Methodist church in the middle of town, blocks away. It pulled something small, kicking and too far away to hear, out of the belfry and then slid down and away.

"I'm telling you it's—" Jerry said again.

Peering through the binoculars, Suzie again hushed him, but not before he finished: "—just like my father's trick."

They spent that night in the attic with the window cracked open for air. The ropy thing was outside, moving under the light of the moon. Twice it came close, once breaking the big picture window on the ground floor, then shooting up just in front of the attic window, tickling the opening with its tip, making Jerry, who was watching, gasp, but then flying away.

They found a box of crackers and ate them. The ropy thing's passings in front of the moon made vague, dark-gray shadows on the attic's ceiling and walls.

"Do you think it's happening everywhere?" Jerry asked.

"What do you think?" Suzie replied, and then Jerry remembered Dad's battery shortwave radio that pulled in stations from all over the world. It was in the back of the attic near the box of flashlights.

He got it and turned it on, and up and down the dial there was nothing but hissing.

"Everywhere . . . " Jerry whispered.

"Looks that way," Suzie answered.

"It can't be . . . " Jerry said.

Suzie ate another cracker.

Suddenly, Jerry dropped the radio and began to cry. "But it was just a trick my father played on me! It wasn't real!"

"It seemed real at the time, didn't it?" Suzie asked.

Jerry continued to sob. "He was always playing tricks on me! After I swallowed a cherry pit he hid a bunch of leaves in his hand and made believe he pulled them from my ear—he told me the cherry it had grown inside and that I was now filled with a cherry tree! Another time he swore that a spaceship was about to land in the backyard, then he made me watch out the big picture window while he snuck into the back and threw a toy rocket over the roof so that it came down in front of me!" He looked earnest and confused. "He was always doing things like that!"

"You believed the tricks while they were happening, didn't you?" Suzie asked.

"Yes! But—"

"Maybe if you believe something hard enough, it happens for real."

Jerry was frantic. "But it was just a trick! You were with me, you saw what he did! He buried a piece of rope in the backyard, then brought us out and pulled the rope partway out of the ground, and said it was part of a giant monster, the Ropy Thing, which filled up the entire Earth until it was just below the surface—and that anytime it wanted it would throw out its ropy tentacles and grab everybody, and pull them down and absorb them into its pulsating jelly body—"

He looked at Suzie with a kind of pleading on his face. "It wasn't real!"

"You believed."

"It was just a trick!"

"But you believed it was real," Suzie said quietly. She was staring at the floor. "Maybe because my mother was moving, taking me away from you, you believed so hard that you made it real." She looked up at him. "Maybe that's why it hasn't gotten us—because you did it."

She went to him and held him, stroking his hair with her long, thin fingers.

"Maybe you did it because you love me," she said.

Jerry looked up at her, his eyes still wet with tears. "I do love you," he said.

They ate all the food in the house after a week, and then moved to the Myers' house and ate all their food, and then to the Janzens next door to the Myers'. They ate their way, uninvited guests, down one block and up the next. They ran from house to house at twilight or dawn. The ropy thing never came near them, busy now with catching all the neighborhood's dogs and cats.

Even when they did see the ropy thing, it stayed away, poking into a house on the next block, straining up straight, nearly touching the clouds, black and almost oily in the sun, like an antennae. It disappeared for days at a time, and once they saw a second ropy thing, through the telescope in the house they were living in, so far away from their own now that they didn't even know their host's names. They were near the edge of town, and the next town over had its own ropy thing curling up into the afternoon, rising up like a shoot here and there, pausing for a moment before bending midriff to point at the ropy thing in their own neighborhood. Their own ropy thing bent and pointed back at it.

Suzie looked at Jerry, who wanted to cry.

"Everywhere," she said.

As the summer wore on the squirrels disappeared, and then the birds and crickets and gnats and mosquitoes. Jerry and Suzie moved from house to house, town to town, and sometimes when they were out they saw the ropy thing pulling dragonflies into the ground, swatting flies dead and yanking them away. Everywhere it was the same: the ropy thing had rid every town, every house, every place, of people and animals and insects. Even the bees in the late summer were gone, as if the ropy thing had saved them for last, and now pulled them into its jelly body along with everything else alive. In one town they found a small zoo, and paused to look with wonder at the empty cages, the clean gorilla pit, the lapping water empty of seals.

There was plenty to eat, and water to drink, and soda in cans, and finally when they were done with the towns surrounding their town they rode a train, climbing up into its engine and getting the diesel to fire and studying the controls and making it move. The engine made a sound like caught thunder. Even Jerry laughed then, putting his head out of the cab to feel the wind like a living thing on his face. Suzie fired the horn, which bellowed like a bullfrog. They passed a city, and then another, until the train ran out of fuel and left them in another town much like their own.

They moved on to another town after that, and then another after that, and always the ropy thing was there, following them, a sentinel in the distance, rising above the highest buildings, its end twitching.

Summer rolled toward autumn. Now, even when he looked at Suzie, Jerry never smiled any more. His eyes became hollow, and his hands trembled, and he barely ate.

Autumn arrived, and still they moved on. In one nameless town, in one empty basement of an empty house, Jerry walked trembling to the workbench and took down from its pegboard a pair of pliers. He handed them to Suzie and said, "Make me stop believing."

"What do you mean?"

"Get the ropy thing out of my head."

Suzie laughed, went to the workbench herself and retrieved a flashlight, which she shined into Jerry's ears.

"Nothing in there but wax," she said.

"I don't want to believe anymore," Jerry said listlessly, sounding like a ghost.

"It's too late," Suzie said.

Jerry lay down on the floor and curled up into a ball.

"Then I want to die," he whispered.

Winter snapped at the heels of autumn. The air was apple cold, but there were no more apples. The ropy thing spent the fall yanking trees and bushes and late roses and grass into the ground.

It was scouring the planet clean of weeds and fish and amoebas and germs.

Jerry stopped eating, and Suzie had to help him walk.

Idly, Jerry wondered what the ropy thing would do after it had killed the Earth.

Suzie and Jerry stood between towns gazing at a field of dirt. In the distance the ropy thing waved and worked, making corn stalks disappear in neat rows. Behind Jerry and Suzie, angled off the highway into a dusty ditch, was the car that Suzie had driven, telephone books propping her up so that she could see over the wheel, until it ran out of gas. The sky was a thin dusty blue-gray, painted with sickly clouds, empty of birds.

A few pale snowflakes fell.

"I want it to end," Jerry whispered hoarsely.

He had not had even a drink of water in days. His clothes were rags, his eyes sunken with grief. When he looked at the sky now his eyeballs ached, as if blinded by light.

"I . . . want it to stop," he croaked.

He sat deliberately down in the dust, looking like an old man in a child's body. He looked up at Suzie, blinked weakly.

When he spoke, it was a soft question: "It wasn't me, it was you who did it."

"Yes," Suzie said. "I believed. I believed because I had to. You were the only one who ever loved me. They were going to take me away from you."

There was silence for a moment. In the distance, the ropy thing finished with the corn field, stood at attention, waiting. Around its base a cloud of weak dust settled.

Quietly, Jerry said, "I don't love you anymore."

For a moment, Suzie's eyes looked sad—but then they turned to something much harder than steel.

"Then there's nothing left," she said.

Jerry sighed, squinting at the sky with his weak eyes.

The ropy thing embraced him, almost tenderly.

And as it pulled him down into its pulsating jelly body, he saw a million ropy things, thin and black, reaching up like angry fingers to the Sun and other stars beyond.

The Third Bear
Jeff VanderMeer

It made its home in the deep forest near the village of Grommin, and all anyone ever saw of it, before the end, would be hard eyes and the dark barrel of its muzzle. The smell of piss and blood and shit and bubbles of saliva and half-eaten food. The villagers called it the Third Bear because they had killed two bears already that year. But, near the end, no one really thought of it as a bear, even though the name had stuck, changed by repetition and fear and slurring through blood-filled mouths to *Theeber*. Sometimes it even sounded like "seether" or "seabird."

The Third Bear came to the forest in mid-summer, and soon most anyone who used the forest trail, day or night, disappeared, carried off to the creature's lair. By the time even large convoys had traveled through, they would discover two or three of their number missing. A straggling horseman, his mount cantering along, just bloodstains and bits of skin sticking to the saddle. A cobbler gone but for a shredded hat. A few of the richest villagers hired mercenaries as guards, but when even the strongest men died, silent and alone, the convoys dried up.

The village elder, a man named Horley, held a meeting to decide what to do. It was the end of summer by then and the leaves had begun to disappear from the trees. The meeting house had a chill to it, a stench of thick earth with a trace of blood and sweat curling through it. All five hundred villagers came to the meeting, from the few remaining merchants to the poorest beggar. Grommin had always been hard scrabble and tough winters, but it was also two hundred years old. It had survived the wars of barons and of kings, been razed twice, only to return.

"I can't bring my goods to market," one farmer said, rising in shadow from beneath the thatch. "I can't be sure I want to send my daughter to the pen to milk the goats."

Horley laughed, said, "It's worse than that. We can't bring in food from the other side. Not for sure. Not without losing men." He had a sudden vision from months ahead, of winter, of ice gravelly with frozen blood. It made him shudder.

"What about those of us who live outside the village?" another farmer asked. "We need the pasture for grazing, but we have no protection."

Horley understood the problem; he had been one of those farmers, once. The village had a wall of thick logs surrounding it, to a height of ten feet. No real defense against an army, but more than enough to keep the wolves out. Beyond that perimeter lived the farmers and the hunters and the outcasts who could not work among others.

"You may have to pretend it is a time of war and live in the village and go out with a guard," Horley said. "We have plenty of able-bodied men, still."

"Is it the witch woman doing this?" Clem the blacksmith asked.

"No," Horley said. "I don't think it's the witch woman."

What Clem and some of the others thought of as a "witch woman," Horley thought of as a crazy person who knew some herbal remedies and lived in the woods because the villagers had driven her there, blaming her for an outbreak of sickness the year before.

"Why did it come?" a woman asked. "Why us?"

No one could answer, least of all Horley. As Horley stared at all of those hopeful, scared, troubled faces, he realized that not all of them yet knew they were stuck in a nightmare.

Clem was the village's strongest man, and after the meeting he volunteered to fight the beast. He had arms like most people's thighs. His skin was tough from years of being exposed to flame. With his full black beard he almost looked like a bear himself.

"I'll go, and I'll go willingly," he told Horley. "I've not met the beast I couldn't best. I'll squeeze the 'a' out of him." And he laughed, for he had a passable sense of humor, although most chose to ignore it.

Horley looked into Clem's eyes and could not see even a speck of fear there. This worried Horley.

"Be careful, Clem," Horley said. And, in a whisper, as he hugged the man: "Instruct your son in anything he might need to know, before you leave. Make sure your wife has what she needs, too."

Fitted in chain mail, leathers, and a metal helmet, carrying an old sword some knight had once left in Grommin by mistake, Clem set forth in search of the Third Bear. The entire village came out to see him go. Clem was laughing and raising his sword and this lifted the spirits of those who saw him. Soon, everyone was celebrating as if the Third Bear had already been killed or defeated.

"Fools," Horley's wife Rebecca said as they watched the celebration with their two young sons.

Rebecca was younger than Horley by ten years and had come from a village far beyond the forest. Horley's first wife had died from a sickness that left red marks all over her body.

"Perhaps, but it's the happiest anyone's been for a month," Horley said.

"All I can think of is that he's taking one of our best horses out into danger," Rebecca said.

"Would you rather he took a nag?" Horley said, but absentmindedly. His thoughts were elsewhere.

The vision of winter would not leave him. Each time, it came back to Horley with greater strength, until he had trouble seeing the summer all around him.

Clem left the path almost immediately, wandered through the underbrush to the heart of the forest, where the trees grew so black and thick that the only glimmer of light came from the reflection of water on leaves. The smell in that place carried a hint of offal.

Clem had spent so much time beating things into shape that he had not developed a sense of fear, for he had never been beaten. But the smell in his nostrils did make him uneasy.

He wandered for some time in the deep growth, where the soft loam of moss muffled the sound of his passage. It became difficult to judge direction and distance. The unease became a knot in his chest as he clutched his sword ever tighter. He had killed many bears in his time, this was true, but he had never had to hunt a man-eater.

Eventually, in his circling, meandering trek, Clem came upon a hill with a cave inside. From within the cave, a green flame flickered. It beckoned like a lithe but crooked finger.

A lesser man might have turned back, but not Clem. He didn't have the sense to turn back.

Inside the cave, he found the Third Bear. Behind the Third Bear, arranged around the walls of the cave, it had displayed the heads of its victims. The heads had been painstakingly painted and mounted on stands. They were all in various stages of rot.

Many bodies lay stacked neatly in the back of the cave. All of them had been defiled in some way. Some of them had been mutilated. The wavery green light came from a candle the Third Bear had placed behind the bodies, to display its handiwork. The smell of blood was so thick that Clem had to put a hand over his mouth.

As Clem took it all in, the methodical nature of it, the fact that the Third Bear had not eaten any of its victims, he found something inside of him tearing and then breaking.

"I . . . " he said, and looked into the terrible eyes of the Third Bear. "I . . . "

Almost sadly, with a kind of ritual grace, the Third Bear pried Clem's sword from his fist, placed the weapon on a ledge, and then came back to stare at Clem once more.

Clem stood there, frozen, as the Third Bear disemboweled him.

The next day, Clem was found at the edge of the village, blood soaked and shit-spattered, legs gnawed away, but alive enough for awhile to, in shuddering lurches, tell those who found him what he had seen, just not coherent enough to tell them *where*.

Later, Horley would wish that he hadn't told them anything.

There was nothing left but fear in Clem's eyes by the time Horley questioned him. Horley didn't remember any of Clem's answers, had to be retold them later. He was trying to reconcile himself to looking *down* to stare into Clem's eyes.

"I'm cold, Horley," Clem said. "I can't feel anything. Is winter coming?"

"Should we bring his wife and son?" the farmer who had found Clem asked Horley at one point.

Horley just stared at him, aghast.

They buried Clem in the old graveyard, but the next week the Third Bear dug him up and stole his head. Apparently, the Third Bear had no use for heroes, except, possibly, as a pattern of heads.

Horley tried to keep the grave robbery and what Clem had said a secret, but it leaked out anyway. By the time most villagers of Grommin learned about it, the details had become more monstrous than anything in real life. Some said Clem had been kept for a week in the bear's lair, while it ate away at him. Others said Clem had had his spine ripped out of his body while he was still breathing. A few even said Clem had been buried alive by mistake and the Third Bear had heard him writhing in the dirt and come for him.

But one thing Horley knew that trumped every tall tale spreading through Grommin: the Third Bear hadn't had to keep Clem alive. *Theeber* hadn't had to place Clem, still breathing, at the edge of the village.

So *Seether* wasn't just a bear.

In the next week, four more people were killed, one on the outskirts of the village. Several villagers had risked leaving, and some of them had even made it through. But fear kept most of them in Grommin, locked into a kind of desperate fatalism or optimism that made their eyes hollow as they stared into some unknowable distance. Horley did his best to keep morale up, but even he experienced a sense of sinking.

"Is there more I can do?" he asked his wife in bed at night.

"Nothing," she said. "You are doing everything you can do."

"Should we just leave?"

"Where would we go? What would we do?"

Few who left ever returned with stories of success, it was true. War and plague and a thousand more dangers lay out there beyond the forest. They'd as likely become slaves or servants or simply die, one by one, out in the wider world.

Eventually, though, Horley sent a messenger to that wider world, to a far-distant baron to whom they paid fealty and a yearly amount of goods.

The messenger never came back. Nor did the baron send any men. Horley spent many nights awake, wondering if the messenger had gotten through and the baron just didn't care, or if Seether had killed the messenger.

"Maybe winter will bring good news," Rebecca said.

Over time, Grommin sent four or five of its strongest and most clever men and women to fight the Third Bear. Horley objected to this waste, but the villagers insisted that something must be done before winter, and those who went were unable to grasp the terrible velocity of the situation. For Horley, it seemed merely a form of taking one's own life, but his objections were over-ruled by the majority.

They never learned what happened to these people, but Horley saw them in his nightmares.

One, before the end, said to the Third Bear, "If you could see the children in the village, you would stop."

Another said, before fear clotted her windpipe, "We will give you all the food you need."

A third, even as he watched his intestines slide out of his body, said, "Surely there is something we can do to appease you?"

In Horley's dreams, the Third Bear said nothing in reply. Its conversation was through its work, and Seether said what it wanted to say very eloquently in that regard.

By now, fall had descended on Grommin. The wind had become unpredictable and the leaves of trees had begun to yellow. A far-off burning smell laced the air. The farmers had begun to prepare for winter, laying in hay and slaughtering and smoking hogs. Horley became more involved in these preparations than usual, driven by his vision of the coming winter. People noted the haste, the urgency, so unnatural in Horley, and to his dismay it sometimes made them panic rather than work harder.

With his wife's help, Horley convinced the farmers to contribute to a communal smoke house in the village. Ham, sausage, dried vegetables, onions, potatoes—they stored it all in Grommin now. Most of the outlying farmers realized that their future depended on the survival of the village.

Sometimes, when they opened the gates to let in another farmer and his mule-drawn cart of supplies, Horley would walk out a ways and stare into the forest. It seemed more unknowable than ever, gaunt and dark, diminished by the change of seasons.

Somewhere out there the Third Bear waited for them.

One day, the crisp cold of coming winter becoming more than a promise, Horley and several of the men from Grommin went looking for a farmer who had not come to the village for a month. The farmer's name was John and he had a wife, five children, and three men who worked for him. John's holdings were the largest outside the village, but he had been suffering because he could not bring his extra goods to market

The farm was a half-hour's walk from Grommin. The whole way, Horley could feel a hurt in his chest, a kind of stab of premonition. Those with him held pitchforks and hammers and old spears, much of it as rust-colored as the leaves now strewn across the path.

They could smell the disaster before they saw it. It coated the air like oil.

On the outskirts of John's farm, they found three mule-pulled carts laden with food and supplies. Horley had never seen so much blood. It had pooled and thickened to cover a spreading area several feet in every direction. The mules had had their throats torn out and then they had been disemboweled. Their organs had been torn out and thrown onto the ground, as if Seether had been searching for something. Their eyes had been plucked from their sockets almost as an afterthought.

John—they thought it was John—sat in the front of the lead cart. The head was missing, as was much of the meat from the body cavity. The hands still held the reins. The same was true for the other two carts, their wheels greased with blood. Three dead men holding reins to dead mules. Two dead men in the back of the carts. All five missing their heads. All five eviscerated.

One of Horley's protectors vomited into the grass. Another began to weep. "Jesus save us," a third man said, and kept saying it for many hours.

Horley was curiously unmoved, his hand and heart steady. He noted the brutal humor that had moved the Third Bear to carefully replace the reins in the men's hands. He noted the wild, savage abandon that had preceded that action. He noted, grimly, that most of the supplies in the carts had been ruined by the wealth of blood that covered them. But, for the most part, the idea of winter had so captured him that whatever came to him moment-by-moment could not compare to the crystalline nightmare of that interior vision.

Horley wondered if his was a form of madness as well.

"This is not the worst," he said to his men. "Not by far."

At the farm, they found the rest of the men and what was left of John's wife, but that is not what Horley had meant.

At this point, Horley felt he should go himself to find the Third Bear. It wasn't bravery that made him put on the leather jerkin and the metal shin guards. It wasn't from any sense of hope that he picked up the spear and put Clem's helmet on his head.

His wife found him there, ready to walk out the door of their home.

"You wouldn't come back," she told him.

"Better," he said. "Still."

"You're more important to us alive. Stronger men than you have tried to kill it."

"I must do something," Horley said. "Winter will be here soon and things will get worse."

"Then do something," Rebecca said, taking the spear from his hand. "But do something *else*."

The villagers of Grommin met the next day. There was less talking this time. Horley tried to gauge their mood. Many were angry, but some now seemed resigned, almost as if the Third Bear were a plague or some other force that could not be controlled or stopped by the hand of Man. In the days that followed, there would be a frenzy of action: traps set, torches lit, poisoned meat left in the forest, but none of it came to anything.

One old woman kept muttering about fate and the will of God.

"John was a good man," Horley told them. "He did not deserve his death. But I was there—I saw his wounds. He died from an animal attack. It may be a clever animal. It may be very clever. But it is still an animal. We should not fear it the way we fear it."

"You should consult with the witch in the woods," Clem's son said.

Clem's son was a huge man of eighteen years, and his word held weight, given the bravery of his father. Several people began to nod in agreement.

"Yes," said one. "Go to the witch. She might know what to do."

The witch in the woods is just a poor, addled woman, Horley thought, but could not say it.

"Just two months ago," Horley reminded them, "you thought she might have made this happen."

"And if so, what of it? If she caused it, she can undo it. If not, perhaps we can pay her to help us."

This from one of the farmers displaced from outside the walls. Word of John's fate had spread quickly, and less than a handful of the bravest or most foolhardy had kept to their farms.

Rancor spread amongst the gathered villagers. Some wanted to take a party of men out to the witch, wherever she might live, and kill her. Others thought this folly—what if the Third Bear found them first?

Finally, Horley raised his hands to silence them.

"Enough! If you want me to go to the witch in the woods, I will go to her."

The relief on their faces, as he looked out at them—the relief that he would take the risk—it was like a balm that cleansed their worries, if only for the moment. Some fools were even smiling.

Later, Horley lay in bed with his wife. He held her tight, taking comfort in the warmth of her body.

"Rebecca? I'm scared."

"I know. I know you are. Do you think I'm not scared too? But neither of us can show it or they will panic, and once they panic, Grommin is lost."

"What can I do?"

"Go see the witch woman, my love. If you go to her, it will make them calmer. And you can tell them whatever you like about what she says."

"If the Third Bear doesn't kill me before I can find her."

If she isn't already dead.

In the deep woods, in a silence so profound that the ringing in his ears had become the roar of a river, Horley looked for the witch woman. He knew that she had been exiled to the southern part of the forest, and so he had started there and worked his way toward the center. What he was looking for, he did not know. A cottage? A tent? What he would do when he found her, Horley didn't know either. His spear, his incomplete armor—these things would not protect him if she truly was a witch.

He tried to keep the vision of the terrible winter in his head as he walked, because concentrating on that more distant fear removed the current fear.

"If not for me, the Third Bear might not be here," Horley had said to Rebecca before he left. It was Horley who had stopped them from burning the witch, had insisted only on exile.

"That's nonsense," Rebecca had replied. "Remember that she's just an old woman, living in the woods. Remember that she can do you no real harm."

It had been as if she'd read his thoughts. But now, breathing in the thick air of the forest, Horley felt less sure about the witch woman. It was true there had been sickness in the village until they had cast her out.

Horley tried to focus on the spring of loam beneath his boots, the clean, dark smell of bark and earth and air. After a time, he crossed a dirt-choked stream. As if this served as a dividing line, the forest became yet darker. The sounds of wrens and finches died away. Above, he could see the distant dark shapes of hawks in the treetops, and patches of light shining down that almost looked more like bog or marsh water, so disoriented had he become.

It was in this deep forest, that he found a door.

Horley had stopped to catch his breath after cresting a slight incline. Hands on his thighs, he looked up and there it stood: a door. In the middle of the forest. It was made of old oak and overgrown with moss and mushrooms, and yet it seemed to flicker like glass. A kind of light or brightness hurtled through the ground, through the dead leaves and worms and beetles, around the door. It was a subtle thing, and Horley half thought he was imagining it at first.

He straightened up, grip tightening on his spear.

The door stood by itself. Nothing human-made surrounded it, not even the slightest ruin of a wall.

Horley walked closer. The knob was made of brass or some other yellowing metal. He walked around the door. It stood firmly wedged into the ground. The back of the door was the same as the front.

Horley knew that if this was the entrance to the old woman's home, then she was indeed a witch. His hand remained steady, but his heart quickened and he thought furiously of winter, of icicles and bitter cold and snow falling slowly forever.

For several minutes, he circled the door, deciding what to do. For a minute more, he stood in front of the door, pondering.

A door always needs opening, he thought, finally.

He grasped the knob, and pushed—and the door opened.

Some events have their own sense of time, and a separate logic. Horley knew this just from the change of seasons every year. He knew this from the growing of the crops and the birthing of children. He knew it from the forest itself, and the cycles it went through that often seemed incomprehensible and yet had their own pattern, if you could only see it. From the first thawed trickle of stream water in the spring to the last hopping frog in the fall, the world held a thousand mysteries. No man could hope to know the truth of them all.

When the door opened and he stood in a room very much like the room one might find in a woodman's cottage, with a fireplace and a rug and a shelf and pots and pans on the wood walls, and a rocking chair—when this happened, Horley decided in the time it took him to blink twice that he had no need for the *why* of it or the *how* of it, even. And this was, he realized later, the only reason he kept his wits about him.

The witch woman sat in the rocking chair. She looked older than Horley remembered, even though no more than a year had passed since he had last seen her. Seeming made of ash and soot, her black dress lay flat against her sagging skin. She was blind, eye sockets bare, but her wrinkled face strained to look at him any way.

There was a buzzing sound.

"I remember you," she said. Her voice was croak and whisper both.

Her arms were mottled with age spots, her hands so thin and cruel-looking that they could have been talons. She gripped the rocking chair as if holding onto the world.

There was a buzzing sound. It came, Horley finally realized, from a halo of black hornets that circled the old woman's head, their wings beating so fast they could hardly be seen.

"Are you Hasghat, who used to live in Grommin?" Horley asked.

"I remember you," the witch woman said again.

"I am the elder of the village of Grommin."

The woman spat to the side. "Those that threw poor Hasghat out."

"They would have done much worse if I'd let them."

"They'd have burned me if they could. And all I knew then were a few charms, a few herbs. Just because I wasn't one of them. Just because I'd seen a bit of the world."

Hasghat was staring right at him and Horley knew that, eyes or no eyes, she could see him.

"It was wrong," Horley said.

"It was wrong," she said. "I had nothing to do with the sickness. Sickness comes from animals, from people's clothes. It clings to them and spreads through them."

"And yet you are a witch?"

Hasghat laughed, although it ended with coughing. "Because I have a hidden room? Because my door stands by itself?"

Horley grew impatient.

"Would you help us if you could? Would you help us if we let you return to the village?"

Hasghat straightened up in the chair and the halo of hornets disintegrated, then reformed. The wood in the fireplace popped and crackled. Horley felt a chill in the air.

"Help you? Return to the village?" She spoke as if chewing, her tongue a thick gray grub.

"A creature is attacking and killing us."

Hasghat laughed. When she laughed, Horley could see a strange double image in her face, a younger woman beneath the older.

"Is that so? What kind of creature?"

"We call it the Third Bear. I do not believe it is really a bear."

Hasghat doubled over in mirth. "Not really a bear? A bear that is not a bear?"

"We cannot seem to kill it. We thought that you might know how to defeat it."

"It stays to the forest," the witch woman said. "It stays to the forest and it is a bear but not a bear. It kills your people when they use the forest paths. It kills your people in the farms. It even sneaks into your graveyards and takes the heads of your dead. You are full of fear and panic. You cannot kill it, but it keeps murdering you in the most terrible of ways."

And that was winter, coming from her dry, stained lips.

"Do you know of it then?" Horley asked, his heart fast now from hope not fear.

"Ah yes, I know it," Hasghat said, nodding. "I know the Third Bear, *Theeber, Seether*. After all I brought it here."

The spear moved in Horley's hand and it would have driven itself deep into the woman's chest if Horley had let it.

"For revenge?" Horley asked.

Hasghat nodded. "Unfair. It was unfair. You should not have done it."

You're right, Horley thought. *I should have let them burn you.*

"You're right," Horley said. "We should not have done it. But we have learned our lesson."

"I was once a woman of knowledge and learning," Hasghat said. "Once I had a real cottage in a village. Now I am old and the forest is cold and uncomfortable. All of this is illusion." She gestured at the fireplace, at the walls of the cottage. "There is no cottage. No fireplace. No rocking chair. Right now, we are both dreaming among the worms and the beetles and the dirt. My back is sore and patterned by leaves. This is no place for someone as old as me."

"I'm sorry," Horley said. "You can come back to the village. You can live among us. We'll pay for your food. We'll give you a house to live in."

Hasghat frowned. "And some logs, I'll warrant. Some logs and some rope and some fire to go with it, too!"

Horley took off his helmet, stared into Hasghat's eye sockets. "I'll promise you whatever you want. No harm will come to you. If you'll help us. A man has to realize when he's beaten, when he's done wrong. You can have whatever you want. On my honor."

Hasghat brushed at the hornets ringing her head. "Nothing is that easy."

"Isn't it?"

"I brought it from a place far distant. In my anger. I sat in the middle of the forest despairing and I called for it from across the miles, across the years. I never expected it would come to me."

"So you can send it back?"

Hasghat frowned, spat again, and shook her head. "No. I hardly remember how I called it. And some day it may even be my head it takes. Sometimes it is easier to summon something than to send it away."

"You cannot help us at all?"

"If I could, I might, but calling it weakened me. It is all I can do to survive. I dig for toads and eat them raw. I wander the woods searching for mushrooms. I talk to the deer and I talk to the squirrels. Sometimes the birds tell me things about where they've been. Someday I will die out here. All by myself. Completely mad."

Horley's frustration heightened. He could feel the calm he had managed to keep leaving him. The spear twitched and jerked in his hands. What if he killed her? Might that send the Third Bear back where it had come from?

"What can you tell me about the Third Bear? Can you tell me anything that might help me?"

Hasghat shrugged. "It acts as to its nature. And it is far from home, so it clings to ritual even more. Where it is from, it is no more or less bloodthirsty than any other creature. There they call it 'Mord.' But this far from home, it appears more horrible than it is. It is merely making a pattern. When the pattern is finished, it will leave and go someplace else. Maybe the pattern will even help send it home."

"A pattern of heads."

"Yes. A pattern with heads."

"Do you know when it will be finished?"

"No."

"Do you know where it lives?"

"Yes. It lives *here*."

In his mind, he saw a hill. He saw a cave. He saw the Third Bear.

"Do you know anything else?"

"No."

Hasghat grinned up at him.

He drove the spear through her dry chest.

There was a sound like twigs breaking.

Horley woke covered in leaves, in the dirt, his body curled up next to the old woman. He jumped to his feet, picking up his spear. The old woman, dressed in a black dress and dirty shawl, was dreaming and mumbling in her sleep.

Dead hornets had become entangled in her stringy hair. She clutched a dead toad in her left hand. A smell came from her, of rot, of shit.

There was no sign of the door. The forest was silent and dark.

Horley almost drove the spear into her chest again, but she was tiny, like a bird, and defenseless, and staring down at her he could not do it.

He looked around at the trees, at the fading light. It was time to accept that there was no reason to it, no *why*. It was time to get out, one way or another.

"A pattern of heads," he muttered to himself all the way home. "A pattern of heads."

Horley did not remember much about the meeting with the villagers upon his return. They wanted to hear about a powerful witch who could help or curse them, some force greater than themselves. Some glint of hope through the trees, a light in the dark. He could not give it to them. He gave them the truth instead, as much as he dared, but when they asked questions could not stand the truth, either, and hinted that the witch had told him how to defeat the Third Bear.

Did it do much good? He didn't know. He could still see winter before them. He could still see blood. And they'd brought it on themselves. That was the part he didn't tell them. That a poor old woman with the ground for a bed and dead leaves for a blanket thought she had, through her anger, brought the Third Bear down upon them. Theeber. *Seether*.

"You must leave," he told Rebecca after the meeting. "Take a wagon. Take a mule. Load it with supplies. Don't let yourself be seen. Take our two sons. Bring that young man who helps chop firewood for us. If you can trust him."

Rebecca stiffened beside him. She was quiet for a very long time.

"Where will you be?" she asked.

Horley was forty-seven years old. He had lived in Grommin his entire life.

"I have one thing left to do, and then I will join you."

"I know you will, my love." Rebecca said, holding onto him tightly, running her hands across his body as if as blind as the old witch woman, remembering, remembering.

They both knew there was only one way Horley could be sure Rebecca and his sons made it out of the forest safely.

Horley started from the south, just up-wind from where Rebecca had set out along an old cart trail, and curled in toward the Third Bear's home. After a long trek, Horley came to a hill that might have been a cairn made by his ancestors. A stream flowed down it and puddled at his feet. The stream was red and carried with it gristle and bits of marrow. It smelled like black pudding frying. The blood mixed with the deep green of the moss and turned it purple. Horley watched the blood ripple at the edges of his boots for a moment, and then he slowly walked up the hill.

He'd been carelessly loud for a long time as he walked through the leaves. About this time, Rebecca would be more than half-way through the woods, he knew.

In the cave, surrounded by all that Clem had seen and more, Horley disturbed Theeber at his work. Horley's spear had long since slipped through numb fingers. He'd pulled off his helmet because it itched and because he was sweating so much. He'd had to rip his tunic and hold the cloth against his mouth.

Horley had not meant to have a conversation; he'd meant to try to kill the beast. But now that he was there, now that he *saw*, all he had left were words.

Horley's boot crunched against half-soggy bone. Theeber didn't flinch. Theeber already knew. Theeber kept licking the fluid out of the skull in his hairy hand.

Theeber did look a little like a bear. Horley could see that. But no bear was that tall or that wide or looked as much like a man as a beast.

The ring of heads lined every flat space in the cave, painted blue and green and yellow and red and white and black. Even in the extremity of his situation, Horley could not deny that there was something beautiful about the pattern.

"This painting," Horley began in a thin, stretched voice. "These heads. How many do you need?"

Theeber turned its bloodshot, carious gaze on Horley, body swiveling as if made of air, not muscle and bone.

"How do you know not to be afraid?" Horley asked. Shaking. Piss running down his leg. "Is it true you come from a long way away? Are you homesick?"

Somehow, not knowing the answers to so many questions made

Horley's heart sore for the many other things he would never know, never understand.

Theeber approached. It stank of mud and offal and rain. It made a continual sound like the rumble of thunder mixed with a cat's purr. It had paws but it had thumbs.

Horley stared up into its eyes. The two of them stood there, silent, for a long moment. Horley trying with everything he had to read some comprehension, some understanding into that face. Those eyes, oddly gentle. The muzzle wet with carrion.

"We need you to leave. We need you to go somewhere else. Please."

Horley could see Hasghat's door in the forest in front of him. It was opening in a swirl of dead leaves. A light was coming from inside of it. A light from very, very far away.

Theeber held Horley against his chest. Horley could hear the beating of its mighty heart, loud as the world. Rebecca and his sons would be almost past the forest by now.

Seether tore Horley's head from his body. Let the rest crumple to the dirt floor.

Horley's body lay there for a good long while.

Winter came—as brutal as it had ever been—and the Third Bear continued in its work. With Horley gone, the villagers became ever more listless. Some few disappeared into the forest and were never heard from again. Others feared the forest so much that they ate berries and branches at the outskirts of their homes and never hunted wild game. Their supplies gave out. Their skin became ever more pale and they stopped washing themselves. They believed the words of madmen and adopted strange customs. They stopped wearing clothes. They would have relations in the street. At some point, they lost sight of reason entirely and sacrificed virgins to the Third Bear, who took them as willingly as anyone else. They took to mutilating their bodies, thinking that this is what the third bear wanted them to do. Some few in whom reason persisted had to be held down and mutilated by others. A few cannibalized those who froze to death, and others who had not died almost wished they had. No relief came. The baron never brought his men.

Spring came, finally, and the streams unthawed. The birds returned, the trees regained their leaves, and the frogs began to sing their mating songs. In the deep forest, an old wooden door lay half-buried in moss and dirt, leading nowhere, all light fading from it. On an overgrown hill, there lay an empty cave with nothing but a few old bones scattered across the dirt floor.

The Third Bear had finished its pattern and moved on, but for the remaining villagers he would always be there.

IT CAME FOR US

Monsters aren't always indiscriminate. For every juggernaut that tornadoes across the page, leaving a body count in the double-digits, there is another creature that takes more care in choosing its victims, and while the eventual tally of its murders may approach or even exceed that of its less selective cousin, every death is a step on the way to its eventual goal: us. Perhaps the beast has fallen in love with us. Perhaps we have trespassed against it in ways intentional or accidental. Perhaps it has recognized in us a threat to itself that must be addressed. Whatever the cause, the monster's notice has settled on us, and it will not rest until it has us. It is as if that secret, narcissistic sense we have as children, that the world revolves around us—which we are supposed to outgrow but never leaves us completely—is being validated in the most horrible of fashions. Yet whatever dark thrill such attention might bring, it must be qualified by our fear at the end result of this attention, as well as by some measure of guilt over its damage to those around us.

So in this third section, Kelly Link's "Monster" gives us the monster as the terrible protector we longed for as children, without ever considering what the cost of such a guardian might be. In comparison, the mysterious entities at work in Genevieve Valentine's "Keep Calm and Carillon" appear more benevolent, except for the rather odd task they require of the people they've saved from certain death, which rapidly moves from amusing in the direction of disturbing. The father in Robert McCammon's "The Deep End" wages a very personal campaign against the water-beast that took his son from him; the sea serpent in F. Brett Cox's "The Serpent and the Hatchet Gang" portends another kind of conflict. In "Blood Makes Noise" and "The Machine Is Perfect, the Engineer Is Nobody," Gemma Files and Brett Alexander Savory, respectively, write of monsters that seem to know more about their intended victims than the victims do, themselves. Laird Barron's "Proboscis" confronts us with monsters content to dwell amongst us unnoticed, until one of us sees more than he should.

The protagonists of all these stories share a kind of election. However terrible it might be, they have been chosen, singled out for a glimpse of the world's hidden engines. The monster that threatens our flesh threatens our understanding, too, its fractured outrage tearing vents in the life we thought we knew.

MONSTER
Kelly Link

No one in Bungalow 6 wanted to go camping. It was raining, which meant that you had to wear garbage bags over your backpacks and around the sleeping bags, and even that wouldn't help. The sleeping bags would still get wet. Some of the wet sleeping bags would then smell like pee, and the tents already smelled like mildew, and even if they got the tents up, water would collect on the ground cloths. There would be three boys to a tent, and only the boy in the middle would stay dry. The other two would inevitably end squashed up against the sides of the tent, and wherever you touched the nylon walls of the tent, water would come through from the outside.

Besides, someone in Bungalow 4 had seen a monster in the woods. Bungalow 4 had been telling stories ever since they got back. It was a no-win situation for Bungalow 6. If Bungalow 6 didn't see the monster, Bungalow 4 would keep the upper hand that fate had dealt them. If Bungalow 6 did see a monster—but who wanted to see a monster, even if it meant that you got to tell everyone about it? Not anyone in Bungalow 6, except for James Lorbick, who thought that monsters were awesome. But James Lorbick was a geek and he had a condition that made his feet smell terrible. That was another thing about camping. Someone would have to share a tent with James Lorbick and his smelly feet.

And even if Bungalow 6 did see the monster, well, Bungalow 4 had seen it first, so there was nothing special about that, seeing a monster after Bungalow 4 went and saw it first. And maybe Bungalow 4 had pissed off that monster. Maybe that monster was just waiting for more kids to show up at the Honor Lookout where all the pine trees leaned backwards in a circle around the bald hump of the hill in a way that made you feel dizzy when you lay around the fire at night and looked up at them.

"There wasn't any monster," Bryan Jones said, "and anyway if there was a monster, I bet it ran away when it saw Bungalow 4." Everybody nodded.

What Bryan Jones said made sense. Everybody knew that the kids in Bungalow 4 were so mean that they had made their counselor cry like a girl. The Bungalow 4 counselor was a twenty-year-old college student named Eric who had terrible acne and wrote poems about the local girls who worked in the kitchen and how their breasts looked lonely but also beautiful, like melted ice cream. The kids in Bungalow 4 had found the poetry and read it out loud at morning assembly in front of everybody, including some of the kitchen girls.

Bungalow 4 had sprayed a bat with insect spray and then set fire to it and almost burned down the whole bungalow.

And there were worse stories about Bungalow 4.

Everyone said that the kids in Bungalow 4 were so mean that their parents sent them off to camp just so they wouldn't have to see them for a few weeks.

"I heard that the monster had big black wings," Colin Simpson said. "Like a vampire. It flapped around and it had these long fingernails."

"I heard it had lots of teeth."

"I heard it bit Barnhard."

"I heard he tasted so bad that the monster puked after it bit him."

"I saw Barnhard last night at dinner," Colin Simpson's twin brother said. Or maybe it was Colin Simpson who said that and the kid who was talking about flapping and fingernails was the other twin. Everybody had a hard time telling them apart. "He had a Band-Aid on the inside of his arm. He looked kind of weird. Kind of pale."

"Guys," their counselor said. "Hey guys. Enough talk. Let's pack up and get going." The Bungalow 6 counselor was named Terence, but he was pretty cool. All of the kitchen girls hung around Bungalow 4 to talk to Terence, even though he was already going out with a girl from Ohio who was six-foot-two and played basketball. Sometimes before he turned out the lights, Terence would read them letters that the girl from Ohio had written. There was a picture over Terence's camp bed of this girl sitting on an elephant in Thailand. The girl's name was Darlene. Nobody knew the elephant's name.

"We can't just sit here all day," Terence said. "Chop chop."

Everyone started complaining.

"I know it's raining," Terence said. "But there are only three more days of camp left and if we want our overnight badges, this is our last chance. Besides it could stop raining. And not that you should care, but everyone in Bungalow 4 will say that you got scared and that's why you didn't want to go. And I don't want to everyone to think that Bungalow 6 is afraid of some stupid Bungalow 4 story about some stupid monster."

It didn't stop raining. Bungalow 4 didn't exactly hike; they waded. They splashed. They slid down hills. The rain came down in clammy, cold, sticky sheets. One of the Simpson twins put his foot down at the bottom of a trail and the mud went up all the way to his knee and pulled his tennis shoe right off with a loud sucking noise. So they had to stop while Terence lay down in the mud and stuck his arm down, fishing for the Simpson twin's shoe.

Bryan Jones stood next to Terence and held out his shirt so the rain wouldn't fall in Terence's ear. Bryan Jones was from North Carolina. He was a big tall kid with a friendly face, who liked paint guns and pulling down his pants and mooning people and putting hot sauce on toothbrushes.

Sometimes he'd sit on top of James Lorbick's head and fart, but everybody knew it was just Bryan being funny, except for James Lorbick. James Lorbick hated Bryan even more than he hated the kids in Bungalow 4. Sometimes James pretended that Bryan Jones's parents died in some weird accident while camp was still going on and that no one knew what to say to Bryan and so they avoided him until James came up to Bryan and said exactly the right thing and made Bryan feel better, although of course he wouldn't really feel better, he'd just appreciate what James had said to him, whatever it was that James had said. And of course then Bryan would feel bad about sitting on James's head all those times. And then they'd be friends. Everybody wanted to be friends with Bryan Jones, even James Lorbick.

The first thing that Terence pulled up out of the mud wasn't the Simpson twin's shoe. It was long and round and knobby. When Terence knocked it against the ground, some of the mud slid off.

"Hey. Wow," James Lorbick said. "That looks like a bone."

Everybody stood in the rain and looked at the bone.

"What is that?"

"Is it human?"

"Maybe it's a dinosaur," James Lorbick said. "Like a fossil."

"Probably a cow bone," Terence said. He poked the bone back in the mud and fished around until it got stuck in something that turned out to be the lost shoe. The Simpson twin took the shoe as if he didn't really want it back. He turned it upside down and mud oozed out like lonely, melting soft-squeeze ice cream.

Half of Terence was now covered in mud, although at least, thanks to

Bryan Jones, he didn't have water in his ear. He held the dubious bone as if he was going to toss it off in the bushes, but then he stopped and looked at it again. He put it in the pocket of his rain jacket instead. Half of it stuck out. It didn't look like a cow bone.

By the time they got to Honor Lookout, the rain had stopped. "See?" Terence said. "I told you." He said it as if now they were fine. Now everything would be fine. Water plopped off the needles of the pitiful pine trees that leaned eternally away from the campground on Honor Lookout.

Bungalow 6 gathered wood that would be too wet to use for a fire. They unpacked their tents and tent poles, and tent pegs, which descended into the sucking mud and disappeared forever. They laid out their tents on top of ground cloths on top of the sucking, quivering, nearly-animate mud. It was like putting a tent up over chocolate pudding. The floor of the tents sank below the level of the mud when they crawled inside. It was hard to imagine sleeping in the tents. You might just keep on sinking.

"Hey," Bryan Jones said, "look out! Snowball fight!" He lobbed a brown mudball which hit James just under the chin and splashed up on James's glasses. Then everyone was throwing mudballs, even Terence. James Lorbick even threw one. There was nothing else to do.

When they got hungry, they ate cold hot dogs for lunch while the mud dried and cracked and fell off their arms and legs and faces. They ate graham crackers with marshmallows and chocolate squares and Terence even toasted the marshmallows with a cigarette lighter for anyone who wanted. Since they couldn't make a fire, they made mud sculptures instead. Terence sculpted an elephant and a girl on top. The elephant even looked like an elephant. But then one of the Simpson twins sculpted an atom bomb and dropped it on Terence's elephant and Terence's girlfriend.

"That's okay," Terence said. "That's cool." But it wasn't cool. He went and sat on a muddy rock and looked at his bone.

The twins had made a whole stockpile of atom bombs out of mud. They decided to make a whole city with walls and buildings and everything. Some of the other kids from Bungalow 6 helped with the city so that the twins could bomb the city before it got too dark.

Bryan Jones had put mud in his hair and twisted it up in muddy spikes. There was mud in his eyebrows. He looked like an idiot, but that didn't matter, because he was Bryan Jones and anything that Bryan Jones did wasn't stupid. It was cool. "Hey man," he said to James. "Come and see what I stole off the clothes line at camp."

James Lorbick was muddy and tired and maybe his feet did smell bad, but he was smarter than most of the kids in Bungalow 6. "Why?" he asked.

"Just come on," Bryan said. "I don't want anyone else to see this yet."

"Okay," James said.

It was a dress. It had big blue flowers on it and James Lorbick got a bad feeling.

"Why did you steal a dress?" he said.

Bryan shrugged. He was smiling as if the whole idea of a dress made him happy. It was a big, happy, contagious smile, but James Lorbick didn't smile back. "Because it will be funny," Bryan said. "Put it on and we'll go show everybody."

"No way," James said. He folded his muddy arms over his muddy chest to show he was serious.

"I dare you," Bryan said. "Come on, James, before everybody comes over here and sees it. Everybody will laugh."

"I know they will," James said. "No."

"Look, I'd put it on, I swear, but it wouldn't fit me. No way would it fit. So you've got to do it. Just do it, James."

"No," James said.

James Lorbick wasn't sure why his parents had sent him off to camp in North Carolina. He hadn't wanted to go. It wasn't as if there weren't trees in Chicago. It wasn't as if James didn't have friends in Chicago. Camp just seemed to be one of those things parents could make you do, like violin lessons, or karate, except that camp lasted a whole month. Plus, he was supposed to be thankful about it, like his parents had done him a big favor. Camp cost money.

So he made leather wallets in arts and crafts, and went swimming every other day, even though the lake smelled funny and the swim instructor was kind of weird and liked to make the campers stand on the high diving board with their eyes closed. Then he'd creep up and push them into the water. Not that you didn't know he was creeping up. You could feel the board wobbling.

He didn't make friends. But that wasn't true, exactly. He was friendly, but nobody in Bungalow 6 was friendly back. Sometimes right after Terence turned out the lights, someone would say, "James, oh, James, your hair looked really excellent today" or "James, James Lorbick, I wish I were as good at archery as you" or "James, will you let me borrow your water canteen tomorrow?" and then everyone would laugh while James pretended to be asleep, until Terence would flick on the lights and say, "Leave James alone—go to sleep or I'll give everyone five demerits."

James Lorbick knew it could have been worse. He could have been in Bungalow 4 instead of Bungalow 6.

At least the dress wasn't muddy. Bryan let him keep his jeans and T-shirt on. "Let me do your hair," Bryan said. He picked up a handful of mud pushed it around on James's head until James had sticky mud hair just like Bryan's.

"Come on," Bryan said.

"Why do I have to do this?" James asked. He held his hands out to the side so that he wouldn't have to touch the dress. He looked ridiculous. He felt worse than ridiculous. He felt so terrible that he didn't even care anymore that he was wearing the dress.

"You didn't have to do this," Bryan said. He sounded like he thought it was a big joke, which it was. "I didn't make you do it, James."

One of the Simpson twins was running around, dropping atom bombs on the sagging, wrinkled tents. He skidded to a stop in front of Bryan and James. "Why are you wearing a dress?" the Simpson twin said. "Hey, James is wearing a dress!"

Bryan gave James a shove. Not hard, but he left a muddy handprint on the dress. "Come on," he said. "Pretend that you're a zombie. Like you're a kitchen girl zombie who's come back to eat the brains of everybody from Bungalow 6, because you're still angry about that time we had the rice pudding fight with Bungalow 4 out on the porch of the dining room. Like you just crawled out of the mud. I'll be a zombie too. Let's go chase people."

"Okay," James Lorbick said. The terrible feeling went away at the thought of being a zombie. Suddenly the flowered dress seemed magical to him. It gave him the strength of a zombie, only faster. He staggered with Bryan along toward the rest of Bungalow 6, holding out his arms. Kids said things like, "Hey, look at James! James is wearing a DRESS!" as if they were making fun of him, but then they got the idea. They realized that James and Bryan were zombies and they ran away. Even Terence.

After a while, everybody had become a zombie. So they went for a swim. Everybody except for James Lorbick, because when he started to take off the dress, Bryan Jones stopped him. Bryan said, "No, wait. Keep it on. I dare you to wear that dress until we get back to camp tomorrow. I dare you. We'll show up at breakfast and say that we saw a monster and it's chasing us, and then you come in the dining room and it will be awesome. You look completely spooky with that dress and all the mud."

"I'll get my sleeping bag all muddy," James said. "I don't want to sleep in a dress. It's dumb."

Everybody in the lake began to yell things.

"Come on, James, wear the dress, okay?"

"Keep the dress on! Do it, James!"

"I dare you," said Bryan.

"I dare you," James said.

"What?" Bryan said. "What do you dare me to do?"

Terence was floating on his back. He lifted his head. "You tell him, James. Don't let Bryan talk you into anything you don't want to do."

"Come on," Bryan said. "It will be so cool. Come on."

So everybody in Bungalow 6 went swimming except for James Lorbick. They splashed around and washed off all the mud and came out of the pond and James Lorbick was the only kid in Bungalow 6 who was still covered in crusty mud. James Lorbick was the only one who still had mud spikes in his hair. James Lorbick was the only one wearing a dress.

The sun was going down. They sat on the ground around the campfire that wouldn't catch. They ate the rest of the hotdogs and the peanut butter sandwiches that the kitchen girls always made up when the bungalows went on overnight hikes. They talked about how cool it would be in the morning, when James Lorbick came running into the dining room back at camp, pretending to be a monster.

It got darker. They talked about the monster.

"Maybe it's a werewolf."

"Or a were-skunk."

"Maybe it's from outer space."

"Maybe it's just really lonely," James Lorbick said. He was sitting between Bryan Jones and one of the Simpson twins, and he felt really good, like he was really part of Bungalow 6 at last, and also kind of itchy, because of the mud.

"So how come nobody's ever seen it before?"

"Maybe some people have, but they died and so they couldn't tell anybody."

"No way. They wouldn't let us camp here if somebody died."

"Maybe the camp doesn't want anybody to know about the monster, so they don't say anything."

"You're so paranoid. The monster didn't do anything to Bungalow 4. Besides, Bungalow 4 is a bunch of liars."

"Wait a minute, do you hear that?"

They were quiet, listening. Bryan Jones farted. It was a sinister, brassy fart.

"Oh, man. That's disgusting, Bryan."

"What? It wasn't me."

"If the monster comes, we'll just aim Bryan at it."

"Wait, what's that?"

Something was ringing. "No way," Terence said. "That's my cell phone. No way does it get reception out here. Hello? Hey, Darlene. What's up?" He turned on his flashlight and shone it at Bungalow 6. "Guys, I gotta go down the hill for a sec. She sounds upset. Something about her car and a Chihuahua."

"That's cool."

"Be careful. Don't let the monster sneak up on you."

"Tell Darlene she's too good for you."

They watched Terence pick his way down the muddy path in a little circle of light. The light got smaller and smaller, farther and farther away, until they couldn't see it any more.

"What if it isn't really Darlene?" a kid named Timothy Ferber said.

"What?"

"Like what if it's the monster?"

"No way. That's stupid. How would the monster know Terence's cell phone number?"

"Are there any marshmallows left?"

"No. Just graham crackers."

They ate the graham crackers. Terence didn't come back. They couldn't even hear his voice. They told ghost stories.

"And she puts her hand down and her dog licks it and she thinks everything is okay. Except that then, in the morning, when she looks in the bathtub, her dog is in there and he's dead and there's lots of blood and somebody has written 'HA HA I REALLY FOOLED YOU' with the blood."

"One time my sister was babysitting and this weird guy called and wanted to know if Satan was there and she got really freaked out."

"One time my grandfather was riding on a train and he saw a naked woman standing out in a field."

"Was she a ghost?"

"I don't know. He used to like to tell that story a lot."

"Were there cows in the field?"

"I don't know, how should I know if there were cows?"

"Do you think Terence is going to come back soon?"

"Why? Are you scared?"

"What time is it?"

"It's not even 10:30. Maybe we could try lighting the fire again."

"It's still too wet. It's not going to catch. Besides, if there was a monster and if the monster was out there and we got the fire lit, then the monster could see us."

"We don't have any marshmallows, anyway."

"Wait, I think I know how to get it started. Like Bungalow 4 did with the bat. If I spray it with insecticide, and then—"

Bungalow 6 fell reverently silent.

"Wow. That's awesome, Bryan. They should have a special merit badge for that."

"Yeah, to go with the badge for toxic farts."

"It smells funny," James Lorbick said. But it was nice to have a fire going. It made the darkness seem less dark. Which is what fires are supposed to do, of course.

"You look really weird in the firelight, James. That dress and all the mud. It's kind of funny and kind of creepy."

"Thanks."

"Yeah, James Lorbick should always wear dresses. He's so hot."

"James Lorbick, I think you are so hot. Not."

"Leave James alone," Bryan Jones said.

"I had this weird dream last year," Danny Anderson said. Danny Anderson was from Terre Haute, Indiana. He was taller than anyone else in Bungalow 6 except for Terence. "I dreamed that I came home from school one day and nobody was there except this man. He was sitting in the living room watching TV and so I said, 'Who are you? What are you doing here?' And he looked up and smiled this creepy smile at me and he said, 'Hey Danny, I'm Angelina Jolie. I'm your new dad."

"No way. You dreamed your dad was Angelina Jolie?"

"No," Danny Anderson said. "Shut up. My parents aren't divorced or anything. My dad's got the same name as me. This guy said he was my new dad. He said he was Angelina Jolie. But he was just some guy."

"That's a dumb dream."

"I know it is," Danny Anderson said. "But I kept having the it, like, every night. This guy is always hanging out in the kitchen and talking to me about what we're going to do now that I'm his kid. He's really creepy. And the thing is, I just got a phone call from my mom, and she says that she and my dad are getting divorced and I think maybe she's got a new boyfriend."

"Hey, man. That's tough."

Danny Anderson looked as if he might be about to cry. He said, "So what if this boyfriend turns out to be my dad? Like in the dream?"

"One time I had a dream James Lorbick was wearing a dress."

"What's that noise?"

"I didn't hear anything."

"Terence has been gone a long time."

"Maybe he went back to camp. Maybe he left us out here."

"The fire smells really bad."

"It reeks."

"Isn't insect stuff poisonous?"

"Of course not. Otherwise they wouldn't be able to sell it. Because you put it on your skin. They wouldn't let you put poison on your skin."

"Hey, look up. I think I saw a shooting star."

"Maybe it was a space ship."

They all looked up at the sky. The sky was black and clear and full of bright stars. It was like that for a moment and then they noticed how clouds were racing across the blackness, spilling across the sky. The stars disappeared. Maybe if they hadn't looked, the sky would have stayed clear. But they did look. Then snow started to fall, lightly at first, just dusting the muddy ground and the campfire and Bungalow 6 and then there was more snow falling. It fell quietly and thickly. It was going to be the tenth of July tomorrow, the next-to-last day of camp, the day that James Lorbick wearing a dress and a lot of mud was going to show up and scare everyone in the dining room.

The snow was the weirdest thing that had ever happened to Bungalow 6.

One of the Simpson twins said, "Hey, it's snowing!"

Bryan Jones said, "I don't believe this."

James Lorbick looked up at the sky, which had been so clear a minute ago. Fat snowflakes fell on his upturned face. He wrapped his crumbly mud-covered arms around himself. "It's kind of beautiful," he said.

"Terence! Hey Terence! It's snowing!"

"Nobody is going to believe us."

"Maybe we should go get in our sleeping bags."

"We could build a snow fort."

"No, seriously. What if it gets really cold and we freeze to death? All I brought is my windbreaker."

"No way. It's going to melt right away. It's summer. This is just some kind of weather event. We should take a picture so we can show everybody."

So far they had taken pictures of mud, of people pretending to be mud-covered zombies, of James Lorbick pretending to be a mud-haired, dress-wearing monster. Terence had taken a picture of the bone that wasn't a cow bone. One of the Simpson twins had put a dozen marshmallows in his mouth and someone took a picture of that. Someone had a digital photo of Bryan Jones's big naked butt.

"So why didn't anyone from Bungalow 4 take a picture of the monster?"

"They did. But you couldn't see anything."

"Snow is cooler anyway."

"No way. A monster is way better."

"I think it's weird that Terence hasn't come back up yet."

"Hey, Terence! Terence!"

They all yelled for Terence for a few minutes. The snow kept falling. They did little dances in the snow to keep warm. The fire got thinner and thinner and started to go out. But before it went out, the monster came up the muddy, snowy path. It smiled at them and it came up the path and Danny Anderson shone his flashlight at it and they could all see it was a monster and not Terence pretending to be a monster. No one in Bungalow 6 had ever seen a monster before, but they all knew that a monster was what it was. It had a white face and its hands were red and dripping. It moved very fast.

You can learn a lot of stuff at camp. You learn how to wiggle an arrow so that it comes out of a straw target without the metal tip coming off. You learn how to make something out of yarn and twigs called a skycatcher, because there's a lot of extra yarn and twigs in the world, and someone had to come up with something to do with it. You learn how to jam your feet up into the mattress of the bunk above you, while someone is leaning out of it, so that they fall out of bed. You learn that if you are riding a horse and the horse sees a snake on the trail, the horse will stand on its hind legs. Horses don't like snakes. You find out that tennis rackets are good for chasing bats. You find out what happens if you leave your wet clothes in your trunk for a few days. You learn how to make rockets and you learn how to pretend if someone takes your rocket and stomps on it. You learn to pretend to be asleep when people make fun of you. You learn how to be lonely.

The snow came down and people ran around Honor Lookout. They screamed and waved their arms around and fell down. The monster chased them. It moved so quickly that sometimes it seemed to fly. It was laughing like this was an excellent, fun game. The snow was still coming down and it was dark which made it hard to see what the monster did when it caught people. James Lorbick sat still. He pretended that he was asleep or not there. He pretended that he was writing a letter to his best friend in Chicago who was spending the summer playing video games and hanging out at the library and writing and illustrating his own comic book. "Dear Alec, how are you? Camp is almost over, and I am so glad. This has been the worst summer ever. We went on a hike and it rained and my counselor found a bone. This kid made me put on a dress. There was a monster that ate everybody. How is your comic book coming? Did you put in the part I wrote about the superhero who can only fly when he's asleep?"

The monster had one Simpson twin under each arm. The twins were screaming. The monster threw them down the path. Then it bent over Bryan Jones, who was lying half inside one of the tents, half in the snow. There were slurping noises. After a minute it stood up again. It looked back and saw James Lorbick. It waved.

James Lorbick shut his eyes. When he opened them again, the monster was standing over him. It had red eyes. It smelled like rotting fish and kerosene. It wasn't actually all that tall, the way you'd expect a monster to be tall. Except for that, it was even worse than Bungalow 4 had said.

The monster stood and looked down and grinned. "You," it said. It had a voice like a dead tree full of bees: sweet and dripping and buzzing. It poked James on the shoulder with a long black nail. "What are you?"

"I'm James Lorbick," James said. "From Chicago."

The monster laughed. Its teeth were pointed and terrible. There was a smear of red on the dress where it had touched James. "You're the craziest thing I've ever seen. Look at that dress. Look at your hair. It's standing straight up. Is that mud? Why are you covered in mud?"

"I was going to be a monster," James said. He swallowed. "No offense."

"None taken," the monster said. "Wow, maybe I should go visit Chicago. I've never seen anything as funny as you. I could look at you for hours and hours. Whenever I needed a laugh. You've really made my day, James Lorbick."

The snow was still falling. James shivered and shivered. His teeth were clicking together so loudly he thought they might break. "What are you doing here?" he asked. "Where's Terence? Did you do something to him?"

"Was he the guy who was down at the bottom of the hill? Talking on a cell phone?"

"Yeah," James said. "Is he okay?"

"He was talking to some girl named Darlene," the monster said. I tried to talk to her, but she started screaming and then she hung up. Do you happen to know where she lives?

"Somewhere in Ohio," James said.

"Thanks," the monster said. He took out a little black notebook and wrote something down.

"What are you?" James said. "Who are you?"

"I'm Angelina Jolie," the monster said. It blinked.

James's heart almost stopped beating. "Really?" he said. "Like in Danny Anderson's dream?"

"No," the monster said. "Just kidding."

"Are you the monster that Bungalow 4 saw?" James said.

"Were those the kids who were here a few days ago?"

"Yeah," James said.

"We hung out for a while," the monster said. "Were they friends of yours?"

"No," James said. "Those kids are real jerks. Nobody likes them."

"That's a shame," the monster said. Even when it wasn't belching, it smelled worse than anything James had ever smelled before. Fish and kerosene and rotting maple syrup poured over him in waves. He tried not to breathe.

The monster said, "I'm sorry about the rest of your bungalow. Your friends. Your friends who made you wear a dress."

"Are you going to eat me?" James said.

"I don't know," the monster said. "Probably not. There were a lot of you. I'm not actually that hungry anymore. Besides, I would feel silly eating a kid in a dress. And you're really filthy."

"Why didn't you eat Bungalow 4?" James said. He felt sick to his stomach. If he looked at the monster he felt sick, and if he looked away, there was Danny Anderson, lying facedown under a pine tree with snow on his back and if he looked somewhere else, there were Bryan Jones's legs poking out of the tent. There was Bryan Jones's head. One of Bryan's shoes had come off and that made James think of the hike, the way Terence had lain down in the mud to fish for the Simpson twin's shoe. "Why didn't you eat them? They're mean. They do terrible things and nobody likes them."

"Wow," the monster said. "I didn't know that. I would have eaten them if I'd known, maybe. Although most of the time I can't worry about things like that."

"Maybe you should," James said. "I think you should."

The monster scratched its head. "You think so? I saw you guys eating hot dogs earlier. So do you worry about whether those were good dogs or bad dogs when you're eating them? Do you only eat dogs that were mean? Do you only eat bad dogs?"

"Hot dogs aren't really made from dogs," James said. "People don't eat dogs."

"I never knew that," the monster said. "But, see, if I worried about that kind of thing, whether the person I was eating was a nice guy or a jerk, I'd never eat anyone. And I get hungry a lot. So to be honest, I don't worry. All I really notice is whether the person I'm chasing is big or small or fast or slow. Or if they have a sense of humor. That's important, you know. A sense of humor. You have to laugh about things. When I was hanging out with Bungalow 4, I was just having some fun. I was just playing around. Bungalow 4 mentioned that you guys were going to show up. I was joking about how I was going to eat them and they said I should eat you guys instead. They said it would be really funny. I have a good sense of humor. I like a good joke."

It reached out and touched James Lorbick's head.

"Don't do that!" James said.

"Sorry," said the monster. "I just wanted to see what the mud spikes felt like. Do you think it would be funny if I wore a dress and put a lot of mud on my head?"

James shook his head. He tried to picture the monster wearing a dress, but all he could picture was somebody climbing up to Honor Lookout. Somebody finding pieces of James scattered everywhere like pink and red confetti. That somebody would wonder what had happened and be glad that it hadn't happened to them. Maybe someday people would tell scary stories about what had happened to Bungalow 6 when they went camping. Nobody would believe the stories. Nobody would understand why one kid had been wearing a dress.

"Are you shivering because you're cold or because you're afraid of me?" the monster said.

"I don't know," James said. "Both. Sorry."

"Maybe we should get up and run around," the monster said. "I could chase you. It might warm you up. Weird weather, isn't it? But it's pretty, too. I love how snow makes everything look nice and clean."

"I want to go home," James said.

"That's Chicago, right?" the monster said. "That's what I wrote down."

"You wrote down where I live?" James said.

"All those guys from the other bungalow," the monster said. "Bungalow 4. I made them write down their addresses. I like to travel. I like to visit people. Besides, if you say that they're jerks, then I should go visit them? Right? It would serve them right."

"Yeah," James said. "It would serve them right. That would be really funny. Ha ha ha."

"Excellent," the monster said. It stood up. "It was great meeting you, James. Are you crying? It looks like you're crying."

"I'm not crying. It's just snow. There's snow on my face. Are you leaving?" James said. "You're going to leave me here? You aren't going to eat me?"

"I don't know," the monster said. It did a little twirl, like it was going to go running off in one direction, and then as if it had changed its mind, as if it was going to come rushing back at James. James whimpered. "I just can't decide. Maybe I should flip a coin. Do you have a coin I can flip?"

James shook his head.

"Okay," the monster said. "How about this. I'm thinking of a number between one and ten. You say a number and if it's the same number, I won't eat you."

"No," James said.

"Then how about if I only eat you if you say the number that I'm thinking of? I promise I won't cheat. I probably won't cheat."

"No," James said, although he couldn't help thinking of a number. He thought of the number four. It floated there in his head like a big neon sign, blinking on and off and back on. Four, four, four. Bungalow 4. Or six. Bungalow 6. Or was that too obvious? Don't think of a number. He would have bet anything that the monster could read minds. Maybe the monster had put the number four in James's head. Six. James changed the number to six hundred so it wouldn't be a number between one and ten. Don't read my mind, he thought. Don't eat me.

"I'll count to six hundred," the monster said. "And then I'll chase you. That would be funny. If you get back to camp before I catch you, you're safe. Okay? If you get back to camp first, I'll go eat Bungalow 4. Okay? I tell you what. I'll go eat them even if you don't make it back. Okay?"

"But it's dark," James said. "It's snowing. I'm wearing a dress."

The monster looked down at its fingernails. It smiled like James had just told an excellent joke. "One," it said. "Two, three, four. Run, James! Pretend I'm chasing you. Pretend that I'm going to eat you if I catch you. Five, six. Come on, James, run!"

James ran.

Keep Calm and Carillon
Genevieve Valentine

Turned out the courthouse elevators had been having problems for weeks, but of course they didn't tell anybody to lay off and use the stairs, and my sister's elevator was packed when it crashed.

(The cops' statement said something about the amazing elasticity of the human body and acts of God and relief, and they were going to look into the elevator system right away. They left out that if you felt like contesting that traffic ticket now you'd have to walk up four flights, so you might as well just pay it and shut up.)

When Shelly finally came out, she was at the head of a knot of people who would be nicknamed the "Elevator Nine," and they were all smiling and talking and really did not look like they had just free-fallen eight stories.

She hugged us (Dad, then me), and pulled back smiling. "We're starting a handbell choir!" she said.

Shelly had gone in for a parking ticket; Dad had made her go alone to teach her a lesson about responsibility.

Catherine was the high school secretary and was there for a custody hearing with her ten-year-old Danny. I think she and Danny had a lot of problems before the elevator, but afterwards they just stood around smiling and hugging each other in front of the cameras like a laxative ad.

Jake was one year older than I was, and to celebrate his college acceptance, he'd wrapped his dad's Beemer around a tree. He probably should have wrapped himself around it while he was at it; he was a jerk before the elevator and he stayed one, shoulder-gripping Danny and saying things like, "Man, it's just, like, awesome!" every time the cameras turned on him.

Judge Thomas Warner had been on the bench for seventeen years, and when he announced his resignation to play handbells with a bunch of strangers everyone thought that was normal enough. The clerks threw him a big party; he'd been a decent judge.

Morgan was really thin and pulled her hair compulsively, blonde strands one by one. She never told anyone what she was there for, but because she was on TV for days staring at the camera and dazedly talking about how life is precious, people got curious. When whatdidmorgando.com launched, the top two most-voted guesses were "institutionalized" and "witness protection."

Eugene was in the courthouse to check on the status of his green card, and he joked to reporters that he'd better get one now, since elevators never broke in Belgium and he might go back. He had a green card in six days, and that got the county into more trouble than the elevator had, because if a green card only took six days, how come people had been waiting eight months?

Grace worked at a think tank and was on jury duty for a zoning thing. Grace never made it on TV because she wasn't as pretty as Morgan, and I figured she'd have something to say about that, but every time the cameras clicked off and they group-hugged, Grace was right in there with the rest of them.

Steve was a mechanic, and he never set foot in front of the cameras and never said a word to the papers. He just asked for access to the scene before the construction crew began, and he spent four days poking around the elevator shaft. When I asked Shelly what he could have been looking for, she shrugged and said, "He had his eyes closed."

Dad and I were beside Shelly nonstop during the little Elevator Nine tour, since Shelly was a minor and had to get Dad's signature for all the interviews. The first big flurry died out after a week or so, but then Eugene got his green card and it all came back up again, and then Danny's dad paid his deadbeat child care and tried to leverage it into an interview with *People* about the importance of being a good guy, but the Judge made a few phone calls and put the stopper on that story in about ten minutes, and that turned into a whole thing about judicial powers until Catherine pointed out that *People* magazine folded like a greeting card for any publicist in the world, and it took about three months for everything to settle down.

By then Dad had forgotten about the handbell thing—it sounded like the sort of thing you said when you were in shock, so I guess I don't blame him—and he was surprised all over again when Shelly reminded him that the first practice was on Thursday and she needed white gloves.

(I'd wanted to learn guitar since I was twelve, and that didn't really pan out, which—Eugene's nice and everything, but I understand how people got angry because they'd been waiting for a green card for eight months and Eugene got his in a week. I'm just saying.)

Shelly got assigned middle C and the B-flat above it, but switched to F-sharp from B-flat because Danny kept making jokes about her chest. By the time they got together for their first practice, there was already talk of adding another octave, but Grace was the only one who could line up five bells and remember where they were in time to ring them. Shelly insisted she could handle the G too, but when Grace handed it over Shelly got nervous and sounded the C during scales when it should have been the G.

They tried scales for three hours without getting it right—even Jake managed to mess up, and he only had the one huge bell that took two hands to gong—but after all that the Judge called to arrange the lease for the bells and everyone hugged and smiled and went home.

"I can't wait to start practicing," Shelly said on the way home, and Dad said, "That's great, honey," and he must not have been paying attention, because come on.

I took up theatre, not so much because I liked the theatre, but because it would keep me out of the house when she was practicing. I got to be in The Importance of Being Earnest as Lady Bracknell, which they said was because I looked "mature" for seventeen. They meant I looked old; living with Shelly gave me gray hair.

Every day when I came home she was standing in the dining room, frowning at the sheet music propped up on the dining table, ringing middle C and F-sharp at random intervals with big sweeping arm motions that looked like she was shoving the bells through molasses. Sometimes she clapped one bell against her chest to cut off the note, and I heard a quick thud, then nothing.

Shelly didn't have to go to school because of the trauma, and when her friends came over she would sit around and be nice for a while (nicer than she had been) and then say, "Hey, I play handbells now! Wanna hear?" They always said yes, because they thought she was just coping, and they'd wave to me on the way out like nothing was wrong, and it was comforting to know that Shelly's friends were as clueless as they had always been.

We ate dinner together since Dad had nearly lost one of us. I had to explain to the director, and he got angry and made Dad come in and explain it, but after Dad mentioned the elevator a few times they made an exception for me, since I wasn't in the middle of the play anyway. I would go onstage, run home, eat, and come back for the big finish.

Shelly would always ask, "How's it going?" and no matter what I said she'd say, "That's so cool! Like my handbells!"

"She's getting really good," Dad would put in, every time, and as soon as he said it, the phone would ring, every time, and it was one of the Elevator Nine. (Dad used to forbid phone calls during family dinner when we even had it, but now everyone was fine except Jake, who kept hitting on Shelly right in front of Dad, and even Dad noticed that, so, no calls from Jake.)

And Shelly would hop up and grab the phone and laugh without even asking who it was, and stand there grinning into the phone and saying, "I know, me too!" and "It's beautiful" and "I can't wait", and as I ran out the door she'd wave at me and sort of bounce on her heels like it was her sixth birthday again, an inhuman gleam in her eye.

I got more "mature" as the weeks went on, and by the time we were doing costumed rehearsals, the makeup girls didn't even need to draw wrinkles.

It wasn't all smiles and hugs among the Elevator Nine, though smiling and hugging constituted a frighteningly large percentage of the time they spent together. They fought over the music for their first concert: the Judge wanted "Jesu, Joy of Man's Desiring"; Jake said it sounded gay. They fought about the group name: it ended up being "Resoun-Ding," though Grace's "Nine-in-Hand" was my favorite. It might have passed the vote if anyone else could handle more than three bells.

They fought over costumes: Catherine thought the "Ring it!" shirts sounded too much like a jewelry ad, "And besides, T-shirts are tacky." Danny refused to wear a button-down, Eugene vetoed short sleeves. They ended up in v-neck sweaters that made them look like escapees from a Mr. Rogers concert. I figured at least Morgan would complain, but she pulled out some hair and smiled and hugged Jake, and I sat in the back of the church hall where they practiced and watched them all dinging on cue under Judge Warner's direction.

Danny had three of the little bells. Grace had her five, Jake had the one bell he rang two-handed. Almost everyone else handled two notes except Steve, who rang his one bell evenly in time—he didn't even have one specific note; he had to be assigned whatever bell rang at the beginning of every measure, because he didn't like random timing.

When he practiced his part (he always came early to practice) the tones came out clear and steady, like a church bell. He never did as well when they were all there staring at the Judge and swinging their arms, with Steve standing awkwardly at one end, sounding the beat.

As soon as the play was over I lost the excuse of going to rehearsals and I had to go back to the church hall and sit through handbelling again, and if it wasn't for Steve and his one steady note I'd have been peeling pages out of the hymnal for tinder to torch myself with.

One Thursday Grace invited everyone over ("We should carpool," Catherine said, then "No, Jake, you can't drive, go with Eugene"), and on the way to the car, Steve and I ended up alone.

"Steve, why handbells?"

"It's what they need," he said, then bit his lip like he'd said something he shouldn't have, and I felt vindicated for guessing that the handbells were no good.

"I already knew that part, don't worry," I lied, "Shelly sort of blabs, I just don't get the bells."

"Me neither," he said, and we smiled at each other in front of the car until Shelly and Dad showed up.

Steve and Shelly insisted I sit in the front, and I could feel Steve getting in the car behind me, ready for a silent ride, and I felt his door close before he really shut it—a quick thud, then nothing.

We were all surprised the day the movie offer came.

"We want to do a documentary," said the guy who showed up at the hall, "it's such an amazing story, and now with the concert coming up—"

"We have to go," said Morgan, clutching the E to her chest, and behind her Grace said, "If you ask us again we're going to consider it harassment and have our attorneys involved," and when the door closed, somehow Dad and I were on the wrong side of it. For a second I was angry—I mean, I'd hated sitting through the rehearsals, but why were they treating us like we'd invited the producers?

The guys asked, "Is it true about the lawyers?"

"Yes," Dad said, and I nodded. It wasn't, but we were both angry at these guys for getting us thrown out of rehearsal.

We got ice cream while we waited for Shelly, and halfway through Dad said, "I'm really getting sick of her practicing."

"I'm glad we got kicked out," I said.

"Me too," he said.

I went back to the courthouse, even though everything had been fixed for a long time and there wasn't a chance of me finding anything. Steve was there, too, and the two of us stood side by side and watched people hopping in and out of the elevators.

"What really happened to you?"

He shrugged. "I don't know. My eyes were closed."

"But the bells," I said, and he shoved his hands in his pockets and shook his head, and he looked suddenly sixteen and not in his thirties.

So I didn't say anything else, because it wasn't like there was anything I could do, and we stood next to each other a little while longer, listening to the sound of people's shoes on the marble. I liked it; but by then I liked any sound that wasn't a brass bell.

Eventually he turned around and said without looking at me, "I can give you a ride," and I said yes, because it was better than the bus, and because it felt like a date, even though that was sort of weird.

He had a beat-up truck, and as I got into the passenger seat he yanked something out from under the windshield wipers.

When he was inside he handed me the thin stack of paper, and as he pulled out I sorted through it.

A note in lipstick—NEVER FORGET THE 9 WE LOVE YO, and whoever it was had run out of space. Nice one. A lottery ticket, already scratched off with a two-dollar win; I put it on the dash. A receipt with FUCK OFF scrawled on the back. The business card from those movie guys.

It felt strange to handle these things; Shelly's life for the last months had been the Nine's, not ours, so Dad and I didn't really know what was happening with her. I wondered what kind of notes she got; if people were nice to her, or if she had a stack of receipts in her room that read FUCK OFF on the back, and she wrapped the bells in them to keep them safe.

We weren't allowed into rehearsals after that.

I joined the next play, because Dad had gotten lucid for a moment without the bells in his head and said he totally supported both his kids. It was Oliver Twist, and I got to be Nancy's friend, so my job was mostly to sit around and look poor. Dad came to the first full run-through like he wanted to support us both equally, one daughter with a bit part in a play and one daughter who had survived an elevator crash and rang handbells ten hours a day.

I told Shelly about the play two nights before her concert, at the dinner table. (Morgan or Catherine dropped her off after rehearsals these days; we weren't even allowed to drive her around.)

She smiled and said, "That's so awesome!"

She didn't say, "Like my handbells," and that's when I really started to worry.

That night I pretended to be asleep until the ringing started; then I crept down the stairs and peered into the dining room.

Shelly was looking out at the street; with her hair pulled back into a pony-tail I could see her rapturous profile, and as she struck each note she kept her arm in front of her, holding the bell like a torch, like the sound was a signal, like she was using the bell to catch rain.

The sounds were irregular —melodic, not rhythmic like Steve, so it was a five-second pause and then suddenly two notes on top of each other, the most uneasy thing I'd ever heard —but I sat on the stairs and watched her for a long time, and after long enough I began to hear a weird reverb, like somehow the bells both rang together, mingled, and made the whole carillon, and whenever it happened Shelly closed her eyes, grinned even wider, until she looked like her ninth-grade Homecoming picture.

I went back up the stairs and sat in bed, shivering, until I heard Shelly's bedroom door close.

All that night I couldn't sleep, because I could hear her through the walls, and her breathing had taken on the weird, halting pattern of the bells—a small sound, a quick thud, then nothing.

The Deep End
Robert R. McCammon

Summer was dying. The late afternoon sky wept rain from low, hovering clouds, and Glenn Calder sat in his Chevy station wagon, staring at the swimming pool where his son had drowned two weeks ago.

Neil was just sixteen years old, Glenn thought. His lips were tight and gray, and the last of his summer tan had faded from his gaunt, hollowed face. Just *sixteen.* His hands tightened around the steering wheel, the knuckles bleaching white. *It's not fair. My son is dead—and* you're *still alive. Oh, I know you're there. I've figured it all out. You think you're so damned smart. You think you've got everybody fooled. But not me. Oh no—not me.*

He reached over the seat beside him and picked up his pack of Winstons, chose a cigarette and clamped the filter between his lips. Then he punched the cigarette lighter in and waited for it to heat up.

His eyes, pale blue behind a pair of horn-rimmed glasses, remained fixed on the Olympic-sized public swimming pool beyond the high chain link fence. A sign on the admissions gate said in big, cheerful red letters: CLOSED FOR THE SEASON! SEE YOU NEXT SUMMER! Beyond the fence were bleachers and sundecks where people had lolled in the hot, sultry summer of north Alabama, and there was a bandstand where an occasional rock band had played at a pool party on a Saturday night. Steam rose from the glistening concrete around the pool and, in the silence between the patter of raindrops, with his windows rolled down and the moody smell of August's last hours inside the car, he thought he could hear ghostly music from that bandstand, there under the red canopy where he himself had danced as a kid in the late fifties.

He imagined he could hear the shouts, squeals and rowdy laughter of the generations of kids that had come to this pool, here in wooded Parnell Park, since it had been dug out and filled with water back in the mid-forties. He cocked his head to one side, listening, and he felt sure that one of these

230

ghostly voices belonged to Neil, and Neil was speaking like a ripple of water down a drain, calling "Dad? *Dad?* It killed me, Dad! I didn't drown! I was always a good swimmer, Dad! *You* know that, don't you . . . ?"

"Yes," Glenn answered softly, and tears filled his eyes. "I know that."

The lighter popped out. Glenn got his cigarette going and returned the lighter to the dashboard. He stared at the swimming pool as a tear crept down his cheek. Neil's voice ebbed and faded, joining the voices of the other ghosts that were forever young in Parnell Park.

If he had a dollar for every time he'd walked through that admissions gate he'd be a mighty rich man today. At least he'd have a lot more money, he mused, than running the Pet Center at Brookhill Mall paid him. But he'd always liked animals, so that was okay, though when he'd been young enough to dream he'd had plans of working for a zoo in a big city like Birmingham, travelling the world and collecting exotic animals. His father had died when he was a sophomore at the University of Alabama, and Glenn had returned to Barrimore Crossing and gone to work because his mother had been hanging on the edge of a nervous breakdown. He'd always planned on going back to college but the spool of time just kept unwinding: he'd met Linda, and they'd fallen in love. And then they'd gotten married and Neil was born four years later, and . . .

Well, that was just the story of life, wasn't it?

There were little flecks of rain on his glasses, caused when the drops ricocheted off the edge of the rolled-down window. Glenn took them off to wipe the lenses with a handkerchief. Without the glasses, everything was kind of fuzzy, but he could still see all right.

His hands were trembling. He was afraid, but not terrified. Funny. He'd thought for sure he'd be scared shitless. Of course, it wasn't time yet. Oh, no. Not yet. He put his glasses back on, drew deeply at his cigarette and let the smoke leak from his mouth. Then he touched the heavy-duty chain cutter that lay on the seat beside him.

Today—the last day of summer—he had brought his own admission ticket to the pool.

Underneath his trousers he was wearing his bathing suit—the red one, the one that Linda said he'd better not wear around the bull up in Howard Mackey's pasture. Glenn smiled grimly. If he hadn't had Linda these past two weeks it might've made him slip right off the deep end. She said they were strong, that they would go on and learn to live with Neil's death, and Glenn had agreed—but that was before he'd started thinking.

That was before he'd started reading and studying about the Parnell Park swimming pool.

That was before he *knew*.

After Neil had drowned, the town council had closed the pool and park. Neil had been its third victim of the summer; back in June a girl named Wanda Shackleford had died in the pool, and on the fourth of July it had been Tom Dunnigan. Neil had known Wanda Shackleford. And Glenn remembered that they'd talked about the incident at home one night.

"Seventeen years old!" Glenn had said, reading from a copy of the Barrimore Crossing *Courier*. "What a waste!" He was sitting in his Barcalounger in the den, and Linda was on the sofa doing her needlepoint picture for Sue Ann Moore's birthday. Neil was on the floor in a comfortable sprawl, putting together a plastic model of a space ship he'd bought at Brookhill Mall that afternoon. "Says here that she and a boy named Paul Buckley decided to climb the fence and go swimming around midnight." He glanced over at Linda. "Is that Alex Buckley's boy? The football player?"

"I think so. Do you know, Neil?"

"Yeah. Paul Buckley's a center for Grissom High." Neil glued a triangular weapons turret together and put it aside to dry, then turned to face his father. Like Glenn, the boy was thin and lanky and wore glasses. "Wanda Shackleford was his girlfriend. She would've been a senior next year. What else does it say?"

"It's got a few quotes from Paul Buckley and the policeman who pulled the girl's body out. Paul says they'd had a six pack and then decided to go swimming. He says he never even knew she was gone until he started calling her and she didn't answer. He thought she was playing a trick on him." He offered his son the paper.

"I can't imagine wanting to swim in dark water," Linda said. Her pleasant oval face was framed with pale blond hair, and her eyes were hazel, the same color as Neil's. She concentrated on making a tricky stitch and then looked up. "That's the first one."

"The first one? What do you mean?"

Linda shrugged uneasily. "I don't know. Just . . . well they say things happen in threes." She returned to her work. "I think the City should fill in that swimming pool."

"Fill in the *pool?*" There was alarm in Neil's voice. "Why?"

"Because last June the Happer boy drowned in it, remember? It happened the first weekend school was out. Thank God we weren't there to see it. And two summers before that, the McCarrin girl drowned in four feet of water. The lifeguard didn't even see her go down before somebody stepped on her." She shivered and looked at Glenn. "Remember?"

Glenn drew on his cigarette, staring through the rain-streaked windshield at the pool. "Yes," he said softly. "I remember." But at the time, he'd told Linda that people—especially kids—drowned in pools, ponds and lakes every summer. People even drown in their own bathtubs! He'd said. The city shouldn't close Parnell Park pool and deprive the people of Barrimore Crossing, Leeds, Cooks Springs and the other surrounding communities. Without Parnell Park, folks would have to drive either to Birmingham or go swimming in the muddy waters of nearby Logan Martin lake on a hot summer afternoon!

Still, he'd remembered that a man from Leeds had drowned in the deep end the summer before Gil McCarrin's daughter died. And hadn't two or three other people drowned there as well?

"You think you're so damned smart," Glenn whispered. "But I know. You killed my son, and by God you're going to pay."

A sullen breeze played over the pool, and Glenn imagined he could hear the water giggle. Off in the distance he was sure he heard Neil's voice, floating to him through time and space: "It killed me, Dad! I didn't drown . . . I didn't drown . . . I didn't . . . I—"

Glenn clamped a hand to his forehead and squeezed. Sometimes that made the ghostly voice go away, and this time it worked. He was getting a whopper of a headache, and he opened the glove compartment and took a half-full bottle of Excedrin from it. He popped it open, put a tablet on his tongue and let it melt.

Today was the last day of August, and tomorrow morning the city workmen would come and open the big circular metal-grated drain down in the twelve-foot depths of the deep end. An electric pump would flood the water through pipes that had been laid down in 1945, when the pool was first dug out. The water would continue for more than two miles, until it emptied into a cove on Logan Martin lake. Glenn knew the route that water would take very well, because he'd studied the yellowed engineering diagrams in Barrimore Crossing's City Hall. And then, the last week of May, when the heat had come creeping back and summer was about to blaze like a nova, the pipes would start pumping Logan Martin lake water back through another system of filtration tanks and sanitation filters and when it spilled into the Parnell Park swimming pool it would be fresh, clean and sparkling.

But it would *not* be lifeless.

Glenn chewed a second Excedrin, crushed his cigarette out in the ashtray. This was the day. Tomorrow would be too late. Because tomorrow, the thing that lurked in the public swimming pool would slither away down the drain and get back to the lake where it would wait in the mud for another summer season and the beckoning rhythm of the pump.

Glenn's palms were wet. He wiped them on his trousers. Tom Dunnigan had drowned in the deep end on the fourth of July, during the big annual celebration and barbecue. Glenn and Linda had been eating sauce-sloppy barbecues when they'd heard the commotion at the pool, and Linda had screamed, "Oh my God! *Neil!*"

But it was not Neil who lay on his stomach as the lifeguard tried to force breath back into the body. Neil had been doing cannonballs off the high dive when Tom's wife had shouted for help. The pool had been crowded with people, but no one had seen Tom Dunnigan slip under; he had not cried out, had not even left a ripple in the water. Glenn got close enough through the onlookers to see Tom's body as the lifeguard worked on him. Tom's eyes were open, and water was running between the pale blue lips. But Glenn had found himself staring at a small, circular purple bruise at the back of Tom's neck, almost at the base of the brain; the bruise was pinpricked with scarlet, as if tiny veins in the skin had been ruptured. He'd wondered what could have caused a bruise like that, but it was so small it certainly wasn't important. Then the ambulance attendants wheeled Tom away, covered with a sheet, and the pool closed down for a week.

It was later—much later—that Glenn realized the bruise could've been a bite mark.

He'd been feeding a chameleon in the pet store when the lizard, which had turned the exact shade of green as the grass at the bottom of his tank, had decided to give him a bite on his finger. A chameleon has no teeth, but the pressure of the lizard's mouth had left a tiny circular mark that faded almost at once. Still the little mark bothered Glenn until he'd realized what it reminded him of.

He'd never really paid much attention to the chameleon before that, but suddenly he was intrigued by how it changed colors so quickly, from grass-green to the tan shade of the sand heaped up in the tank's corner. Glenn put a large gray rock in there as well, and soon the chameleon would climb up on it and bloom gray; in that state, he would be invisible but for the tiny, unblinking black circles of his eyes.

"I know what you are," Glenn whispered. "Oh, yeah. I sure do."

The light was fading. Glenn looked in the rear seat to check his gear: a snorkel, underwater mask, and fins. On the floorboard was an underwater light—a large flashlight sealed in a clear plastic enclosure with an upraised red off-on switch. Glenn had driven to the K-Mart in Birmingham to buy the equipment in the sporting goods department. No one knew him there. And wrapped up in a yellow towel in the back seat was his major purchase. He reached over for it, carefully picked it up, and put it across his lap. Then he began to unfold the towel, and there it was—clean, bright, and deadly.

"Looks wicked, doesn't it?" the K-Mart clerk had asked.

Glenn had agreed that it did. But then, it suited his needs.

"You couldn't get *me* underwater," the clerk had said. "Nossir! I like my feet on solid ground! What do you catch with that thing?"

"Big game," Glenn had told him. "So big you wouldn't believe it."

He ran his hands over the cool metal of the spear gun in his lap. He'd read all the warnings and instructions, and the weapon's barbed spear was ready to fire. All he had to do was move a little lever with his thumb to unhook the safety, and then squeezing the trigger was the same as any other gun. He'd practiced on a pillow in the basement, late at night when Linda was asleep. She'd really think he was crazy if she found what was left of that tattered old thing.

But she thought he was out of his mind anyway, so what did it matter? Ever since he'd told her what he knew was true, she'd looked at him differently. It was in her eyes. She thought he'd slipped right off the deep end.

"We'll see about that." There was cold sweat on his face now, because the time was near. He started to get out of the station wagon, then froze. His heart was pounding. A police car had turned into the parking lot, and was heading toward him.

Oh, Jesus! he thought. No! He visualized Linda on the phone to the police: "Officer, my husband's gone crazy! I don't know what he'll do next. He's stopped going to work, he has nightmares all the time and can't sleep, and he thinks there's a monster in the Parnell Park swimming pool! He thinks a monster killed our son, and he won't see a doctor or talk to anybody else about—"

The police car was getting closer. Glenn hastily wrapped the towel around the spear gun, put it down between the seat and the door. He laid the chain cutter on the floorboard and then the police car was pulling up right beside him and all he could do was sit rigidly and smile.

"Having trouble, sir?" the policeman on the passenger side asked through his rolled-down window.

"No. No trouble. Just sitting here." Glenn heard his voice tremble. His smile felt so tight his face was about to rip.

The policeman suddenly started to get out of the car, and Glenn knew he would see the gear on the back seat. "I'm fine!" Glenn protested. "Really!" But the police car's door was opening and the man was about to walk over and see—

"Hey, is that *you*, Mr. Calder?" the policeman sitting behind the wheel asked. The other one hesitated.

"Yes. I'm Glenn Calder."

"I'm Mike Ward. I bought a cocker spaniel puppy from you at the first of the summer. Gave it to my little girl for her birthday. Remember?"

"Uh . . . yes! Sure." Glenn recalled him now. "Yes! How's the puppy?"

"Fine. We named him Bozo because of those big floppy feet. I'll tell you, I never knew a puppy so small could eat so much!"

Glenn strained to laugh. He feared his eyes must be bulging with inner pressure. Mike Ward was silent for a few seconds, and then he said something to the other man that Glenn couldn't make out. The second policeman got back into the car and closed the door, and Glenn released the breath he'd been holding.

"Everything okay, Mr. Calder?" Mike asked; "I mean . . . I know about your son, and—"

"I'm fine!" Glenn said. "Just sitting here. Just thinking." His head was about to pound open.

"We were here the day it happened," Mike told him. "I'm really sorry."

"Thank you." The whole, hideous scene unfolded again in Glenn's mind: he remembered looking up from his Sports Illustrated magazine and seeing Neil going down the aluminum ladder on the left side of the pool, down at the deep end. "I hope he's careful," Linda had fretted and then she'd called to him. "Be careful!" Neil had waved and gone on down the ladder into the sparkling blue water.

There had been a lot of people there that afternoon. It had been one of the hottest days of the summer.

And then Glenn remembered that Linda suddenly set aside her needle-point, her face shaded by the brim of her straw hat, and said the words he could never forget: *"Glenn? I don't see Neil anymore."*

Something about the world had changed in that moment. Time had been distorted and the world had cracked open, and Glenn had seen the horror that lies so close to the surface.

They brought Neil's body up and tried mouth-to-mouth resuscitation, but he was dead. Glenn could tell that right off. He was dead. And when they turned his body over to try to pound the life back into him, Glenn had seen the small purple bruise at the back of his son's neck, almost at the base of the brain.

Oh God, Glen had thought. *Something stole the life right out of him.*

And from that moment on, maybe he *had* gone crazy. Because he'd looked across the surface of the pool, and he had realized something very odd.

There was no aluminum ladder on the left side of the pool down at the deep end. On the pool's right side there was a ladder—but not on the left.

"He was a good boy," Glenn told the two policemen. There was still a fixed smile on his face, and he could not make it let go. "His mother and I loved him very, very much."

"Yes sir. Well . . . I guess we'll go on, then. You sure you're all right? You . . . uh . . . haven't been drinking, have you?"

"Nope. Clean as a whistle. Don't you worry about me, I'll go home soon. Wouldn't want to get Linda upset, would I?"

"No sir. Take care, now." Then the police car backed up, turned around in the parking lot and drove away along the wooded road.

Glenn had a splitting headache. He chewed a third Excedrin, took a deep breath, and reached down for the chain cutter. Then he got out of the car, walked to the admissions gate and cleaved the chain that locked it. The chain rattled to the concrete, and the gate swung open.

And now there was nothing between him and the monster in the swimming pool. He returned to the car and threw the clippers inside, shucked off his shoes, socks and trousers. He let them fall in a heap beside the station wagon, but he kept his blue-striped shirt on. It had been a present from Neil. Then he carried his mask, fins and snorkel into the pool area, walked the length of the pool and laid the gear on a bleacher. Rain pocked the dark surface, and on the pool's bottom were the black lines of swimming lanes, sometimes used for area swim-meets Ceramic tiles on the bottom made a pattern of dark blue, aqua and pale green.

There were thousands of places for it to hide, Glenn reasoned. It could be lying along a black line, or compressed flat and smooth like a stingray on one of the colored tiles. He looked across the pool where the false ladder had been—the monster could make itself resemble a ladder, or it could curl up and emulate the drain, or lie flat and still in a gutter waiting for a human form to come close enough. Yes. It had many shapes, many colors, many tricks. But the water had not yet gone back to the lake, and the monster that had killed Neil was still in there. Somewhere.

He walked back to the car, got the underwater light and the spear gun. It was getting dark, and he switched the light on.

He wanted to make sure the thing found him once he was in the water—and the light should draw it like a neon sign over a roadside diner.

Glenn sat on the edge of the pool and put on his fins. He had to remove his glasses to wear the facemask; everything was out of focus, but it was the best he could do. He fit the snorkel into his mouth, hefted the underwater light in his left hand, and slowly eased himself over the edge.

I'm ready, he told himself. He was shaking, couldn't stop. The water, untended for more than two weeks, was dirty—littered with Coke cups, cigarette butts, dead waterbugs. The carcass of a bluejay floated past his face, and Glenn thought that it appeared to have been crushed.

He turned over on his stomach, put his head underwater, and kicked off against the pool's side, making a splash that sounded jarringly loud. He began to drift out over the drain, directing the light's yellow beam through the water. Around and beneath him was gray murk. But the light suddenly glinted off something, and Glenn arched down through the chill to see what it was—a beer can on the bottom. Still, the monster could be anywhere. *Anywhere.* He slid to the surface, expelling water through the snorkel like a whale. Then he continued slowly across the pool, his heartbeat pounding in his ears and the sound of his breathing like a hellish bellows through the snorkel. In another moment his head bumped the other side of the pool. He drifted in another direction, guiding himself with an occasional thrust of a fin.

Come on, damn you! Glenn thought. I know you're here!

But nothing moved in the depths below. He shone the light around, seeking a shadow.

I'm not crazy, he told himself. I'm really not. His head was hurting again, and his mask was leaking, the water beginning to creep up under his nose. Come out and fight me, damn you! I'm in your element now, you bastard! Come on!

Linda had asked him to see a doctor in Birmingham. She said she'd go with him, and the doctor would listen. There was no monster in the swimming pool, she'd said. And if there *was* where had it come from?

Glenn knew. Since Neil's death, Glenn had done a lot of thinking and reading. He'd gone back through the *Courier* files, searching for any information about the Parnell Park swimming pool. He'd found that, for the last five years, at least one person had died in the pool every summer. Before that you had to go back eight years to find a drowning victim—an elderly man who'd already suffered one heart attack.

But it had been in a copy of the Birmingham *News,* dated October tenth six years ago, that Glenn had found his answer.

The article's headline read *"Bright Light" Frightens Lake Residents.*

On the night of October ninth, a sphere of blue fire had been seen by a dozen people who lived around Logan Martin lake. It had flashed across the sky, making a noise—as one resident put it—"like steam whistling out of a cracked radiator." The blue light had gone down into the lake, and for the next two days, dead fish washed up on shore.

You found the pipes that brought you up into our swimming pool, didn't you? Glenn thought as he explored the gray depths with his light. Maybe you came from somewhere that's all water, and you can't live on land. Maybe you can suck the life out of a human body just as fast and easy as some of us step on ants. Maybe that's what you live on—but by God I've come to stick you, and I'll find you if I have to search all—

Something moved.

Down in the gloom, below him. Down near the drain. A shadow . . . *something.* Glenn wasn't sure what it was. He just sensed a slow, powerful uncoiling.

He pushed the spear gun's safety off with his thumb. He couldn't see anything, dead bugs floated through the light like a dust storm, and a sudden newspaper page drifted up from the bottom, flapped in his face and sank out of sight again. Glenn's nerves were near snapping, and he thought with a touch of hysterical mirth that it might have been an obituaries page.

He lowered his head and descended.

Murky clouds swirled around him. He probed with the light, alert for another movement. The water felt thick, oily; a contaminated feel. He continued to slide down into the depths, and they closed over him. His fins stirred more pool silt, and the clouds refused the light. He stayed down as long as he could, until his lungs began to heave, and then he rose toward the surface like a flabby arrow.

When he reached the top, something grasped his head.

It was a cold, rubbery thing, and Glenn knew it was the grip of death. He couldn't help it; he shrieked around the snorkel's mouthpiece, twisted violently in the water and caught sight of slick green flesh. His frantic movement dislodged the facemask, and water flooded in. He was blinded, water was pressing up his nostrils and the thing was wrapped around his shoulders. He heard his gurgling underwater scream, flailed the thing off him and thrashed desperately away.

Glenn kicked to the edge of the pool, raising geysers. The aluminum ladder was in front of him, and he reached up to haul himself out.

No! he thought, wrenching his hand back before it touched the metal—or what was supposed to pass as metal. That's how it had killed Neil. It had emulated the other ladder and entwined itself around Neil as he entered the water, and it had taken him under and killed him in an instant while everyone else was laughing and unaware.

He swam away from the ladder and hung to the gutter's edge. His body convulsed, water gurgling from his nostrils. His dangling legs were vulnerable, and he drew them up against his chest, so fast he kneed himself in the chin. Then he dared to look around and aim the light at the monster.

About ten feet away, bouncing in the chop of his departure, was a child's deflated rubber ring, the green head of a seahorse with a grinning red mouth lying in the water. Glenn laughed, and spat up more of the pool. Brave man, he thought. Real brave. Oh Jesus, if Linda had been here to see this! I was scared shitless of a kid's toy! His laughter got louder, more strident. He laughed until it dawned on him that he was holding his facemask's strap around his right wrist, and his right hand gripped the gutter.

In his left hand was the underwater light.

He had lost his snorkel. And the spear gun.

His laughter ceased on a broken note.

Fear shot up his spine. He squinted, saw the snorkel bobbing on the surface five or six feet away. The spear gun had gone to the bottom.

He didn't think about getting out of the pool. His body just did it, scrabbling up over the sloshing gutter to the concrete, where he lay on his belly in the rain and shivered with terror.

Without the spear gun, he had no chance. I can use the chain cutter, he thought. Snap the bastard's head off! But no, no: the chain cutter needed two hands, and he had to have a hand free to hold the light. He thought of driving back to Birmingham, buying another spear gun, but it occurred to him that if he got in the car and left Parnell Park, his guts might turn to jelly on the highway and Neil's voice would haunt him: *"You know I didn't drown, don't you, Dad? You know I didn't . . . "*

He might get in that car and drive away and never come back, and today was the last day of summer, and when they opened the drain in the morning, the monster would go back to the lake and await another season of victims.

He knew what he had to do. Must do. Must. He had to put the facemask back on, retrieve the snorkel, and go down after that spear gun. He lay with his cheek pressed against the concrete and stared at the black water; how many summer days had seen him in that pool, basking like a happy whale? As a kid, he couldn't wait for the clock of seasons to turn around and point him to this pool—and now, everything had changed. Everything, and it could never be the same again.

Neil was dead, killed by the monster in the swimming pool. The creature had killed part of him, too, Glenn realized. Killed the part that saw this place as a haven of youthful dreams, an anchor-point of memories. And next summer, when the monster came back, someone else's dreams would die as well.

He had to go down and get the spear gun. It was the only way.

It took him another minute or so to make his body respond to his mind's command. The chill shocked his skin again as he slipped over the side; he moved slowly, afraid of noise or splashes. Then he put the mask on, swam carefully to the snorkel with his legs drawn up close to the surface; he bit down hard on the mouthpiece, thinking suddenly that if there was really a monster here it could have emulated the snorkel, and both of them would've gotten a very nasty surprise. But the snorkel remained a snorkel, as Glenn blew the water out of it.

If there was really a monster here. The thought caught him like a shock. *If.* And there it was. What if Linda was right? he asked himself. What if there's nothing here, and I'm just treading dirty water? What if everything I've thought is wrong—and I'm losing my mind? No, no, I'm right. I know I am. Dear God. I *have* to be right.

He took a deep breath, exhaled it. The collapsed green seahorse seemed to be drifting toward him again. Was its grin wider? Did it show a glint of teeth? Glenn watched the rubber ring move through the light's beam, and then he took another breath and slid downward to find the spear gun.

His thrashing had stirred up more debris. The water seemed alive with reaching, darting shadows as he kicked to the bottom and skimmed along it, his belly brushing the tiles. The light gleamed off another beer can, off a scatter of pennies left by children who'd been diving for them. Something bony lay on the bottom, and Glenn decided it was a chicken drumstick somebody had tossed over the fence. He kept going, slowly swinging his light in an arc before him.

The dirty clouds opened under his waving hand, and more metal glinted. Another crushed beer can—no, no, it wasn't. His heart kicked. He fanned the murk away, and caught sight of the spear gun's handle. Gripped it in his right hand with a flood of relief. Thank God! he thought. Now he felt powerful again, and the shadows seemed to flee before him. He turned in a circle, illuminating the darkness at his back. Nothing there. Nothing. To his right the newspaper page flapped like a manta ray, and to his left the clouds parted for a second to show him a glimpse of the drain. He was in the twelve-foot depth. The deep end, that place where parents warned their kids not to go.

And about three feet from the drain lay something else. Something that made Glenn's throat catch and bubbles spill from his nostrils.

And that was when the thing that had taken the shape of a spear gun in his hand burst into its true form, all camouflage done. Ice-white tentacles tightened around Glenn's wrist as his fingers spasmed open.

The bubbles of a scream exploded from Glenn's mouth, but his jaws clamped shut before all his air was lost. As he tried to lunge upward, a third and fourth tentacle—pale, almost translucent and as tough as piano-wire—shot out, squeezing into the drain's grate and locked there.

Glenn fought furiously, saw the monster's head taking shape from its gossamer ghost of a body; the head was triangular, like a cobra's, and from it emerged a single scarlet, blazing eye with a golden pupil. Below the eye was a small round mouth full of suction pads like the underside of a starfish. The mouth was pulsating rapidly, and began to turn from white to crimson.

The single eye stared into Glenn's face with clinical interest. And suddenly the thing's neck elongated and the mouth streaked around for the back of Glenn's neck.

He'd known that's where it was going to strike, and he'd flung his left arm up to ward off the blow an instant before it came. The mouth sealed to his shoulder like a hot kiss, hung there for a second and withdrew with a *sputt* of distaste. The monster's head weaved back and forth as Glenn hunched his shoulders up to protect the back of his neck and spinal cord. His lungs heaved; his mouth was full of water, the snorkel spun away in the turbulence. Water was streaming into his mask, and the light had dropped from the fingers of his left hand and lay on the bottom, sending rays through the roiling clouds like a weird sunset through an alien atmosphere.

The thing's head jerked forward, its mouth aiming at Glenn's forehead; he jerked aside as much as he could, and the mouth hit the facemask glass. Glenn felt tentacles slithering around his body, drawing him closer, trying to crack his ribs and squeeze the last of his air out. He pressed his left hand to the back of his neck. The monster's eye moved in the socket, seeking a way to the juices it craved. The mouth was bright red now, and deep in the folds of its white body, Glenn saw a crimson mass that pulsated at the same rhythm as its mouth.

Its heart, he realized. Its heart.

The blood thundered in his head. His lungs were seizing, about to grab for water. He looked down, saw the real spear gun a few feet away. He had no time for even a second's hesitation, and he knew that if he failed he was dead.

He took his hand away from the back of his neck and reached for the gun, his own heartbeat about to blow the top of his skull off.

The creature's head came around like a whip. The suckers fixed to the base of Glenn's brain, and for an instant there was an agony that he thought would end only when his head split open; but then there was a numbing, floating, novocained sensation, and Glenn felt himself drifting toward death.

But he had the spear gun in his hand.

The monster shivered with hungry delight. From between the suction cups tiny needle-like teeth began to drill through the pores of its prey's flesh, toward the spinal cord at the base of the brain.

One part of Glenn wanted to give up. Wanted to drift and sleep. Wanted to join Neil and the others who had gone to sleep in this pool. It would be so easy . . . so easy . . . But the part of him that clung to life and Linda and the world beyond this pool made him lift the gun, press the barbed spear against the monster's pulsing heart and squeeze the trigger.

Sharp, head-clearing pain ripped through him. A black cloud of blood spilled into the water. The spear had pierced the creature's body and gone into his own forearm. The monster released his neck, its head whipping and the eye wide and stunned. Glenn saw that the spear had gone right through the thing's heart—if that's indeed what the organ was—and then he wrenched at his arm with all his remaining strength. The spear and the heart tore out of the monster's writhing body. The pupil of its eye had turned from gold to black, and its tattered body began to ooze through the drain's grate like strands of opaque jelly.

Glenn's lungs lurched. Pulled in water. He clawed toward the surface, his arm puffing blood. The surface was so far, so terribly far. The deep end had him, was not going to let him go. He strained upward, as dark gnawed at him and his lungs hitched and the water began to gurgle in his throat.

And then his head emerged into night air, and as he drew a long, shuddering breath he heard himself cry out like a victorious beast.

He didn't remember reaching the pool's side. Still would not trust the ladder. He tried to climb out and fell back several times. There seemed to be a lot of blood, and water still rattled in his lungs. He didn't know how long it was, but finally he pulled himself out and fell on his back on the wet concrete.

Sometime later, he heard a hissing sound.

He wearily lifted his head, and coughed more water out. At the end of the spear, the lump of alien flesh was sizzling. The heart shriveled until it resembled a piece of coal—and then it fell apart like black ash, and there was nothing left.

"Got you," Glenn whispered. "Got you . . . didn't I?"

He lay on his back for a long time, as the blood continued to stream from the wound in his arm, and when he opened his eyes again he could see the stars.

"Crazy fella busted in here last night," one of the overall-clad workmen said to the other as he lit a cigarette. "Heard it on the news this mornin'. Radio said a fella broke in here and went swimmin'. That's why the chain's cut off the gate."

"Is that right? Lord, Jimmy, this is some crazy world!" The second workman, whose name was Leon, sat on the concrete beside the little brick enclosure housing an iron wheel that opened the drain and a switch that operated the electric pump. They'd spent an hour cleaning the pool out before they'd turned the wheel, and this was the first chance to sit down and rest. They'd filled a garbage bag with beer cans, dead bugs, and other debris that had collected at the bottom. Now the water was draining out, the electric pump making a steady thumping sound. It was the first morning of September, and the sun was shining through the trees in Parnell Park.

"Some folks are just born fools," Jimmy offered, nodding sagely. "Radio said that fella shot himself with a *spear*. Said he was ravin' and crazy and the policeman who found him couldn't make heads or butts outta anythin' he was sayin'."

"Musta wanted to go swimmin' awful bad. Hope they put him in a nice asylum with a swimmin' pool."

Both men thought that was very funny, and they laughed. They were still laughing when the electric pump made a harsh gasping moan and died.

"Oh, my achin' ass!" Jimmy stood up, flicked his cigarette to the concrete. "We musta missed somethin'! Drain's done clogged for sure!" He went over to the brick enclosure and picked up a long-handled, telescoping tool with a hooked metal tip on the end. "Let's see if we can dig whatever it is out. If we can't, then somebody named Leon is goin' swimmin'."

"Uh uh, not me! I don't swim in nothin' but a bathtub!"

Jimmy walked to the edge of the low diving board and reached into the water with his probe. He telescoped the handle out and began to dig down at the drain's grate, felt the hook slide into something that seemed . . . rubbery. He brought the hook up and stood gawking at what dangled from it.

Whatever it was, it had an eye.

"Go . . . call somebody," he managed to tell Leon. "Go call somebody right *quick!*"

Leon started running for the pay phone at the shuttered concessions stand.

"Hey, Leon!" Jimmy called, and the other man stopped. "Tell 'em I don't know what it is . . . but tell 'em I think it's dead! And tell 'em we found it in the deep end!"

Leon ran on to make the phone call.

The electric pump suddenly kicked on again, and with a noise like a heartbeat began to return water to the lake.

The Serpent
and the Hatchet Gang
F. Brett Cox

The serpent in the sea was nothing compared to the serpent in the hearts of men. The serpent in the sea may or may not find you, Esther Lane said, may or may not be there at all. But the corruption in a man's heart, the malicious weakness that disguises itself as passion and autonomy, then drowns itself and all around it in liquor and violence and failure—that is inescapable. Its effects can be lessened, its power can be curbed, but it can never be banished entirely. Put the men in chains and pour their liquor out on the ground, she continued, and they will still find a way to do you harm. The serpent in their hearts will not be defeated. Better to take your chances with the monster offshore.

Julia Brooks listened attentively. The others, though steadfast in their commitment, were long used to Esther's grand pronouncements and greeted them placidly, nodding in agreement as they waited for the old woman's rhetoric to run its course. But to Julia, the youngest among them, Esther's words flowed like the tide into Sandy Bay, and as they all sat—in three cases, stood—crammed liked netted mackerel into Rachel and Stephen Perkins' parlor, the temperate July night turned sweltering in such close quarters, she waited eagerly for Esther to continue.

Instead, there was the sound of an elderly throat clearing, and Julia turned with the rest of them to see Hannah Jumper look up from her knitting. "Don't say that, Esther. The whole point is to pour the liquor out. Ain't that why we're here?"

Esther looked momentarily annoyed, but quickly composed herself and said, "Of course, Hannah. I do get carried away sometimes. Of course we remain united in our purpose. Don't we, everyone?"

They all voiced their agreement. Tonight, only the leaders gathered for one last coordinated review of their plan. But come tomorrow, fully sixty of the women of Rockport, Massachusetts, would bring moral and economic sense back to the community. The half-hearted attempts of the town's agents to regulate liquor sales had been a miserable failure, and it was now up to the women who bore the worst of the burden, and the handful of men who understood what was at stake, to deal themselves with this public nuisance. No more men lying about in drunken indolence when the winter storms and summer doldrums kept the fishing boats docked; no more backbreaking grocery bills whose main item was rum. No more bruises to hide, Julia thought. No more knowing the back of your husband's hand better than his heart.

They had been meeting for weeks, in secret. And while Esther's eloquence kept them inspired, Hannah kept them going. She was not well-spoken, and seventy-five years old in the bargain. But it was she who had called the first meeting, she who had kept record as the conspirators discovered, and chalked, with white X's that would not be seen by those not looking for them, every spot in Rockport where liquor would be found. It was Hannah who had invoked their Revolutionary ancestors, the twenty women who had banded together some eighty years back and raided Colonel Foster's supply store in Gloucester after their men marched off to Bunker Hill promising to bring back liberty but leaving their fishing boats idle and their families improvident and shivering. And it was Hannah who convinced them that hatchets were the only sufficient instrument for dispatching, if not the men who defied decency and the law, at least the wretched barrels of rum.

Mary Hale, at thirty-seven the next youngest after Julia, had objected. "Is there not too great a risk of injury? We don't want anyone to get hurt, do we?"

"Desperate cases need desperate remedies," replied Hannah, and continued with her knitting.

Now, on the eve of their action, the old woman sat calmly, the motion of her needles and yarn so smooth and continuous it scarcely seemed motion at all. Although she sat to the side, against the wall, the room seemed centered around her.

"But why all this talk of sea serpents?" asked Stephen Perkins, leaning forward from his perch on the edge of the room's only sofa. "Haven't we enough to do without digging up all that nonsense?"

"I agree," said Mary Knowlton. Her husband had enjoyed great success transporting stone south to Boston, prosperity that set her apart from the fishermen's wives and daughters who filled the room; some were surprised that she had joined enthusiastically in their conspiracy. But when Mrs. Knowlton was Mary Clarkson she had been a schoolteacher, and Julia, one of her students, still remembered the impromptu temperance lectures with which the young teacher would punctuate even a math lesson. "Do we want to be laughed at again? To the rest of the world we might as well have been Indians chasing spirits in the woods, and the nineteenth century might as well never have arrived. What we're doing is too important—"

"I was scarcely speaking publicly for the Boston papers," said Esther. "I merely invoked the serpent as a figure to dramatize my point. We're gathered here, after all, because of the depravity of men—"

"We're gathered here because of rum," Hannah said without looking up from her work. "Rum is real. So's our hatchets. Let's stick to them."

"Please, friends," said Mary Hale, "Hannah, Esther—we're all here for the same reason. Let us not divide ourselves from ourselves." She stood and brushed straight the skirt of her grey dress. There were some of the younger matrons in town who had left their Puritan ancestors firmly behind. Betsey Andrews, the current schoolteacher, periodically took the steamboat down to Boston to inspect the latest fashions, while Judy MacQuestion was rumored to own at least one hat imported from Paris. Mary was not among their number: the neatness of her clothing was matched only by its plainness. "Mrs. Knowlton is right. The task before us is too important. Esther, we all admire your eloquence, and are grateful for it. Who of us could have framed the issues so compellingly? How many will there be on the streets tomorrow because of your persuasion?" Esther smiled and nodded her head every so slightly.

"And if Esther's silver tongue has put people in the streets, it is Hannah's courage and strength that has put us all in this room. Please don't worry, Hannah. We know what needs to be done, and we shall do it."

Hannah did not reply. They all knew by now that, in a group at least, Hannah would speak only to prod forward or to object; her silence testified that the disagreement was settled. Mary sat and smoothed her skirts again.

"Well, then," said Mr. Perkins. "Are we concluded, then?"

They agreed that, barring unforeseen circumstances, this would be their last meeting; the plan was set and would be implemented tomorrow.

As they adjourned, James Babson, who had kept silent throughout, offered to escort Julia home. As an agent of the Granite Company, Mr. Babson had access to all manner of tools and an income not dependent on the vagaries of the ocean; both made him an invaluable ally. He was also corpulent and ill-kept, and the breath that whistled through two missing teeth was foul. Julia had had to accustom herself to such attentions in the two years since her husband's ship had returned to port with its flag at half-staff, and she had no real reason to consider Mr. Babson's offer as anything other than honorable.

Still. "Many's the time, ma'am, when I saw your late husband, God rest him, with his hand so reverently on your arm as you walked home of an evening. I would be honored to assume that duty—even if only momentarily, this evening," he added hastily.

Julia instinctively leaned away from him, then steadied herself, sighed, and was about to agree when Hannah stepped in. "Walk home with me, child. I reckon I could use the company."

Hannah had no more need of company, Julia believed, than did Squam Lighthouse. But she quickly accepted the old woman's offer and left Mr. Babson standing in the middle of the parlor, Esther heading casually but directly toward him, already talking.

The night felt almost chilly after the warmth of the overcrowded parlor, and Julia pulled her shawl close about her shoulders. Inside, Hannah's presence had filled the room; outside, her great height remained—Julia came barely to the old woman's shoulder—but, free of the press of walls and bodies, Hannah seemed reduced, distant. It was like walking with a scarecrow, Julia thought, although a most strong and determined one.

As they made their way down High Street, Julia, still full of the meeting and the righteousness of their cause, reiterated much of the evening's discussion. Hannah remained silent, her heavy shoes clopping on the cobblestones. When they reached the Inner Harbor, rather than turning right to continue to their respective homes, Hannah stopped, facing the water. Julia followed the old woman's gaze into the harbor. The fishing boats rested at their moorings, looking like charcoal drawings beneath the dim light of the half moon. They had not been out to sea for over a month. On one of the larger boats, at the outer edge of the harbor, several figures moved around the deck. Julia could not make them out individually, but she heard rough laughter, the shattering of glass, a bellowing voice: "She was mine, damn ya! Who said you could get under her skirts afore me?" More laughter, and the sawing of a fiddle. Although she knew it was impossible at such a distance, she could almost swear she smelled their liquor across the brine.

Julia shuddered. "After tomorrow perhaps we'll have less of that."

Hannah stared out past the boats and the profanity. Julia looked up at her. For a moment, the old woman's face was obliterated by the darkness, and she looked like her bonnet and her dress and nothing else. "They should stay on the boats," Hannah said. "They should stay on the ocean. They can't harm the ocean."

"Maybe the serpent will get them," Julia said, and then instantly remembered Hannah's harsh dismissal of Esther at the meeting. "Oh, I know, Hannah, it's just nonsense, forgive me."

Hannah said nothing in response. Then she turned sharply away and said, "Long past time we were home, child."

They proceeded down Mt. Pleasant Street, past Hannah's house. Julia tried to get Hannah to stop and let her make the remaining short walk on her own, but the old woman refused. As they turned down Long Cove Lane, Hannah asked, somewhat to Julia's surprise, if the chamomile she had sent to Julia's Aunt Martha had helped with her digestive difficulties. The women of Rockport paid Hannah to mend their dresses, but far more valuable, and free in the bargain, was the harvest of Hannah's herb garden. Horseradish for a sore throat, catnip to sleep, pennyroyal for a chill, pipsissewa leaves for the heart.

Julia replied that her aunt was much better and expressed her admiration for Hannah's skills. "I wish I could cultivate herbs as well as you. I tried planting some rosemary last season and it just didn't take."

"Put rosemary close to the high-water mark. It gets its strength from the sea."

At Julia's doorstep, Hannah bade the young woman good night. "Rest well, child. You'll need all your wits about you tomorrow." Julia promised that she would and watched the old woman retrace her path down the street and disappear around the corner.

Later, with the lamps an hour dark and sleep nowhere close, Julia stood before her open bedroom window. The moon was gone, and the land and the ocean and the horizon were a dark unbroken carpet over the world. But she heard the ocean, and felt it in the breeze that chilled her through her nightclothes, and smelled it. If she opened her mouth, she knew she could taste it.

There was nothing to see, but much to remember. Two years ago next month.

She had heard the stories; everyone had. The summer of 1817, fourteen years before her own birth. Hundreds down in Gloucester, most more reliable than not, had seen it. From Ten Pound Island to Western Harbor they had shielded their children and grabbed their telescopes, or set out in their boats. The reports were almost all the same: fifty to one hundred feet long, thick as a barrel, dark on top, lighter on what of its belly could be seen when it raised itself from the water. A head the size of a horse's. Some claimed it was segmented; others noted its vertical undulations. It could turn on a dime and raced away when approached. Several had tried to kill it, of course, even as one newspaper suggested they should be grateful to it for driving herring into the harbor.

The Linnaean Society of New England had formed a committee—Harvard men, of course—to investigate, but, being too busy living inside their own heads to come and see for themselves, the committee members had sent a list of questions to the Justice of the Peace with a request for him to interview the witnesses and send them the results.

Things might have held steady at that point, or even faded away, but a couple of months later the Colbeys found a humpbacked snake, over a yard long, on the ground near Loblolly Cove. They killed and examined it, and they remembered one or two people claimed to have seen two serpents in the harbor. Could this be offspring? The Linnaeans got hold of it, dissected it, gave it a Latin name, and declared that, well, yes, it might be kin to the creature in the harbor. But then another Harvard man came along and proved that it was just a deformed black snake.

The next summer there were more sightings in the harbor, and things looked as if they were getting heated up again. But when the creature came up to Squam Bar, near the lighthouse, and a Boston captain chased it down in a whaleboat, only to discover that he had harpooned a horse mackerel, most of Cape Ann was ready to forget anything ever happened. The following year, dozens more saw the same thing just off the shore down at Nahant, but by then the Linaaeans had given up, the Boston captain had disappeared, and people were making fun of the gullible Yankees all the way down to Charleston.

They were all just stories Julia had grown up with, and she didn't regard them as anything more, or less. And then she saw it herself.

Her husband Joshua had been out with the boats, and she had not been sorry to see him go. The summer doldrums had lasted longer than usual, giving him more time to drink, and curse the fish because they weren't there, and her because she was. It could have been worse. Abigail Hancock's husband used her so badly that both the town constables had intervened, and Mr. Hancock, after he sobered up, left abruptly for a rumored family in the Maine woods. But the memories of the young man of promise and passion she had married, against the sullen wreck who stared emptily out at the waves as he swigged his rum, were almost as bad as the bruises she managed most of the time to hide.

Almost. A hundred fifty-seven dollars for nine months' work was no life for anyone; she understood, felt his entrapment. But he had no right to take it out on her. He had no right to do that.

She had been out on the rocks at Bearskin Neck in the early morning, looking out into Sandy Harbor. She had emptied the liquor as soon as he left and no longer cared how angry he would be when he returned. It was a clear morning and the sun was warm on her face, but the water still looked hard and grey.

She blinked, and felt as if she had just missed something. She looked intently out into the bay, and seconds later it rose up in front of her.

Immediately, she knew what it was. All the stories she had always heard, with all of their divergent details, now merged and came to life not fifty yards in front of her. It was black, and it undulated vertically through the water, and it did indeed seem about as big around as a barrel, and its head did in fact look about the size of a horse's. Its front end was several feet out of the water, and the sound of its churning and splashing was louder than the tide lapping against the rocks beneath her feet. The serpent splashed and glistened in the sun, and she reached out as if to touch it.

In an unbroken motion, it turned and plunged toward shore. Before she could even consider backing away, it was directly in front of her. It raised itself up from the water, its head level with her own. Its liquid grey eyes regarded her calmly. There was a hissing sound, but not that of a snake; rather of wind blowing through an enclosed space, or her husband's breath beside her when he slept without drinking.

Her heart felt as if it would hammer through her chest, but she was not frightened. At that moment she had no problems; there was nothing in her life but this wonder. She kept her arm outstretched, leaned forward.

And as quickly as it had come to her, it left. By the time she lowered her arm, it was gone. The water seemed scarcely disturbed. She turned away and went back through town to her home.

Two days later came the news that her husband was lost.he wept properly at his funeral and gave his clothes away.

She had never told anyone, ever, what she had seen, not even when it had been sighted a week later out from Loblolly Cove, and later that same month further south near Hull. It was not so much that she feared ridicule as that she wanted to keep the event for herself. She had given everything to her family and her husband while they lived, but that moment at Bearskin Cove, that splash of water and shining strange skin, was hers alone. Let the learned men have their theories, and let the foolish men try to hunt it like a whale. For her, the creature was not a disruption of the natural order; it was a reassurance, a guarantee of possibility.

And she so needed that guarantee. When her grandmother had died, she and Joshua had claimed the old woman's house. (Grandmother had loathed him, thought him beneath her only granddaughter; Joshua swore she had lasted as long as she did solely to keep him out of her home.) Modest as it was, it did for them, and certainly it had for Julia by herself. There was, of course, no pension for a dead fisherman, but there was still a bit left of the small inheritance she had from her parents, and it went farther without Joshua working his way through it a bottle at a time.

But it would not last forever. Sooner or later, Julia knew she would have to choose among gloomy options: join the relatives in Boston whom she barely knew but who had grand visions of her becoming a governess on Beacon Hill; strike off on her own and seek work in the inland factories; or cast her lot with the likes of Mr. Babson. These were not choices; these were sentences for the crime of being a widow.

Now, as she leaned out her open window into the dark, she breathed deeply of the ocean and thought about a new and wonderful possibility: a town without rum. A community of responsible and sober men who cared for their families. Surely in such a place, there would be true choices. She and Hannah and the rest would make it happen. Julia closed the window, buried herself under the bedclothes, and dreamed of swimming with the serpent, giving it sweet herbs from Hannah's garden.

By nine the next morning, Dock Square was more or less awake. The boats languished in the harbor waiting for July to pass and the winds to return, and the men who were about were already in the taverns. The shopkeepers had their doors open for business and what breeze might come off the harbor. But business almost always came from the women, and as Julia waited in front of Deacon Burns' shop, there were none anywhere in sight. Here were two men playing checkers in front of Johnson's Hall hotel; there was a cluster of neighboring merchants discussing the merits of Fillmore's audacious embrace of the Know-Nothings. An isolated scholar took his leisure near the checker players and perused the latest collection of Mr. Emerson's essays.

But where were the women? Julia smiled graciously at the merchants and restrained herself from wringing her hands. Where were they?

Then she saw a figure approaching from School Street, and two more down Broadway. Margaret Thurston, two of the Choate sisters. Then a group turned off High Street, Mary Knowlton among them, and more down Broadway, and when Julia looked up Mt. Pleasant she saw Hannah marching across the cobblestones, her hands hidden beneath the folds of her shawl.

As Julia moved to join the women, there was a commotion down past Jim Brown's shop. She turned and saw what looked like a small battalion moving in her direction, men as well as women. The women marched silently toward Dock Square, but Julia heard the cries of the men: "Watch out! They're coming for the rum! The women are going for the rum shops! Think they'll do it? Never in hell! Oh, yes they will, too! Ha! Let's go! Better hurry, boys!"

They're coming for the rum? How could these men know? She and the others had gone to such lengths to keep the plan secret. But as Julia saw more women treading resolutely toward the square, marching silently past the shouting men, she had a sudden sense of her own naiveté, and of the scope of what was about to happen. Of course others had found out. Not everyone. But enough. How could they not know what the problem was? How could they not see the ruinous effects of the rum in the idle men, in the drawn and haggard faces of the women? She moved quickly to join the others.

By now there must have been two hundred women on the square. Everyone from the meetings, of course, but plenty of others as well. The younger men stood to the harbor side and jeered. At least one woman, whom Julia did not recognize, complained loudly at being caught up in this lawless mob and swore to head straight for the constable's office. A few men were now gathered with the women: Stephen Perkins, Newell Burnham, James Babson—the latter of whom, to Julia's consternation, found her in the crowd, smiled, and tipped his hat. Joe Griffin, who worked for Perkins, waved an American flag.

Julia had expected Hannah to take command, but it was Esther Lane who separated from the crowd and planted herself to speak. Now the men as well as the women fell silent. The sun beat down on their heads as the gulls screamed over the harbor. Julia rearranged her shawl, and prepared for a lengthy discourse.

Esther started to speak, stopped, removed a hand from her shawl to wipe a tear from her eye. Julia marveled at the intensity of the old woman's face:

for once, Esther Lane seemed to be yielding to what she felt, rather than to the sound of her own voice. "We know why we are here," she said, her voice quavering but loud enough for all to hear. "We are here to take back our town and our families and our lives." She paused, removed her other hand from beneath her shawl, and held aloft a hatchet. "Not one bottle left!"

In unison, every woman present produced a hatchet from beneath her shawl and raised it high. Every family in Rockport had one, or more—the common land was now mostly sold off to private hands, but most of the fishermen still cut their own wood as best they could from the ever-thinning landscape. To see them all at once, in the hands of these women, took Julia's breath away. As Joe Griffin waved his flag, Sally Norwood raised the banner she had promised to make: a cotton rectangle she held aloft bore a hatchet in black paint.

Julia held her own weapon over her head. She thought of Joshua and gripped the hatchet tighter. "Not one bottle left!"

With that, Hannah stepped forward beside Esther and shouted, "Let's get to work!"

The young men who had been so noisy before gaped as the women fell into formation, four abreast, and began their march down the street. Julia tensed when she saw the town's two constables, who had but recently arrived, but they looked on with the other men, and did no more to stop the women than they had done to enforce the liquor laws.

As they passed by Deacon Burns' shop, he stood in the doorway, his face twisted with rage. He looked like Joshua used to after a session with the rum, and Julia's step almost faltered. "Shame!" Burns shouted. "Where are your husbands? Are they men? Shame! There's nothing here for you! Go home!"

There was a sudden movement from the marching column, and Betsey Andrews darted toward Burns. Julia was shocked to see that the school-teacher's latest fashion was a skirt that came just below her knee, exposing light yellow bloomers that ruffled down to her shoes. But the lack of a full skirt left her free to maneuver past Burns while holding a hatchet in each hand. She waved to the women, and as most of the column continued down the street, several broke ranks, shoved the deacon aside, and charged into his shop.

Julia followed them in, and they began rolling barrels out into the street, one after the other: rum, brandy, ale, beer. As Burns screamed and cursed in a manner not befitting a leader of the church, the women took their hatchets and went to work. The young men who had followed them from the Square were now cheering: "That's it, girls! Have at it! Damn, look at Burns! Better pour some on the Deacon, ladies—he needs cooling off, by God! Serves him right! Hurrah for the hatchet gang!"

Julia tried to weigh in with her own weapon, but there were too many women ahead of her. The aroma of the spilled liquor was overpowering, and she tried in vain to wipe off the rum that had splashed on her dress. She was mortified by the crude encouragement of the young men and unsettled by the gleam in the eyes of the women as they swung their hatchets down, again and again and again, on Deacon Burns' stock. Their hands were growing bloody, but they did not even seem to notice.

When she heard a voice from inside the shop announce, "That's the last one," Julia moved to rejoin the column. The gang now moved as with a mind of its own: several women would peel off to attack a shop or tavern, then rejoin the column as it wound through the streets. They took care of the Stage Coach Inn, the Laf-a-Lot cottage, Johnson Hall. When they got to Jim Brown's shop, they found him sitting atop a barrel, swearing, daring them to take his livelihood from him. They swept him onto his own front steps, smashed the barrel, and slopped over the foaming ale to get inside. Brown had hidden many bottles, and they found them all.

"Damn you!" Brown cried. "Whores! Devils! What are you trying to do? What do you want? Is this going to makes things better? Will this make the winds blow? Are your hatchets going to fill our ships? Give your men work? I'll be restocked in a month! We all will!"

They brushed past him and moved on to John Hooper's basement, reportedly the largest holdings in town. Julia stepped over a man she recognized as one of Stephen Perkins' crewmen as he lay beneath Brown's steps and tried to catch the dripping ale in his mouth. Mary Hale, her plain dress drenched with alcohol, evidently thought the man injured. She paused and tried to help him up, but he shoved her away.

And so it went for the rest of the morning. They ceased around noon, lining up to drink from the town pump, and then they resumed their work. They had marked many places with their subtle white X's, and they dispatched them all. As they moved through the town, the young men following them were joined by children, by dogs. The stench of liquor in the streets was suffocating, made worse by the boiling sun. The women's dresses were soaked through. With each stop, their eyes grew brighter, their hatchets cut deeper. Their laughter was punctuated by screams that might have been of anger or of joy. Some sang hymns that sounded here and now as rough as the sailors' chanteys.

Julia had never been so weary in her life. Her dress was ruined; her shoes squished from the spilled liquor. She had marched with the others from the square to Bearskin Neck and back, the fear she had felt at the beginning of the violence turning to exhilaration, and then back to fear as the violence continued, and then finally to numbness. The certainty of their cause, the care of their planning, her ache for a better life for them all—none of that had prepared her for the reality of smashed barrels and broken glass, the curses of the men, the jeers of the boys, the consuming ferocity that possessed the women. The unshielded, naked emotion on both sides. One of the merchants had actually wept as they smashed his bottles of brandy on the cobblestones. She had never before seen a man weep.

And still the women were on the hunt, and still the men did not try to stop them. Not really. She had heard one man shout to anyone who would listen that they should go down to the armory and come back and teach these women a lesson, but another man cuffed him on the head and called him a damned scoundrel. The women moved at will through the town. "Not a bottle left!"

Julia found herself staggering away from the hatchet gang down Long Cove Lane, her head spinning from the heat and the fumes, her hands bloody from her turns at the barrels. She had been unsure at first, and then she had thought about Joshua and the times she had tried and failed to fight back, and then her hatchet sank as deep as anyone's. Now she was in front of Hannah's house. Her head was so heavy. Her hands were trembling. It was so hot. Perhaps it would be cooler by the inner harbor. She walked around the house and through the back yard, past the herb garden, to the water's edge.

The sun was still relentless, but the wind had picked up, and the water was choppy. Julia shook her head as if to stir the air some more. She let her shawl drop from her shoulders. She did not know what had become of her hatchet. Behind her she could still hear the occasional sound of breaking glass, distant shouting. She stepped out onto the rocks. She wanted to be closer to the water.

Which churned, and bubbled, and produced the serpent. No sighting, no warning. The enormous head rose in front of her. The same grey eyes; the same hissing sound. And why not, on this mad day? Julia reached out to the serpent, as she had before. She leaned closer, and her soaked shoes on the slick rocks betrayed her.

The water was shockingly cold, and almost immediately her head struck one of the submerged rocks. Everything went away for an instant, and then she rose out of the water, and above it. The serpent's skin was like nothing she had ever felt before. She adhered to it without effort; she did not have to try to hold on.

As the serpent moved with her out into the harbor, she wondered dimly where she might be going, but a destination truthfully did not seem all that important. The stench of the liquor had been replaced with something equally strong, but it was the smell of the sea and not the weakness of men or the violence of women. To her still-spinning head, that was a great comfort. Esther's words came to her from what seemed like some other world: *The serpent in their hearts will not be defeated. Better to take your chances with the monster offshore.*

They raced through the harbor, plunging beneath the surface for seconds at the time, then rising, then plunging down again. It seemed the most natural thing in the world. Once the serpent paused on the surface and she could see the shore behind her. A figure appeared. A blotch on the horizon, but Julia dimly registered the outlines of a dress, a bonnet. Hannah? Was it over? Had they won? The serpent plunged again, but this time it stayed down. Julia held her breath and closed her eyes against the salt water.

When they surfaced, Julia opened her eyes. She was still facing the shore, but now it was different. The shore was yards and yards away, and yet she saw with perfect clarity as if looking through a telescope whose lens encompassed the whole world. Hannah stood motionless at the water's edge while behind her the houses, the shops, the cobblestones, all melted away, leaving no trace, leaving only a field of white, an appalling empty whiteness before which Hannah stood frozen like a carving before a piece of blank paper.

The serpent dove again. Julia closed her eyes and prepared to drown.

But when the serpent brought her to the surface she still breathed, and when she opened her eyes Hannah was still there on the shore, and the buildings had returned. Some of them. There was Hannah's house, and others. But now the telescope lens had become a stereopticon, and she could see past the houses on the shore to buildings she had never seen before, and bizarrely-shaped carriages that moved by themselves, without horses, and men and women dressed in bright colors, with some of the women dressed like men and some in nothing but what appeared to be undergarments. Before it all stood Hannah, still, and Julia heard a voice that was Hannah's, and was something else altogether. *Our victory will outlive us! It will outlive this century, and the next!*

The serpent was gone. Julia had never been particularly adept in the water, but she floated comfortably, without difficulty. She would not have noticed if fifty serpents had appeared. She did not know what she saw, but she knew that within this impossible scene was a cleanliness, a tolerance, a prosperity beyond anything she could ever have hoped, and at the same time a danger, an inexplicable poison that frightened her to the bone. There were options after all. It made no sense at all, and it made perfect sense.

Julia shut her eyes against the salt and the sun and the knowledge, good and bad, which overwhelmed her. She felt a hundred miles from shore and wondered if Joshua lay somewhere beneath her. She thought how pleasant it would be to remain floating there, like a leaf, like a hatchet, away from women and men.

When she opened her eyes again, the strange buildings and machines and people were gone, and so was Hannah, and her town as she knew it spilled down to the water's edge. She felt a gentle pressure on her back grow more insistent. She tried to keep floating, but soon her heels dragged the bottom, and she was returned to the shore.

Julia looked back to the water. The serpent was gone. So she turned and made her way over the rocks and across the yard and went back to the options that awaited, to the triumph and the wreckage of her town.

For "The Serpent and the Hatchet Gang," I'm deeply indebted to Eleanor C. Parsons' Hannah and the Hatchet Gang: Rockport's Revolt Against Rum (1975) and Rockport: The Making of a Tourist Treasure (1998), and to J.P. O'Neill's The Great New England Sea Serpent (1999). The town of Rockport, Massachusetts remained dry until 2005.

Blood Makes Noise
Gemma Files

Depth drunkenness brings strange thoughts—stranger than usual, at least. Right at the moment, it's like I'm seeing my deaf paternal grandmother's hands hover in this darkening air, signing the scenes of my life away syllable by syllable: Old, new, in and out of order.

These slippery reminiscences, repetitive and elusive—squid-ink images written on oil, squirming from close examination. A memory flip-book, curling at the corners: Nanny Book's crepe-paper skin, laced with pale blue veins; the vestigial webs between her arthritic fingers, spread to catch the light.

My unit bracing to take their turn—pulses shallow, impatient with dismay, most of them more terrified to gauge the true limits of their shameful, mounting fear than consider the circumstances prompting it—as Captain Kiley lies propped up against his bunk, making rabbit-shadows on the holding cell wall.

The sky over Pittsburgh when I was five years old, dirty as a bed of nails.

A map I saw once of the twin moons of Mars.

Hit, flash: Popped bulb, clicked lens—image, then absence. Whispers in my skull, like the roar inside an empty shell: Blood echoes. Music to—in—my ears.

And just what the hell is that word for the fear of fear, anyway?

Fear: Phobos. Fear of: Phobia.

Phobophobia?

. . . must be it.

I press my eyes closed, momentarily forgetting to remember just how deep we must already be. HPNS regulations at least breached, for certain-sure, if not exceeded—more than deep enough to check my hands for tremors, and count off the rest of those prospective High Pressure Nervous Syndrome symptoms our mission literature listed: Increased excitability, motor reflex decay; aphasia. Mental glitches.

. . . under the deep black sea, who loves to die with me . . .

—glitches. Psychosis. Cyanosis.

And eventually . . .

I slam my head back, skull on wall, hard enough to ring myself true—short, sharp shock, broken left incisor into lip, tweak of clarifying pain. Instant coherence. Kiley's rules, channeling themselves: Keep alert. Tell it through. No opinion without research. No solution without . . .

. . . with—out . . .

"Book," the Doctor whispers, beside me. I shift a bit towards him, deliberately trying to find the floor's sharpest angle, to bend my hip in such a way as to make the pain flare just so, girdling my pelvis. Making myself uncomfortable.

"Doctor," I answer.

"Book, Regis. American. No . . . registered rank."

"Specialist."

He coughs. "I . . . didn't know that."

"No reason you would."

The Doctor gives a snuffling gasp, a liquid retch. Something catches in his throat, rattles there briefly—then flicks out again, splattering the floor between us with wet, red bile. I glance back at the wall I just used for a memory aid, which could frankly use a few shadow animals right about now. And as though he's read my mind—

—which may, I suspect, no longer be quite as hard to do as it once was—

"Black . . . Ops . . . operative. 'Wet . . . boy.' Yes? C . . . I . . . A—puppet."

I smile, thinly. "Whatever."

But at least you know my *first name.*

"You . . . are a—coward, Book," the Doctor tells me. Then lets all his breath out in one big rush, ragged with the effort, like he expects me to pause, to take note—to congratulate him on his sudden insight, his startling perspicacity.

As though this were really some big revelation.

Okay: Step back. Start over.

To call the situation bleak would be an understatement. Down to our last few hours of oxygen, high on our own fumes and drifting blind:

Trapped inside a lost, crewless, experimental submarine—make and model strictly classified, even if it mattered—trolling rudderless, black and silent, along a smoking ridge of volcanic fissures at the bottom of the Subeja Trench. Engines blown, no fuel reserves, interior lights dimmed down to a thread or two of emergency luminance along the hallways. With nobody left to tell the whole tale but me and the Doctor, enemies in an undeclared Lukewarm War, huddled across from each other behind the blackout blinds, the two-way mirrored walls, of what we used to call the Waiting Room.

Me sitting quiet, chin on knees, cradled by a weak but quenchless glow that emanates from somewhere deep inside me—quivering, almost imperceptibly, against the back corner of my former prison. Watching him, on the floor, slumped in on himself—curled, fetal. Broken. Moving just enough, every once in a while, to give up the occasional cough—weak and wet, greased with pinkish phlegm; visible fallout from a buried hematoma, a crushed rib, a punctured lung.

Blood whispering in my inner ear, static between stations: Radio Tintinitus, the voice of the virus. Of that indefinite thing to whom I owe my freedom, my breath and life itself, but whose true nature remains as much a mystery to me now as when they finally threw me into this same room, head-first, to sweat and scream out my appointment with its presence behind a triple-mag-locked door.

The barely-there voice of my master, my soon-to-be savior.

It cajoles, flatters. It says: *My love.* It says: *You know I will honor my promises.* It says: *Time means nothing.* And in the same non-breath, self-contradictory, it says: *Soon.*

Soon, soon.

And I sit here, still, not answering. My whole body nothing but a thin skin suit, stretched tight over an endless scream.

When three of the Doctor's largest "orderlies" finally dragged me down to the Waiting Room, they had to break two fingers just to get me through the door. I lurched, tripped, came down face-down and felt my bottom lip split open on impact against the floor, left eyetooth cracking right in half like a piece of candy-corn.

Mouth full, head tolling, I spat, swallowed, screamed back at them—and him, for all I couldn't see him through the two-way's glare—every invective phrase I could form in their wonderfully poetic native language: "May goats rut on your grave! May nuns use your bones for dildos! May God fill your heart with shit and drown your grandchildren in blood!"

And then, reverting under the stress of the moment to pure all-American: "Fuck you! Motherfuckers! Fuck, fuck, FUCK *ALL* Y'ALL!"

Unlike the rest of my former unit, you see, I knew exactly what to expect—because I'd already been there behind the mirror myself, helping the Doctor record what happened to each and every one.

I felt like I'd broken the rest of my fingers on that fucking door, before the pain calmed me far enough down to get me thinking straight again.

So: Slowly, I turned. Made myself look back.

And there it was, in the Waiting Room's far corner—almost close enough to touch.

The thing.

They found it at the bottom of the sea somewhere, in relatively shallow water. Took it out real deep to test it, just in case—a fairly good idea, in my personal opinion. Given what I've seen it do.

White coil of unknown—metal? Bone?

Silence. Compressed dust.

What*ever*, Doctor.

A funnelled, calcified glass shell, an empty tube-worm knot, utterly alien. Shedding icy light the way we shed blood, and looking somehow slick while doing it. Somehow . . . unclean.

But that might just have been the fear talking.

Blink-flash fast, I conjured a mental image of the Doctor comfortably ensconced behind that mirror, taking his notes, making his calculations, running his useless experiments; the same fucking data, over and over:

You go in. And it sits there. And you sit with it.

And then—the glow begins to change. To grow.

And then—

—you die.

Five times out of five. Granted, I'm a traitor, not a scientist—but to me, those odds do suggest a certain pattern.

I felt myself freeze, then, settling instinctively into much the same position I hold now, except with my back up against the door instead of the corner. Freeze and listen, straining for a hidden warning, some cold whisper beating up through the rush and gasp of my own hot blood—a hum *beneath* the hum.

Beneath the *human*.

The flutter of my pulse, quick and light with morbid anticipation. The—

(Phobo)

—inescapable fear—

(phobia)

—of my own fear.

. . . and why do I keep forgetting that *fucking* word?

Oh yeah, right; brain melting. Memory—drowning.

Terror-struck, I held my breath, tried to slow it down. Closed my eyes and prayed to simply disappear, before the sheer, dull, palpable horror of it all ate me alive.

But I didn't piss my actual pants until the first time I heard that noise in my blood begin to talk.

Two weeks, ten days and five other men ago . . . five men I knew well—my trusting comrades, my trusted co-operatives . . . five men plus dear, dead Captain Kiley, that old Cold War-horse, who once let slip (in strictest confidence) how he considered me his second son . . .

The call came straight from the top, wherever that is: A need-to-know mission with an unstated goal, just a set of coordinates and a schedule on a sheet of flammable fax-paper.

Search and destroy, no questions asked. So we smuggled ourselves into the area, clinging barnacle-fast to the hull of a rented ship—dropped blind, docked ourselves at the base of volcano 037, got equalized with the pressure, and spent the rest of the day marking off time. And when the sub's shadow fell over us, we swam to meet it in perfect formation, convinced—like the brave little hardbodied boy scouts our training had made us—that the computerized codes we'd been issued with would be enough to trick our way inside. Which they were, of course; when you're working for folks who routinely drop $50 million or so on new toilet paper dispensers, a string of numbers probably comes comparatively cheap.

No, it wasn't the codes that betrayed us, or got us captured within an insulting half-hour. The codes didn't give us up to the Doctor, to serve as cannon-fodder in his continuing quest to find out what that thing in the Waiting Room was—aside from almost-instant death for anybody he threw in with it.

'Cause codes, you see, don't really come equipped for treason—hold no political opinions, weigh no options, covet no raise in monetary reward.

Risk nothing and nobody on the simple hope of getting pee-ay-ei-dee-paid.

So who?

Well . . .

Like participants in any arranged marriage, The Doctor and I agreed to consummate our vows only after an exhaustively negotiated ritual of long-distance courtship. Acting under Kiley's orders, I used my satellite access as the unit's translator and intelligence liaison to track the sub's location and eavesdrop on its internal mutterings—and when his back was turned, I used the same good ol' U.S. technology to slip inside the Doctor's laptop, read his notes. Send him e-mail. Tell him he could protect his precious project, and gain a core group of experimental subjects, for the one-time-only price of a hefty Swiss bank-account deposit, a trip back to the surface and an artfully-faked sole survivor scenario: Me cast momentarily adrift in the unit's life-pod, beacon on, with an enemy bullet lodged in some suitably fleshy body-part (exact location to be determined later on, at both our conveniences).

"You tellin' me all this's about money?" Kiley demanded. And I just shrugged, snapping back: "What *else*?"

Thinking, all the while: *Disappointed? Well, fuck you, dead man. You can yap all you want about honor, and duty, and the idiot joy of the holy patriotic Cause—but from where I stand, you're nothing but worm-food with an attitude. So go ahead, strike that pose. When you're being buried with full military honors, I'll be cutting myself a slice of apple pie and negotiating a thousand-dollar blow-job.*

"You know when the Old Ma'am and the rest of those REMFs back at HQ find out, they're gonna cancel your sorry ass."

I smirked. "Find out from who?"

"Ain't you got no pride at all, boy?"

"Well. I guess *not*."

Behind me, somebody spit on the floor. All of them glaring through me, turned back first: If looks could eviscerate. Even fey little Ed LoCaso, the training camp's token cocksucker, suddenly pumped full of indifferent hauteur and undying contempt—if the situation hadn't been just a little too butch to bear it, he looked like he might have given me the finger-snap, or maybe just the finger.

"You just better be ready to live with yourself, Book," Kiley told me, finally, right before they hauled his kneecapped ass onto that medical stretcher and took him down the hall to meet our mystery guest. Last words, and he knew it, so he thought he had to make them count—make his point before it was too late for me to repent, and come to an impressive eleventh-hour understanding of the error of my ways.

"Is that meant to be some kind of challenge?"

A frown—a wince, almost. Like: *Jesus*, Regis!

"History—"

"Yeah, right. Now, let's see: Who is it writes history, again, exactly?"

We both knew the answer, and so did everybody else—it'd been one of Kiley's favorite saws, back up top. So no one bothered to reply.

Not even him.

Distant echoes, as the dim lights fade further: Roils and rumblings, metal gamelan trills. The odd hollow clang, barely audible, as the Waiting Room floor's dip slowly steepens. Behind the two-way, I hear the Doctor's autopsy equipment start to skitter down the counter, catch and clatter on the fixtures—all those poor lonely clamps and scalpels, laid out in eager anticipation of my corpse.

And cheated instead: Cheated, cheated.

For now.

The voice seems to smile, seems to agree. And tells me:

Soon.

Oh, Book, Book—shape up, soldier. You think you really got all the time in the world? You believe everything some fossil full of prehistoric bacteria tells you?

. . . can't believe I even just *thought* that sentence . . .

So talk it out straight, for once, you crooked motherfucker—before your brain turns irretrievably to mush.

Regis Aaron Book: Me. 28 years old. Specialist rank 4, Lang-Intel. Cheat and smart-ass. Traitor.

Coward.

Born in Louisiana, raised in Pittsburgh; deaf grandma, absent Mom—gone so long, all the photos burned, I barely remember if she had a face. But I suspect she was probably pretty; I sure am.

After she ran off, Dad re-enlisted, went to Germany. Got all ripped on LSD one night and drove his tank into the Rhine. The government sent us a letter. I got to it before Nanny Book could see, read it, and flushed it down the toilet.

No great conversationalist, my Nan, and that wasn't all because of her pronunciation problems. She did teach me ASL before I was five, though.

Ever see the sign for drowning? It's kind of cute.

I played football in high school, got a university scholarship. Fucked my left foot (deliberately, I must confess)—hairline fracture, long-healed now. Transferred streams. Did languages: French, German, Hungarian, Romanian, five different Slavic variants—the USSR grand tour, they used to call it. Which is how I caught certain people's eye.

When I went ROTC, I told people it was because the recruiting officers said they'd kick me $40,000 toward the rest of my fees. But that was a lie. I joined the army so I could kill people—after which I joined the CIA, so I could do it for no good reason and be virtually assured of getting away with it.

I'm an American, born and bred. I like money. I like power. I like sex, as long as it doesn't lead to anything too permanent. I—

. . . blood in my . . .

—what else? Anything relevant?

(*there*'s a concept)

Oh, fuck: Shut up. Will you just shut the hell *up*, already?

. . . noise. In my . . .

My name is Book, Regis—Regis Book—and yes, I am a coward. And you know why? Because the proper synonym for coward, in this messed-up post-Berlin Wall world of ours, is "smart person." Cowards always come out on top. We try harder, and when we screw up it hurts worse, so we make damn sure it never happens again. We're the ones who live to fight another day—or just to live.

. . . blood.

Stay alive: My sole, my only legitimate consideration. The only one that matters.

Five more minutes, five more hours. Five more days, more years. Fifty. Five hundred—I don't discriminate. But I *am* selfish: Oh, yes. You damn betcha.

Because I'm not going to die, not here—never here, never like this. Watching image and word meaning shuffle off into disintegration as my mental deck of cards deals me a dead man's hand, and the air runs out.

Watching the Doctor cough his life away. Watching the lights dim, and hearing this thing inside me hold its figurative breath, waiting for me to get so loopy I don't care whether or not I'm part of it, or it's part of me. Or if there's any me still left for it to be a part of.

No. I'm not going to die like this—or any other way, if I can help it. I'm coming out of this sub just the same way I came in, the same way the Doctor and company found me when they opened the Waiting Room's mag-locked door, after the mandatory five hours had finally elapsed: Alive alive-oh, just like sweet Molly Malone . . .

. . . before the fever, that is. Before the last verse.

Yeah, well, whatEVER; folk music was never my strong suit.

Alive, spelled ay-ell-ei-vee-ee.

Anything else is gravy.

The Doctor has lapsed into some kind of half-sleep. In the two-way, I catch a glimpse of my fine new self, post-*thing*: My bone-blonde hair, my bleached-out skin. My eyes like bruises, cilia purple with broken blood-vessels. I sniff the air, and decide that my skin has begun to smell like hash packed in sulfur.

And this glow, this glow, around and inside me. This inmost light.

The whispers tell me: *You are a chrysalis.* And I counter by forcing myself to think hard about the shrivelled husks I saw left behind in Nanny Book's back yard, after the butterflies had gone on their merry way. I imagine my mouth splitting slowly open, ripping. Bending like vinyl under the eruptive strain, as a hitherto-hidden larva sloughs me off like so much deluded dead skin.

I feel the fear rise up in me again like wine, like flame—the salt and spices of it distributing themselves through my body while I struggle in its slow-cooking flame, rendering me ever more tender, more juicy. More appetizing.

'Cause fear is what this thing goes for, see? It loves it. Eats it. Got it in little tiny jolts from Kiley and the boy scouts, one by one by one; suck 'em dry and move along, bub. Skin packets, lit and hollowed from within, irradiated with detritus radiance. One big bruise, left to rot: An empty, man-sized wrapper, stuffed full of crumbly bones.

And why was I the only one, apparently, to ever figure this particular connection out?

Just my luck, I guess.

Dribs and drabs, after the long drought on the sea-bottom—aside from stealing the occasional muffled howl from a passing, boneless thing or two, in between geological epochs. From me, though, a veritable stream of terror, so constant as to skirt actual satiety. Fear-engine Book, running on empty: C'mon in and make yourself at home.

The Doctor turns his head again, heavier. Barely able to open his eyes. And tries to ask:

"What . . . happened . . . to—the—?"

"The shell?" I shrug. "Dust in the wind, Doc." Adding, as though in explanation: "It was old."

"Pre- . . . Pleistocene."

"Yeah, that sounds about right."

A wheeze; a cough. "And—what was . . . inside . . . ?"

To which I smile, curling back my bruised lower lip. Showing the tips of all my remaining upper teeth—my ill-set front caps, my jagged, half-missing left incisor. And reply:

" . . . went—inside *me*."

And hey, there's even evidence: The Doctor taped it all, obsessively anal to the last, with a camcorder installed (as per tradition) behind the two-way— images skipping and fading between intermittent washes of static. I wound it back, watched it, in those first dim eons after I knew for sure that no matter what, the sub would just keep right on drifting further down and faster. Talk about post-modern: My cruel apotheosis, shot by shot, in all its real-time glory.

Hour one: Me pounding, pleading. Slumping. Turning.

Hour two: Me and the shell.

Hour three: The glow, beginning. Spreading.

Hour four: My hypnotized attention. Our conversation, me and it—that *thing*; not something which really seems to register, actually, on the purely visual scale.

Cajoling, flattering. Saying: *My love.* Saying: *You know I will honor my promises.*

The glow increasing steadily throughout, meanwhile; a slimy glitter. A blazing smokeless cloud, pillar of salt-white fire. A certain sense of boiling. Of moving outward, then—inward. Saying: *Soon.*

Soon, soon.

And in hour five . . .

The Waiting Room door clicks open, admits four—Doctor and goons, the original three-pack, already braced for action. They see me on the floor, face-down; the declining line of my limp back, head clutched in hands, shadow-rapt. No more light, bright or otherwise. No more shell.

. . . this quintessence of dust . . .

"Bastard ate the fucking thing, fuck your mother," I hear one blurt. And think:

You could say that.

The Doctor kneels, waves them closer. One kicks me over. They see my face, hesitate as one—

. . . this noise . . .

—and I feel my hands knot, my insides furl. I feel them start to reel away from me, then stop dead—sway, dazed. Instantaneously lulled. All of them, Doctor included, plunged into a kind of half-intoxicated trance brought on by my—(its)—proximity. Like standing next to a generator, invisible energy pouring off me in waves. Drowsiness seeping in through the pores.

I feel their fear, like I feel my own. And I feel what was once inside the shell—what's now inside me—sniffing at it: My mental tastebuds, gearing for the feast. My mouth, watering. The glow rekindling, a slow flame under my skin. This radiance looking out through my eyes, bruising them from the inside with the pressure of its glare.

. . . in my blood . . .

Disconnected, surfing the current: A battery. A contained conflagration, run on incipient panic. I lever myself up with both hands, mirroring the Doctor. Look around. See them return my look, all of them—helpless *not* to.

"Bet you wish we were back in El Salvador *now*, fellas," I remark. Conversationally.

And I feel it let go of me, the thing, exploding outward like a concussion bomb-blast: Blow out the bridge, bring the bulkheads down. Crush the goons back against the Waiting Room walls. Crumple the Doctor in on himself. A surge of pent-up energy, driving me upward—haloed, paralyzed, cocooned in power. Catapulted into some pupa stage, lapped in adrenaline and brain-opiates. I feel the shell's former inhabitant slip away from me, in search of fresher fields, and my terror surges, babbling. I match it, promise for promise—set myself up as its carrier, its willing Judas Goat.

Succor and repair me—love me for real, like you love yourself—and I will bring you prey and praise.

A modern Prometheus for the century's end: Eat my fear anew each day, that I may live forever. Trying my level best to make it understand, through instinct rather than intelligence, that I'm not just a host—not just some new flesh shell for it to hide and sleep in, hibernating until the next best thing comes along. Wordlessly eloquent, I vow to trade keeping myself in a constant state of fear and pain for a vaccination—however temporary—against the whole concept of death: Death by drowning, by slow suffocation, death here at the bottom of the deep black sea, in the pressure-drunken final fathoms.

Making sure to also point out—with strictest possible attention to detail—that if I lose my personal identity, then I won't know what I have to be scared of anymore.

And you'll starve.

I hover, wait for its reply. Until the words come, soft as necrosis. Cells collapsing. A lie for a lie:

Time means nothing . . .

Yeah, yeah: To you.

. . . to us.

Which brings us, I believe, right back to where we started.

"Book," the Doctor whispers, now—so soft I can barely hear him, over my own constant internal whisper.

"Doctor," I reply. The word not meaning quite what it used to: Two empty syllables, ringing hollow in my skull. Language no longer seeming *necessary*, even as a nervous tic.

He clears his throat, or tries to, blood rattling in his lungs. Spits, or tries to. And shapes the words, with a last feeble breath:

" . . . I'm . . . a—fraid."

I shift my gaze back to him, slowly. Take a moment to remember his title, his significance. Then nod. And think:

But not as much as me.

Thankfully.

Here on the Subeja Trench's second shelf, already too far down to hope for rescue—anytime soon, at least—we drift past holes belching black lava, coral mountains crusted five arms deep with vivid, fleshy anemones. Everything watches us go by, large or small. They give us sidelong glances, and bare their teeth. And we keep on slipping down, fathom by fathom, until the foliage thins and the light falls away. Until there's nothing to note our descent but a congregation of boneless, blazing things which regard us with a total lack of curiosity.

While I note the Doctor's broken corpse, sprawled and sloughed on the floor beside me. Feeling similarly little.

Wondering: *Did I really strike a bargain, just then? Or do I only THINK I did?*

But if I can still think coherently enough to even consider the question, I guess, it probably just doesn't matter all that much.

The sub buckles, twisting in on itself deck by deck. But I hold fast, foot-loose and evidence-free, to the improbable notion that I have been promised exemption—that even when the water seeps in under the Waiting Room door, this *thing's* infernal patronage will render me impermeable, slicked with infection. No swelling, no softening, no gentle nibbles from passing teeth; just a long sleep, a long, long dream. One long nightmare, a phobo-phobic haze, during which I can jim in my own stew—

(you fucker, you promised)

—stew—*swim* in my own . . . juices. Awhile.

. . . *a while, a minute, a century* . . .

And when they (the CIA, the Doctor's bunch, a salvage crew, whoever) finally find us, and pry open this busted can, how very sweet I'll be. Well-marinaded, and ready to serve: To be my prehistoric savior's chosen liaison, its translator. Its face prepared to meet the faces it will eat.

Or maybe we'll just stay down here, forever, unfound and unmourned, until entropy eats us both.

I raise my hand, look at my fingers. See my vision narrow. My pressure-drunk brain, squeezing itself flat. Glitches, sparking and fading: Images fizzling. Kiley's shadow-animals. Nanny's hands.

The two moons of Mars, on that childhood chart. Deimos and—

(Phobo)

—Phobos. Meaning panic—

(phobia)

—and fear.

Fear, my motive, my spur. My dark and guiding star.

All my life, I think, my fear has driven me to take the easiest way. And where does the easiest way lead, usually?

Well, that would probably be—down.

Down here, at the bottom. Where there are a lot of things, and most of them glow . . .

Thinking: *When you get what you ask for, you really have no right to be surprised.*

    . . . including me.

The Machine is Perfect, The Engineer is Nobody
Brett Alexander Savory

When she touches him, he flinches awake. Lying on a filthy mattress, he stares up at the low rock ceiling, listening to the sounds of machinery. Her breathing close to his ear blends with the mechanical sounds, nearly indistinguishable from one another.

"What do you think they're doing out there?" she asks.

He sighs. "We've been over this a thousand times. I don't know what—"

"Yes, yes, but what do you *think* they're doing?"

He turns on his side, away from her.

Outside their little cave, gears grind, engines roar deep and throaty. The stench of oil exhaust permeates everything.

A few moments later, she touches him again. He does not flinch this time, does not respond at all. In all the time they've been here, she has not asked this question, has not had the courage to do so, but now she does, now she feels she needs to: "Are we going to die in here?"

He turns back to her, cups her cheek with one hand, and kisses her gently. It is the first time they've kissed.

They fall asleep, their backs touching.

Four months ago, when they first arrived, they'd thought to escape through the small vent in the ceiling, but when they'd finally gotten the vent cover off and shined a lamp inside, they saw that the shaft went straight up as far as they could see. It probably only went up a dozen metres or so, but they had no way of getting a grip to climb up its metal sides, and it was small enough that either of them could've easily gotten stuck.

Piled in one corner of the cave was a supply of lamps and kerosene; in another corner, they'd found canned food and bottles of water, stacked nearly

274

to the ceiling. A toilet-size hole was dug into the floor, in a tiny cul-de-sac, as far away from the bed as possible. As with the vent, they couldn't see how far it extended. Within the first week, they'd run their hands over every part of the walls, ceiling, and floor and could not discover how they'd gotten in. When they'd asked each other what they remembered about getting to this cave, neither could recall. One of them felt that the other was lying.

Several hours after kissing her, he gets up from the mattress, lights a kerosene lamp. Yellow-orange light dances on the walls until the flame settles. The vent in the ceiling flaps with the strength of the wind outside.

He looks into the corners of the room, these corners that used to be completely stuffed with food, water, and kerosene. Now only four bottles of water and six cans of food sit in one corner; two containers of kerosene are left. He goes back and sits on the edge of the mattress with a can of food and a bottle of water. He pulls his utility knife from his belt, cracks the can open, pulls up the edge of the lid, and scoops out the beans with his fingers, shovels them into his mouth. He hopes she doesn't wake up to see him eating a whole can to himself in one sitting.

When he finishes the beans, he neatly and quietly stacks the empty can in another corner of the cave. He sits back on the mattress, facing her, and sips his water. She stirs when he sits, knuckles her eyes, turns and grins sleepily at him.

"What's for breakfast?" she asks.

He smiles briefly, but it quickly slips. "There're only five cans left."

She yawns, sits up, says, "I know. You don't have to tell me. I know."

They are both so thin that their cheeks are sunken and their vertebrae poke through their thin black shirts.

"Do you want to talk about the kiss?" he asks. Despite their situation, he still, absurdly, blushes.

"What is there to talk about?" she says. "It was nice. Isn't that enough?"

His eyes fall to the floor. "Well, what I mean is—"

She suddenly brushes past him, picks up a can of beans, holds it at arm's length in his direction. "Can you please open this?"

He has had control of the utility knife the entire time they've been here. Now he pulls it from his belt, extends his arm toward her, palm open, upturned. She looks at him strangely for a moment, then gently takes the knife from his hand.

Later, they are lying on the mattress, trying to sleep, but both wide awake. The machines pound and they pound and they pound. Sometimes small bits of rock fall from the ceiling, sprinkling them, their mattress, the floor. It is one of the only things that makes this experience seem real to her. She says, "If that vent just goes straight up and out, why can't we ever see daylight when we look up it? It doesn't make any sense. I don't understand."

He waits a moment before he responds, fiddles with his watch—the watch that tells the time and date. The number "22" sits in the little window, on its way to "23." Glancing at the remaining supplies, he knows they probably won't live to see much of next month.

"We don't ever see daylight when we look up the shaft because the daylight is gone," he says. "It's gone."

They sleep again, but this time their backs do not touch.

A couple of days later, eating and drinking, trying to ration what little they have left. They sit on the bed, cross-legged, facing each other. The man thinks of it as their attempt at creating a civilized dinner-table situation. The woman simply thinks of it as heartbreaking and squalid.

"What did you mean when you said the daylight is gone?" the woman asks, licking beans from her fingertips.

"I mean that the daylight is gone; it no longer exists," the man answers. He does not look at her when he speaks.

"So what happened? Does it have something to do with the machines outside? Or maybe something to do with what they're digging for?"

"I don't know. I really don't." He wipes bean sauce off the inside of the can with his index finger, angling it so he doesn't cut himself on the sharp edges.

"Sometimes I feel like you're not telling me something."

The man finally looks up from his can. "Like what?"

"I don't know." She reaches a hand out, touches his knee lightly. "You wouldn't hide anything from me, would you? We're in this together, aren't we? I want to think that I can trust you."

The man grins a little, touches the woman's hand with his own. He plays with her fingers like they've known each other for years, gently stroking the tops, curling down to slide under her palm. His familiarity simultaneously excites and disturbs the woman.

"Yes. Yes, we're in this together. I'm glad you think so. I really am. I know I haven't said it before, but I'm very happy you're here with me."

Something about the phrasing of this statement makes the woman pull her hand away from the man. *Happy you're here with me*, she thinks. *What does that mean?*

Something like suspicion crawls across her scalp, settles deep at the base of her skull.

When they fall asleep that night, one of her hands is curled into a tight fist, nestled next to her heart; the other hand wraps around the fist, pulsating in time with the grind of the machines.

He is awakened by more pounding, but this time it's much closer and not nearly as deep. Not the bone-rattling pounding of the machines outside, but a machine inside—or at least very nearly inside.

He springs from the bed—a movement he wouldn't have thought himself capable of anymore—and reaches down to his belt for his utility knife. *Fuck*, he thinks. *I knew I shouldn't have—*

"Here," she says. "Calm down, it's right here." Awake now, too, she hands him the knife. He snatches it from her hand, flicks open the longest blade with his thumbnail.

The noise comes from beneath them. A drill. Louder with every passing moment. The floor shakes. He is very aware of the knife in his hand, his thumping heart, blood pounding through his system. She yells something at him from where she sits on the bed.

"What?" he bellows back, the floor now buckling. The faint outline of a manhole-size circle forms.

She takes a deep breath and shouts, "I said, why do you want to kill this person? Maybe he's here to rescue us. What's wrong with you? What's *wrong* with you?"

The tip of the enormous drill finally breaks through, scattering pieces of rock across the floor of the cave. The drill then recedes. Muttering voices as it's passed from the driller down to someone below him. The driller tentatively pops his head into the cave. He eyes the man and the woman in the room. He raises himself up a little more, bringing a gun into view.

For nearly a full half-minute, no one says anything. Just heavy breathing, wild-eyed stares, and the sounds of the machinery growling outside the cave walls.

Then: "Nearly out of water, I see," the driller says. He's wearing a heavily scuffed hardhat and dark goggles. "Food, too."

The man with the knife just stares, still in defensive posture.

The woman speaks: "Are you here to rescue us? We've been here for so long."

The driller does not look at her.

"Sir," he says. "We have to get you out of here. They're getting closer, they've nearly drilled down to where they think it is. But they're getting bizarre readings, indications of something no one expected to find this deep and—"

"I'm not leaving," the man with the knife says.

The woman's brow furrows. "What are you *talking* about? And what is *he* talking about?" She moves her head in the direction of the driller. "What is this 'sir' shit? What's going on here? What—"

"Doctor Farrid, listen," the driller says, cutting the woman off. He steps up out of the hole in the floor, kicks aside chunks of rock to get a firm foothold. "We don't have time for this. We need to leave *now*. They're getting close, and I know you wanted to see it, but—"

Farrid steps forward quickly, pushes the knife out in front of him, hisses through clenched teeth, "I'm not. *Fucking*. Leaving. I need to see this. I need to know what it is. And *do not* say my name again, understood?"

"Sir," the driller says, clearly intimidated, even though he holds the gun. "No disrespect intended, but these are orders from higher up—higher than both of us. We need to get you to a safe place, somewhere through the service tunnels, maybe to the first check post, where we can—"

Farrid steps forward quickly, slashes the knife across the driller's throat as hard and as fast as he can, then steps back. Blood bubbles out of the driller's throat, his eyes wide, throat gurgling. He drops his gun, slumps forward onto the floor. Twitches once and is silent.

Farrid pockets the knife, picks up the driller's gun, points it at the woman's face. "Not one sound, do you hear me? Not one sound."

But the woman isn't thinking about speaking, screaming, or any other sounds. Only one thought runs through her mind: *He kidnapped me. He kidnapped me. He kidnapped me.*

Someone calls up from below: "Derek? Everything all right, brother? What's going on up there?"

Another few moments of silence as the man below waits for an answer that will never come. Then booted feet clanging on metal ladder steps, coming up. Farrid points the gun at the hole, but keeps his eyes trained on the woman.

The man, far from expecting to see his colleague's dead body, comes up fairly quickly through the hole, glances at the woman and Farrid before casting his eyes down to see his fallen partner. Shocked, his mouth just flaps a couple of times, then his hand instinctively reaches for the gun on his belt.

"Don't," is all Farrid says, shakes his head once.

The woman, finally finding her voice, says, "Why did you do this to me? We don't know each other. I don't understand." Her hands flutter like curious butterflies at her sides. "Why did you do it? What sort of sense does it make to—"

Farrid motions with his gun at the woman, speaks to the man: "Take her. Go."

There is fury in the man's eyes, a tightness around his lips. He wants to go for his gun. Farrid sees that he desperately wants to try. Farrid shakes his head again. "I will shoot you both before you even get your revolver halfway out of its holster, son. Just take the girl and leave me. I'm sorry about your friend. Really, I am. I did not mean for things to turn out like this."

Farrid sees wetness on the man's eyelids. The face hardens further. Farrid squeezes the trigger a little, sensing movement of the man's hand toward his holster. Then the man's eyes drop to his friend again; they remain there for a few moments before he lifts them to the woman. Frightened, confused. Her breath comes in hitches. The man holds his hand out to her. The butterflies at the ends of her arms settle a little. One of the woman's hands comes up slowly, then before her and the man's fingers touch, she says quietly, "Are you here to rescue me? You're here to save me, aren't you?"

The man does not react, only keeps his hand out for her to take.

The woman takes the man's hand, steps over the blood-soaked body of the driller, focuses her attention on Farrid once more. "Liar. Murderer," she says.

Farrid nods.

The woman's lip trembles, but she does not cry.

Outside, the machines seem closer, the earth shaking more than any other time since he's been here. Concerned voices drift down the airshaft. Farrid cannot make out the words, only the tone. Curiosity. Fear.

The man steps out of the hole, moves aside, helps the woman find the top rung of the ladder several feet down. Once she's safely on her way, the man lowers himself to the top rung, locks eyes with Farrid, says, "I'm taking the body."

Farrid nods again.

The man pulls his friend's legs toward him, maneuvers them so they're aligned with his back, rests the torso on his shoulder in a fireman's carry. He descends slowly with the body, making sure not to bump the head on anything.

Farrid lowers the gun, stares at the red streak of blood leading to the hole, the congealing pool a few feet away, the flecks spattered across the jumbled rocks.

Liar. Murderer, he thinks, and knows the truth of it, but is unable to dig out of himself anything resembling remorse.

Farrid picks his way through the rocks to the stained mattress, sits down softly. For a brief moment, he imagines the gun in his mouth, the knife sliding along his wrists. He feels this is what he should be thinking about, but he is not. He is thinking only of what the machines have found. What he has waited his whole life to see.

The ground suddenly shakes like a bomb has gone off. The kerosene lamp flickers out. Darkness wraps him in a stifling blanket. He cannot breathe, but he does not want to breathe; he wants only to see it, hear it, feel it near him. If he can just have a taste of its presence, this will all have been worth it.

The machines outside suddenly stop, every one of them powering down. The silence is enormous, as if all life on the planet has suddenly been vacuumed out into space. It fills Farrid's ears, his heart, his mind. Batters at his skull to get out. Then a massive throbbing sound, of blood pumping through gigantic veins.

They found it. They found it, and it's alive.

He feels it awaken, senses its life in his mind, through his entire body. It cries out, once—a deep, lonely, mournful sound. It does not want to be here. It does not belong.

Farrid is the only one who hears it.

Proboscis
Laird Barron

1.

After the debacle in British Columbia, we decided to crash the Bluegrass festival. Not we—Cruz. Everybody else just shrugged and said yeah, whatever you say, dude. Like always. Cruz was the alpha-alpha of our motley pack.

We followed the handmade signs onto a dirt road and ended up in a muddy pasture with maybe a thousand other cars and beat-to-hell tourist buses. It was a regular extravaganza—pavilions, a massive stage, floodlights. A bit farther out, they'd built a bonfire, and Dead Heads were writhing with pagan exuberance among the cinder-streaked shadows. The brisk air swirled heavy scents of marijuana and clove, of electricity and sex.

The amplified ukulele music was giving me a migraine. Too many people smashed together, limbs flailing in paroxysms. Too much white light followed by too much darkness. I'd gone a couple beers over my limit because my face was Novocain-numb and I found myself dancing with some sloe-eyed coed who'd fixed her hair in corn rows. Her shirt said *MILK*.

She was perhaps a bit prettier than the starlet I'd ruined my marriage with way back in the days of yore, but resembled her in a few details. What were the odds? I didn't even attempt to calculate. A drunken man cheek to cheek with a strange woman under the harvest moon was a tricky proposition.

"Lookin' for somebody, or just rubberneckin'?" The girl had to shout over the hi-fi jug band. Her breath was peppermint and whiskey.

"I lost my friends," I shouted back. A sea of bobbing heads beneath a gulf of night sky and none of them belonged to anyone I knew. Six of us had piled out of two cars and now I was alone. Last of the Mohicans.

The girl grinned and patted my cheek. "You ain't got no friends, Ray-bo."

I tried to ask how she came up with that, but she was squirming and pointing over my shoulder.

"My gawd, look at all those stars, will ya?"

Sure enough the stars were on parade; cold, cruel radiation bleeding across improbable distances. I was more interested in the bikers lurking near the stage and the beer garden. Creepy and mean, spoiling for trouble. I guessed Cruz and Hart would be nearby, copping the vibe, as it were.

The girl asked me what I did and I said I was an actor between jobs. Anything she'd seen? No, probably not. Then I asked her and she said something I didn't quite catch. It was either etymologist or entomologist. There was another thing, impossible to hear. She looked so serious I asked her to repeat it.

"Right through your meninges. Sorta like a siphon."

"What?" I said.

"I guess it's a delicacy. They say it don't hurt much, but I say nuts to that."

"A delicacy?"

She made a face. "I'm goin' to the garden. Want a beer?"

"No, thanks." As it was, my legs were ready to fold. The girl smiled, a wistful imp, and kissed me briefly, chastely. She was swallowed into the masses and I didn't see her again.

After a while I staggered to the car and collapsed. I tried to call Sylvia, wanted to reassure her and Carly that I was okay, but my cell wouldn't cooperate. Couldn't raise my watchdog friend, Rob in LA. He'd be going bonkers too. I might as well have been marooned on a desert island. Modern technology, my ass. I watched the windows shift through a foggy spectrum of pink and yellow. Lulled by the monotone thrum, I slept.

Dreamt of wasp nests and wasps. And rare orchids, coronas tilted towards the awesome bulk of clouds. The flowers were a battery of organic radio telescopes receiving a sibilant communiqué just below my threshold of comprehension.

A mosquito pricked me and when I crushed it, blood ran down my finger, hung from my nail.

2.

Cruz drove. He said, "I wanna see the Mima Mounds."

Hart said, "Who's Mima?" He rubbed the keloid on his beefy neck.

Bulletproof glass let in light from a blob of moon. I slumped in the tricked-out back seat, where our prisoner would've been if we'd managed to bring him home. I stared at the grille partition, the leg irons and the doors with no handles. A crusty vein traced black tributaries on the floorboard. Someone had scratched R+G and a fanciful depiction of Ronald Reagan's penis. This was an old car. It reeked of cigarette smoke, of stale beer, of a million exhalations.

Nobody asked my opinion. I'd melted into the background smear.

The brutes were smacked out of their gourds on junk they'd picked up on the Canadian side at the festival. Hart had tossed the bag of syringes and miscellaneous garbage off a bridge before we crossed the border. That was where we'd parted ways with the other guys—Leon, Rufus and Donnie. Donnie was the one who had gotten nicked by a stray bullet in Donkey Creek, earned himself bragging rights if nothing else. Jersey boys, the lot; they were going to take the high road home, maybe catch the rodeo in Montana.

Sunrise forged a pale seam above the distant mountains. We were rolling through certified boondocks, thumping across rickety wooden bridges that could've been thrown down around the Civil War. On either side of busted up two-lane blacktop were overgrown fields and hills dense with maples and poplar. Scotch broom reared on lean stalks, fire-yellow heads lolling hungrily. Scotch broom was Washington's rebuttal to kudzu. It was quietly everywhere, feeding in the cracks of the earth.

Road signs floated nearly extinct; letters faded, or bullet-raddled, dimmed by pollen and sap. Occasionally, dirt tracks cut through high grass to farmhouses. Cars passed us head-on, but not often, and usually local rigs—camouflage-green flatbeds with winches and trailers, two-tone pickups, decrepit jeeps. Nothing with out-of-state plates. I started thinking we'd missed a turn somewhere along the line. Not that I would've broached the subject. By then I'd learned to keep my mouth shut and let nature take its course.

"Do you even know where the hell they are?" Hart said. Hart was sour about the battle royale at the wharf. He figured it would give the bean counters an excuse to waffle about the payout for Piers' capture. I suspected he was correct.

"The Mima Mounds?"

"Yeah."

"Nope." Cruz rolled down the window, squirted beechnut over his shoulder, contributing another racing streak to the paint job. He twisted the radio dial and conjured Johnny Cash confessing that he'd "shot a man in Reno just to watch him die."

"Real man'd swallow," Hart said. "Like Josey Wales."

My cell beeped and I didn't catch Cruz's rejoinder. It was Carly. She'd seen the bust on the news and was worried, had been trying to reach me. The report mentioned shots-fired and a wounded person, and I said yeah, one of our guys got clipped in the ankle, but he was okay, I was okay and the whole thing was over. We'd bagged the bad guy and all was right with the world. I promised to be home in a couple of days and told her to say hi to her mom. A wave of static drowned the connection.

I hadn't mentioned that the Canadians contemplated jailing us for various legal infractions and inciting mayhem. Her mother's blood pressure was already sky-high over what Sylvia called my, "midlife adventure." Hard to blame her—it was my youthful "adventures" that set the torch to our unhappy marriage.

What Sylvia didn't know, couldn't know, because I lacked the grit to bare my soul at this late stage of our separation, was during the fifteen-martini lunch meeting with Hart, he'd showed me a few pictures to seal the deal. A roster of smiling teenage girls that could've been Carly's schoolmates. Hart explained in graphic detail what the bad man liked to do to these kids. Right there it became less of an adventure and more of a mini-crusade. I'd been an absentee father for fifteen years. Here was my chance to play Lancelot.

Cruz said he was hungry enough to eat the ass-end of a rhino and Hart said stop and buy breakfast at the greasy spoon coming up on the left, materializing as if by sorcery, so they pulled in and parked alongside a rusted-out Pontiac on blocks. Hart remembered to open the door for me that time. One glimpse of the diner's filthy windows and the coils of dogshit sprinkled across the unpaved lot convinced me I wasn't exactly keen on going in for the special.

But I did.

The place was stamped 1950s from the long counter with a row of shiny black swivel stools and the too-small window booths, dingy Formica peeling at the edges of the tables, to the bubble-screen TV wedged high up in a corner alcove. The TV was flickering with grainy black and white images of a talk show I didn't recognize and couldn't hear because the volume was turned way down. Mercifully I didn't see myself during the commercials.

I slouched at the counter and waited for the waitress to notice me. Took a while—she was busy flirting with Hart and Cruz, who'd squeezed themselves into a booth, and of course they wasted no time in regaling her with their latest exploits as hardcase bounty hunters. By now it was purely mechanical; rote bravado. They were pale as sheets and running on fumes of adrenaline and junk. Oh, how I dreaded the next twenty-four to thirty-six hours.

Their story was edited for heroic effect. My private version played a little differently.

We finally caught the desperado and his best girl in the Maple Leaf Country. After a bit of "slap and tickle," as Hart put it, we handed the miscreants over to the Canadians, more or less intact. Well, the Canadians more or less took possession of the pair.

The bad man was named Russell Piers, a convicted rapist and kidnaper who'd cut a nasty swath across the great Pacific Northwest and British Columbia. The girl was Penny Aldon, a runaway, an orphan, the details varied, but she wasn't important, didn't even drive; was along for the thrill, according to the reports. They fled to a river town, were loitering wharf-side, munching on a fish basket from one of six jillion Vietnamese vendors when the team descended.

Piers proved something of a Boy Scout—always prepared. He yanked a pistol from his waistband and started blazing, but one of him versus six of us only works in the movies and he went down under a swarm of blackjacks, tasers and fists. I ran the hand-cam, got the whole jittering mess on film.

The film.

That was on my mind, sneaking around my subconscious like a night prowler. There was a moment during the scrum when a shiver of light distorted the scene, or I had a near-fainting spell, or who knows. The men on the sidewalk snapped and snarled, hyenas bringing down a wounded lion. Foam spattered the lens. I swayed, almost tumbled amid the violence. And Piers looked directly at me. Grinned at me. A big dude, even bigger than the troglodytes clinging to him, he had Cruz in a headlock, was ready to crush bones, to ravage flesh, to feast. A beast all right, with long, greasy hair, powerful hands scarred by prison tattoos, gold in his teeth. Inhuman, definitely. He wasn't a lion, though. I didn't know what kingdom he belonged to.

Somebody cold-cocked Piers behind the ear and he switched off, slumped like a manikin that'd been bowled over by the holiday stampede.

Flutter, flutter and all was right with the world, relatively speaking. Except my bones ached and I was experiencing a not-so-mild wave of paranoia that hung on for hours. Never completely dissipated, even here in the sticks at a godforsaken hole in the wall while my associates preened for an audience of one.

Cruz and Hart had starred on *Cops* and *America's Most Wanted*; they were celebrity experts. Too loud, the three of them honking and squawking, especially my ex brother-in-law. Hart resembled a hog that decided to put on a dirty shirt and steel toe boots and go on its hind legs. Him being high as a kite wasn't helping. Sylvia tried to warn me, she'd known what her brother was about since they were kids knocking around on the wrong side of Des Moines.

I didn't listen. *'C'mon, Sylvie, there's a book in this. Hell, a Movie of the Week!'* Hart was on the inside of a rather seamy yet wholly marketable industry. He had a friend who had a friend who had a general idea where Mad Dog Piers was running. Money in the bank. See you in a few weeks, hold my calls.

"Watcha want, hon?" The waitress, a strapping lady with a tag spelling Victoria, poured translucent coffee into a cup that suggested the dishwasher wasn't quite up to snuff. Like all pro waitresses she pulled off this trick without looking away from my face. "I know you?" And when I politely smiled and reached for the sugar, she kept coming, frowning now as her brain began to labor. "You somebody? An actor or somethin'?"

I shrugged in defeat. "Uh, yeah. I was in a couple TV movies. Small roles. Long time ago."

Her face animated, a craggy talking tree. "Hey! You were on that comedy, one with the blind guy and his seein' eye dog. Only the guy was a con man or somethin', wasn't really blind and his dog was an alien or somethin', a robot, don't recall. Yeah, I remember you. What happened to that show?"

"Cancelled." I glanced longingly through the screen door to our ugly Chevy.

"Ray does shampoo ads," Hart said. He said something to Cruz and they cracked up.

"Milk of magnesia!" Cruz said. "And 'If you suffer from erectile dysfunction, now there's an answer!' " He delivered the last in a passable radio announcer's voice, although I'd heard him do better. He was hoarse.

The sun went behind a cloud, but Victoria still wanted my autograph, just in case I made a comeback, or got killed in a sensational fashion and then my signature would be worth something. She even dragged Sven the cook out to shake my hand and he did it with the dedication of a zombie following its mistress's instructions before shambling back to whip up eggs and hash for my comrades.

The coffee tasted like bleach.

The talk show ended and the next program opened with a still shot of a field covered by mossy hummocks and blackberry thickets. The black and white imagery threw me. For a moment I didn't register the car parked between mounds was familiar. Our boxy Chevy with the driver-side door hanging ajar, mud-encrusted plates, taillights blinking SOS.

A grey hand reached from inside, slammed the door. A hand? Or something like a hand? A B-movie prosthesis? Too blurry, too fast to be certain.

Victoria changed the channel to *All My Children*.

3.

Hart drove.

Cruz navigated. He tilted a road map, trying to follow the dots and dashes. Victoria had drawled a convoluted set of directions to the Mima Mounds, a one-star tourist attraction about thirty miles over. Cruise on through Poger Rock and head west. Real easy drive if you took the local shortcuts and suchlike.

Not an unreasonable detour; I-5 wasn't far from the site—we could do the tourist bit and still make the Portland night scene. That was Cruz's sales pitch. Kind of funny, really. I wondered at the man's sudden fixation on geological phenomena. He was a NASCAR and *Soldier of Fortune Magazine* type personality. Hart fit the profile too, for that matter. Damned world was turning upside down.

It was getting hot. Cracks in the windshield dazzled and danced.

The boys debated cattle mutilations and the inarguable complicity of the Federal government regarding the Grey Question and how the moon landing was fake and remember that flick from the 1970s, *Capricorn One*, goddamned if O.J wasn't one of the astronauts. Freakin' hilarious.

I unpacked the camera, thumbed the playback button, and relived the Donkey Creek fracas. Penny said to me, "Reduviidea—any of a species of large insects that feed on the blood of prey insects and some mammals. They are considered extremely beneficial by agricultural professionals." Her voice was made of tin and lagged behind her lip movements, like a badly dubbed foreign film. She stood on the periphery of the action, scrawny fingers pleating the wispy fabric of a blue sundress. She was smiling. "The indices of primate emotional thresholds indicate the [*click-click*] process is traumatic. However, point oh-two percent vertebrae harvest corresponds to non-[*click-click*] purposes. As an X haplotype you are a primary source of [*click-click*]. Lucky you!"

"Jesus!" I muttered and dropped the camera on the seat. *Are you talkin' to me?* I stared at too many trees while Robert DeNiro did his mirror schtick as a low frequency monologue in the corner of my mind. Unlike DeNiro, I'd never carried a gun. The guys wouldn't even loan me a taser.

"What?" Cruz said in a tone that suggested he'd almost jumped out of his skin. He glared through the partition, olive features drained to ash. Giant drops of sweat sparkled and dripped from his broad cheeks. The light wrapped his skull, halo of an angry saint. Withdrawals something fierce, I decided.

I shook my head, waited for the magnifying glass of his displeasure to swing back to the road map. When it was safe I hit the playback button. Same scene on the view panel. This time when Penny entered the frame she pointed at me and intoned in a robust, Slavic accent, "Supercalifragilisticexpialidocious is Latin for a death god of a primitive Mediterranean culture. Their civilization was buried in mudslides caused by unusual seismic activity. If you say it loud enough—" I hit the kill button. My stomach roiled with rancid coffee and incipient motion-sickness.

Third time's a charm, right? I played it back again. The entire sequence was erased. Nothing but deep-space black with jags of silvery light at the edges. In the middle, skimming by so swiftly I had to freeze things to get a clear image, was Piers with his lips nuzzling Cruz's ear, and Cruz's face was corpse-slack. And for an instant, a microsecond, the face was Hart's too; one of those three-dee poster illusions where the object changes depending on the angle. Then, more nothingness, and an odd feedback noise that faded in and out, like Gregorian monks chanting a litany in reverse.

Okay. ABC time.

I'd reviewed the footage shortly after the initial capture in Canada. There was nothing unusual about it. We spent a few hours at the police station answering a series of polite yet penetrating questions. I assumed our cameras would be confiscated, but the inspector simply examined our equipment in the presence of a couple suits from a legal office. Eventually the inspector handed everything back with a stern admonishment to leave dangerous criminals to the authorities. Amen to that.

Had a cop tampered with the camera, doctored it in some way? I wasn't a film-maker, didn't know much more than point and shoot and change the batteries when the little red light started blinking. So, yeah, Horatio, it was possible someone had screwed with the recording. Was that likely? The answer was no—not unless they'd also managed to monkey with the television at the diner. More probable one of my associates had spiked the coffee with a miracle agent and I was hallucinating. Seemed out of character for those greedy bastards, even for the sake of a practical joke on their third wheel—dope was expensive and it wasn't like we were expecting a big payday.

The remaining options weren't very appealing.

My cell whined, a dentist's drill in my shirt pocket. It was Rob Fries from his patio office in Gardena. Rob was tall, bulky, pink on top and garbed according to his impression of what Miami vice cops might've worn in a bygone era, such as the '80s. Rob also had the notion he was my agent despite the fact I'd fired him ten years ago after he handed me one too-many scripts for laxative testimonials. I almost broke into tears when I heard his voice on the buzzing line. "Man, am I glad you called!" I said loudly enough to elicit another scowl from Cruz.

"Hola, compadre. What a splash y'all made on page 16. *'American Yahoos Run Amok!'* goes the headline, which is a quote of the Calgary rag. Too bad the stupid bastards let our birds fly the coop. Woulda been better press if they fried 'em. Well, they don't have the death penalty, but you get the point. Even so, I see a major motion picture deal in the works. Mucho dinero, Ray, buddy!"

"Fly the coop? What are you talking about?"

"Uh, you haven't heard? Piers and the broad walked. Hell, they probably beat you outta town."

"You better fill me in." Indigestion was eating the lining of my esophagus.

"Real weird story. Some schmuck from Central Casting accidentally turned 'em loose. The paperwork got misfiled or some such bullshit. The muckety-mucks are po'd. Blows your mind, don't it?"

"Right," I said in my actor's tone. I fell back on this when my mind was in neutral but etiquette dictated a polite response. Up front, Cruz and Hart were bickering, hadn't caught my exclamation. No way was I going to illuminate them regarding this development—Christ, they'd almost certainly consider pulling a u-turn and speeding back to Canada. The home office would be calling any second now to relay the news; probably had been trying to get through for hours—Hart hated phones, usually kept his stashed in the glovebox.

There was a burst of chittery static. "—returning your call. Keep getting the answering service. You won't believe it—I was having lunch with this chick used to be one of Johnny Carson's secretaries, yeah? And she said her best friend is shacking with an exec who just frickin' adored you in *Clancy & Spot*. Frickin' adored you! I told my gal pal to pass the word you were riding along on this bounty hunter gig, see what shakes loose."

"Oh, thanks, Rob. Which exec?"

"Lemmesee—uh, Harry Buford. Remember him? He floated deals for the *Alpha Team*, some other stuff. Nice as hell. Frickin' adores you, buddy."

"Harry Buford? Looks like the Elephant Man's older, fatter brother, loves pastels and lives in Mexico half the year because he's fond of underage Chicano girls? Did an expose piece on the evils of Hollywood, got himself blackballed? That the guy?"

"Well, yeah. But he's still got an ear to the ground. And he frickin'—"

"Adores me. Got it. Tell your girlfriend we'll all do lunch, or whatever."

"Anywhoo, how you faring with the gorillas?"

"Um, great. We're on our way to see the Mima Mounds."

"What? You on a nature study?"

"Cruz's idea."

"The Mima Mounds. Wow. Never heard of them. Burial grounds, huh?"

"Earth heaves, I guess. They've got them all over the world—Norway, South America, Eastern Washington—I don't know where all. I lost the brochure."

"Cool." The silence hung for a long moment. "Your buddies wanna see some, whatchyacallem—?"

"Glacial deposits."

"They wanna look at some rocks instead of hitting a strip club? No bullshit?"

"Um, yeah."

It was easy to imagine Rob frowning at his flip-flops propped on the patio table while he stirred the ice in his rum and coke and tried to do the math. "Have a swell time, then."

"You do me a favor?"

"Yo, bro'. Hit me."

"Go on the Net and look up X haplotype. Do it right now, if you've got a minute."

"X-whatsis?"

I spelled it and said, "Call me back, okay? If I'm out of area, leave a message with the details."

"Be happy to." There was a pause as he scratched pen to pad. "Some kinda new meds, or what?"

"Or what, I think."

"Uh, huh. Well, I'm just happy the Canucks didn't make you an honorary citizen, eh. I'm dying to hear the scoop."

"I'm dying to dish it. I'm losing my signal, gotta sign off."

He said not to worry, bro', and we disconnected. I worried anyway.

4.

Sure enough, Hart's phone rang a bit later and he exploded in a stream of repetitive profanity and dented the dash with his ham hock of a fist. He was still bubbling when we pulled into Poger Rock for gas and fresh directions. Cruz, on the other hand, accepted the news of Russell Piers' "early parole" with a Zen detachment demonstrably contrary to his nature.

"Screw it. Let's drink," was his official comment.

Poger Rock was sunk in a hollow about fifteen miles south of the state capitol in Olympia. It wasn't impressive—a dozen or so antiquated buildings moldering along the banks of a shallow creek posted with NO SHOOTING signs. Everything was peeling, rusting or collapsing toward the center of the earth. Only the elementary school loomed incongruously—a utopian brick and tile structure set back and slightly elevated, fresh paint glowing through the alders and dogwoods. Aliens might have landed and dedicated a monument.

Cruz filled up at a mom and pop gas station with the prehistoric pumps that took an eon to dribble forth their fuel. I bought some jerky and a carton of milk with a past-due expiration date to soothe my churning guts. The lady behind the counter had yellowish hair and wore a button with a fuzzy picture of a toddler in a bib. She smiled nervously as she punched keys and furiously smoked a Pall Mall. Didn't recognize me, thank God.

Cruz pushed through the door, setting off the ding-dong alarm. His gaze jumped all over the place and his chambray shirt was molded to his chest as if he'd been doused with a water hose. He crowded past me, trailing the odor of armpit funk and cheap cologne, grunted at the cashier and shoved his credit card across the counter.

I raised my hand to block the sun when I stepped outside. Hart was leaning on the hood. "We're gonna mosey over to the bar for a couple brewskis." He coughed his smoker's cough, spat in the gravel near a broken jar of marmalade. Bees darted among the wreckage.

"What about the Mima Mounds?"

"They ain't goin' anywhere. 'Sides, it ain't time, yet."

"Time?"

Hart's ferret-pink eyes narrowed and he smiled slightly. He finished his cigarette and lighted another from the smoldering butt. "Cruz says it ain't."

"Well, what does that mean? It 'ain't time'?"

"I dunno, Ray-bo. I dunno fuckall. Why'nchya ask Cruz?"

"Okay." I took a long pull of tepid milk while I considered the latest developments in what was becoming the most bizarre road trip of my life. "How are you feeling?"

"Groovy."

"You look like hell." I could still talk to him, after a fashion, when he was separated from Cruz. And I lied, "Sylvia's worried."

"What's she worried about?"

I shrugged, let it hang. Impossible to read his face, his swollen eyes. In truth, I wasn't sure I completely recognized him, this wasted hulk swaying against the car, features glazed into gargoyle contortions.

Hart nodded wisely, suddenly illuminated regarding a great and abiding mystery of the universe. His smile returned.

I glanced back, saw Cruz's murky shadow drifting in the station window.

"Man, what are we doing out here? We could be in Portland by three." What I wanted to say was, let's jump in the car and shag ass for California. Leave Cruz in the middle of the parking lot holding his pecker and swearing eternal vengeance for all I cared.

"Anxious to get going on your book, huh?"

"If there's a book. I'm not much of a writer. I don't even know if we'll get a movie out of this mess."

"Ain't much of an actor, either." He laughed and slapped my shoulder with an iron paw to show he was just kidding. "Hey, lemme tell'ya. Did'ya know Cruz studied geology at UCLA? He did. Real knowledgeable about glaciers an' rocks. All that good shit. Thought he was gonna work for the oil companies up in Alaska. Make some fat stacks. Ah, but you know how it goes, doncha, Ray-bo?"

"He graduated UCLA?" I tried not to sound astonished. It had been the University of Washington for me. The home of medicine, which wasn't my specialty, according to the proctors. Political science and drama were the last exits.

"Football scholarship. Hard hittin' safety with a nasty attitude. They fuckin' grow on trees in the ghetto."

That explained some things. I was inexplicably relieved.

Cruz emerged, cutting a plug of tobacco with his pocket knife. "C'mon, H. I'm parched." And precisely as a cowboy would unhitch his horse to ride across the street, he fired the engine and rumbled the one quarter block to Moony's Tavern and parked in a diagonal slot between a hay truck and a station wagon plastered with anti-Democrat, pro-gun bumper stickers.

Hart asked if I planned on joining them and I replied maybe in a while, I wanted to stretch my legs. The idea of entering that sweltering cavern and bellying up to the bar with the lowlife regulars and mine own dear chums made my stomach even more unhappy.

I grabbed my valise from the car and started walking. I walked along the street, past a row of dented mailboxes, rust-red flags erect; an outboard motor repair shop with a dusty police cruiser in front; the Poger Rock Grange, which appeared abandoned because its windows were boarded and where they weren't, kids had broken them with rocks and bottles, and maybe the same kids had drawn 666 and other satanic symbols on the whitewashed planks, or maybe real live Satanists did the deed; Bob's Liquor Mart, which was a corrugated shed with bars on the tiny windows; the Laundromat, full of tired women in oversized tee-shirts, and screeching, dirty-faced kids racing among the machinery while an A.M. radio broadcast a Rush Limbaugh rerun; and a trailer loaded with half-rotted firewood for 75 BUCKS! I finally sat on a rickety bench under some trees near the lone stoplight, close enough to hear it clunk through its cycle.

I drew a manila envelope from the valise, spread sloppy typed police reports and disjointed photographs beside me. The breeze stirred and I used a rock for a paper weight.

A whole slew of the pictures featured Russell Piers in various poses, mostly mug shots, although a few had been snapped during more pleasant times. There was even one of him and a younger brother standing in front of the Space Needle. The remaining photos were of Piers' latest girlfriend—Penny Aldon, the girl from Allen Town. Skinny, pimply, mouthful of braces. A flower child with a suitably vacuous smirk.

Something cold and nasty turned over in me as I studied the haphazard data, the disheveled photo collection. I felt the pattern, unwholesome as damp cobwebs against my skin. Felt it, yet couldn't put a name to it, couldn't put my finger on it and my heart began pumping dangerously and I looked away, thought of Carly instead, and how I'd forgotten to call her on her seventh birthday because I was in Spain with some friends at a Lipizzaner exhibition. Except, I hadn't forgotten, I was wired for sound from a snort of primo Colombian blow and the thought of dialing that long string of international numbers was too much for my circuits.

Ancient history, as they say. Those days of fast-living and superstar dreams belonged to another man, and he was welcome to them.

Waiting for cars to drive past so I could count them, I had an epiphany. I realized the shabby buildings were cardboard and the people milling here and there at opportune junctures were macaroni and glue. Dull blue construction paper sky and cotton ball clouds. And I wasn't really who I thought of myself as—I was an ant left over from a picnic raid, awaiting some petulant child god to put his boot down on my pathetic diorama existence.

My cell rang and an iceberg calved in my chest.

"Hey, Ray, you got any Indian in ya?" Rob asked.

I mulled that as a brand new Cadillac convertible paused at the light. A pair of yuppie tourists mildly argued about directions—a man behind the wheel in stylish wraparound shades and a polo shirt, and a woman wearing a floppy, wide-brimmed hat like the Queen Mum favored. They pretended not to notice me. The woman pointed right and they went right, leisurely, up the hill and beyond. "Comanche," I said. Next was a shiny green van loaded with Asian kids. Sign on the door said THE EVERGREEN STATE COLLEGE. It turned right and so did the one that came after. "About one thirty-second. Am I eligible for some reparation money? Did I inherit a casino?"

"Where the hell did the Comanche sneak in?"

"Great grandma. Tough old bird. Didn't like me much. Sent me a straight razor for Christmas. I was nine."

Rob laughed. "Cra-zee. I did a search and came up with a bunch of list-ings for genetic research. Lemme check this . . . " he shuffled paper close to the receiver, cleared his throat. "Turns out this X haplogroup has to do with mitochondrial DNA, genes passed down on the maternal side—and an X-haplogroup is a specific subdivision or cluster. The university wags are tryin' to use female lineage to trace tribal migrations and so forth. Some-thing like three percent of Native Americans, Europeans and Basque belong to the X-group. Least, according to the stuff I thought looked reputable. Says here there's lots of controversy about its significance. Usual academic crap. Whatch you were after?"

"I don't know. Thanks, though."

"You okay, bud? You sound kinda odd."

"Shucks, Rob, I've been trapped in a car with two redneck psychos for weeks. Might be getting to me, I'll admit."

"Whoa, sorry. Sylvia called and started going on—"

"Everything's hunky-dory, All right?"

"Cool, bro." Rob's tone said nothing was truly cool, but he wasn't in any position to press the issue. There'd be a serious Q&A when I returned, no doubt about it.

Cruz's dad was Basque, wasn't he? Hart was definitely of good, solid German stock only a couple generations removed from the motherland.

Stop me if you've heard this one—a Spaniard, a German and a Comanche walk into a bar—

After we said goodbye, I dialed my ex and got her machine, caught myself and hung up as it was purring. It occurred to me then, what the pattern was, and I stared dumbly down at the fractured portraits of Penny and Piers as their faces were dappled by sunlight falling through a maze of leaves.

I laughed, bitter.

How in God's name had they ever fooled us into thinking they were people at all? The only things missing from this farce were strings and zippers, a boom mike.

I stuffed the photos and the reports into the valise, stood in the weeds at the edge of the asphalt. My blood still pulsed erratically. Shadows began to crawl deep and blue between the buildings and the trees and in the wake of low-gliding cumulus clouds. Moony's Tavern waited, back there in the golden dust, and Cruz's Chevy before it, stolid as a coffin on the altar.

Something was happening, wasn't it? This thing that was happening, had been happening, could it follow me home if I cut and ran? Would it follow me to Sylvia and Carly?

No way to be certain, no way to tell if I had simply fallen off my rocker—maybe the heat had cooked my brain, maybe I was having a long-overdue nervous breakdown. Maybe, shit. The sinister shape of the world contracted around me, gleamed like the curves of a great killing jar. I heard the lid screwing tight in the endless ultraviolet collisions, the white drone of insects.

I turned right and walked up the hill.

5.

About two hours later, a guy in a vintage farm truck stopped. The truck had cruised by me twice, once going toward town, then on the way back. And here it was again. I hesitated; nobody braked for hitchhikers unless the hitcher was a babe in tight jeans.

I thought of Piers and Penny, their expressions in the video, drinking us with their smiling mouths, marking us. And if that was true, we'd been weighed, measured and marked, what was the implication? Piers and Penny were two from among a swarm. Was it open season?

The driver studied me with unsettling intensity, his beady eyes obscured by thick, black-rimmed glasses. He beckoned.

My legs were tired already and the back of my neck itched with sunburn. Also, what did it matter anyway? If I were doing anything besides playing out the hand, I would've gone into Olympia and caught a southbound Greyhound. I climbed aboard.

George was a retired civil engineer. Looked the part—crewcut, angular face like a piece of rock, wore a dress shirt with a row of clipped pens and a tie flung over his shoulder, and polyester slacks. He kept NPR on the radio at a mumble. Gripped the wheel with both gnarled hands.

He seemed familiar—a figure dredged from memories of scientists and engineers of my grandfather's generation. He could've *been* my grandfather.

George asked me where I was headed. I said Los Angeles and he gave me a glance that said LA was in the opposite direction. I told him I wanted to visit the Mima Mounds—since I was in the neighborhood.

There was a heavy silence. A vast and unfathomable pressure built in the cab. At last George said, "Why, they're only a couple miles farther on. Do you know anything about them?"

I admitted that I didn't and he said he figured as much. He told me the Mounds were declared a national monument back in the '60s; the subject of scholarly debate and wildly inaccurate hypotheses. He hoped I wouldn't be disappointed—they weren't glamorous compared to real natural wonders such as Niagara Falls, the Grand Canyon or the California Redwoods. The preserve was on the order of five hundred acres, but that was nothing. The Mounds had stretched for miles and miles in the old days. The land grabs of the 1890s reduced the phenomenon to a pocket, surrounded it with rundown farms, pastures and cows. The ruins of America's agrarian era.

I said that it would be impossible to disappoint me.

George turned at a wooden marker with a faded white arrow. A nicely paved single lane wound through temperate rain forest for a mile and looped into a parking lot occupied by the Evergreen vans and a few other vehicles. There was a fence with a gate and beyond that, the vague border of a clearing. Official bulletins were posted every six feet, prohibiting dogs, alcohol and firearms.

"Sure you want me to leave you here?"

"I'll be fine."

George rustled, his clothes chitin sloughing. "X marks the spot."

I didn't regard him, my hand frozen on the door handle, more than slightly afraid the door wouldn't open. Time slowed, got stuck in molasses. "I know a secret, George."

"What kind of secret?" George said, too close, as if he'd leaned in tight.

The hairs stiffened on the nape of my neck. I swallowed and closed my eyes. "I saw a picture in a biology textbook. There was this bug, looked exactly like a piece of bark, and it was barely touching a beetle with its nose. The one that resembled bark was what entomologists call an assassin bug and it was draining the beetle dry. Know how? It poked the beetle with a razor sharp beak thingy—"

"A rostrum, you mean."

"Exactly. A rostrum, or a proboscis, depending on the species. Then the assassin bug injected digestive fluids, think hydrochloric acid, and sucked the beetle's insides out."

"How lovely," George said.

"No struggle, no fuss, just a couple bugs sitting on a branch. So I'm staring at this book and thinking the only reason the beetle got caught was because it fell for the old piece of bark trick, and then I realized that's how lots of predatory bugs operate. They camouflage themselves and sneak up on hapless critters to do their thing."

"Isn't that the way of the universe?"

"And I wondered if that theory only applied to insects."

"What do you suppose?"

"I suspect that theory applies to everything."

Zilch from George. Not even the rasp of his breath.

"Bye, George. Thanks for the ride." I pushed hard to open the door and jumped down; moved away without risking a backward glance. My knees were unsteady. After I passed through the gate and approached a bend in the path, I finally had the nerve to check the parking lot. George's truck was gone.

I kept going, almost falling forward.

The trees thinned to reveal the humpbacked plain from the TV picture. Nearby was a concrete bunker shaped like a squat mushroom—a park information kiosk and observation post. It was papered with articles and diagrams under Plexiglas. Throngs of brightly-clad Asian kids buzzed around the kiosk, laughing over the wrinkled flyers, pointing cameras and chattering enthusiastically. A shaggy guy in a hemp sweater, presumably the professor, lectured a couple of wind-burned ladies who obviously ran marathons in their spare time. The ladies were enthralled.

I mounted the stairs to the observation platform and scanned the environs. As George predicted, the view wasn't inspiring. The mounds spread beneath my vantage, none greater than five or six feet in height and largely engulfed in blackberry brambles. Collectively, the hillocks formed a dewdrop hemmed by mixed forest, and toward the narrowing end, a dilapidated trailer court, its structures rendered toys by perspective. The paved footpath coiled unto obscurity.

A radio-controlled airplane whirred in the trailer court airspace. The plane's engine throbbed, a shrill metronome. I squinted against the glare, couldn't discern the operator. My skull ached. I slumped, hugged the valise to my chest, pressed my cheek against damp concrete, and drowsed. Shoes scraped along the platform. Voices occasionally floated by. Nobody challenged me, my derelict posture. I hadn't thought they would. Who'd dare disturb the wildlife in this remote enclave?

My sluggish daydreams were phantoms of the field, negatives of its buckled hide and stealthy plants, and the whispered words *Eastern Wash-*

ington, South America, Norway. Scientists might speculate about the geological method of the mounds' creation until doomsday. I knew this place and its sisters were unnatural as monoliths hacked from rude stone by primitive hands and stacked like so many dominos in the uninhabited spaces of the globe. What were they? Breeding grounds, feeding grounds, shrines? Or something utterly alien, something utterly incomprehensible to match the blighted fascination that dragged me ever closer and consumed my will to flee.

Hart's call yanked me from the doldrums. He was drunk. "You shoulda stuck around, Ray-bo. We been huntin' everywhere for you. Cruz ain't in a nice mood." The connection was weak, a transmission from the dark side of Pluto. Batteries were dying.

"Where are you?" I rubbed my gummy eyes and stood.

"We're at the goddamned Mounds. Where are *you*?"

I spied a tiny glint of moving metal. The Chevy rolled across the way where the road and the mobile homes intersected. I smiled—Cruz hadn't been looking for me; he'd been trolling around on the wrong side of the park, frustrated because he'd missed the entrance. As I watched, the car slowed and idled in the middle of the road. "I'm here."

The cell phone began to click like a Geiger counter that'd hit the mother lode. Bits of fiddle music pierced the garble.

The car jolted from a savage tromp on the gas and listed ditchward. It accelerated, jounced and bounded into the field, described a haphazard arc in my direction. I had a momentary terror that they'd seen me atop the tower, were coming for me, were planning some unhinged brand of retribution. But no, the distance was too great. I was no more than a speck, if I was anything. Soon, the car lurched behind the slope of intervening hillocks and didn't emerge.

"Hart, are you there?"

The clicking intensified and abruptly chopped off, replaced by smooth, bottomless static. Deep sea squeals and warbles began to filter through. Bees humming. A castrati choir on a gramophone. Giggling. Someone, perhaps Cruz, whispering a Latin prayer. I was grateful when the phone made an electronic protest and expired. I hurled it over the side.

The college crowd had disappeared. Gone too, the professor and his admirers. I might've joined the migration if I hadn't spotted the cab of George's truck mostly hidden by a tree. It was the only rig in the parking lot. I couldn't tell if anyone was behind the wheel.

The sun hung low and fat, reddening as it sank. The breeze had cooled. It plucked at my hair, dried my sweat, chilled me a little. I listened for the roar of the Chevy, buried to the axles in loose dirt, high-centered on a stump; or perhaps they'd abandoned the vehicle. Thus I strained to pick my companions from among the blackberry patches and softly undulating clumps of scotch broom that had invaded this place too.

Quiet.

I went down the stairs and let the path take me. I went as a man in a stupor, my muscles lethargic with dread. The lizard subprocessor in my brain urged me to sprint for the highway, to scuttle into a burrow. It possessed a hint of what waited over the hill, had possibly witnessed this melodrama many times before. I whistled a dirge through clenched teeth and the mounds closed ranks behind me.

Ahead, came the dull clank of a slamming door.

The car was stalled at the foot of a steep slope, its hood buried in a tangle of brush. The windows were dark as a muddy aquarium and festooned with fleshy creepers and algid scum.

I took root a few yards from the car, noting that the engine was dead, yet the vehicle rocked on its springs from some vigorous activity. A rhythmic motion that caused metal to complain. The brake lights stuttered.

Hart's doughy face materialized on the passenger side, bumped against the glass with the dispassion of a pale, exotic fish, and withdrew, descending into a marine trench. His forehead left a starry impact. Someone's palm smacked the rear window, hung there, fingers twitching.

I retreated. Ran, more like. I may have shrieked. Somewhere along the line the valise flew open and its contents spilled—a welter of files, the argyle socks Carly gave me for Father's Day, my toiletries. A handful of photographs pinwheeled in a gust. I dropped the bag. Ungainly, panicked, I didn't get far, tripped and collapsed as the sky blackened and a high-pitched keening erupted from several locations simultaneously. In moments all ambient light had been sucked away; I couldn't see the thorny bush gouging my neck as I wriggled for cover, couldn't make out my own hand before my eyes.

The keening ceased. Peculiar echoes bounced in its wake, gave me the absurd sensation of lying on a sound stage with the kliegs shut off. I received the impression of movement around my hunkered self, although I didn't hear footsteps. I shuddered, pressed my face deeper into musty soil. Ants investigated my pants cuffs.

Cruz called my name from the throat of a distant tunnel. I knew it wasn't him and kept silent. He cursed me and giggled the unpleasant giggle I'd heard on the phone. Hart tried to coax me out, but this imitation was even worse. They went down the entire list and despite everything I was tempted to answer when Carly began crying and hiccupping and begging me to help her, daddy please, in a baby girl voice she hadn't owned for several years. I stuffed my fist in my mouth, held on while the chorus drifted here and there and eventually receded into the buzz and chirr of field life.

The sun flickered on and the world was restored piecemeal—one root, one stump, one hill at a time. My head swam; reminded me of waking from anesthesia.

Dusk was blooming when I crept from the bushes and tasted the air, cocked an ear for predators. The Chevy was there, shimmering in the twilight. Motionless now.

I could've crouched in my blind forever, wild-eyed as a hare run to ground in a ruined shirt and piss-stained slacks. But it was getting cold and I was thirsty, so I slunk across the park at an angle that took me to the road near the trailer court. I went, casting glances over my shoulder for pursuit that never came.

6.

I told a retiree sipping ice tea in a lawn chair that my car had broken down and he let me use his phone to call a taxi. If he witnessed Cruz crash the Chevy into the Mounds, he wasn't saying. The police didn't show while I waited and that said enough about the situation.

The taxi driver was a stolid Samoan who proved not the least bit interested in my frightful appearance or talking. He drove way too fast for comfort, if I'd been in a rational frame of mind, and dropped me at the Greyhound depot in downtown Olympia.

I wandered inside past the rag-tag gaggle of modern gypsies who inevitably haunted these terminals, studied the big board while the ticket agent pursed her lips in distaste. Her expression certified me as one of the unwashed mob.

I picked Seattle at random, bought a ticket. The ticket got me the key to the restroom, where I splashed my welted flesh, combed cat tails from my hair and looked almost human again. Almost. The fluorescent tube crackled and sizzled, threatened to plunge the crummy toilet into darkness, and in the discotheque flashes, my haggard face seemed strange.

The bus arrived an hour late and it was crammed. I shared a seat with a middle-aged woman wearing a shawl and scads of costume jewelry. Her ivory skin was hard and she smelled of chlorine. I didn't imagine she wanted to sit by me, judging from the flare of her nostrils, the crimp of her over-glossed mouth.

Soon the bus was chugging into the wasteland of night and the lights clicked off row by row as passengers succumbed to sleep. Except some guy near the front who left his overhead lamp on to read, and me. I was too exhausted to close my eyes.

I surprised myself by crying.

And the woman surprised me again by murmuring, "Hush, hush, dear. Hush, hush." She patted my trembling shoulder. Her hand lingered.

It Came From Us

Unsnarl the etymology, and you find that "monster" and "demonstrate" share a common root, the Latin *monstrum*, whose meanings include "sign" or "portent." As Umberto Eco notes in *On Ugliness* (2007), the traditional view of the monster has been as an indication of something else, often a divine message. The monster is simultaneously that which snaps its misshapen jaws in front of us, and a signpost pointing us towards some additional significance. (Indeed, the idea of the *monstrum* might be a very profitable way to discuss how it is that horror stories function.) Often enough, the meaning a monster points to lies outside the self, in anxiety at the world's threats and failings, the harm it poses to us physically and mentally. Certainly, the stories in the first three sections of this anthology offer a host of such meanings.

There is, of course, another direction to which the signpost might point, and that is at us. This is the monster as mirror, reflecting our own ugliness and shortcomings back at us. The stories in the fourth and final section of this anthology hold up the glass to humanity, and record what is found in its depths. China Miéville's "Familiar" begins with a witch's disappointment in the creature he has wrought from his flesh, and then follows the discarded lump as it remakes itself from its urban surroundings. In Lisa Tuttle's "Replacements," a strange new pet becomes the obsession of women all over London, much to the disgust and confusion of the men in their lives. Stephen Graham Jones's "Little Monsters" is an exercise in the challenges of monster-construction, while Sarah Langan's "The Changeling" presents an unwanted and neglected child who becomes a child-snatching monster in the service of the dead. Nathan Ballingrud's "The Monsters of Heaven" asks to what ends we might employ our monsters in the expiation of our most terrible mistakes. And in the anthology's powerful closing story, Nadia Bulkin's "Absolute Zero," eight-year-old Max is given a Polaroid picture of his missing father, a stag-headed avatar of the wild. As Max grows and tries to build a future by searching for pieces of his past, including his monstrous father, he discovers that the worlds of the human and the monster are hopelessly blurred.

To one degree or another, all the stories in this final section touch on ideas of parents and children. Given that family is the means by which we enter the world, and by which the world first enters us, it is not so surprising that stories about our monstrousness should involve the family. If this anthology has an overarching theme, it might be that monsters are our family, always closer to us than is really comfortable, the twisted limbs on our family tree.

Familiar
China Miéville

A witch needed to impress his client. His middleman, who had arranged the appointment, told him that the woman was very old—"hundred at least"—and intimidating in a way he could not specify. The witch intuited something unusual, money or power. He made careful and arduous preparations. He insisted that he meet her a month later than the agent had planned.

His workshop was a hut, a garden shed in the shared allotments of north London. The woman edged past plots of runner beans, tomatoes, failing root vegetables and trellises, past the witch's neighbours, men decades younger than her but still old, who tended bonfires and courteously did not watch her.

The witch was ready. Behind blacked-out windows his little wooden room was washed. Boxes stowed in a tidy pile. The herbs and organic accoutrements of his work were out of the way but left visible—claws, skins like macabre facecloths, bottles stopped up, and careful piles of dust and objects. The old woman looked them over. She stared at a clubfooted pigeon chained by its good leg to a perch.

"My familiar."

The woman said nothing. The pigeon sounded and shat.

"Don't meet his eye, he'll steal your soul out of you." The witch hung a black rag in front of the bird. He would not look his client clear on. "He's basilisk, but you're safe now. He's hidden."

From the ceiling was a chandelier of unshaped coat hangers and pieces of china, on which three candles scabbed with dripping were lit. Little pyramids of wax lay on the wooden table beneath them. In their guttering the witch began his consultation, manipulating scobs of gris-gris—on the photographs his client provided he sprinkled leaf flakes, dirt, and grated remnants of plastic with an herb shaker from a pizzeria.

The effects came quickly so that even the cold old woman showed interest. Air dried up and expanded until the shed was stuffy as an aeroplane. There were noises from the shelves: mummied detritus moved anxious. It was much more than happened at most consultations, but the witch was still waiting.

In the heat the candles were moist. Strings of molten wax descended. They coated each other and drip-dripped in instantly frozen splashes. The stalactites extended, bearding the bottom of the candelabrum. The candles burnt too fast, pouring off wax, until the wire was trimmed with finger-thick extrusions.

They built up matter unevenly, curling out away from the table, and then they sputtered and seemed not to be dripping grease but drooling it from mouths that stretched open stringy within the wax. Fluttering tongues emerged and colourless eyes from behind nictitating membranes. For moments the things were random sculptures and then they were suddenly and definitively organic. At their ends, the melted candles' runoff was a fringe of little milk-white snakes. They were a few inches of flesh. Their bodies merged, anchored, with wax. They swayed with dim predatory intent and whispered.

The old woman screamed and so did the witch. He turned his cry though into a declamation and wavered slightly in his chair, so that the nest of dangling wax snakes turned their attention to him. The pigeon behind its dark screen called in distress. The snakes stretched vainly from the candles and tried to strike the witch. Their toxin dribbled onto the powder of his hex, mixed it into wet grime under which the woman's photographs began to change.

It was an intercession, a series of manipulations even the witch found tawdry and immoral: but the pay was very good, and he knew that for his standing he must impress. The ceremony lasted less than an hour, the grease-snakes leaking noise and fluid, the pigeon ceaselessly frightened. At the end the witch rose weakly, his profuse sweat making him gleam like the wet wax. Moving with strange speed, too fast to be struck, he cut the snakes off where their bodies became candle, and they dropped onto the table and squirmed in death, bleeding thick pale blood.

His client stood and smiled, taking the corpses of the half-snakes and her photographs, carefully leaving them soiled. She was clear-eyed and happy and she did not wince at light as the witch did when he opened the door to her and gave her instructions for when to return. He watched her go through the kitchen gardens and only closed his shed door again when she was out of sight.

The witch drew back the screen from before the terrified pigeon and was about to kill it, but he stared at the stubs of wax where the snakes had been and instead he opened a window and let the bird out. He sat at the table and breathed heavily, watching the boxes at the back of the hut. The air settled. The witch could hear scratching. It came from inside a plastic toolbox, where he had stashed his real familiar.

He had called a familiar. He had been considering it for a long time. He had had a rough understanding that it would give him a conduit to a fecundity, and that had bolstered him through the pain and distaste of what the conjuration had needed. Listening to the curious scritch-scritch he fingered the scabs on his thighs and chest. They would scar.

The information he had found on the technique was vague—passed-on vagrants' hedge-magic, notepad palimpsests, marginalia in phone books. The mechanics of the operation had never been clear. The witch consoled himself that the misunderstanding was not his fault. He had hoped that the familiar, when it came, would fit his urban practice. He had hoped for a rat, big and dirty-furred, or a fox, or a pigeon such as the one he had displayed. He had thought that the flesh he provided was a sacrifice. He had not known it was substance.

With the lid off, the toolbox was a playpen, and the familiar investigated it. The witch looked at it, queasy. It had coated its body in the dust, so it no longer left wetness. Like a sea slug, ungainly, flanged with outgrowths of its own matter. Heavy as an apple, it was an amalgam of the witch's scraps of fat and flesh, coagulated with his sputum, cum, and hoodoo. It coiled, rolled itself busy into corners of its prison. It clutched towards the light, convulsing its pulp.

Even in its container, out of sight, the witch had felt it. He had felt it groping in the darkness behind him, and as he did with a welling up like blood he had made the snakes come, which he could not have done before. The familiar disgusted him. It made his stomach spasm, it left him ill and confounded, and he was not sure why. He had flensed animals for his calling, alive sometimes, and was inured to that. He had eaten shit and roadkill when liturgy demanded. But that little rag of his own flesh gave him a kind of passionate nausea.

When the thing had first moved he had screamed, realising what his familiar would be, and spewed till he was empty. And still it was almost beyond him to watch it, but he made himself, to try to know what it was that revolted him.

The witch could feel the familiar's enthusiasm. A feral fascination for things held it together, and every time it tensed and moved by peristalsis around its plastic cell the contractions of its dumb and hungry interest passed through the witch and bent him double. It was stupid: wordless and searingly curious. The witch could feel it make sense of the dust, now that it had rolled in it, randomly then deliberately, using it for something.

He wanted the strength to do again what he had done for the woman, though making the snakes had exhausted him. His familiar manipulated things, was a channel for manipulation; it lived to change, use, and know. The witch very much wanted that power it had given him, and he closed his eyes and made himself sure he could, he could steel himself. But looking at the nosing dusted red thing he was suddenly weak and uncertain. He could feel its mindless mind. To have his own effluvia maggot through him with every experience, he could not bear it, even with what it gave him. It made him a sewer. Every few seconds in his familiar's presence he was swallowing his own bile. He felt its constant eager interest like foulness, God knew why. It was not worth it. The witch decided.

It could not be killed, or if it could he did not know how. The witch took a knife to it but it investigated the blade avidly, only parting and re-forming under his efforts. It tried to grip the metal.

When he bludgeoned it with a flatiron it recoiled and regrouped its matter, moved over and around the weapon, soiling it with itself, and making the iron into a skate on which it tried to move. Fire only discomfited it, and it sat tranquil in acid. It studied every danger as it had dust, trying to use it, and the echo of that study turned the witch's gut.

He tipped the noisome thing into a sack. He could feel it shove itself at the fabric's pores, and he moved quickly. The witch drove, hessian fumbling in the toolbox beside him (he could not put it behind him, where he could not see it, where it might get out and conduct its investigations near his skin).

It was almost night when he stopped by the Grand Union Canal. In the municipal gardens of west London, between beat-up graffitied bridges, in earshot of the last punk children in the skate park, the witch tried to drown his familiar. He was not so stupid as to think it would work, but to drop the thing, weighted with rocks and tied up, into the cool and dirty water, was a relief so great he moaned. To see it drunk up by the canal. It was gone from him. He ran.

Cosseted by mud, the familiar tried to learn. It sent out temporary limbs to make sense of things. It strained without fear against the sack.

It compared everything it found to everything it knew. Its power was change. It was tool-using; it had no way of knowing except to put to use. The world was infinite tools. By now the familiar understood dust well, and had a little knowledge of knives and irons. It felt the water and the fibrous weave of the bag, and did things with them to learn that they were not what it had used before.

Out of the sack, in muddy dark, it swam ugly and inefficient, learning scraps of rubbish and little life. There were hardy fish even in so grubby a channel, and it was not long before it found them. It took a few carefully apart, and learned to use them.

The familiar plucked their eyes. It rubbed them together, dangled them from their fibres. It sent out microscopic filaments that tickled into the blood-gelled nerve stalks. The familiar's life was contagious. It sucked the eyes into itself and suddenly as visual signals reached it for the first time, though there was no light (it was burrowing in the mud) it *knew* that it was in darkness. It rolled into shallows, and with its new vitreous machines it saw streetlamp light cut the black water.

It found the corpses of the fish again (using sight, now, to help it). It unthreaded them. It greased itself with the slime on their skins. One by one it broke off the ribs like components of a model kit. It embedded them in its skin (its minute and random blood vessels and muscle fibres insinuating into the bone). It used them to walk, with the sedate pick-picking motion of an urchin.

The familiar was tireless. Over hours it learned the canal bed. Each thing it found it used, some in several ways. Some it used in conjunction with other pieces. Some it discarded after a while. With each use, each manipulation (and only with that manipulation, that change) it read meanings. The familiar accumulated brute erudition, forgetting nothing, and with each insight the next came easier, as its context grew. Dust had been the first and hardest thing to know.

When the familiar emerged from the water with the dawn, it was poured into a milk-bottle carapace. Its clutch of eyes poked from the bottleneck. It nibbled with a nail clipper. With precise little bullets of stone it had punc-tured holes in its glass sides, from which legs of waterlogged twig-wood and broken pens emerged. To stop it sinking into wet earth its feet were coins and flat stones. They looked insecurely attached. The familiar dragged the brown sack that had contained it. Though it had not found a use for it, and though it had no words for the emotion, it felt something like sentiment for the hessian.

All its limbs were permanently reconfigured. Even those it tired of and kicked off were wormed with organic ruts for its juices. Minuscule muscles and tendons the thickness of spider-silk but vastly stronger rooted through the components of its bric-a-brac body, anchoring them together. The flesh at its centre had grown.

The familiar investigated grass, and watched the birds with its inadequate eyes. It trouped industrious as a beetle on variegated legs.

Through that day and night the familiar learned. It crossed paths with small mammals. It found a nest of mice and examined their parts. Their tails it took for prehensile tentacles; their whiskers bristled it; it upgraded its eyes and learned to use ears. It compared what it found to dust, blades, water, twigs, fish ribs, and sodden rubbish: it learned mouse.

It learned its new ears, with focused fascination. Young Londoners played in the gardens, and the familiar stayed hidden and listened to their slang. It heard patterns in their sequenced barks.

There were predators in the gardens. The familiar was the size of a cat, and foxes and dogs sometimes went for it. It was now too big for the bottle-armour, had burst it, but had learned instead to fight. It raked with shards of china, nails, and screws—not with anger, but with its unchanging beatific interest. It was impossibly sure-footed on its numerous rubbish legs. If an attacker did not run fast enough, the familiar would learn it. It would be used. The familiar had brittle fingertips, made of dogs' teeth.

The familiar moved away from the gardens. It followed the canal bank to a graveyard, to an industrial sidings, to a dump. It gave itself a shape with wheels, plunging its veins and tissue into the remnants of a trolley. When later it discarded them, pulling them out, the wheels bled.

Sometimes it used its tools like their original owners, as when it took its legs from birds (scampering over burnt-out cars like a rock rabbit on four or six avian feet). It could change them. In sun, the familiar shaded its eyes with flanges of skin that had been cats' ears.

It had learned to eat. Its hunger, its feeding was a tool like dust had been: the familiar did not need to take in nourishment but doing so gave it satisfaction, and that was enough. It made itself a tongue from strips of wet towel, and made a mouth full of interlocking cogs. These teeth rotated in its jaw, chewing, driving food scraps back towards the throat.

In the small hours of morning, in a waste lot stained by chemical spill, the familiar finally made a tool of the sack that had delivered it. It found two broken umbrellas, one skeletal, the other ragged, and it busied itself with them, holding them tight with hair-grip hands, manipulating them with rat tails. It secured the sackcloth to them with its organic roots. After hours of calculated tinkering, during which it spoke English words in the mind it had built itself, the reshaped umbrellas spasmed open and shut on analogues of shoulders, and with a great gust the familiar flew.

Its umbrellas beat like scooping bat wings, and the greased hessian held it. It flew random as a butterfly, staring at the moon with cats' and dogs' eyes, its numerous limbs splayed. It hunted with urban bramble, thorned stalks that whipped and pinioned prey from the air and the ground. It scoured the scrubland of cats. It spasmed between tower blocks, each wing contraction jerking it through the air. It shouted the words it had learned, without sound.

There were only two nights that it could fly, before it was too large, and it loved them. It was aware of its pleasure. It used it as it grew. The summer became unusually hot. The familiar hid in the sudden masses of buddleia. It found passages through the city. It lived in wrecking yards and sewers, growing, changing, and using.

Though it replaced them regularly, the familiar kept its old eyes, moving them down itself so that its sight deteriorated along its back. It had learned caution. It was educated: two streets might be empty, but not identically so, it knew. It parsed the grammar of brick and neglected industry. It listened at doors, cupping the cones of card, the plastic funnels with which it extended its ears. Its vocabulary increased. It was a Londoner.

Every house it passed it marked like a dog: the familiar pissed out its territory with glands made from plastic bottles. Sniffing with a nose taken from a badger, it sprayed a liquid of rubbish-tip juices and the witch's blood in a rough circle across the flattened zones of the north city, where the tube trains emerged from underground. The familiar claimed the terraced landscape.

It seemed a ritual. But it had watched the little mammals of the landfills and understood that territory was a tool, and it used it and learned it, or thought it did until the night it was tracing its limits into suburban spaces, and it smelt another's trail.

The familiar raged. It was maddened. It thrashed in a yard that reeked of alien spoor, chewing tires and spitting out their rags. Eventually, it hunkered down to the intruder's track. It licked it. It bristled throughout its body of witch flesh and patchwork trash. The new scent was sharper than its own, admixed with different blood. The familiar hunted.

The trail ran across back gardens, separated by fences that the familiar vaulted easily, trickled across toys and drying grass, over flowerbeds and rockeries. The prey was old and tough: it told in the piss. The familiar used the smell to track, and learned it, and understood that it was the newcomer here.

In the sprawl of the outer city the stench became narcotic. The familiar stalked silently on rocks like hooves. The night was warm and overcast. Behind empty civic halls, tags, and the detritus of vandalism. It ended there. The smell was so strong, it was a fight-drug. It blistered the familiar's innards. Cavities opened in it, rudimentary lungs like bellows: it made itself breathe, so that it could pant to murder.

Corrugated iron and barbed wire surrounds. The witch's familiar was the intruder. There were no stars, no lamplight. The familiar stood without motion. It breathed out a challenge. The breath drifted across the little arena. Something enormous stood. Debris moved. Debris rose and turned and opened its mouth and caught the exhalation. It sucked it in out of all the air, filled its belly. It learned it.

Dark expanded. The familiar blinked its eyelids of rain-wet leather offcuts. It watched its enemy unfold.

This was an old thing, an old familiar, the bull, the alpha. It had escaped or been banished or lost its witch long ago. It was broken bodies, wood and plastic, stone and ribbed metal, a constellation of clutter exploding from a mass of skinless muscle the size of a horse. Beside its wet bloody eyes were embedded cameras, extending their lenses, powered by organic current. The mammoth shape clapped some of its hand-things.

The young familiar had not known until then that it had thought itself alone. Without words, it wondered what else was in the city—how many other outcasts, familiars too foul to use. But it could not think for long as the monstrous old potentate came at it.

The thing ran on table legs and gripped with pincers that were human jaws. They clenched on the little challenger and tore at its accrued limbs.

Early in its life the familiar had learned pain, and this attack gave it agony. It felt itself lessen as the attacker ingested gulps of its flesh. The familiar understood in shock that it might cease.

Its cousin taught it that with its new mass it could bruise. The familiar could not retreat. Even bleeding and with arms, legs gone, with eyes crushed and leaking and something three times its size opening mouths and shears and raising flukes that were shovels, the intoxicant reek of a competitor's musk forced it to fight.

More pain and the loss of more self. The little insurgent was diminishing. It was awash in rival stink. A notion came to it. It pissed up in its adversary's eyes, spraying all the bloody muck left in it and rolling away from the liquid's arc. The hulking thing clamoured silently. Briefly blinded, it put its mouth to the ground and followed its tongue.

Behind it, the familiar was motionless. It made tools of shadows and silence, keeping dark and quiet stitched to it as the giant tracked its false trail. The little familiar sent fibres into the ground, to pipework inches below. It connected to the plastic with tentacles quickly as thick as viscera, made the pipe a limb and organ, shoving and snapping it a foot below its crouching opponent. It drove the ragged end up out of the earth, its plastic jags spurs. It ground it into the controlling mass of the old familiar, into the dead centre of meat, and as the wounded thing tried to pull itself free, the guileful young familiar sucked through the broken tube.

It ballooned cavities in itself, gaping vacuums at the ends of its new pipe intestine. The suction pinioned its enemy, and tore chunks of bloody matter from it. The familiar drew them through the buried duct, up into its own body. Like a glutton it swigged them.

The trapped old one tried to raise itself but its wood and metal limbs had no purchase. It could not pull itself free, and the pipe was too braced in earth to tear away. It tried to thread its own veins into the tubing and vie for it, to make its own oesophagus and drink down its attacker, but the vessels of the young familiar riddled the plastic, and the dying thing could not push them aside, and with all the tissue it had lost to the usurper, they were now equal in mass, and now the newcomer was bigger, and now bigger still.

Tissue passed in fat pellets into the swelling young familiar sitting anchored by impromptu guts. Venting grave little breaths, the ancient one shrivelled and broke apart, sucked into a plughole. The cobweb of its veins dried up from all its borrowed limbs and members, and they disaggregated, nothing but hubcaps again, and butcher's remnants, a dead television, tools, mechanical debris, all brittled and sucked clean of life. The limbs were arranged around clean ground, from which jagged a shard of piping.

All the next day, the familiar lay still. When it moved, after dark, it limped though it replaced its broken limbs: it was damaged internally, it ached with every step it took, or if it oozed or crawled. All but a few of its eyes were gone, and for nights it was too weak to catch and use any animals to fix that. It took none of its opponent's tools, except one of the human jaws that had been pincers. It was not a trophy, but something to consider.

It metabolised much of the flesh-matter it had ingested, burnt it away (and the older familiar's memories, of self-constitution on Victorian slag-heaps, troubled it like indigestion). But it was still severely bloated. It pierced its distended body with broken glass to let out pressure, but all that oozed out of it was its new self.

The familiar still grew. It had been enlarging ever since it emerged from the canal. With its painful victory came a sudden increase in its size, but it knew it would have reached that mass anyway.

Its enemy's trails were drying up. The familiar felt interest at that, rather than triumph. It lay for days in a car-wrecking yard, using new tools, building itself a new shape, listening to the men and the clatter of machines, feeling its energy and attention grow, but slowly. That was where it was when the witch found it.

An old lady came before it. In the noon heat the familiar sat loose as a doll. Over the warehouse and office roofs, it could hear church bells. The old lady stepped into its view and it looked up at her.

She was glowing, with more, it seemed, than the light behind her. Her skin was burning. She looked incomplete. She was at the edge of something. The familiar did not recognise her but it remembered her. She caught its eye and nodded forcefully, moved out of sight. The familiar was tired.

"There you are."

Wearily the familiar raised its head again. The witch stood before it.

"Wondered where you got to. Buggering off like that."

In the long silence the familiar looked the man up and down. It remembered him, too.

"Need you to get back to things. Job to finish."

The familiar's interest wandered. It picked at a stone, looked down at it, sent out veins and made it a nail. It forgot the man was there, until his voice surprised it.

"Could feel you all the time, you know." The witch laughed without pleasure. "How we found you, isn't it?" Glanced back at the woman out of the familiar's sight. "Like following me nose. Me gut."

Sun baked them all.

"Looking well."

The familiar watched him. It was inquisitive. It felt things. The witch moved back. There was a purr of summer insects. The woman was at the edge of the clearing of cars.

"Looking well," the witch said again.

The familiar had made itself the shape of a man. Its flesh centre was several stone of spread-out muscle. Its feet were boulders again, its hands bones on bricks. It would stand eight feet tall. There was too much stuff in it and on it to itemise. On its head were books, grafted in spine-first, their pages constantly riffling as if in wind. Blood vessels saturated their pages, and engorged to let out heat. The books sweated. The familiar's dog eyes focused on the witch, then the gently cooking wrecks.

"Oh Jesus."

The witch was staring at the bottom of the familiar's face, half pointing.

"Oh Jesus what you *do?*"

The familiar opened and closed the man-jaw it had taken from its opponent and made its own mouth. It grinned with third-hand teeth.

"What you fucking *do* Jesus *Christ*. Oh shit man. Oh no."

The familiar cooled itself with its page-hair.

"You got to come back. We need you again." Pointing vaguely at the woman, who was motionless and still shining. "Ain't done. She ain't finished. You got to come back.

"I can't *do it* on my own. Ain't got it. She ain't paying me no more. She's fucking *ruining me*." That last he screamed in anger directed backwards, but the woman did not flinch. She reached out her hand to the familiar, waved a clutch of mouldering dead snakes. "Come back," said the witch.

The familiar noticed the man again and remembered him. It smiled.

The man waited. "Come *back*," he said. "Got to come *back*, fucking *back*." He was crying. The familiar was fascinated. "Come *back*." The witch tore off his shirt. "You been *growing*. You been fucking *growing* you won't stop, and I can't do nothing without you now and you're *killing* me."

The woman with the snakes glowed. The familiar could see her through the witch's chest. The man's body was faded away in random holes. There was no blood. Two handspans of sternum, inches of belly, slivers of arm-meat all faded to nothing, as if the flesh had given up existing. Entropic wounds. The familiar looked in interest at the gaps. He saw into the witch's stomach, where hoops of gut ended where they met the hole, where the spine became hard to notice and did not exist for a space of several vertebrae. The man took off his trousers. His thighs were punctuated by the voids, his scrotum gone.

"You got to come back," he whispered. "I can't do nothing without you, and you're killing me. Bring me back."

The familiar touched itself. It pointed at the man with a chicken-bone finger, and smiled again.

"Come *back*," the witch said. "She wants you; I need you. You fucking *have* to come back. Have to *help* me." He stood cruciform. The sun shone through the cavities in him, breaking up his shadow with light.

The familiar looked down at black ants labouring by a cigarette end, up at the man's creased face, at the impassive old woman holding her dead snakes like a bouquet. It smiled without cruelty.

"Then *finish*," the witch screamed at it. "If you ain't going to come back then fucking *finish*." He stamped and spat at the familiar, too afraid to touch but raging. "You *fucker*. I can't stand this. Finish it for me you *fucker*." The witch beat his fists against his naked holed sides. He reached into a space below his heart. He wailed with pain and his face spasmed, but he fingered the inside of his body. His wound did not bleed, but when he drew out his shaking hand it was wet and red where it had touched his innards. He cried out again and shook blood into the familiar's face. "That what you *want*? That do you? You fucker. Come *back* or make it *stop*. Do *something* to *finish*."

From the familiar's neck darted a web of threads, which fanned out and into the corona of insects that surrounded it. Each fibre snaked into a tiny body and retracted. Flies and wasps and fat bees, a crawling handful of chitin was reeled in to the base of the familiar's throat, below its human jaw. The hair-thin tendrils scored through the tumour of living insects and took them over, used them, made them a tool. They hummed their wings loudly in time, clamped to the familiar's skin.

The vibrations resonated through its boccal cavity. It moved its mouth as it had seen others do. The insectile voice box echoed through it and made sound, which it shaped with lips.

"Sun," it said. Its droning speech intrigued it. It pointed into the sky, over the nude and fading witch's shoulder, up way beyond the old woman. It closed its eyes. It moved its mouth again and listened closely to its own quiet words. Rays bounced from car to battered car, and the familiar used them as tools to warm its skin.

Replacements
Lisa Tuttle

Walking through gray north London to the tube station, feeling guilty that he hadn't let Jenny drive him to work and yet relieved to have escaped another pointless argument, Stuart Holder glanced down at a pavement covered in a leaf-fall of fast-food cartons and white paper bags and saw, amid the dog turds, beer cans, and dead cigarettes, something horrible.

It was about the size of a cat, naked-looking, with leathery, hairless skin and thin, spiky limbs that seemed too frail to support the bulbous, ill-proportioned body. The face, with tiny bright eyes and a wet slit of a mouth, was like an evil monkey's. It saw him and moved in a crippled, spasmodic way. Reaching up, it made a clotted, strangled noise. The sound touched a nerve, like metal between the teeth, and the sight of it, mewling and choking and scrabbling, scaly claws flexing and wriggling, made him feel sick and terrified. He had no phobias, he found insects fascinating, not frightening, and regularly removed, unharmed, the spiders, wasps, and mayflies which made Jenny squeal or shudder helplessly.

But this was different. This wasn't some rare species of wingless bat escaped from a zoo, it wasn't something he would find pictured in any reference book. It was something that should not exist, a mistake, something alien. It did not belong in his world.

A little snarl escaped him and he took a step forward and brought his foot down hard.

The small, shrill scream lanced through him as he crushed it beneath his shoe and ground it into the road.

Afterward, as he scraped the sole of his shoe against the curb to clean it, nausea overwhelmed him. He leaned over and vomited helplessly into a red-and-white-striped box of chicken bones and crumpled paper.

He straightened up, shaking, and wiped his mouth again and again with his pocket handkerchief. He wondered if anyone had seen, and had a furtive look around. Cars passed at a steady crawl. Across the road a cluster of schoolgirls dawdled near a man smoking in front of a newsagent's, but on this side of the road the fried chicken franchise and bathroom suppliers had yet to open for the day and the nearest pedestrians were more than a hundred yards away.

Until that moment, Stuart had never killed anything in his life. Mosquitoes and flies of course, other insects probably, a nest of hornets once, that was all. He had never liked the idea of hunting, never lived in the country. He remembered his father putting out poisoned bait for rats, and he remembered shying bricks at those same vermin on a bit of waste ground where he had played as a boy. But rats weren't like other animals; they elicited no sympathy. Some things had to be killed if they would not be driven away.

He made himself look to make sure the thing was not still alive. Nothing should be left to suffer. But his heel had crushed the thing's face out of recognition, and it was unmistakably dead. He felt a cool tide of relief and satisfaction, followed at once, as he walked away, by a nagging uncertainty, the imminence of guilt. Was he right to have killed it, to have acted on violent, irrational impulse? He didn't even know what it was. It might have been somebody's pet.

He went hot and cold with shame and self-disgust. At the corner he stopped with five or six others waiting to cross the road and because he didn't want to look at them he looked down.

And there it was, alive again.

He stifled a scream. No, of course it was not the same one, but another. His leg twitched; he felt frantic with the desire to kill it, and the terror of his desire. The thin wet mouth was moving as if it wanted to speak.

As the crossing-signal began its nagging blare he tore his eyes away from the creature squirming at his feet. Everyone else had started to cross the street, their eyes, like their thoughts, directed ahead. All except one. A woman in a smart business suit was standing still on the pavement, looking down, a sick fascination on her face.

As he looked at her looking at it, the idea crossed his mind that he should kill it for her, as a chivalric, protective act. But she wouldn't see it that way. She would be repulsed by his violence. He didn't want her to think he was a monster. He didn't want to be the monster who had exulted in the crunch of fragile bones, the flesh and viscera merging pulpily beneath his shoe.

He forced himself to look away, to cross the road, to spare the alien life. But he wondered, as he did so, if he had been right to spare it.

Stuart Holder worked as an editor for a publishing company with offices an easy walk from St. Paul's. Jenny had worked there, too, as a secretary, when they met five years ago. Now, though, she had quite a senior position with another publishing house, south of the river, and recently they had given her a car. He had been supportive of her ambitions, supportive of her learning to drive, and proud of her on all fronts when she succeeded, yet he was aware, although he never spoke of it, that something about her success made him uneasy. One small, niggling, insecure part of himself was afraid that one day she would realize she didn't need him anymore. That was why he picked at her, and second-guessed her decisions when she was behind the wheel and he was in the passenger seat. He recognized this as he walked briskly through more crowded streets toward his office, and he told himself he would do better. He would have to. If anything drove them apart it was more likely to be his behavior than her career. He wished he had accepted her offer of a ride today. Better any amount of petty irritation between husband and wife than to be haunted by the memory of that tiny face, distorted in the death he had inflicted. Entering the building, he surreptitiously scraped the sole of his shoe against the carpet.

Upstairs two editors and one of the publicity girls were in a huddle around his secretary's desk; they turned on him the guilty-defensive faces of women who have been discussing secrets men aren't supposed to know.

He felt his own defensiveness rising to meet theirs as he smiled. "Can I get any of you chaps a cup of coffee?"

"I'm sorry, Stuart, did you want . . . ?" As the others faded away, his secretary removed a stiff white paper bag with the NEXT logo printed on it from her desktop.

"Joke, Frankie, joke." He always got his own coffee because he liked the excuse to wander, and he was always having to reassure her that she was not failing in her secretarial duties. He wondered if Next sold sexy underwear, decided it would be unkind to tease her further.

He felt a strong urge to call Jenny and tell her what had happened, although he knew he wouldn't be able to explain, especially not over the phone. Just hearing her voice, the sound of sanity, would be a comfort, but he restrained himself until just after noon, when he made the call he made every day.

Her secretary told him she was in a meeting. "Tell her Stuart rang," he said, knowing she would call him back as always.

But that day she didn't. Finally, at five minutes to five, Stuart rang his wife's office and was told she had left for the day.

It was unthinkable for Jenny to leave work early, as unthinkable as for her not to return his call. He wondered if she was ill. Although he usually stayed in the office until well after six, now he shoved a manuscript in his briefcase and went out to brave the rush hour.

He wondered if she was mad at him. But Jenny didn't sulk. If she was angry she said so. They didn't lie or play those sorts of games with each other, pretending not to be in, "forgetting" to return calls.

As he emerged from his local underground station Stuart felt apprehensive. His eyes scanned the pavement and the gutters, and once or twice the flutter of paper made him jump, but of the creatures he had seen that morning there were no signs. The body of the one he had killed was gone, perhaps eaten by a passing dog, perhaps returned to whatever strange dimension had spawned it. He noticed, before he turned off the high street, that other pedestrians were also taking a keener than usual interest in the pavement and the edge of the road, and that made him feel vindicated somehow.

London traffic being what it was, he was home before Jenny. While he waited for the sound of her key in the lock he made himself a cup of tea, cursed, poured it down the sink, and had a stiff whiskey instead. He had just finished it and was feeling much better when he heard the street door open.

"Oh!" The look on her face reminded him unpleasantly of those women in the office this morning, making him feel like an intruder in his own place. Now Jenny smiled, but it was too late. "I didn't expect you to be here so early."

"Nor me. I tried to call you, but they said you'd left already. I wondered if you were feeling all right."

"I'm fine!"

"You look fine." The familiar sight of her melted away his irritation. He loved the way she looked: her slender, boyish figure, her close-cropped, curly hair, her pale complexion and bright blue eyes.

Her cheeks now had a slight hectic flush. She caught her bottom lip between her teeth and gave him an assessing look before coming straight out with it. "How would you feel about keeping a pet?"

Stuart felt a horrible conviction that she was not talking about a dog or a cat. He wondered if it was the whiskey on an empty stomach which made him feel dizzy.

"It was under my car. If I hadn't happened to notice something moving down there I could have run over it." She lifted her shoulders in a delicate shudder.

"Oh, God, Jenny, you haven't brought it home!"

She looked indignant. "Well, of course I did! I couldn't just leave it in the street—somebody else might have run it over."

Or stepped on it, he thought, realizing now that he could never tell Jenny what he had done. That made him feel even worse, but maybe he was wrong. Maybe it was just a cat she'd rescued. "What is it?"

She gave a strange, excited laugh. "I don't know. Something very rare, I think. Here, look." She slipped the large, woven bag off her shoulder, opening it, holding it out to him. "Look. Isn't it the sweetest thing?"

How could two people who were so close, so alike in so many ways, see something so differently? He only wanted to kill it, even now, while she had obviously fallen in love. He kept his face carefully neutral although he couldn't help flinching from her description. *"Sweet?"*

It gave him a pang to see how she pulled back, holding the bag protectively close as she said, "Well, I know it's not pretty, but so what? I thought it was horrible, too, at first sight. . . . " Her face clouded, as if she found her first impression difficult to remember, or to credit, and her voice faltered a little. "But then, then I realized how *helpless* it was. It needed me. It can't help how it looks. Anyway, doesn't it kind of remind you of the Psammead?"

"The what?"

"Psammead. You know, *The Five Children and It*?"

He recognized the title but her passion for old-fashioned children's books was something he didn't share. He shook his head impatiently. "That thing didn't come out of a book, Jen. You found it in the street and you don't know what it is or where it came from. It could be dangerous, it could be diseased."

"Dangerous," she said in a withering tone.

"You don't know."

"I've been with him all day and he hasn't hurt me, or anybody else at the office, he's perfectly happy being held, and he likes being scratched behind the ears."

He did not miss the pronoun shift. "It might have rabies."

"Don't be silly."

"Don't *you* be silly; it's not exactly native, is it? It might be carrying all sorts of foul parasites from South America or Africa or wherever."

"Now you're being racist. I'm not going to listen to you. *And* you've been drinking." She flounced out of the room.

If he'd been holding his glass still he might have thrown it. He closed his eyes and concentrated on breathing in and out slowly. This was worse than any argument they'd ever had, the only crucial disagreement of their marriage. Jenny had stronger views about many things than he did, so her wishes usually prevailed. He didn't mind that. But this was different. He wasn't having that creature in his home. He had to make her agree.

Necessity cooled his blood. He had his temper under control when his wife returned. "I'm sorry," he said, although she was the one who should have apologized. Still looking prickly, she shrugged and would not meet his eyes. "Want to go out to dinner tonight?"

She shook her head. "I'd rather not. I've got some work to do."

"Can I get you something to drink? I'm only one whiskey ahead of you, honest."

Her shoulders relaxed. "I'm sorry. Low blow. Yeah, pour me one. And one for yourself." She sat down on the couch, her bag by her feet. Leaning over, reaching inside, she cooed, "Who's my little sweetheart, then?"

Normally he would have taken a seat beside her. Now, though, he eyed the pale, misshapen bundle on her lap and, after handing her a glass, retreated across the room. "Don't get mad, but isn't having a pet one of those things we discuss and agree on beforehand?"

He saw the tension come back into her shoulders, but she went on stroking the thing, keeping herself calm. "Normally, yes. But this is special. I didn't plan it. It happened, and now I've got a responsibility to him. Or her." She giggled. "We don't even know what sex you are, do we, my precious?"

He said carefully, "I can see that you had to do something when you found it, but keeping it might not be the best thing."

"I'm not going to put it out in the street."

"No, no, but . . . don't you think it would make sense to let a professional have a look at it? Take it to a vet, get it checked out . . . maybe it needs shots or something."

She gave him a withering look and for a moment he faltered, but then he rallied. "Come on, Jenny, be reasonable! You can't just drag some strange animal in off the street and keep it, just like that. You don't even know what it eats."

"I gave it some fruit at lunch. It ate that. Well, it sucked out the juice. I don't think it can chew."

"But you don't know, do you? Maybe the fruit juice was just an aperitif, maybe it needs half its weight in live insects every day, or a couple of small, live mammals. Do you really think you could cope with feeding it mice or rabbits fresh from the pet shop every week?"

"Oh, Stuart."

"Well? Will you just take it to a vet? Make sure it's healthy? Will you do that much?"

"And then I can keep it? If the vet says there's nothing wrong with it, and it doesn't need to eat anything too impossible?"

"Then we can talk about it. Hey, don't pout at me; I'm not your father, I'm not telling you what to do. We're partners, and partners don't make unilateral decisions about things that affect them both; partners discuss things and reach compromises and . . . "

"There can't be any compromise about this."

He felt as if she'd doused him with ice water. "What?"

"Either I win and I keep him or you win and I give him up. Where's the compromise?"

This was why wars were fought, thought Stuart, but he didn't say it. He was the picture of sweet reason, explaining as if he meant it, "The compromise is that we each try to see the other person's point. You get the animal checked out, make sure it's healthy and I, I'll keep an open mind about having a pet, and see if I might start liking . . . him. Does he have a name yet?"

Her eyes flickered. "No . . . we can choose one later, together. If we keep him."

He still felt cold and, although he could think of no reason for it, he was certain she was lying to him.

In bed that night as he groped for sleep Stuart kept seeing the tiny, hideous face of the thing screaming as his foot came down on it. That moment of blind, killing rage was not like him. He couldn't deny he had done it, or how he had felt, but now, as Jenny slept innocently beside him, as the creature she had rescued, a twin to his victim, crouched alive in the bathroom, he tried to remember it differently.

In fantasy, he stopped his foot, he controlled his rage and, staring at the memory of the alien animal, he struggled to see past his anger and his fear, to see through those fiercer masculine emotions and find his way to Jenny's feminine pity. Maybe his intuition had been wrong and hers was right. Maybe, if he had waited a little longer, instead of lashing out, he would have seen how unnecessary his fear was.

Poor little thing, poor little thing. It's helpless, it needs me, it's harmless so I won't harm it.

Slowly, in imagination, he worked toward that feeling, *her* feeling, and then, suddenly, he was there, through the anger, through the fear, through the hate to . . . not love, he couldn't say that, but compassion. Glowing and warm, compassion filled his heart and flooded his veins, melting the ice there and washing him out into the sea of sleep, and dreams where Jenny smiled and loved him and there was no space between them for misunderstanding.

He woke in the middle of the night with a desperate urge to pee. He was out of bed in the dark hallway when he remembered what was waiting in the bathroom. He couldn't go back to bed with the need unsatisfied, but he stood outside the bathroom door, hand hovering over the light switch on this side, afraid to turn it on, open the door, go in.

It wasn't, he realized, that he was afraid of a creature no bigger than a football and less likely to hurt him; rather, he was afraid that he might hurt it. It was a stronger variant of that reckless vertigo he had felt sometimes in high places, the fear, not of falling, but of throwing oneself off, of losing control and giving in to self-destructive urges. He didn't *want* to kill the thing—had his own feelings not undergone a sea change, Jenny's love for it would have been enough to stop him—but something, some dark urge stronger than himself, might make him.

Finally he went down to the end of the hall and outside to the weedy, muddy little area which passed for the communal front garden and in which the rubbish bins, of necessity, were kept, and, shivering in his thin cotton pajamas in the damp, chilly air, he watered the sickly forsythia, or whatever it was, that Jenny had planted so optimistically last winter.

When he went back inside, more uncomfortable than when he had gone out, he saw the light was on in the bathroom, and as he approached the half-open door, he heard Jenny's voice, low and soothing. "There, there. Nobody's going to hurt you, I promise. You're safe here. Go to sleep now. Go to sleep."

He went past without pausing, knowing he would be viewed as an intruder, and got back into bed. He fell asleep, lulled by the meaningless murmur of her voice, still waiting for her to join him.

Stuart was not used to doubting Jenny, but when she told him she had visited a veterinarian who had given her new pet a clean bill of health, he did not believe her.

In a neutral tone he asked, "Did he say what kind of animal it was?"

"He didn't know."

"He didn't know what it was, but he was sure it was perfectly healthy."

"God, Stuart, what do you want? It's obvious to everybody but you that my little friend is healthy and happy. What do you want, a birth certificate?"

He looked at her "friend," held close against her side, looking squashed and miserable. "What do you mean, 'everybody'?"

She shrugged. "Everybody at work. They're all jealous as anything." She planted a kiss on the thing's pointy head. Then she looked at him, and he realized that she had not kissed him, as she usually did, when he came in. She'd been clutching that thing the whole time. "I'm going to keep him," she said quietly. "If you don't like it, then . . . " Her pause seemed to pile up in solid, transparent blocks between them. "Then, I'm sorry, but that's how it is."

So much for an equal relationship, he thought. So much for sharing. Mortally wounded, he decided to pretend it hadn't happened.

"Want to go out for Indian tonight?"

She shook her head, turning away. "I want to stay in. There's something on telly. You go on. You could bring me something back, if you wouldn't mind. A spinach bahjee and a couple of nans would do me."

"And what about . . . something for your little friend?"

She smiled a private smile. "He's all right. I've fed him already."

Then she raised her eyes to his and acknowledged his effort. "Thanks."

He went out and got take-away for them both, and stopped at the off-license for the Mexican beer Jenny favored. A radio in the off-license was playing a sentimental song about love that Stuart remembered from his earliest childhood: his mother used to sing it. He was shocked to realize he had tears in his eyes.

That night Jenny made up the sofa bed in the spare room, explaining, "He can't stay in the bathroom; it's just not satisfactory, you know it's not."

"He needs the bed?"

"I do. He's confused, everything is new and different, I'm the one thing he can count on. I have to stay with him. He needs me."

"He needs you? What about me?"

"Oh, Stuart," she said impatiently. "You're a grown man. You can sleep by yourself for a night or two."

"And that thing can't?"

"Don't call him a thing."

"What am I supposed to call it? Look, you're not its mother—it doesn't need you as much as you'd like to think. It was perfectly all right in the bathroom last night—it'll be fine in here on its own."

"Oh? And what do you know about it? You'd like to kill him, wouldn't you? Admit it."

"No," he said, terrified that she had guessed the truth. If she knew how he had killed one of those things she would never forgive him. "It's not true, I don't—I couldn't hurt it any more than I could hurt you."

Her face softened. She believed him. It didn't matter how he felt about the creature. Hurting it, knowing how she felt, would be like committing an act of violence against her, and they both knew he wouldn't do that. "Just for a few nights, Stuart. Just until he settles in."

He had to accept that. All he could do was hang on, hope that she still loved him and that this wouldn't be forever.

The days passed. Jenny no longer offered to drive him to work. When he asked her, she said it was out of her way and with traffic so bad a detour would make her late. She said it was silly to take him the short distance to the station, especially as there was nowhere she could safely stop to let him out, and anyway, the walk would do him good. They were all good reasons, which he had used in the old days himself, but her excuses struck him painfully when he remembered how eager she had once been for his company, how ready to make any detour for his sake. Her new pet accompanied her everywhere, even to work, snug in the little nest she had made for it in a woven carrier bag.

"Of course things are different now. But I haven't stopped loving you," she said when he tried to talk to her about the breakdown of their marriage.

"It's not like I've found another man. This is something completely different. It doesn't threaten you; you're still my husband."

But it was obvious to him that a husband was no longer something she particularly valued. He began to have fantasies about killing it. Not, this time, in a blind rage, but as part of a carefully thought-out plan. He might poison it, or spirit it away somehow and pretend it had run away. Once it was gone he hoped Jenny would forget it and be his again.

But he never had a chance. Jenny was quite obsessive about the thing, as if it were too valuable to be left unguarded for a single minute. Even when she took a bath, or went to the toilet, the creature was with her, behind the locked door of the bathroom. When he offered to look after it for her for a few minutes she just smiled, as if the idea was manifestly ridiculous, and he didn't dare insist.

So he went to work, and went out for drinks with colleagues, and spent what time he could with Jenny, although they were never alone. He didn't argue with her, although he wasn't above trying to move her to pity if he could. He made seemingly casual comments designed to convince her of his change of heart so that eventually, weeks or months from now, she would trust him and leave the creature with him—and then, later, perhaps, they could put their marriage back together.

One afternoon, after an extended lunch break, Stuart returned to the office to find one of the senior editors crouched on the floor beside his secretary's empty desk, whispering and chuckling to herself.

He cleared his throat nervously. "Linda?"

She lurched back on her heels and got up awkwardly. She blushed and ducked her head as she turned, looking very unlike her usual high-powered self. "Oh, uh, Stuart, I was just—"

Frankie came in with a pile of photocopying. "Uh-huh," she said loudly.

Linda's face got even redder. "Just going," she mumbled, and fled.

Before he could ask, Stuart saw the creature, another crippled bat-with-out-wings, on the floor beside the open bottom drawer of Frankie's desk. It looked up at him, opened its slit of a mouth and gave a sad little hiss. Around one matchstick-thin leg it wore a fine golden chain which was fastened at the other end to the drawer.

"Some people would steal anything that's not chained down," said Frankie darkly. "People you wouldn't suspect."

He stared at her, letting her see his disapproval, his annoyance, disgust, even. "Animals in the office aren't part of the contract, Frankie."

"It's not an animal."

"What is it, then?"

"I don't know. You tell me."

"It doesn't matter what it is, you can't have it here."

"I can't leave it at home."

"Why not?"

She turned away from him, busying herself with her stacks of paper. "I can't leave it alone. It might get hurt. It might escape."

"Chance would be a fine thing."

She shot him a look, and he was certain she knew he wasn't talking about *her* pet. He said, "What does your boyfriend think about it?"

"I don't have a boyfriend." She sounded angry but then, abruptly, the anger dissipated, and she smirked. "I don't have to have one, do I?"

"You can't have that animal here. Whatever it is. You'll have to take it home."

She raised her fuzzy eyebrows. "Right now?"

He was tempted to say yes, but thought of the manuscripts that wouldn't be sent out, the letters that wouldn't be typed, the delays and confusions, and he sighed. "Just don't bring it back again. All right?"

"Yowza."

He felt very tired. He could tell her what to do but she would no more obey than would his wife. She would bring it back the next day and keep bringing it back, maybe keeping it hidden, maybe not, until he either gave in or was forced into firing her. He went into his office, closed the door, and put his head down on his desk.

That evening he walked in on his wife feeding the creature with her blood.

It was immediately obvious that it was that way round. The creature might be a vampire—it obviously was—but his wife was no helpless victim. She was wide-awake and in control, holding the creature firmly, letting it feed from a vein in her arm.

She flinched as if anticipating a shout, but he couldn't speak. He watched what was happening without attempting to interfere and gradually she relaxed again, as if he wasn't there.

When the creature, sated, fell off, she kept it cradled on her lap and reached with her other hand for the surgical spirit and cotton wool on the table, moistened a piece of cotton wool and tamped it to the tiny wound. Then, finally, she met her husband's eyes.

"He has to eat," she said reasonably. "He can't chew. He needs blood. Not very much, but . . . "

"And he needs it from you? You can't . . . ?"

"I can't hold down some poor scared rabbit or dog for him, no." She made a shuddering face. "Well, really, think about it. You know how squeamish I am. This is so much easier. It doesn't hurt."

It hurts me, he thought, but couldn't say it. "Jenny . . . "

"Oh, don't start," she said crossly. "I'm not going to get any disease from it, and he doesn't take enough to make any difference. Actually, I like it. We both do."

"Jenny, please don't. Please. For me. Give it up."

"No." She held the scraggy, ugly thing close and gazed at Stuart like a dispassionate executioner. "I'm sorry, Stuart, I really am, but this is nonnegotiable. If you can't accept that you'd better leave."

This was the showdown he had been avoiding, the end of it all. He tried to rally his arguments and then he realized he had none. She had said it. She had made her choice, and it was nonnegotiable. And he realized, looking at her now, that although she reminded him of the woman he loved, he didn't want to live with what she had become.

He could have refused to leave. After all, he had done nothing wrong. Why should he give up his home, this flat which was half his? But he could not force Jenny out onto the streets with nowhere to go; he still felt responsible for her.

"I'll pack a bag, and make a few phone calls," he said quietly. He knew someone from work who was looking for a lodger, and if all else failed, his brother had a spare room. Already, in his thoughts, he had left.

He ended up, once they'd sorted out their finances and formally separated, in a flat just off the Holloway Road, near Archway. It was not too far to walk if Jenny cared to visit, which she never did. Sometimes he called on her, but it was painful to feel himself an unwelcome visitor in the home they once had shared.

He never had to fire Frankie; she handed in her notice a week later, telling him she'd been offered an editorial job at The Women's Press. He wondered if pets in the office were part of the contract over there.

He never learned if the creatures had names. He never knew where they had come from, or how many there were. Had they fallen only in Islington? (Frankie had a flat somewhere off Upper Street.) He never saw anything on the news about them, or read any official confirmation of their existence, but he was aware of occasional oblique references to them in other contexts, occasional glimpses.

One evening, coming home on the tube, he found himself looking at the woman sitting opposite. She was about his own age, probably in her early thirties, with strawberry-blond hair, greenish eyes, and an almost translucent complexion. She was strikingly dressed in high, soft-leather boots, a long black woolen skirt, and an enveloping cashmere cloak of cranberry red. High on the cloak, below and to the right of the fastening at the neck, was a simple, gold circle brooch. Attached to it he noticed a very fine golden chain which vanished inside the cloak, like the end of a watch fob.

He looked at it idly, certain he had seen something like it before, on other women, knowing it reminded him of something. The train arrived at Archway, and as he rose to leave the train, so did the attractive woman. Her stride matched his. They might well leave the station together. He tried to think of something to say to her, some pretext for striking up a conversation. He was, after all, a single man again now, and she might be a single woman. He had forgotten how single people in London contrived to meet.

He looked at her again, sidelong, hoping she would turn her head and look at him. With one slender hand she toyed with her gold chain. Her cloak fell open slightly as she walked, and he caught a glimpse of the creature she carried beneath it, close to her body, attached by a slender golden chain.

He stopped walking and let her get away from him. He had to rest for a little while before he felt able to climb the stairs to the street.

By then he was wondering if he had really seen what he thought he had seen. The glimpse had been so brief. But he had been deeply shaken by what he saw or imagined, and he turned the wrong way outside the station. When he finally realized, he was at the corner of Jenny's road, which had once also been his. Rather than retrace his steps, he decided to take the turning and walk past her house.

Lights were on in the front room, the curtains drawn against the early winter dark. His footsteps slowed as he drew nearer. He felt such a longing to be inside, back home, belonging. He wondered if she would be pleased at all to see him. He wondered if she ever felt lonely, as he did.

Then he saw the tiny, dark figure between the curtains and the window.

It was spread-eagled against the glass, scrabbling uselessly; inside, longing to be out.

As he stared, feeling its pain as his own, the curtains swayed and opened slightly as a human figure moved between them. He saw the woman reach out and pull the creature away from the glass, back into the warm, lighted room with her, and the curtains fell again, shutting him out.

Little Monsters
Stephen Graham Jones

We built the monster from leftover pieces of other monsters. A beak here, a tentacle there, claws all over. Gina kept pushing for bilateral symmetry, and I held my tongue for as long as I could—this wasn't her idea, after all—but finally had to say it over ordered-in boxes of noodles: that this is a nightmare creature we're foisting on the world, right? It's not *supposed* to conform to biology as we know it. That's specifically what's terrifying. Gina chopsticked another mouthful in, showing off that she could—of the two of us, I'm the barbarian—then shrugged and explained that bilateralism is particular to two things (chew, chew): whether or not the monster walks upright, might need to *balance* in some 'crazy, unmagical' way, and what gravity field it developed in. And of course it had to walk upright. Chase scenes are completely unexciting when the creature's just clumping and oozing and looming behind. Sometimes I hate her. But I wouldn't be doing this with anybody else, either. So, again, I told her sure, sure, this monster was going to be terrestrial, definitely, homegrown, and it was also going to get around without leaving a slime trail. And then I forked another bite in, let it swell until I had to close my eyes to swallow. The creature I'd been dreaming of for so long now, I told myself, maybe I'd been hiding it half in the shadows of my mind on purpose, so I didn't have to get into stupid details like gravity. I guess what I wanted was the effect—people in the streets falling to their knees, screaming, the whole city stopping what it's doing, looking around to this new thing in its midst. Except, then, two days later, Gina stepped back, kind of rubbed her lips with the side of her hand, and said something was wrong. "What?" I asked, squinting in dread. "Peter," she said, cranking the garage door up to let us breathe, "so it, you know, it eats random citizens, pets, the occasional shrub or mailbox." I nodded. Hated it when she called me by my full name. It never tokened well for what was coming. This time was no

333

exception: our monster needed some means of elimination. If not, then it would bulge, teeter, finally explode. And, if it was going to have that kind of apparatus, then we might as well assign it a sex, right? Unless of course we wanted to pioneer a third, fourth, or fifth gender—but we were already pushing it with the tentacles, wouldn't I say? I closed my eyes, could feel things collapsing inside me. We had to go to the kitchen to hash this out, and it took days, sketch after sketch. Not just the bathroom habits of monsters, but the mating practices. The dimorphism between the sexes—we were unimaginative, finally stuck with just the two we knew—and which sex was likely to be the most fierce, the most terrifying. The most successful. So the beaks had to go, turned out to just be vestigial, movie-inspired ornamentation. Driving to get more noodles that night, I hammered the steering wheel with the heel of my hand and cried, called myself *Peter* over and over. The next morning, then—I'd like to say after a night of furious lovemaking, but, well: more like acrimonious sitcom watching—we walked into the garage, found we'd forget to disconnect the fibers from the switchboard. We salvaged what we could, our hands working in a unison we thought gone forever, but still, at the end of that terrible day, our monster was maybe a sixteenth of its former mass. The tentacles were still disconcerting, sure, but the claws were outsized now, had to go. "I'm sorry," Gina said into my chest, "it was me, it was me," but it had been both of us. I'm adult enough to know that, at least. So we did what we could with what we had. Again. Gina pulled back-to-back eighteen hours days just getting the eyes right—if it wasn't going to be fast, it at least needed to be able to spot its prey from a distance, have that kind of advantage—and I decided to save the tentacles (our last complete set) for next time around, and promised myself to harbor zero malice toward this monster, for not having been worthy of them. And then, finally, all of summer behind us now, it was done. Sure, we could tinker here, adjust that, shade this over a scratch, but the good artist knows when to put the brush down. And we could pretend to be good artists, anyway. "Well?" Gina said, her arm around my side, my arm draped down across her far shoulder—you love whoever you climb the mountain with, right?—and I nodded, hit the button in my hand, and the garage door creaked up behind us, bathing the slick cement floor in early morning sunlight, and, just like the two times before, our little monster hitched its backpack into the right place and we unleashed it on the world, out into the river of children leading to the playground, to kindergarten, each of them perfectly designed to wreak its own particular brand of havoc on the world, to never ever *ever* stop until the helicopters made it. And, if the city's breath caught in its throat a bit when our garage door came up, if it looked our way for maybe a moment longer than usual, then we never knew it. Were too busy watching her walk away ourselves.

The Changeling
Sarah Langan

She peered through the window at the slumbering cherub. Pale skin and black lashes. A nightlight shone against the red drapes, and tinted the walls bloody. It was warm inside that nursery, she imagined. Snug, like the house where she'd once lived. But that was a long time ago. She did not remember her name anymore, or the person she'd once been. Only the job, the houses she visited each night. The faces of the children she stole.

This place was familiar, its weeping willows and honeyed air. The roots of giant trees had fissured the wide sidewalks into strips of pebbles. Swaths of grass lazed on lawns like Kudzu's wealthy cousin. The house was a brick Victorian with stained glass eyes. Yes, this terrain was familiar. Like a tune she couldn't place, or the scent of a stranger wearing an old friend's skin.

The cherub startled and sat up. They had a sixth sense sometimes, and knew when she was near. He threw off his Batman bed sheets, and she readied herself for the scream, the hurried entry she would have to make, the kicks and bites he would inflict as she carried him away.

He didn't scream. The boy scooted out of the small bed and approached the window. The tip of his nose flattened like a mushroom against the glass, and he squinted into the dark. "Sister," his red lips mouthed. The word rattled like ice against her hollow bones: she knew this boy.

She'd stolen thousands. Brown eyes, blue eyes, green eyes, hazel. She'd seen cockroach-candied mattresses, mobiles that twisted overhead to the tune of Mozart's Figaro, dirt floors, hand-knit blankets so soft and sweet-smelling that more than once she'd been tempted to steal them along with the child. At first they'd been missions of mercy. The starving, the sick. Better to carry them away. And then she'd graduated to the unwanted. Their mothers cursed their every breath. And now, finally, the loved. They were the most valuable in the scheme of things. The most satisfying meal.

She delivered the children to a place deep underground. Set them down inside a mouth of rocks. The dead smelled the scent of young flesh and came quickly, smacking their lips. They bent over the infants until their whimpers were piercing howls that suddenly went silent.

Twice she'd taken pity. A little girl from New Hyde Park, Long Island had caressed the webbing of her fingers as if trying to heal it. She'd held the girl, and kissed her cheek. Another time she'd spared a sleeping baby. The child's crib had looked especially warm, and though she'd done it hundreds of times before, her mind had set like a strip of steel. She would not steal the child from a happy dream. She would rather have died. But these had happened long ago. The years had suckled her pity dry. This was just a job now. A thing she did out of necessity, like shit and sleep. Corruption is the eyes, the nose, the sense of touch. Corruption is the salve, and its irritant.

She remembered everything, even the womb. Her parents were a young couple with healthy good looks. Tall and brunette and glowing from summers spent at the helms of boats and winters at the gym. They'd looked alike. Could have been siblings and in a way, were. They'd married within their town, their social set, their country club.

She was their first child. Born too quickly for a hospital. A labor in two-hours and without an afterbirth. Ravenous, she'd chewed her way down the canal. Their faces at the sight of her had been all smiles. Their perfect child. Their perfect life. And then the mid-wife bathed her, and they saw gray skin, gaunt body, and long limbs. Her crown of black curls like the laurels of an illegitimate queen. Forgetting her professional demeanor, the midwife dropped the baby in the sink, and made the sign of the cross.

From her first breath she cried without relent. At first they crooned lullabies and rocked her. Shook stuffed giraffes and elephants and bears at her angular face. Wept over the stygian squeals transmitted through their Walkie-Talkies (How could she cry for so long? Was she sick? Hurt? Frightened?). But soon their concern became exhaustion. She did not take her mother's milk, but only formula. Over the weeks and then months of her endless shrieks, her body remained gaunt. Any material other than burlap gave her a rash, and if she wore the cashmere blanket her mother had knit, her skin opened up and began to bleed.

There were doctors. Trips to Universities where women in white pricked her toes with needles. But she did not stop crying. She did not learn to speak. She did not smile. To muffle her constant wails, they nailed rugs to the walls of her nursery. But still they heard her, and no one in that house slept. They stopped seeing friends, stopped speaking on the phone, stopped loving the child that bore not their looks, but their name. After her second birthday, they started adding fingers of whiskey to her milk. Boozy, she did not fall asleep, but instead drifted away.

Once, her father sneaked into the room and lifted her into his arms. A hairy little girl with feathery down on her chin. *How could this child belong to him?* He must have wondered. He ran his fingers along the seams of her limbs. Not a tender touch. He recoiled even as he did it. "What are you?" he asked when she was only two years old, and if she could have given him an answer, she would have.

She'd been crying for two days straight when her mother delivered the bottle full of brown whiskey. Medicine, they called it, but her mind was more fertile than they knew. Her eyes were focused, watchful. She understood the things they did. Since drinking the whiskey, her hair had fallen out. Her mother held her. Squeezed her nose and mouth against her dry bosom. Tighter. Tighter. Tighter. So tight she hitched, and her lungs emptied, and she stopped breathing. Her eyes bulged, and she could not name the emotion she felt. She did not know what emotions meant. "Why won't you go away?" her mother whispered, and then threw her back into the crib.

They stopped kissing her good-night. They stopped opening her bedroom blinds in the morning so that she could witness the rising sun. With stealth they sped past her room. They resumed the vacations they'd missed. Trips to sun-dappled islands surrounded by tropical fish, and sides of mountains where their downward skiing was rewarded with mugs of hot chocolate in front of warm fires. They went out at night with friends again, and left her to wail until she fell asleep.

They went through new nannies almost every week until they'd contacted every agency in town, and there were no more nannies to be hired. None could endure her endless shrieks, her strange body, her knowing eyes. They started paying the woman who cleaned house to feed and change her once a day. The woman did as she was instructed, but wore gloves so as never to touch her gray skin. She remembered watching things back then. The twisting mobile that she could not reach. The sky that thickened like soup in the summer heat. The designs on the blanket in her crib that were blue posies. She thought about death.

When she was four, the gloved woman called her parents, who were away on vacation, to tell them that the child's cries had not ceased for two days.

In broken English she explained that she could not stay another second. She was leaving.

In a daze, they packed their bags. They called the airline. They headed for a taxi, and then they stopped. They were hungry, and it was better to eat before a long trip. They ordered eggs from room service. They watched the news and learned that another Kennedy had died. At the last minute they decided to attend a cocktail party that was important for his career, where they drank too much wine, and had to stay overnight at the hotel. When thirsty headaches woke them the next morning, something insidious slipped between them. A thing that would gnaw at them without cease until all that remained was the husks of their bodies. They looked at each other and this thing coiled itself between then, nourished by their mutual madness. They did not go home for their child.

Alone, she cried until her lungs gave out, and her throat burned from thirst, and her stomach began to digest itself. The posies on her blanket looked like death. The shadows in her room looked like death.

The dead came to her, then. They entered the cabin like a fog that slipped through the cracks under the nursery door. Their bodies were conjoined, each starting before the other ended. Faces looked down at her while she wept, so hungry, in her crib. By luck they had found her. A meal. A chance to live another day. But when they saw her, they stopped. There was something kindred in her. Something they understood. In their mercy they adopted her as one of their own.

One of them, a woman, saw the child's hunger, and ran her teeth along the inside of her palm until her cold flesh opened wide. She suckled the dead woman's blood. Black nourishment filled her belly like sleeping snakes. She stopped crying, and never cried again. They carried her to the window, this foundling. This child that had been born not quite human. They carried her away.

Even the dead have honor, and to show their disdain for what the parents had done, they replaced the changeling's body with the carcass of a pig.

She lived with them for fifteen years. Spent her days with them in the dark underground. They came out at night after feeding to spy on the living. Listen to old stories, visit old loves. They fixated on the epithets written on their headstones, and fomented old grudges, and sometimes wandered the floors of malls, their steps in synch with Barry Manlow tunes. They refused to let go, and so they lingered in a world they had no place. To keep their shadows from losing shape, to give them the semblance of flesh, they fed off the lives of children.

But she was not one of them. They offered her the bodies of broken-necked squirrels and small birds from above, and the meat from roots that grew underground. Once, they even found a jar of apple sauce. She could not keep any of it in her stomach, and so they took turns cutting open their hands and feeding her their blood. She was stronger than them, and in return for their blood, she learned to steal.

They made her in their image. To help her to climb the sides of houses, they bound and shredded her hands and toes until the flaps of skin on them became webbed. The sustenance of their cold blood gave her strength, but her nourishment had been neglected for so long that her bones were hollow, and when she moved, she ached. The dark had made her eyes and skin so sensitive that she couldn't tolerate natural sunlight. She'd lived for so long without human touch that she did not know how to feel. Only to steal, to watch through windows, to skirt between two worlds, coveting both the living and the dead.

This was her story. A changeling raised with less humanity than a pig.

Now, the little boy smiled. She did not smile back. She suctioned her webbed fingers against the window and soundlessly opened it. She climbed inside. This place was familiar. So familiar. The boy was brunette, and had the glow of health. Wide brown eyes. Victorian house. She knew this place. She remembered this place.

She entered the room. On his bed was a blanket with blue posies. He didn't scream. Perhaps he had been born different, too. Could sense in her their kinship.

She lowered her hands over the lids of his eyes and closed them. He thought they were playing a game. Hide and seek. Peek-a-boo. So trusting. So sweet she could lick him.

She wondered if she had ever left this house. If the dead were an invention she'd dreamed in this very nursery, too ignorant to recognize that she'd gone mad. The feeling was like rocks in her stomach, rooting her deeply to the floor, drowning her here. The memories of this place. She should have jettisoned them long ago, and yet they persisted.

The boy climbed into her arms, and she thought about taking him away.

Saving him the way she wished she'd been saved. They'd enter the sunlight together. She carried him to the window. But down below the dead had risen early, and followed her here. They reached their arms up to catch him, this boy. To feed from him. A test. The dead had sent her here to test her loyalty. The boy hugged her tightly, and her hollow bones ached.

Behind her the door opened and she saw a couple, older now. Sadder, now. A man and a woman. They stopped in the doorway. There was recognition, and then it closed like an eye winking, and they forgot. They did not know her.

What had they done with the pig?

She dangled the child out the window. Trusting her, he did not fight. The dead clamored. The couple shouted. The boy did not blink. Such a sweet thing. Brown eyes, brown hair. A cold snake coiled inside her belly, and *she* knew that she loved him. This, her opposite. This thing too perfect to be human. And yet, together, they were whole.

She dropped him into the arms of the dead. He was too surprised to scream. Wide-eyed, he fell with his arms extended, as if convinced that at the last moment she would reach out and catch him. And then the thud and moan when he landed, a startled sound. And then the crunch, and the smacking lips, and the snakes in her stomach writhed like rage.

The couple was weeping when she turned to them. Their eyes became the opposite of stars. They went from wet and shining, to black. They looked at her, and their recognition returned. Then she climbed inside the tiny bed, and took her rightful place as their firstborn child.

The Monsters of Heaven
Nathan Ballingrud

"Who invented the human heart, I wonder? Tell me,
then show me the place where he was hanged."
—Lawrence Durrell, *Justine*

For a long time, Brian imagined reunions with his son. In the early days, these fantasies were defined by spectacular violence. He would find the man who stole him and open his head with a claw hammer. The more blood he spilled, the further removed he became from his own guilt. The location would often change: a roach-haunted tenement building; an abandoned warehouse along the Tchoupitoulas wharf; a pre-fab bungalow with an American flag out front and a two-door hatchback parked in the driveway.

Sometimes the man lived alone, sometimes he had his own family. On these latter occasions Brian would cast himself as a moral executioner, spraying the walls with the kidnapper's blood but sparing his wife and child—freeing them, he imagined, from his tyranny. No matter the scenario, Toby was always there, always intact; Brian would feel his face pressed into his shoulders as he carried him away, feel the heat of his tears bleed into his shirt. You're safe now, he would say. Daddy's got you. Daddy's here.

After some months passed, he deferred the heroics to the police. This marked his first concession to reality. He spent his time beached in the living room, drinking more, working less, until the owner of the auto shop told him to take time off, a lot of time off, as much as he needed. Brian barely noticed. He waited for the red and blue disco lights of a police cruiser to illuminate the darkness outside, to give some shape and measure to the night. He waited for the phone to ring with a glad summons to the station. He played out scenarios, tried on different outcomes, guessed at his own reactions. He gained weight and lost time.

Sometimes he would get out of bed in the middle of the night, careful not to wake his wife, and get into the car. He would drive at dangerous speeds through the city, staring into the empty sockets of unlighted windows. He would get out of the car and stand in front of some of these houses, looking and listening for signs. Often, the police were called. When the officers realized who he was, they were usually as courteous as they were adamant. He'd wonder if it had been the kidnapper who called the police. He would imagine returning to those houses with a gun.

This was in the early days of what became known as the Lamentation. At this stage, most people did not know anything unusual was happening. What they heard, if they heard anything, was larded with rumor and embellishment. Fogs of gossip in the barrooms and churches. This was before the bloodshed. Before their pleas to Christ clotted in their throats.

Amy never told Brian that she blamed him. She elected, rather, to avoid the topic of the actual abduction, and any question of her husband's negligence. Once the police abandoned them as suspects, the matter of their own involvement ceased to be a subject of discussion. Brian was unconsciously grateful, because it allowed him to focus instead on the maintenance of grief. Silence spread between them like a glacier. In a few months, entire days passed with nothing said between them.

It was on such a night that Amy rolled up against him and kissed the back of his neck. It froze Brian, filling him with a blast of terror and bewilderment; he felt the guilt move inside of him, huge but seemingly distant, like a whale passing beneath a boat. Her lips felt hot against his skin, sending warm waves rolling from his neck and shoulders all the way down to his legs, as though she had injected something lovely into him. She grew more ardent, nipping him with her teeth, breaking through his reservations. He turned and kissed her. He experienced a leaping arc of energy, a terrifying, violent impulse; he threw his weight onto her and crushed his mouth into hers, scraping his teeth against hers. But there immediately followed a cascade of unwelcome thought: Toby whimpering somewhere in the dark, waiting for his father to save him; Amy, dressed in her bedclothes in the middle of the day, staring like a corpse into the sunlight coming through the windows; the playground, and the receding line of kindergarteners. When she reached under the sheets she found him limp and unready. He opened his mouth to apologize but she shoved her tongue into it, her hand working at him with a rough urgency, as though more depended on this than he knew. Later he would learn that it did. Her teeth sliced his lip and blood eeled into his mouth. She was pulling at him too hard, and it was starting to hurt. He wrenched himself away.

"Jesus," he said, wiping his lip. The blood felt like an oil slick in the back of his throat.

She turned her back to him and put her face into the pillow. For a moment he thought she was crying. But only for a moment.

"Honey," he said. "Hey." He put his fingers on her shoulder; she rolled it away from him.

"Go to sleep," she said.

He stared at the landscape of her naked back, pale in the streetlight leaking through the blinds, feeling furious and ruined.

The next morning, when he came into the kitchen, Amy was already up. Coffee was made, filling the room with a fine toasted smell, and she was leaning against the counter with a cup in her hand, wearing her pink terrycloth robe. Her dark hair was still wet from the shower. She smiled and said, "Good morning."

"Hey," he said, feeling for a sense of her mood.

Dodger, Toby's dog, cast him a devastated glance from his customary place beneath the kitchen table. Amy had wanted to get rid of him—she couldn't bear the sight of him anymore, she'd said—but Brian wouldn't allow it. When Toby comes back, he reasoned, he'll wonder why we did it. What awful thing guided us. So Dodger remained, and his slumping, sorrowful presence tore into them both like a hungry animal.

"Hey boy," Brian said, and rubbed his neck with his toe.

"I'm going out today," Amy said.

"Okay. Where to?"

She shrugged. "I don't know. The hardware store. Maybe a nursery. I want to find myself a project."

Brian looked at her. The sunlight made a corona around her body. This new resolve, coupled with her overture of the night before, struck him as a positive sign. "Okay," he said.

He seated himself at the table. The newspaper had been placed there for him, still bound by a rubberband. He snapped it off and unfurled the front page. Already he felt the gravitational pull of the Jack Daniels in the cabinet, but when Amy leaned over his shoulder and placed a coffee cup in front of him, he managed to resist the whiskey's call with an ease that surprised and gratified him. He ran his hand up her forearm, pushing back the soft pink sleeve, and he kissed the inside of her wrist. He felt a wild and incomprehensible hope. He breathed in the clean, scented smell of her. She stayed there for a moment, and then gently pulled away.

They remained that way in silence for some time—maybe fifteen minutes or more—until Brian found something in the paper he wanted to share with her. Something being described as "angelic"—"apparently not quite a human man," as the writer put it—had been found down by the Gulf Coast, in Morgan City; it had been shedding a faint light from under two feet of water; whatever it was had died shortly after being taken into custody, under confusing circumstances. He turned in his chair to speak, a word already gathering on his tongue, and he caught her staring at him. She wore a cadaverous, empty look, as though she had seen the worst thing in the world and died in the act. It occurred to him that she had been looking at him that way for whole minutes. He turned back to the table, his insides sliding, and stared at the suddenly indecipherable glyphs of the newspaper. After a moment he felt her hand on the back of his neck, rubbing him gently. She left the kitchen without a word.

This is how it happened:

They were taking Dodger for a walk. Toby liked to hold the leash—he was four years old, and gravely occupied with establishing his independence—and more often than not Brian would sort of half-trot behind them, one hand held indecisively aloft should Dodger suddenly decide to break into a run, dragging his boy behind him like a string of tin cans. He probably bit off more profanities during those walks than he ever did changing a tire. He carried, as was their custom on Mondays, a blanket and a picnic lunch. He would lie back in the sun while Toby and the dog played, and enjoy not being hunched over an engine block. At some point they would have lunch. Brian believed these afternoons of easy camaraderie would be remembered by them both for years to come. They'd done it a hundred times.

A hundred times.

On that day a kindergarten class arrived shortly after they did. Toby ran up to his father and wrapped his arms around his neck, frightened by the sudden bright surge of humanity; the kids were a loud, brawling tumult, crashing over the swings and monkey bars in a gabbling surf. Brian pried Toby's arms free and pointed at them.

"Look, screwball, they're just kids. See? They're just like you. Go on and play. Have some fun."

Dodger galloped out to greet them and was received as a hero, with joyful cries and grasping fingers. Toby observed this gambit for his dog's affections and at last decided to intervene. He ran toward them, shouting, "That's my dog! That's my dog!" Brian watched him go, made eye contact with the teacher and nodded hello. She smiled at him—he remembered thinking she was kind of cute, wondering how old she was—and she returned her attention to her kids, gamboling like lunatics all over the park. Brian reclined on the blanket and watched the clouds skim the atmosphere, listened to the sound of children. It was a hot, windless day.

He didn't realize he had dozed until the kindergarteners had been rounded up and were halfway down the block, taking their noise with them. The silence stirred him.

He sat up abruptly and looked around. The playground was empty. "Toby? Hey, Toby?"

Dodger stood out in the middle of the road, his leash spooled at his feet. He watched Brian eagerly, offered a tentative wag.

"Where's Toby?" he asked the dog, and climbed to his feet. He felt a sudden sickening lurch in his gut. He turned in a quick circle, a half-smile on his face, utterly sure that this was an impossible situation, that children didn't disappear in broad daylight while their parents were *right fucking there*. So he was still here. Of course he was still here. Dodger trotted up to him and sat down at his feet, waiting for him to produce the boy, as though he were a hidden tennis ball.

"Toby?"

The park was empty. He jogged after the receding line of kids. "Hey. *Hey*! Is my son with you? *Where's my son?*"

One morning, about a week after the experience in the kitchen, Brian was awakened by the phone. Every time this happened he felt a thrill of hope, though by now it had become muted, even dreadful in its predictability. He hauled himself up from the couch, nearly overturning a bottle of Jack Daniels stationed on the floor. He crossed the living room and picked up the phone.

"Yes?" he said.

"Let me talk to Amy." It was not a voice he recognized. A male voice, with a thick rural accent. It was the kind of voice that inspired immediate prejudice: the voice of an idiot; of a man without any right to make demands of him.

"Who is this?"

"Just let me talk to Amy."

"How about you go fuck yourself."

There was a pause as the man on the phone seemed to assess the obstacle. Then he said, with a trace of amusement in his voice, "Are you Brian?"

"That's right."

"Look, dude. Go get your wife. Put her on the phone. Do it now, and I won't have to come down there and break your fucking face."

Brian slammed down the receiver. Feeling suddenly lightheaded, he put his hand on the wall to steady himself, to reassure himself that it was still solid, and that he was still real. From somewhere outside, through an open window, came the distant sound of children shouting.

It was obvious that Amy was sleeping with another man. When confronted with the call, she did not admit to anything, but made no special effort to explain it away, either. His name was Tommy, she said. She'd met him once when she was out. He sounded rough, but he wasn't a bad guy. She chose not to elaborate, and Brian, to his amazement, found a kind of forlorn comfort in his wife's affair. He'd lost his son; why not lose it all?

On television the news was filling with the creatures, more of which were being discovered all the time. The press had taken to calling them angels. Some were being found alive, though all of them appeared to have suffered from some violent experience.

At least one family had become notorious by refusing to let anyone see the angel they'd found, or even let it out of their home. They boarded their windows and warned away visitors with a shotgun.

Brian was stationed on the couch, staring at the television with the sound turned down to barely a murmur. He listened to the familiar muted clatter from the medicine cabinet as Amy applied her make-up in the bathroom. A news program was on, and a handheld camera followed a street reporter into someone's house. The JD bottle was empty at his feet, and the knowledge that he had no more in the house smoldered in him.

Amy emerged from the kitchen with her purse slung over her arm and made her way to the door. "I'm going out," she said.

"Where?"

She paused, one hand on the doorknob. She wavered there, in her careful make-up and her push-up bra. He tried to remember the last time he'd seen her look like this and failed dismally. Something inside her seemed to collapse—a force of will, perhaps, or a habit of deception. Maybe she was just too tired to invent another lie.

"I'm going to see Tommy," she said.

"The redneck."

"Sure. The redneck, if that's how you want it."

"Does it matter how I want it?"

She paused. "No," she said. "I guess not."

"Well well. The truth. Look out."

She left the door, walked into the living room. Brian felt a sudden trepidation; this is not what he imagined would happen. He wanted to get a few weak barbs in before she walked out, that was all. He did not actually want to talk.

She sat on the rocking chair across from the couch. Beside her, on the television, the camera focused on an obese man wearing overalls smiling triumphantly and holding aloft an angel's severed head.

Amy shut it off.

"Do you want to know about him?" she said.

"Let's see. He's stupid and violent. He called my home and threatened me. He's sleeping with my wife. What else is there to know?"

She appraised him for a moment, weighing consequences. "There's a little more to know," she said. "For example, he's very kind to me. He thinks I'm beautiful." He must have made some sort of sound then, because she said, "I know it must be very hard for you to believe, but some men still find me attractive. And that's important to me, Brian. Can you understand that?"

He turned away from her, shielding his eyes with a hand, although without the TV on there was very little light in the room. Each breath was laced with pain.

"When I go to see him, he talks to me. Actually talks. I know he might not be very smart, according to your standards, but you'd be surprised how much he and I have to talk about. You'd be surprised how much more there is to life—to my life—than your car magazines, and your tv, and your bottles of booze."

"Stop it," I said.

"He's also a very considerate lover. He paces himself. For my sake. For me. Did you *ever* do that, Brian? In all the times we made love?"

He felt tears crawling down his face. Christ. When did that start?

"I can forget things when I sleep with him. I can forget about . . . I can forget about everything. He lets me do that."

"You cold bitch," he rasped.

"You passive little shit," she bit back, with a venom that surprised him. "You let it happen, do you know that? You let it all happen. Every awful thing."

She stood abruptly and walked out the door, slamming it behind her. The force of it rattled the windows. After a while—he had no idea how long—he picked up the remote and turned the TV back on. A girl pointed to moving clouds on a map.

Eventually Dodger came by and curled up at his feet. Brian slid off the couch and lay down beside him, hugging him close. Dodger smelled the way dogs do, musky and of the earth, and he sighed with the abiding patience of his kind.

Violence filled his dreams. In them he rent bodies, spilled blood, painted the walls using severed limbs as gruesome brushes. In them he went back to the park and ate the children while the teacher looked on. Once he awoke after these dreams with blood filling his mouth; he realized he had chewed his tongue during the night. It was raw and painful for days afterward. A rage was building inside him and he could not find an outlet for it. One night Amy told him she thought she was falling in love with Tommy. He only nodded stupidly and watched her walk out the door again. That same night he kicked Dodger out of the house. He just opened the door to the night and told him to go. When he wouldn't—trying instead to slink around his legs and go back inside—he planted his foot on the dog's chest and physically pushed him back outside, sliding him backwards on his butt. "*Go find him!*" he yelled. "*Go find him! Go and find him!*" He shut the door and listened to Dodger whimper and scratch at it for nearly an hour. At some point he gave up and Brian fell asleep. When he awoke it was raining. He opened the door and called for him. The rain swallowed his voice.

"Oh no," he said quietly, his voice a whimper. "Come back! I'm sorry! Please, I'm so sorry!"

When Dodger did eventually return, wet and miserable, Brian hugged him tight, buried his face in his fur, and wept for joy.

Brian liked to do his drinking alone. When he drank in public, especially at his old bar, people tried to talk to him. They saw his presence as an invitation to share sympathy, or a request for a friendly ear. It got to be too much. But tonight he made his way back there, endured the stares and the weird silence, took the beers sent his way, although he wanted none of it. What he wanted tonight was Fire Engine, and she didn't disappoint.

Everybody knew Fire Engine, of course; if she thought you didn't know her, she'd introduce herself to you post haste. One hand on your shoulder, the other on your thigh. Where her hands went after that depended on a quick negotiation. She was a redhead with an easy personality, and was popular with the regular clientele, including the ones that would never buy her services. She claimed to be twenty-eight but looked closer to forty. At some unfortunate juncture in her life she had contrived to lose most of her front teeth, either to decay or to someone's balled fist; either way common wisdom held she gave the best blowjob in downtown New Orleans.

Brian used to be amused by that kind of talk. Although he'd never had an interest in her he'd certainly enjoyed listening to her sales pitch; she'd become a sort of bar pet, and the unselfconscious way she went about her life was both endearing and appalling. Her lack of teeth was too perfect, and too ridiculous. Now, however, the information had acquired a new kind of value to him. He pressed his gaze onto her until she finally felt it and looked back. She smiled coquettishly, with gruesome effect. He told the bartender to send her a drink.

"You sure? She ain't gonna leave you alone all night."

"Fuck yeah, I'm sure."

All night didn't concern him. What concerned him were the next ten minutes, which was what he figured ten dollars would buy him. After the necessary negotiations and bullshit they left the bar together, trailing catcalls; she took his hand and led him around back, into the alley.

The smell of rotting garbage came at him like an attack, like a pillowcase thrown over his head. She steered him into the alley's dark mouth, with its grime-smeared pavement and furtive skittering sounds, and its dumpster so stuffed with straining garbage bags that it looked like some fearsome monster choking on its dinner. "Now you know I'm a lady," she said, "but sometimes you just got to make do with what's available."

That she could laugh at herself this way touched Brian, and he felt a wash of sympathy for her. He considered what it would be like to run away with her, to rescue her from the wet pull of her life; to save her.

She unzipped his pants and pulled his dick out. "There we go, honey, that's what I'm talking about. Ain't you something?"

After a couple of minutes she released him and stood up. He tucked himself back in and zipped his pants, afraid to make eye contact with her.

"Maybe you just had too much to drink," she said.

"Yeah."

"It ain't nothing."

"I know it isn't," he said harshly.

When she made no move to leave, he said, "Will you just get the fuck away from me? Please?"

Her voice lost its sympathy. "Honey, I still got to get paid."

He opened his wallet and fished out a ten dollar bill. She plucked it from his fingers and walked out of the alley, back toward the bar. "Don't get all bent out of shape about it," she called. "Shit happens, you know?"

He slid down the wall until his ass hit the ground. He brought his hand to his mouth and choked out a sob, his eyes squeezed shut. He banged his head once against the brick wall behind him and then thought better of it. Down here the stench was a steaming blanket, almost soothing in its awfulness. He felt like he deserved to be there, that it was right that he should sleep in shit and grime. He listened to the gentle ticking of the roaches in the dark. He wondered if Toby was in a place like this.

Something glinted further down the alley.

He strained to see it. It was too bright to be merely a reflection.

It moved.

"Son of a—" he said, and pushed himself to his feet.

It lay mostly hidden; it had pulled some stray garbage bags atop itself in an effort to remain concealed, but its dim luminescence worked against it. Brian loped over to it, wrenched the bags away; its clawed hands clutched at them and tore them open, spilling a clatter of beer and liquor bottles all over the ground. They caromed with hollow music through the alley, coming at last to silent rest, until all Brian could hear was the thin, high-pitched noise the creature made through the tiny O-shaped orifice he supposed passed for a mouth. Its eyes were black little stones. The creature—*angel*, he thought, *they're calling these things angels*—was tall and thin, abundantly male, and it shed a thin light that illuminated exactly nothing around it. *If you put some clothes on it*, Brian thought, *hide its face, gave it some gloves, it might pass for a human.*

Exposed, it held up a long-fingered hand, as if to ward him off. It had clearly been hurt: its legs looked badly broken, and it breathed in short, shallow gasps. A dark bruise spread like a mold over the right side of its chest.

"Look at you, huh? You're all messed up." He felt a strange glee as he said this; he could not justify the feeling and quickly buried it. "Yeah, yeah, somebody worked you over pretty good."

It managed to roll onto its belly and it scrabbled along the pavement in a pathetic attempt at escape. It loosed that thin, reedy cry. Calling for help? Begging for its life?

The sight of it trying to flee from him catalyzed some deep predatory impulse, and he pressed his foot onto the angel's ankle, holding it easily in place. "No you don't." He hooked the thing beneath its shoulders and lifted it from the ground; it was astonishingly light. It mewled weakly at him. "Shut up, I'm trying to help you." He adjusted it in his arms so that he held it like a lover, or a fainted woman. He carried it back to his car, listening for the sound of the barroom door opening behind him, of laughter or a challenge chasing him down the sidewalk. But the door stayed shut. He walked in silence.

Amy was awake when he got home, silhouetted in the doorway. Brian pulled the angel from the passenger seat, cradled it against his chest. He watched her face alter subtly, watched as some dark hope crawled across it like an insect, and he squashed it before it could do any real harm.

"It's not him," he said. "It's something else."

She stood away from the door and let him come in.

Dodger, who had been dozing in the hallway, lurched to his feet with a sliding and skittering of claws and growled fiercely at it, his lips curled away from his teeth.

"Get away, you," Brian said. He eased past him, bearing his load down the hall.

He laid it in Toby's bed. Together he and Amy stood over it, watching as it stared back at them with dark flat eyes, its body twisting away from them as if it could fold itself into another place altogether. Its fingers plucked at the train-spangled bed sheets, wrapping them around its nakedness. Amy leaned over and helped to tuck she sheets around it.

"He's hurt," she said.

"I know. I guess a lot of them are found that way."

"Should we call somebody?"

"You want camera crews in here? Fuck no."

"Well. He's really hurt. We need to do something."

"Yeah. I don't know. We can at least clean him up, I guess."

Amy sat on the mattress beside it; it stared at her with its expression-less face. Brian couldn't tell if there were thoughts passing behind those eyes, or just a series of brute reflex arcs. After a moment it reached out with one long dark fingernail and brushed her arm. She jumped as though shocked.

"Jesus! Be careful," said Brian.

"What if it's him?"

"What?" It took him a moment to understand her. "Oh my god. Amy. It's not him, okay? It's *not him*."

"But what if it is?"

"It's *not*. We've seen them on the news, okay? It's a, it's a *thing*."

"You shouldn't call it an 'it.' "

"*How do I know what the fuck to call it?*"

She touched her fingers to its cheek. It pressed its face into them, making some small sound.

"Why did you leave me?" she said. "You were everything I had."

Brian swooned beneath a tide of vertigo. Something was moving inside him, something too large to stay where it was. "It's an angel," he said. "Nothing more. Just an angel. It's probably going to die on us, since that's what they seem to do." He put his hand against the wall until the dizziness passed. It was replaced by a low, percolating anger. "Instead of thinking of it as Toby, why don't you ask it where Toby *is*? Why don't you make it explain to us why it happened?"

She looked at him. "It happened because you let it," she said.

Dodger asked to be let outside. Brian opened the door for him to let him run around the front yard. There was a leash law here, but Dodger was well known by the neighbors and generally tolerated. He walked out of the house with considerably less than his usual enthusiasm. He lifted his leg desultorily against a shrub, then walked down to the road and followed the sidewalk further into the neighborhood. He did not come back.

Over the next few days it put its hooks into them, and drew them in tight. They found it difficult to leave it alone. Its flesh seemed to pump out some

kind of soporific, like an invisible spoor, and it was better than the booze—
better than anything they'd previously known. Its pull seemed to grow
stronger as the days passed. For Amy, especially. She stopped going out,
and for all practical purposes moved into Toby's room with it. When Brian
joined her in there, she seemed to barely tolerate his presence. If he sat beside
it she watched him with naked trepidation, as though she feared he might
damage it somehow.

It was not, he realized, an unfounded fear. Something inside him became
turbulent in its presence, something he couldn't identify but which sparked
flashes of violent thought, of the kind he had not had since just after Toby
vanished. This feeling came in sharp relief to the easy lethargy the angel
normally inspired, and he was reminded of a time when he was younger,
sniffing heroin laced with cocaine. So he did not object to Amy's efforts at
excluding him.

Finally, though, her vigilance slipped. He went into the bathroom and
found her sleeping on the toilet, her robe hiked up around her waist, her head
resting against the sink. He left her there and crept into the angel's room.

It was awake, and its eyes tracked him as he crossed the room and sat
beside it on the bed. Its breath wheezed lightly as it drew air through its puckered mouth. Its body was still bruised and bent, though it did seem to be
improving.

Brian touched its chest where the bruise seemed to be diminishing. *Why
does it bruise?* he wondered. *Why does it bleed the same way I do? Shouldn't
it be made of something better?* Also, it didn't have wings. Not even vestigial
ones. Why were they called angels? Because of how they made people feel? It
looked more like an alien than a divine being. *It has a cock, for Christ's sake.
What's that all about? Do angels fuck?*

He leaned over it, so his face was inches away, almost touching its nose. He
stared into its black, irisless eyes, searching for some sign of intelligence, some
evidence of intent or emotion. From this distance he could smell its breath;
he drew it into his own lungs, and it warmed him like a shot of whiskey. The
angel lifted its head and pressed its face into his. Brian jerked back and felt
something brush his elbow. He looked behind him and discovered the angel
had an erection.

He lurched out of bed, tripping over himself as he rushed to the door,
dashed through it and slammed it shut. His blood sang. It rose in him like
the sea and filled him with tumultuous music. He dropped to his knees and
vomited all over the carpet.

Later, he stepped into its doorway, watching Amy trace her hands down its face. Through the window he could see that night was gathering in little pockets outside, lifting itself toward the sky. At the sight of the angel his heart jumped in his chest as though it had come unmoored. "Amy, I have to talk to you," he said. He had some difficulty making his voice sound calm.

She didn't look at him. "I know it's not really him," she said. "Not really."

"No."

"But don't you think he is, kind of? In a way?"

"No."

She laid her head on the pillow beside it, staring into its face. Brian was left looking at the back of her head, the unwashed hair, tangled and brittle. He remembered cupping the back of her head in his hand, its weight and its warmth. He remembered her body.

"Amy. Where does he live?"

"Who?"

"Tommy. Where does he live?"

She turned and looked at him, a little crease of worry on her brow. "Why do you want to know?"

"Just tell me. Please."

"Brian, don't."

He slammed his fist into the wall, startling himself. He screamed at her. "*Tell me where he lives! God damn it!*"

Tommy opened the door of his shotgun house, clad only in boxer shorts, and Brian greeted him with a blow to the face. Tommy staggered back into his house, due more to surprise than the force of the punch; his foot slipped on a throw rug and he crashed to the floor. The small house reverberated with the impact. Brian had a moment to take in Tommy's hard physique and imagine his wife's hands moving over it. He stepped forward and kicked him in the groin.

Tommy grunted and seemed to absorb it. He rolled over and pushed himself quickly to his feet. Tommy's fist swung at him and he had time to experience a quick flaring terror before his head exploded with pain. He found himself on his knees, staring at the dust collecting in the crevices of the hardwood floor. Somewhere in the background a television chattered urgently.

A kick to the ribs sent Brian down again. Tommy straddled him, grabbed a fistful of hair, and slammed Brian's face into the floor several times. Brian felt something in his face break and blood poured onto the floor. He wanted to cry but it was impossible, he couldn't get enough air. *I'm going to die*, he thought. He felt himself hauled up and thrown against a wall. Darkness crowded his vision; he began to lose his purchase on events.

Someone was yelling at him. There was a face in front of him, skin peeled back from its teeth in a smile or a grimace of rage. It looked like something from hell.

He awoke to the feel of cold grass, cold night air. The right side of his face burned like a signal flare; his left eye refused to open. It hurt to breathe. He pushed himself to his elbows and spit blood from his mouth; it immediately filled again. Something wrong in there. He rolled onto his back and laid there for a while, waiting for the pain to subside to a tolerable level. The night was high and dark. At one point he felt sure that he was rising from the ground, that something up there was pulling him into its empty hollows.

Somehow he managed the drive home. He remembered nothing of it except occasional stabs of pain as opposing headlights washed across his windshield; he would later consider his safe arrival a kind of miracle. He pulled into the driveway and honked the horn a few times until Amy came out and found him there. She looked at him with horror, and with something else.

"Oh, baby. What did you do? What did you do?"

She steered him toward the angel's room. He stopped himself in the doorway, his heart pounding again, and he tried to catch his breath. It occurred to him, on a dim level, that his nose was broken. She tugged at his hand, but he resisted. Her face was limned by moonlight, streaming through the window like some mystical tide, and by the faint luminescence of the angel tucked into their son's bed. She'd grown heavy over the years, and the past year had taken a harsh toll: the flesh on her face sagged, and was scored by grief. And yet he was stunned by her beauty.

Had she always looked like this?

"Come on," she said. "Please."

The left side of his face pulsed with hard beats of pain; it sang like a war drum. His working eye settled on the thing in the bed: its flat black eyes, its wickedly curved talons. Amy sat beside it and put her hand on its chest. It arched its back, seeming to coil beneath her.

"Come lay down," she said. "He's here for us. He's come home for us."

Brian took a step into Toby's room, and then another. He knew she was wrong; that the angel was not home, that it had wandered here from somewhere far away.

Is heaven a dark place?

The angel extended a hand, its talons flexing. The sheets over its belly stirred as Brian drew closer. Amy took her husband's hands, easing him onto the bed. He gripped her shoulders, squeezing them too tightly. "I'm sorry," he said suddenly, surprising himself. "I'm sorry! I'm sorry!" Once he began he couldn't stop. He said it over and over again, so many times it just became a sound, a sobbing plaint, and Amy pressed her hand against his mouth, entwined her fingers into his hair, saying, "Shhhh, shhhhh," and finally she silenced him with a kiss. As they embraced each other the angel played its hands over their faces and their shoulders, its strange reedy breath and its narcotic musk drawing them down to it. They caressed each other, and they caressed the angel, and when they touched their lips to its skin the taste of it shot spikes of joy through their bodies. Brian felt her teeth on his neck and he bit into the angel, the sudden dark spurt of blood filling his mouth, the soft pale flesh tearing easily, sliding down his throat. He kissed his wife furiously and when she tasted the blood she nearly tore his tongue out; he pushed her face toward the angel's body, and watched the blood blossom from beneath her. The angel's eyes were frozen, staring at the ceiling; it extended a shaking hand toward a wall decorated with a Spider-Man poster, its fingers twisted and bent.

They ate until they were full.

That night, heavy with the sludge of bliss, Brian and Amy made love again for the first time in nearly a year. It was wordless and slow, a synchronicity of pressures and tender familiarities. They were like rare creatures of a dying species, amazed by the sight of each other.

Brian drifts in and out of sleep. He has what will be the last dream about his son. It is morning in this dream, by the side of a small country road. It must have rained during the night, because the world shines with a wet glow. Droplets of water cling, dazzling, to the muzzle of a dog as it rests beside the road, unmenaced by traffic, languorous and dull-witted in the rising heat.

It might even be Dodger. His snout is heavy with blood. Some distance away from him Toby rests on the street, a small pile of bones and torn flesh, glittering with dew, catching and throwing sunlight like a scattered pile of rubies and diamonds.

By the time he wakes, he has already forgotten it.

Absolute Zero
Nadia Bulkin

"If it were only you naked on the grass, who would you be then?
And I said I wasn't really sure, but I would probably be cold."
—Phillip Glass, *Freezing*

When Max Beecham was eight years old, his mother Deena (delirious from antihypertensives) gave him a Polaroid and then lay down on the carpet behind him. Inside the white border of this photograph lurked a thing with the naked body of a gaunt man and the head of a dark, decayed stag. It sat on a tree stump the way neighborhood men sat on bar stools, surrounded by a cavalry of thin, burned trees. Max almost recognized this nightmare place as Digby Forest, a festering infection of wild land on the edge of Cripple Creek. In the dusk the image was shadowless and tense, as if that black-eyed Stag-Man meant to lunge out of its frame. As if it was only waiting for Max to look away.

"What is it?" Max asked.

"That's your father," said Deena. She had her back to him. Her thin cotton dress stretched to translucency across her long torso. He could see the shape of her vertebrae. "You're always asking, so there he is."

He thought she was joking and he turned to prod her, but she had fallen asleep. He put the Polaroid face down on the carpet and pressed his fingers against his eyeballs. It was the first thing in his life that he wished he could unsee. He would hear later that time heals all wounds, but the deep slice in his heart that this picture created never got any better. The next summer Max tried to walk Fallspur Bridge for the right to join the Petrinos on the other side, but halfway across and already wobbling, he looked up and saw the Stag-Man crouched in the trees behind the Petrinos. And the bastard never left him alone; the Stag-Man watched him try to impress the slouching upperclassmen, the tall blonde girls in athletic shorts and shirts that claimed them as the property of Jesus. He might win himself a little respite—when he was concentrating on a math exam, for example—but as soon as his mind unclenched, the Stag-Man would be there: looking in the window, waiting behind the fence.

During this time, his mother went on disability. She nearly drowned in the bathtub twice—when he pulled her out she said she was trying to "get back to herself." This was a lie. He knew that she was trying to get back to that thing, that Stag-Man.

"Why did you tell me?" he'd shout at her when he got older. By that time she had confined herself to her rocking chair, with her gaze fixed on their lopsided black locust tree. No, it was not their tree—it was older than he was, and he knew she wouldn't have planted it. It was no one's tree, and maybe that was why it had grown up crooked. "Why didn't you just keep this shit to yourself? You could have lied to me, you know. It's not like I would've known."

Max flapped the Polaroid in her face—his mother did not respond. He had tried to destroy the photo but every time he took it to the backyard with a lighter, some bony inner feeling stopped him. So it lived in his closet in a taped-up shoebox, supposedly contained.

"Why did you tell me!" he shouted. "Come on, mom!" The urge swelled to seize her and wrestle her to the floor—anything to break her out of the stasis that had closed in around her like a hard coat of amber. He grabbed the chair instead, swung it around so that she couldn't look at the tree anymore. He immediately wished he hadn't. Her miserable, time-eaten gaze felt like the swing of an iron bar.

"You didn't like what you saw?" She was breathing shallowly. When she sighed it sounded like wind rushing through a pipe. "Bummer."

She and the tree died that winter. The end was very hard. Deena fought the hospital staff with long-dormant claws whenever they rolled into her room with needles and droopy bags of liquid medicine. "Fuck your poison," she would say. The hospital was two hours away from Cripple Creek, and the neighbor who drove Max in and out of the city always fish-tailed on the icy roads. The flat white landscape would spin past with no beginning and no end; the neighbor would mumble obscenities, and Max would think ecstatically about dying. At first the tree went on without her, its branches twisting round its trunk, but Max burned it down.

Max's grandmother, Rowena, came down from Vertigo to see him through high school. She shed no tears for the one she called her lost child. "She was gone by the time she walked out of those woods pregnant with you," said Grandma Ro. "So I've been mourning your whole life."

Years later, after Grandma Ro had passed on (she died in her daughter's bedroom; Max taped the door shut afterwards, designating the room "condemned"), Tom Lowell caught something large and alarming on the edge of his property. By then Max was twenty-six and working at Ticonderoga Mills, buying wheat from the ragged, leftover farms of Cripple Creek. Whenever prices dropped, Max would see them leaning heavy against their trucks, eyes to the dirt. Sometimes they cussed him out. Max reasoned that they shouldn't have been clinging to their backwards lifestyle anyway. He hated their excuses: their fathers' fathers had cultivated that land for generations, and now the grains were in their blood. "What if your fathers' fathers have been killing for generations?" he would mutter to himself. "What then?"

Then you strip yourself down to the smallest, purest molecules and rebuild yourself up to something better, that's what. Max thought that he had pretty well succeeded at this—at least he did not see those eyes in the mirror anymore, at least he had a job and a girl and a house (his mother's house, but still)—but then Tom Lowell started running around town saying that he was charging twenty dollars to see the Meanest Looking Thing on Earth, this Devil's Child. Max began to feel the Polaroid staring at him from inside the shoebox again.

Nothing very strange had happened in Cripple Creek in the years between Max's birth and the capture of what Tom Lowell christened The Creeker—aside from the woman who ran the plant nursery, Chastity Dawes, getting pregnant out of nowhere and giving birth to a small fawn. The hospital had the creature euthanized, despite the mother's objections. But other than that, life in Cripple Creek had been normal. Progress continued apace. The racetrack, the shopping mall, the microbrewery. They were on track to match Grand Island in annual revenue. God knew theirs was a community on the rise.

Kevin from work wanted to see The Creeker. He wanted to see it so he could laugh at it, and at Tom Lowell. "It's probably just some two-headed cow," Kevin said. "Lowell's a nut, you know. I heard he went hunting for some Demon Razorback of Arkansas once."

Of course Max knew what this Creeker was, in the bowels of his soul. It was the Stag-Man. It was his . . .

And then he would have to go to the restroom and cradle his head between his knees. Maybe he shouldn't have gone. On the drive over, his stomach was flipping so badly that he couldn't talk. But it would have looked strange if he'd bowed out—he'd gone to mock the "crop circles" out at Rookshire, after all—and besides, his depraved subconscious just couldn't let go of the image of Tom Lowell's farm and the captive creature behind its fence. In the days before they finally went to the farm his world had warped into a tunnel, a vortex like the one at Rapid City, with all furniture and foliage blurring together and everything hurtling toward a pair of eyes like lumps of coal.

Caridee Lowell, sixteen years old with eyes sunken from methamphetamine, sold red tickets out of a tin lunchbox. "To your left," she hissed after taking their bills. There was no need for directions; the bright yellow fireworks tent was visible all the way down Cahokia Drive.

The tent was surprisingly quiet. The dozen people gathered inside would knock heads to whisper to each other, but all their eyes were fixed upon one location: a metal crate on the far side of the tent, large enough to shuttle a cow. "It's one of Murray's old transport cages," Tom Lowell said. Several years ago there had been a short, ugly attempt at a town zoo—both the Ag Department and Fish and Wildlife had to get involved. The surviving animals had all been taken away, supposedly, but one reasonable theory argued that this Creeker was some mutated, mutilated escapee. Angry with man. Hungry for revenge. An old story. "It's for handling wild animals, so don't worry. He won't getcha."

And there, in the cage, was the Stag-Man. After years of staring at a three-inch image in a palm-sized Polaroid, its immense size overwhelmed Max. He would have needed to stoop to get inside that cage, but the Stag-Man had to sit, cramped, its knees to its chin. Its four-foot antlers flared out from its cervine head like skeleton-wings. Max could see immediately that it was too big for this cage, too big for this tent. Its skin was loose—it was not feeding enough. His slow-burning father, the monster. The captive. Why was it just sitting there? What was it thinking? Dread crawled up his throat. He felt fear, yes, but also the early twinges of sympathy.

Max and Kevin heard the nervous mumbling as they pushed to the front— "Where the hell did that thing come from?" "What's it doing here?"—but no one wanted to answer, because no one really wanted to know. Sometimes after they asked these questions they would cough and pat their chests, as if they had accidentally invited themselves down some terrible internal rabbit hole. The ones that simply said, "I don't know what to say" fared better. Kevin whispered "No fucking way" with his eyes glazed, and Max was thinking, *"Father."*

Up close the scent of rank earth nearly knocked them down. Max could barely believe the Stag-Man was real and tangible and capable of bleeding—it had made so much more sense as a dream-spirit, his mother's Boogeyman. He stared at the beast for fifteen minutes, helpless, trapped like a rabbit in a snare. He thought it was because the Stag-Man knew him as a son but post-tent conversation would reveal that everyone in the Creeker's presence thought it was staring them in the eye, holding them rapt.

A little girl standing beside Max clutched the bars as if she was the one imprisoned. She was watching the Creeker breathe, so it seemed, and sobbing quietly the entire time.

There were casualties. Unlike the Big Eats Barbecue, Tom Lowell's show did not spread joy. People left the tent either stone silent or pissing mad, bickering about "that one night in Reno" and "what you did with my father's money." The biggest casualty that night was Pastor Connor from the Good Shepherd Lutheran Church. He had come to pressure Tom Lowell into closing down the show, but of course had to look at the exhibit first. It was a mistake. After staring at the Creeker for several minutes he ran out of the tent, shoving his own parishioners aside, and collapsed on the grass with his hands to his heart. Kevin called an ambulance and Elise Buckley fed him aspirin, but it was too late.

"Ah, geez," said the kid in the paramedic uniform. "I *told* him not to go."

"You've seen the Creeker?" asked Kevin.

"I went opening night," said the paramedic-kid. "I was freaking out for a whole week. Kept thinking about all the squirrels I shot coming back rabid and biting me in my sleep." He tried to laugh. "Fucking weird, right?"

After Pastor Connor was lifted into the back of the ambulance the rest of them stood in a circle with their hands in their pockets. They were more distressed by the Creeker than by Pastor Connor's death, which seemed like a just response to that monstrous aberration. A small child screamed from some parked car—they glanced up, but dropped their chins when they heard the stern voice of a disciplinarian-father. Finally Elise Buckley lit a cigarette and started to talk.

"I guess it was a bad summer, if that thing's wandering out of Digby this time of year. Isn't that what happens with bears? If they're scavenging in October, you gotta figure it's because they didn't get to feed enough in the summer. Feeding on what, I don't know. People's lost dogs, I guess."

After this little burst they fell quiet again, thinking about dogs they had lost, and horses that had supposedly run away, and then the really unpleasant stuff: the missing people. There had been no more than a handful in the past ten years, but how the news stations had dwelled upon those unlucky few. Everyone around for the last census remembered at least one. Even the missing migrant workers were considered tragedies. *They must be cold out there*, people said.

"That thing's not ours," Kevin mumbled into his gloved hands. "It's not our problem."

Elise shook her head, took a big drag, and walked away. "I really hate all of you people."

Then it was just Max and Kevin watching for shadows on the darkened grass. "I saw a chupacabra once," whispered Kevin. "I was visiting my grandparents in Texas. It was the middle of the night when I heard it howling. It killed my favorite goat."

The Stag-Man was some kind of witch, Max decided. In all the years that he had known these people, nothing else had warped them so. He knew what Kevin and Elise and everyone else was feeling—like they were wobbling on the lip of a great dark funnel—because he had suffered the power of the Stag-Man's gaze every night since he was eight. Max wanted to tell them this, but like hell would he admit to his friends and neighbors that he shared any blood with that thing in Tom Lowell's cage. He had a brief moment of panic: what if Kevin saw some familial resemblance between his long features and that of the Stag-Man? He frantically rubbed his face. He was feeling for rough fur and a soft wet snout, but all he got was dry human skin. When he was twelve he had asked his mother if he had anything in common with the Stag-Man, and now he heard her reply: "Believe me," she'd said, with a snort, "You're nothing alike."

Mallory Jablonski taught fifth grade at Cripple Creek Elementary. It was the same school Max had attended, but they were not schoolyard sweethearts—she grew up in Lincoln, and she had the straight teeth and designer

jeans to prove it. She'd been on a school dance squad, which Max understood
to be a mythical troupe of hot girls in black leotards that would never be
permitted at Cripple Creek High, where even the cheerleaders wore turtle-
necks and chastity rings. Mallory had been on a class trip to New York.
She liked sushi. All sorts of things, and still she radiated that earthy glow
of harvest corn. Mallory was cultured; Mallory was genuine. He drove her
around town slowly, with the windows down, because damn if his classmates
wouldn't be surprised that he managed to catch a girl like that. Mallory
always laughed when they stopped at intersections. "Traffic's real bad today,"
she'd say. It was funny because there was no such thing as traffic in Cripple
Creek.

When the Creeker became the talk of the town she asked him to take
her to see it. "All my students are talking about it," she said. "Have you seen
it?"

He thought of the Polaroid. The slow-burning eyes. "Yeah."

"And? Is it scary?" She bit her nails, grinning. She probably thought it
was some pathetic artifact of rural Americana, a cousin of cow-tipping and
haystack rides. "No, don't tell me. I want to see it myself."

Max took her to the Lowell farm that Friday. The carnival tent was
fraying now that the first of the cold fronts were moving in. Mallory had
been talkative as they crossed the pesticide-yellow grass, but in the presence
of the Stag-Man, she approached the cage as if in a trance. She knelt down
at the bars the way she did at Mass and looked soulfully, silently into the
Stag-Man's eyes. Max felt acid bubble into his throat. They were exchanging
secrets and truths, he could just tell. She was in communion with the same
incubus that had seduced his mother. He would have yanked her out of that
deferential pose by her hair, but Mallory stood up just as he was reaching
down. She stuffed her hands in her sweatshirt pockets.

"Let's go, I want to go," she mumbled. "I don't feel well."

A throng of preteens that had set up a devotional camp outside the
Stag-Man's cage leered up at them. They looked like jackals in black
clothes. "Ooh, yeah," said one of them. "Run along and hi-i-ide." Max
sharply told them to go home—trying to sound like a responsible man,
even though his own father was a freak in a cage—but they sang back,
"This *is* home."

He and Mallory walked back to his truck with his arm around her
shoulders. He could feel her trembling. It was a cold sort of relief to see that
she was suffering instead of enraptured. She was nothing like his mother, he

told himself. She was an innocent. Virtuous. Competent. "I shouldn't have brought you here. This stuff's no good." He bit his lips, in guilt. Mallory shook her head absently but didn't speak until they were in the muscular safety of the Chevrolet Colorado, barreling down Cahokia Drive, listening to Doctor Touchdown on KMKO Radio.

"I used to have an imaginary friend."

He turned the volume down. "Huh?"

"But I don't know if she was really imaginary. She came out at night, from the wetlands. She would tap on my window. Glowing like a gravestone. No one else saw her but I . . . saw her more and more after my sister died." Max hadn't known about this sister. "I think she wanted me to go away with her. She said there was a castle under the water at Napoleon Pond. Oh, God." She slumped forward in the passenger seat as if something had punched her in the stomach. Max wondered if this was why she could not sleep facing any windows, why she slept in the pitch-black dark with the sheets over her head. "I never told anybody. But I guess seeing that thing on the farm . . . brought it all back." She looked over at him plaintively. "You think I'm a freak, don't you? Just say it. I know that's what you're thinking."

It was a strange moment. He would dwell upon it later to try to determine what had possessed him to tell her the truth. Maybe he was shocked that a girl as presentable as Mallory could feel his bewildered shame. Maybe he thought shared alienation would deepen their bond. "I don't think you're a freak," he said. "Something even stranger happened to me."

She raised a pale brown eyebrow.

"You know that . . . thing on the farm?" She nodded. "Well, that's my father." He immediately exploded in terrified laughter. The sensible, screaming part of him wanted to backtrack before things got any worse— tack on a quick "Holy shit, just kidding!"—but when he opened his mouth only nonsense dribbled out. "My mother was a strange lady. She was the kind of person that chased tornadoes, you know? No jeep or cameras or nothing, she'd just head out the door and run after them. She's dead now. Died a long time ago."

Mallory was trying to smile. But she was waiting for that "just kidding!" and when it didn't come—when every word that rolled down his chin was a confirmation of the wretched truth—Mallory gathered up the handles of her purse and said to take her home. She looked like she was about to jump out of the truck. "I have a lot of quizzes to grade," she said.

He reached over, teeming with concern, but Mallory recoiled from his hand. It was as if she was saying, *No—I never touched you. I disown you. I don't know who you even are.*

The road dwindled. Her driveway was covered in fallen leaves. "Mallory," he said, hoping to remind her of what they had been sharing for the past six months. "It doesn't change anything."

Mallory's eyes widened; she was probably remembering the same six months in retrospective horror. "I can't do this, Max." The passenger door swung open and the cold rushed in. "I can't do this now."

And then she was gone. He had wanted to marry her. He had visualized himself walking into her parents' house in the old part of Lincoln, all brick walls and roundabouts and leafy trees, and introducing himself to her father the banker. *"My name is Max,"* he would have said, and there would have been no doubt.

He started dreaming about hurting Mallory. He didn't enjoy these dreams, but they satisfied the same ache in his belly that years earlier made him want to shake his mother until her head popped off. The Stag-Man was there too, watching and waiting, and after the floor swallowed Mallory's ruined body, the Stag-Man would remain: bright and powerful and merciless. A fire in the woods, an old whispered force. Sometimes the Stag-Man called him "son." Sometimes Max would curl around the creature's feet because in the dark the Stag-Man was all there was to the world. With its crown of antlers it looked like some wise and wizened tree. And sometimes when Max woke up he would go to the bathroom mirror and rub his forehead to see if his own velvet-covered antlers were growing in.

Tom Lowell had cut the entrance fee in half. Word had spread of the Creeker's negative side effects—*nausea, heartburn, indigestion*—and now the farmer stood alone in the middle of his driveway, hands on his hips, watching for vehicles on Cahokia Drive. "You think it makes 'em feel better to think this stuff doesn't exist?" he asked Max, cocking his head, chicken-like. "Hey, isn't this your third time?" Like the Stag-Man was some ride at Worlds of Fun.

Three drunks in Husker windbreakers were tossing peanut shells at the Stag-Man. They were giving themselves points for contact: five for the body, ten for the head. They did not deign to speak to it even in the way they spoke to their dogs, even though the body they shot at was just a taller, stronger version of their own. Max felt a pang of defensive anger and shame, but the Stag-Man seemed to be smiling back at them. Not that its deer mouth could grin, but its eyes were gleeful.

Max crept up to the cage. It was filthy, and swarming with bronze cock-roaches. He sensed the Stag-Man watching him and his legs wobbled—the last two times he'd been in the tent he'd been able to hold steady, but not now. Moving his center of gravity closer to the earth quelled a little bit of nausea, but still he had to ask the question. "Do you know me?"

A peanut shell hit the back of his head. "That's ten for me!" shouted one drunk; "Get out of the way!" said another. Max hissed at them and did not move. Instead he eased his hands between the bars, gingerly laying them on the floor of the cage. A cockroach ran over his empty ring finger and down his sleeve, but the Stag-Man was silent. Max swallowed. Of course it didn't know him from Adam—God knew how many women from Cripple Creek had gone running into its forest on summer nights. He took out his wallet, and a small secret photo he kept behind his ID. A woman with coiffed black hair and a red Christmas sweater gazed up and out with gorgeous cat-eyes. She was a little drunk but still healthy then, surrounded by cheap tinsel. "This is my mother. Twenty-seven years ago, you . . . "

The Stag-Man looked at the photo and curled its lips back, showing its teeth. Those teeth were pointed. Max shuddered, and one of the drunks started to retch. At first the man spat bile and beer, but upon reaching into the back of his throat, began to pull out a long and thin industrial wire.

Max should have gotten fired that week—not that he would have cared—because he couldn't focus on his paperwork. The window behind his desk let in too much light and too much landscape. Cripple Creek seemed filled with broken pre-war churches and painted-over signs: the skeletons of older towns. No matter where he went—the Kwik Shop, the liquor store—these battered, ghostly layers peeked through the concrete he walked upon. "You remember that lady Chastity Dawes?"

Kevin glanced at him over the crest of a golden taco. Max had tried to bring up the chupacabra, but Kevin would always pretend to be choking on something or getting a phone call. "The one that gave birth to a deer?"

"Yeah. Whatever happened to her? I know the Gordons own the nursery now."

"She killed herself, man. Well, 'died of exposure.' But when you ditch your car off Highway 2 in the middle of a snow storm so you can go walking through a corn field, I don't know how you call it anything else." Kevin shrugged. "I guess once you've given birth to a monster, what the fuck else are you going to do?"

Max tried to picture those cornfields. They were a grim sight in winter—the stalks either pale and withered or draped with silent, crushing snow. "Isn't that right by Digby Forest?"

"Hell if I know. I haven't been *there* since elementary school."

"Field trip," said Max. He remembered his own school-sponsored foray into Digby Forest—or rather, he remembered being terrified that he would see the Stag-Man. He was so frightened, so attuned to any blur of movement and any sound of breaking twigs, that he learned nothing at all about Nebraska's native forests. And here Chastity Dawes had gone running *toward* this doom, just like his mother sinking in the bathtub. At the time he had thought, *Is this world so bad?* but maybe they were onto something. "She was going on a field trip."

"What?" The taco muffled Kevin's words. "You know, Beecham, sometimes you freak me out." He kept talking, but Max was looking out the window. Clouds had swooped in from the south in violent formation, armies of fists against armies of hammers. Something was on its way. Judging by the speed of his heartbeat, it was probably his fate.

Tom Lowell and his daughter Caridee were found murdered in their living room on Tuesday the 20th. Tom on the couch, Caridee on the floor, the television broadcasting an episode of the soap opera *Coming Up Roses*. To say murdered was to put it kindly: they had been disemboweled. The Creeker was gone, its cage bent open like a soup can. Relief washed over Cripple Creek, because people assumed that the malformed beast that shared their name had gone back to Digby Forest. They were duly sorry about Caridee, but at least nobody would have to see that damn thing again. Max alone knew that it was still in town, hiding in collapsed barns and hobbled school buses, and he lay awake at night waiting for it to come crawling through his window. The thought still made his skin crawl, but it was oddly reassuring to feel that he still belonged to someone, something. It was nice to know that he was still someone's son.

At Cabela's, he looked at the Deer Head Mounts. There was a whole wall of them, right beside the Buffalo Mounts and European Mounts. Some had shoulders, some only necks. The replicas were cheaper, but the originals looked at Max with soft and sad fraternal recognition. They were kin to the Stag-Man, his father—only smaller, with fair and innocent faces. They did not look like monsters spat out of hell. They looked like the deer that the Deer Crossing signs warned of, the deer that lived in the narrow strips of woodland between the farms and the roads. He briefly imagined the heads of all the world's beasts mounted upon a giant fortress wall. His own head was among them, bolted to a wooden slab.

The sales clerk was rambling statistics. "That rack's a 17-pointer, with a 30-inch spread. Came off an early season northern whitetail . . . "

"Can you take the skin off?" Max asked.

The sales clerk looked shocked. "No . . . but we've got deer skin rugs."

They had grizzly skin rugs too, as well as wolf skin rugs and cougar skin rugs and muskox skin rugs and child-sized lynx and badger and beaver skin rugs. All had heads attached to their flat and floppy puppet bodies. Unlike the snarling predators—still fighting even in this state of preserved death—the buck's mouth was stitched closed. "It's got a canvas backing. Professionally taxidermied."

"I'll take it," Max said.

That evening he sat on the couch and wrapped himself with the deer skin rug. The buck's head sat upon his own—he had to slouch to keep it from falling down his back. His new skin was so suffocatingly warm that he turned off the heater. Then he exhaled, trying to feel comfortable. He dug his nails into the hide and imagined it to be his own. What were the odds, he wondered, of having been born into a human body? Maybe it was the wrong one. Maybe he should have been a ruminant all along, just like Chastity Dawes' fawn.

A door opened—judging by the hard slap of metal on wood, it was the screen door in the kitchen. He looked up. The Stag-Man, bloody-mouthed, stood in the doorway. Its antlers were scraping the ceiling. At first it was just breathing, staring; then it came gliding forward, never raising its hooves off the fake wood-paneled floor.

"Father," mumbled Max, hoping that it would see him in his deer form. The Stag-Man did look into the false glass eyes of the dead buck, but quickly lowered its gaze to Max's real eyes, all hazel and watery and bursting with nerves. That gaze reached right inside his head and rummaged around. Within this visual stranglehold the house changed and decomposed. Filth rose to the surface. He saw his mother creeping down the stairs out of the corner of his eye. Neither she nor his father saw each other. Her bloated lips called his name. After ten seconds, Max had to look away.

The Stag-Man hovered above him, sniffing deeply, then withdrew with a grunt. It paused at the doorway. It was waiting, Max realized. It grunted again and Max got to his feet. They were sharing a floor now, father and son. It was like sharing an earth.

How new this night-world was. A man with a flashlight could only point out the random human signposts that survived nightfall in the country—the gravel of a driveway, the lawn chairs on a porch. All else was lost in the dark and gnarly mass: the pulsing, growing *stuff* that flashlights could not bear to focus on. Max was in the thick of it now, this world without property fences (only land), without cars (only lights), without houses (only wood). He was not sure if he was running or drowning, and he had lost the deer skin somewhere back on 10th Street. Sometimes he could throw himself fully into this night-run, lose himself in the muscle-searing pursuit of his Stag-Man father who did not run but madly leapt from things that used to be mailboxes to things that used to be trash cans.

And then he would look down at his hands and see his pale, chilled human skin. It made his stomach fold. He was pushing so fast that the ground seemed to roll beneath him, so fast his mind tumbled like a whirligig. And all the while, deep welts grew on his skin where trees had clawed him. With blood in the air, the Stag-Man let out a trembling, hungry, open-throated howl. Max felt it in his spine, as deep and familiar as a knife in a wound. He almost stopped. The boy inside him wanted to crawl home. *This is home*, he told himself. *The others would have found you out eventually. You would have started to stink. So don't mourn. Don't mourn.*

Bill MacAtee was dead, but he was not the one the Stag-Man wanted. The Stag-Man had killed him with a teacher's patience, lingering over the precise angle and depth of the slice across Bill's stomach, encouraging Max to scoop out the viscera. Bill was the kind of asshole that used to drive around town calling quiet men fags, and Max (having been Bill's target once or twice) tried to be glad that Bill was dead. And maybe he was, but not like that, not with long swaths of Bill hanging out and inviting flies, not so Bill could stare up at the clouds like a middle-schooler rolling his eyes. The Stag-Man had already moved onto the true object of its desire: the MacAtees' sheepdog, groomed and collared with hair the color of a Holstein cow. It had come running after Bill, barking indignantly, but when the Stag-Man turned toward the dog with its branch-like arms outstretched and its dirty claws dripping with the master's blood, the domesticated little creature buckled down, whimpering.

At least the Stag-Man killed it quickly. Max wasn't sure why—some hint of tenderness, or pity? The dog might have been wild, in another lifetime. After it collapsed, blood soaking its blue collar black, the Stag-Man squatted down and dug a hole beneath the dog's ribs. Liquid gushed out along with a twitch and a squeak as if the little life was not quite gone. Max pressed his hands against his own belly. The Stag-Man pulled tendons and muscles and gelatinous organs out of this cavity like they were the treasures of the damn Sierra Madre, but all Max saw when the Stag-Man's hands opened was inside-out-dog, all the wet under-the-skin shit that he didn't want to see. And then the smell—putrid, sour, like drowned flowers—hit him.

Max retched. He slapped his hand over his mouth so that when the salt bubbled up his throat he could chase it back down. When he looked up the Stag-Man was standing at full height. The burnt black eyes drilled down into him as if from the pinnacle of a grotesque tower. The steaming, dripping hand was still available; God only knew he tried to take it. His father was grunting at him, thrusting the hand forward, snorting. He had flashbacks of walking across Fallspur Bridge, and the sunburned children on the other side who screamed at him to hurry and cross. The plank wobbled. The world beneath, the great bottomless funnel, rocked and churned. His body failed him now as it had failed him then. The Stag-Man threw the innards at his heart and Max compulsively shuddered, trying to shake the wetness off without getting it under his nails. Maybe it was this final twitch that ruined it, because the Stag-Man turned then, growling: away from Max, back toward the wild tree line. Max hurried after, mewling like a lost animal. He had not realized until then how warm he had felt in his father's presence.

And then his father had him by the neck in a bristling, rough embrace. His ribs were groaning, but Max tried not to struggle. His mother had some-times held him this way. *"Come here. Oh God. Don't cry."* A bark-skin hand clenched the roots of his hair—so tightly that he could feel his scalp peeling off his skull, tears shooting into his eyes, so tightly that he forgot all but this pain and an incomprehensible fear—and ripped Max away. Like a man pulling off a leech. A human would have been disemboweled and a fawn would have been taken along, but Max was just tossed into the winter grass, a formless mess not even a mother could love. It came down like an iron gate between them: *you are nothing of mine.*

Max flinched and curled his muscles, trying to turn his trembling body into a fist. The Stag-Man was gliding away toward the foggy pines. "Don't you dare walk away!" Max shouted. "Hey, you look at me!"

There was no response. He remembered his mother sitting in her rocking chair, staring unshaken at the black locust tree. He could have set himself on fire and not drawn her eye—not until she coughed on his ashes would she realize that the skinny thing she sometimes called her child was gone. He grabbed Bill MacAtee's shotgun, pulling back the cold, thick fingers one by one, and after another warning—another *"Look at me!"*—he fired it at his father. The cartridge opened a hole in the tawny hide of his father's back. Blood-petals sprayed into the frosted dawn like a bridal bouquet, but for a full thirty seconds, the Stag-Man kept walking. What call could be higher than its own survival? Max's eyes began to water and when he looked back after wiping his face, the Stag-Man was gone. A deflated lump so unlike the striking figure in his mother's Polaroid lay in its place. The pines shook and Max hunched over, shivering.

"Bill?" Caroline MacAtee stood on the back porch. Her trembling fingers rose to touch her mouth. Max could not tell—simply could not determine—whether she was staring at him or at the dead things gathered at his feet.

"Everything's okay!" Max shouted, raising the rifle. "It's gone now, I took care of it!"

Caroline MacAtee didn't thank him—she backed into her house and slammed the door. But maybe he couldn't blame her, because here it was starting to snow.

The wild had been tamed, and now they were losing visibility. Max was too busy clenching his teeth and the steering wheel to manipulate the windshield wipers, and he drifted toward what looked like a glory-white horizon before recalling fear and slamming on the brakes. He slid to a stop half-on, half-off the shoulder. "A fire out in Digby Forest . . . " KMKO Radio was starting to cut out. "Not sure if they're going to send the Fire Department on account of . . . hope it doesn't come near us . . . " On the other side of the road, a pudgy man in a green Parks and Recreation jacket stood next to a blinking truck. He was trying to shovel the remains of a very large piece of road kill into the truck's open bed. Black tarp was whipping in the wind.

Max rolled down his window. "What is that?" he shouted.

"Hell if I know," the Parks and Recreation man shouted back. "Guy said it just showed up in the middle of the road, didn't even try to get out of the way."

The corpse was the size of a small horse and covered with icy fur, but elephantine tusks protruded from the garbled carcass.

"Sixth call we've had this hour. I didn't even know we had these many animals to run down." The Parks and Recreation man started laughing, then coughing. "You know there's birds falling out of the sky by the racetrack? Something in the weather, I guess."

Deena used to say that animals could tell when it was time to get the hell out of Dodge. "You'll know when bad times are coming," she whispered, "Because you'll hear them *howling*." Max closed his eyes. He never wanted to think of that name again. Never wanted to see that bewitched smile again. *Stay dead*, he thought. *Stay dead*.

"You hear that Digby's burning down?"

Suddenly tired, Max rested his arms against the steering wheel. "Yeah, I heard."

"I hope they let it burn. That no-good place." The man's lower lip was trembling. "It's just a breeding ground for monsters."

Burning the black locust tree had cauterized some of the wounds in his young heart. Maybe that was all Cripple Creek needed: a good cleansing burn, some scar tissue to seal away the unpleasantness. He nodded. "Get rid of it," he said. "Nothing else you can do." With growing anger, the Parks and Recreation man smashed his shovel against the unknown animal. The creature was fixed to the ice, more figurine than entity, too ugly and beaten to be mounted on somebody's wall. Max looked away.

Both eastbound and westward, cars were diving off the edge of the road into the white expanse. Max counted eight in all. Their doors were open, their seats were empty. He didn't know where those drivers thought they were going—did they really think there was anything left to run away to? The world was smothered with ash and snow.

Mallory's fluorescent windows glared like the beacon of an arctic outpost, so harsh he had to squint. He rang the door bell and listened to her slippered feet approach from the other side. Was she looking through the peep hole? Did she see spatters of blood, any antler stubs? No—she was unlocking the dead bolt, unhooking the security chain. She opened the door, and he was surprised by how empty and sterile her home looked, like a hollow egg. Bare as the sky and the buried fields. *No, not empty*, he told himself. *Safe from monsters*. "Max?" She leaned her listless head against the door. "What are you doing here?"

"I cleaned myself up," he said. "I bashed in those demons. I dropped that baggage . . . feel lighter already. I'm good as new." He realized that he could not feel his lips. But after all these years of feeling, he could use a little numbness. It was a small price to pay for the capacity to forget. "I want to start over. Please, Mallory. We can be happy, I know it."

Mallory's sleepy blue eyes looked him up and down. She smiled faintly. As she parted her lips to speak the wind rose to an ear-splitting shriek, and all the sound in the world went out.

Biographies

Nathan Ballingrud lives in Asheville, NC, with his daughter. His short stories have appeared in *SCIFICTION*, *Inferno: New Tales of Terror*, *Lovecraft Unbound*, *Teeth*, and other places. Several stories have been reprinted in various Year's Best anthologies, and he won the Shirley Jackson Award for "The Monsters of Heaven." He can be found online at nathanballingrud. wordpress.com.

Clive Barker was born in Liverpool in 1952. He is the author of *The Books of Blood* (in six volumes), *The Damnation Game*, *Weaveworld*, *Cabal*, *The Great and Secret Show*, *Imajica*, *Everville* and *Sacrament* as well as writing, directing and producing for the screen—his films include *Hellraiser* and *Nightbreed*. He presently lives in Los Angeles.

Laird Barron's work has appeared in numerous anthologies. Much of it has been collected in two books, *The Imago Sequence* and *Occultation*. He lives in Olympia, Washington.

Nadia Bulkin is a writer and political science student. Her short fiction has appeared in *ChiZine*, *Strange Horizons*, *Fantasy Magazine*, the anthology *Bewere The Night*, and elsewhere; more information is available at nadiabulkin.wordpress.com. She spent her impressionable teen years in the suburban wilds of Nebraska. Her world view (and "Absolute Zero") was greatly influenced by her environmental science minor and the 1982 movie about life out of balance, *Koyaanisqatsi*.

F. Brett Cox's fiction has appeared in numerous publications, including *Century*, *North Carolina Literary Review*, *Lady Churchill's Rosebud Wristlet*, *Postscripts*, and *Phantom*. With Andy Duncan, he co-edited *Crossroads: Tales of the Southern Literary Fantastic* (Tor, 2004). A native of North Carolina, Brett is Associate Professor of English at Norwich University in Northfield,

Vermont, and lives in Roxbury, Vermont, with his wife, playwright Jeanne Beckwith.

Gemma Files's first novel, *A Book of Tongues: Volume One of the Hexslinger Series* (ChiZine Publications), won *Dark Scribe* Magazine's 2010 Black Quill "Small Press Chill" award; its sequel, *A Rope of Thorns*, will be released in May 2011. She also won the 1999 International Horror Guild's Best Short Fiction award for her story "The Emperor's Old Bones." Learn more about her at musicatmidnight-gfiles.blogspot.com.

Jeffrey Ford is the author of the novels, *The Physiognomy, The Portrait of Mrs. Charbuque, The Girl In the Glass, The Shadow Year*, and the story collections, *The Fantasy Writer's Assistant, The Empire of Ice Cream, The Drowned Life*. He lives in the world capital of Creatures, New Jersey, and teaches Fiction Writing and Early American Lit. at Brookdale Community College.

Christopher Golden is the author of such novels as *Of Saints and Shadows, The Myth Hunters, The Boys Are Back in Town, Strangewood* and, with Mike Mignola, *Baltimore, or, The Steadfast Tin Soldier and the Vampire*. His work for teens and young adults includes *The Secret Journeys of Jack London*, co-authored with Tim Lebbon, and the *Body of Evidence* series. His other hats include editor, screenwriter, video game scripter, and comic book creator. Golden was born and raised in Massachusetts, where he still lives with his family. His original novels have been published in more than fourteen languages in countries around the world. Please visit him at www.christophergolden.com.

Stephen Graham Jones is the author of *It Came from Del Rio*, the horror collection *That Ones That Got Away*, and seven other books, with two more on the way from Dzanc. His stories have appeared in *The Year's Best Fantasy and Horror, The Best Horror of the Year*(s), and around a hundred and twenty magazines and journals. Jones teaches in the MFA program at CU Boulder. More at demontheory.net.

Alaya Dawn Johnson is the author of several short stories and three novels: *Moonshine, Racing the Dark* and *The Burning City*. She lives in New York City and can be contacted via her website www.alayadawnjohnson.com.

Michael Kelly is the author of *Scratching the Surface*, and *Undertow and Other Laments*. His short fiction has appeared in a number of journals and anthologies, including *Best New Horror*, *Dark Arts*, *Nemonymous*, *PostScripts*, *Space & Time*, *Supernatural Tales*, and *Tesseracts 13*. Michael edited the anthologies *Apparitions* (for which he was a Shirley Jackson Award finalist), and *Chilling Tales*. He also runs Undertow Publications, and its flagship publication, *Shadows & Tall Trees*.

Carrie Laben, formerly of Buffalo, Ithaca, and Brooklyn, is currently studying for her MFA in Creative Nonfiction at the University of Montana. As a result she has eaten more elk in the past six months than she even considered eating in the first thirty-one years of her life. Her work has previously appeared in venues such as *Clarkesworld*, *Chizine*, *Haunted Legends*, and the anthology *Phantom*. When she is not writing she looks at birds.

John Langan is the author of a novel, *House of Windows* (Night Shade 2009), and a collection of stories, *Mr. Gaunt and Other Uneasy Encounters* (Prime 2008). He lives in upstate New York with his wife, son, dog, and a trio of mutually-suspicious cats.

Sarah Langan is the author of the novels *The Keeper* and *The Missing*, and *Audrey's Door*. She is currently finishing her fourth book, *Empty Houses*. Her work has garnered three Bram Stoker Awards, an ALA Award, a *New York Times Book Review* editor's pick, a *PW* favorite book of the year selection, and been optioned by The Weinstein Company for film. She lives in Brooklyn with her husband, daughter, and rabbit.

Joe R. Lansdale is the author of over thirty novels and eighteen short story collections. His work has appeared in numerous markets here and abroad. His work has been recognized by numerous awards, including The Edgar and seven Bram Stokers. His novella, *Bubba Hotep*, was filmed by Don Coscarelli and has become a cult film.

Kelly Link is the author of three collections, *Pretty Monsters*, *Magic for Beginners* and *Stranger Things Happen*. Her short stories have won three Nebula awards, a Hugo, a Locus and a World Fantasy Award. She was born in Miami, Florida, and once won a free trip around the world by answering the question "Why do you want to go around the world?" ("Because you can't go through it.") Link lives in Northampton, Massachusetts, where she and her husband, Gavin J. Grant, run Small Beer Press and play ping-pong. In 1996 they started the occasional zine *Lady Churchill Rosebud's Wristlet*.

Robert McCammon is the bestselling author of eighteen novels, including the classic horror novels *Swan Song* and *The Wolf's Hour* and the imaginative (tour de force?) *Boy's Life*, which is taught in seventy percent of American schools. McCammon is also the author of the Matthew Corbett mystery/ adventure series, set in Colonial America. His latest novel, *The Five*, will be published in May and follows a rock band on their final and fateful tour across the Southwest as they are pursued by a dark force of destruction. McCammon lives in Birmingham, Alabama.

China Miéville is the author of *King Rat*; *Perdido Street Station*, winner of the Arthur C. Clarke Award and the British Fantasy Award; *The Scar*, winner of the Locus Award and the British Fantasy Award; *Iron Council*, winner of the Locus Award and the Arthur C. Clarke Award; *Looking for Jake*, a collection of short stories; *Un Lun Dun*, his New York Times bestselling book for younger readers; *The City & The City*, named one of the top 100 Books of the Year by *Publishers Weekly*; and most recently the novel *Kraken*. He lives and works in London.

Norman Partridge's fiction includes horror, suspense, and the fantastic—"sometimes all in one story" says his friend Joe Lansdale. Partridge's novel *Dark Harvest* was chosen by *Publishers Weekly* as one of the 100 Best Books of 2006, and two short story collections were published in 2010—*Lesser Demons* from Subterranean Press and *Johnny Halloween* from Cemetery Dance. Other work includes the Jack Baddalach mysteries *Saguaro Riptide* and *The Ten-Ounce Siesta*, plus *The Crow: Wicked Prayer*, which was adapted for film. He can be found on the web at NormanPartridge.com and americanfrankenstein.blogspot.com.

Cherie Priest is the author of ten novels from Bantam, Tor, and Subterranean Press, including *Dreadnought* and *Boneshaker*—which was nominated for a Nebula Award and a Hugo Award, and won the Locus Award for Best Science Fiction Novel—plus *Bloodshot*, the Eden Moore series, *Clementine*, and *Fathom*.

Brett Alexander Savory is the Bram Stoker Award-winning editor-in-chief of *ChiZine: Treatments of Light and Shade in Words*, co-publisher of ChiZine Publications, has had about fifty short stories published, and has written two novels, *The Distance Travelled* and *In and Down*, and one short story collection, *No Further Messages*. He is now at work on his third novel, *Lake of Spaces, Wood of Nothing*. He lives in Toronto with his wife, writer/editor Sandra Kasturi.

David J. Schow's short stories have been regularly selected for over twenty-five volumes of "Year's Best" anthologies across two decades and have won the World Fantasy Award, the ultra-rare Dimension Award from *Twilight Zone* magazine, plus a 2002 International Horror Guild Award for his collection of *Fangoria* columns, *Wild Hairs*. His novels include *The Kill Riff, The Shaft, Rock Breaks Scissors Cut, Bullets of Rain, Gun Work, Internecine* and the forthcoming *Upgunned*. His short stories are collected in *Seeing Red, Lost Angels, Black Leather Required, Crypt Orchids, Eye, Zombie Jam* and *Havoc Swims Jaded*. He is the author of the exhaustively detailed *Outer Limits Companion* and has written extensively for films (*Leatherface: Texas Chainsaw Massacre III, The Crow*) and television (*Perversions of Science, The Hunger, Masters of Horror*). His bibliography and many other fascinating details are available online at his official site, *Black Leather Required*: www.davidjschow.com

Jim Shepard is the author of six novels, including most recently *Project X*, and four story collections, including *Like You'd Understand, Anyway*, which was a finalist for the National Book Award and won The Story Prize, and most recently *You Think That's Bad*, released March 2011. He teaches at Williams College.

Al Sarrantonio is the author of forty-five books. He is a winner of the Bram Stoker Award and has been a finalist for the World Fantasy Award. His novels, spanning many genres, include *Moonbane, The Masters of Mars* trilogy and the *Orangefield* Halloween trilogy. Hailed as "a master anthologist" by *Booklist*, he has edited numerous collections, including the highly acclaimed *999* and, most recently, *Portents* and, with co-editor Neil Gaiman, *Stories*.

Paul Tremblay is the author of the weirdboiled novels *The Little Sleep* and *No Sleep Till Wonderland*, the short story collection *In the Mean Time*, and the novella *The Harlequin and the Train*. His short fiction has appeared in *Weird Tales* and *Year's Best American Fantasy 3*. He's the co-editor of the anthologies *Fantasy*, *Bandersnatch*, and *Phantom*. He still has no uvula and lives somewhere south of Boston with his wife and two kids.

Lisa Tuttle has been writing strange, weird stories nearly all her life, and this year marks the fortieth anniversary of her first professional sale. *Stranger in the House*, the first volume of her "Collected Short Supernatural Fiction" was published by Ash-Tree Press in 2010. Her novels include *Lost Futures*, *The Mysteries* and *The Silver Bough*. A native of Texas, she presently resides with her family in the highlands of Scotland.

Genevieve Valentine's fiction has appeared or is forthcoming in *Clarkesworld*, *Strange Horizons*, *Fantasy Magazine*, *Apex*, and others, and in the anthologies *Federations*, *The Living Dead 2*, *Running with the Pack*, *Teeth*, and more. Her nonfiction has appeared in *Lightspeed*, *Tor.com*, and *Fantasy Magazine*. Her first novel, *Mechanique: A Tale of the Circus Tresaulti*, is forthcoming from Prime Books in 2011. Her appetite for bad movies is insatiable, a tragedy she tracks on her blog: www.genevievevalentine.com.

Jeff VanderMeer is a two-time winner of the World Fantasy Award, with novels published in over twenty languages. His short fiction has appeared in *Asimov's SF Magazine*, *Black Clock*, *Conjunctions*, *Clarkesworld*, and many anthologies. He reviews books for the *New York Times Book Review*, *Los Angeles Times*, *Washington Post*, and many others.

Publication Credits